SAMMY'S HOUSE

SAMMY'S HOUSE

Kristin Gore

NEW YORK

BALLAD OF A THIN MAN
Copyright © 1965 by Warner Bros. Inc.
Copyright renewed 1993 by Special Rider Music.
All rights reserved. International copyright secured.
Reprinted by permission

LAY LADY LAY
Copyright © 1969 by Big Sky Music.
All rights reserved. International copyright secured.
Reprinted by permission.

Library of Congress Cataloging-in-Publication Data

Gore, Kristin
    Sammy's house / Kristin Gore.—1st ed.
        p. cm.
    ISBN: 1-4013-0264-5
    ISBN-13: 978-1-4013-0264-1
    1. United States. Executive Office of the President—Officials and
employees—Fiction.   2. Women—Washington (D.C)—Fiction.   3. Washington
(D.C.)—Fiction.   4. Political fiction.   I. Title.
    PS3607.O5965S25   2007
    813'.6—dc22   20061010441

Hyperion books are available at special quantity discounts
to use as premiums or for special programs, including corporate training.
For details contact Michael Rentas,
Assistant Director, Inventory Operations,
Hyperion, 77 West 66th Street, 12th floor,
New York, New York 10023,
or call 212-456-0133.

Design by Fritz Metsch

FIRST EDITION

1   3   5   7   9   10   8   6   4   2

For my husband, Paul

SAMMY'S HOUSE

Splash

———

IT WAS WHEN SHE STARTED STRIPPING that everyone realized something was wrong. This was an official White House event. A somewhat boring, completely respectable cruise on the Potomac River to thank everyone in the West Wing for the hard work that had won the election. But it was no longer boring.

Until the woman whipped off her tailored black jacket to reveal a star-spangled bra and a surprisingly elaborate dragon tattoo, the only remarkable thing about this cruise was that it was nineteen months late. The celebratory boat ride had been promised long ago, in the first month of our new administration, but no one minded that the business of running the country had continuously delayed its actual launch. Victory was prize enough—who needed a cruise?

I tore my eyes away from the increasingly explicit show to scan the crowd for RG. He'd gone below deck to take a call from President Wye, and I was relieved that he still seemed to be there, unaware of these antics. He was the vice president, and as a member of the White House staff, one of my duties was to protect him from public embarrassment whenever possible. That job had become significantly harder in the last thirty seconds.

I looked quickly around for help, but most people seemed frozen, capable only of staring with wide-open mouths. The stereo system played on, its background hum now transformed into a striptease soundtrack. Someone needed to shut it off. Someone needed to shut *her* off. I searched for the Secret Service agents posted throughout the boat. Would they get involved only if they deemed the stripper a security threat? By now, she'd reached a point where concealed weapons seemed an impossibility.

Upon closer examination, the dragon tatooed on her shoulder appeared to be wearing a tufted pink tutu. I pondered its significance. Perhaps this unknown woman, who until a minute ago everyone had taken for an inhibited waitress offering shrimp dip and taquitos, belonged to a hard-livin', rough-and-tumble gang of rebel ballerinas. She was certainly nimble, judging by the ease with which she was now pirouetting out of her panties.

I was blinking from the flashes, both photographic and pornographic, and had just noticed the tattoo of a tap-dancing minotaur on the stripper's upper thigh when Harry Danson, the president's chief of staff, suddenly pushed through the crowd and covered her with his jacket. She tried to shrug it off, but Harry was very firm. It's in his job description.

"Just what is this all about?" he demanded fiercely, painfully aware of all the photos that had already been taken.

There wasn't any press aboard; the cruise was for staff only. But though everyone was ostensibly loyally intent on protecting the administration from unnecessary scandal, it was hard to keep a story like this from getting out. I myself could think of five people I planned to regale immediately with this sordid tale. It wasn't often that one attended an office function and got entertained by a scantily clad exhibitionist inked with dancing fantasy creatures. It would be selfish to keep this to myself.

"I'm a gift from the Exterminators," the stripper answered. "They say congratulations for making it this far. They didn't think you had it in you."

I watched Harry's jawline stiffen. When he got angry, which was distressingly often, he looked like he'd had steel cheek implants. I'd met few people more ripe for a hernia.

"Thank you, that will be all," he ground out through clenched teeth.

Harry and a couple Secret Service agents ushered the woman through the still-stunned crowd toward the caterers' station. The hushed silence that had accompanied her performance exploded into the sounds of a hundred and seventy-five people talking at once.

The Exterminators were a very disgruntled band of former officials from the previous administration. Most of them had stayed in D.C. to form an opposition think tank, and nothing seemed to please them more than perpetrating juvenile pranks while they worked very seriously to sabotage every policy change we tried to make.

They hadn't named their think tank the Exterminators. That particular moniker derived from one of the many vindictive stunts they'd pulled on their way out of the West Wing, which they had vandalized to the best of their abilities in a rage against their ouster. In addition to rigging booby traps and carving their initials into various pieces of furniture, they had also taken the time to enact a much more elaborate and dastardly scheme.

They'd ordered cases of frozen feeder mice—available on the Internet to pet owners in need of food for raptors and reptiles—and, in an impressive labor of hate, had carefully sewn several hundred of these tiny frozen mice into the hems of all the heavy West Wing drapes.

We'd noticed an unpleasant odor a few days after we'd moved in, but couldn't be positive that wasn't the way the place always smelled. But as the frozen feeder mice had thawed in their thick fabric tombs, the smell had intensified rapidly. In a little over a week, it had become unbearably wretched, rendering the West Wing virtually uninhabitable.

It had been difficult to locate the precise source, since the horrific stench had seemed to emanate from the very walls around us. The maintenance crew had finally discovered the tiny rotting rodent corpses after their fourth thorough search. That very day, a case of champagne had been delivered to the West Wing with a note that read: "To wash down the smell. Enjoy yourselves while you last, because we'll be rid of you before you know it. Love and kisses, the Exterminators." And thus, an annoying nickname had been born.

Even after the discovery and removal of the mice carcasses, the gut-gripping stink had lingered for nearly two months, despite all efforts to eradicate it. To their obnoxious delight, the Exterminators had inflicted a parting gift that had kept on giving.

I knew that my own party was perfectly capable of similar pettiness, because the previous administration had complained instantly to the press when they'd moved into the White House eight years earlier to

find tuna sandwiches locked in all their file cabinets and their comput-
ers rigged to print the chorus of Bob Dylan's "Ballad of a Thin Man"
no matter what the command. Some in the press had privately enjoyed
the specter of then President Pile's political guru Carl Jones battling
rebellious office machinery that taunted him with the words "Because
something is happening here but you don't know what it is. Do you,
Mister Jones?" printed over and over again, but the majority of columns
and articles had chastised the outgoing administration for such child-
ishness.

Had we been as eager to whine to the press, we might have garnered
comparable support, but we weren't the same breed of tattletales. And
even taking pride in that was immature. The whole embarrassing rivalry
gave me flashbacks to junior high.

Which, frankly, didn't seem all that long ago. I was twenty-eight now
and working as a health care advisor to the White House, but I still often felt as awkward and unsure of myself as I had during those halcyon
days of orthodontic headgear and New Kids on the Block fan clubs.
Though I'd spent a few fascinating years as a Capitol Hill staffer to then
Senator Robert Gary (RG to his staff), the White House was an entirely
different universe. The stakes, the pressure, the perpetual potential for
both extraordinary progress and crippling failure—everything was
ratcheted up to a spectacular intensity now that I worked for the president and vice president of the United States. More than ever before, I
felt like I needed to constantly prove myself in a new world full of gossip and cliques and all sorts of social politics. So in some ways, the junior
high flashbacks were apropos. Though perhaps I had slightly more of a
shot at a date with New Kid heartthrob Jordan Knight now. Slightly.

Amid the fear and anxiety, I also felt a certain wide-eyed wonder at
everything I was witnessing. At the inauguration of Wye and RG, I'd
been awed by the sight of democracy in action. After a hard-fought,
nasty election cycle, it had been thrilling and refreshing to observe the
peaceful transfer of power. I'd watched everything from the sidelines,
humbled by the remarkable nature of such an event, and grateful to be
on the happier end of it. Granted, a week later I'd felt considerably less
idealistic about the whole thing when I'd had to wear a surgical mask at
my desk to filter the rancid fumes of decomposing mice.

And now those same clever saboteurs had disrupted our year-and-a-half-late victory cruise by paying a woman to take her clothes off. They were classy, classy folks.

"Everyone resume having fun," Harry Danson barked threateningly at the crowd.

We instantly pretended to obey. I watched several people punching buttons on their cell phones and could practically feel the camera-phone photos whisking away to the world beyond White House control.

I noticed Lincoln Thomas standing by the starboard railing, as far from the heart of the crowd as he could get. As usual, he looked like a frightened stork—ready at the next instant to gather his thin legs and ruffled feathers and take off for calmer waters. Lincoln was my direct superior—the chief domestic policy advisor to the president—and I worked with him all day, every day. I was continually amazed by his excruciating shyness and considered it part of my job to try to help him overcome it.

"What did you make of the show?" I asked, wondering if he might pretend not to hear me. It was an old trick of his.

His eyes flitted to my face briefly, and then away again as he cleared his throat in his nervous way. Every conversation was a cage for him. He'd beat against it for a panicked moment, hoping against hope for escape, before realizing he was trapped.

"Well, it was, er . . . exhilarating," he finally managed. "Not 'exhilarating' in the good, I-was-enjoying-it way," he rushed to mumble. "I just mean it was very, um . . ."

His face had turned red and taken on a desperate sheen.

"Unexpected," I offered.

He breathed in gratefully.

"Exactly. Unexpected," he agreed. "That's more what I meant. Not sexy or titillating or . . ." He trailed off, looking alarmed again.

"So, I think we're all set for the bill signing tomorrow," I threw out.

"Yes. Good," Lincoln answered thankfully.

He was completely in his element when discussing work. It was everything else that he couldn't handle.

"I'll see you then, there. I mean there, then. Bye," he blurted, before moving quickly away.

I watched him walk off to inflict his social awkwardness on someone else, then busied myself with some passing guacamole as I studied the remaining waitstaff. I was no longer fooled by their crisp jackets, which I now knew could be quickly shed like so much feigned politeness.

Where had the stripper gone, anyway? Had she already been removed from the boat, with the help of the D.C. police? After a quick search, I spotted her sitting in a chair, being interrogated by an agent. And what about RG? I was glad Wye wasn't on board. The Exterminators would have felt even more insufferably proud of themselves had they managed to punk the president along with the entire West Wing staff.

I heard RG's familiar deep tones behind me and turned to find him in quiet conversation with Harry Danson, who was obviously briefing him on what he'd missed. Harry was considerably shorter than RG, with a bald, pointy head. He often reminded me of a very angry garden gnome. RG, in contrast, was a good-looking man whose distinguished demeanor conveyed a sense of calm intelligence, though these days his shoulders were too often tensed for conflict. Indeed, I noticed that his hair had grayed further over the past month, and the little lines around his eyes had burrowed deeper. When he'd joined the presidential ticket, he'd looked like a grown-up Boy Scout, but his face was considerably more worn-in now. Observing him, I was reminded of George Orwell's famous quote: "At fifty, everyone has the face he deserves." RG still had a few more years to sculpt his legacy, but his face was beginning to reflect the efforts.

I wondered if RG was bothered by the pace of his aging, whether it even crossed his mind. He blinked his tired eyes, said something I couldn't hear to Harry, and made his way to the center of the main deck. Someone clinked a spoon against a glass. Everyone quieted immediately, though I heard some scattered snickers, perhaps because RG was standing in the same spot where the stripper had begun her routine. It was almost impossible not to imagine what it would be like if he followed suit.

It was a ridiculous visual, and to my horror, I suddenly found myself having to stifle my own inadvertent laughter. Against my will, I was picturing RG helicoptering his jacket around in the air and swiveling his hips as he loosened that trusty red tie. Don't start laughing, I ordered myself sternly. Even as I commanded, I knew it was a lost cause. Trying not to laugh was the one sure way to send me into hysterics, however unwilling or inappropriate. I had yet to recover from a recent incident at my great-aunt's funeral triggered by the prim preacher's involuntary burp during the homily.

I winced at the memory even as I felt insubordinate giggles rising up once again and stuffed an olive in my mouth to keep it occupied. Looking serious, RG began speaking.

"For anyone visualizing me stripping, it ain't gonna happen," he deadpanned.

Everyone laughed, which was a welcome release for my pent-up hilarity.

"I understand there's been some excitement this evening and I'm sure our friends on the other side are very proud of their latest stunt, but our celebration tonight is about a whole lot more than silly games," RG continued. "We were elected, and we're now here in D.C. because of a simple, real truth. The American people want more out of their public servants, and we're going to give it to them. With the extraordinary hearts and minds gathered here today, we can do anything. We're going to help this great country be even better. So on behalf of the president and myself, and the bright future we are all shaping together, I want to thank you. And I want to salute you. For your passion, your commitment, and your fantastic, important work."

I felt a swell of pride and joined the heartfelt clapping, relishing the communal thrill that raced through the crowd. We had all worked incredibly hard to put RG and Wye, and by extension ourselves, into the White House. Though it was easy to forget the greater cause in the midst of the daily grind, luckily it only seemed to take a little well-placed rhetoric to energize us anew. Particularly when it involved flattery.

I suspected that we were so easily rejuvenated because at our cores, we believed we really could change the world. I knew that this didn't make us all that fashionable or cool. Cynicism was definitely much more in vogue. But this crowd had somehow opted out of ironic detachment. For better or for worse, we cared.

And so, though it occurred to me that we all might be suckers, the reality was that a year and a half after commandeering the White House, most of us still felt the blood-tingling, breath-skipping happiness of what we'd pulled off. No amount of criticism, opposition, or sabotage could take that away. At least we hoped not.

"We've accomplished a lot so far, but it's only the beginning," RG continued. "We have an exciting few years ahead of us, so fill up on this shrimp dip. You're gonna need the energy."

I laughed along with the others and helped toast to our future, but RG's shrimp dip comment made me wonder about the possible hazards of the hors d'oeuvres we were consuming. Now that one of the waitresses had turned out to be a hired stripper, I was newly leery of the chefs. It's not like "cruise food" enjoys the most stellar reputation as it is. It seemed to me that I was perpetually coming across news stories about cruise ship passengers stricken by some mystery virus or another, and the sheer number of these incidents was worrisome. As far as I could tell, it was tough to go on a cruise and *not* come down with a hideous food-borne illness.

Good Lord, we were probably surrounded by salmonella. I looked around suspiciously at the dumplings, bruschetta, and crabcakes laid out on their trays like so many invitations to gastroenteritis. We were doomed. I could sense it.

Feeling nauseous, I checked my bag for backup. I had Dramamine, various antihistamines, an eye patch, an EpiPen, some antibacterial ointment and Band-Aids, a Z-Pak in the event I needed to start antibiotics right away, and Tamiflu to combat a sudden outbreak of avian flu. Friends found my first-aid kits creepy, but I considered them reassuring. I spent enough time researching health care issues to have an ever-expanding understanding of the countless mishaps and illnesses that were out there, just waiting to pounce. In light of the omnipresent danger, the best I could do was arm myself. The EpiPen had been the hardest to procure, since I wasn't technically deathly allergic to anything. But you never know, I argued with the doctor. Maybe I was deathly allergic to something obscure that I hadn't yet come across. I needed to be geared up for it when I did.

I reminded myself to stay calm and not get too carried away. I knew deep down that the food was more than likely completely fine. But was that my abdomen cramping? If I'd contracted salmonella, I shouldn't experience symptoms for another six hours. Perhaps this ship was host to a particularly aggressive strain. I looked up from my kit to assess whether a medical helicopter would have enough room to land on the deck and saw that some of my more lubricated colleagues were fashioning a conga line. Should I break up the party to inform them of their intestinal peril?

Behind them, through the dusk, the Kennedy Center lights slid by. My eyes moved to RG, who was a few feet away, extricating himself from a conversation as he moved a safe distance from the conga parade. He happened upon my gaze as he made his way back toward the cabin.

"Seasick?" he inquired, confirming that I looked as bad as I suddenly felt.

"I'm fine, sir," I answered unconvincingly.

The helicopter ride would just make me more nauseous, I'd determined. Best to stick with a speedboat evacuation. Though now that darkness had fallen, any of these maneuvers would be tricky. How much longer were we on this damn cruise anyway?

"Well, we're almost back to shore," RG said lightly, as if reading my thoughts.

I hoped he was right. I didn't want to toss my cookies in front of everyone if I could help it. I'd prefer to get off the boat as soon as possible without causing an embarrassing scene.

"Listen, I was impressed with your latest report on lifestyle drugs," RG continued. "It was very thorough, very intriguing. I'd like to hold a White House conference on them as soon as we can organize it. Write up a proposal, will you?"

"Yes, sir." I nodded, pleased that my briefing had made the desired impact. I'd worked hard on it. And it was about time he started tuning in to the issue.

And now that he had, I clearly couldn't afford the time deficit a full-fledged salmonella infection would create. I couldn't be bedridden for days when I finally had the chance to spearhead a White House conference. Okay, deep breaths, I instructed myself. I'd really only had some chips and guacamole and a few olives, nothing dairy or fish-based. Plus, this wasn't actually a cruise ship—just a riverboat hired for the evening. There was a chance I'd live.

Just as I began to settle down and feel a sense of eerie calm, an explosion of shots rang out.

Reflecting back, it might have been my musing on mortality that was to blame for my reaction. Or a freshly fueled sense of paranoia thanks to the stripper's reminder of the saboteurs who meant us harm. Or perhaps I really had contracted salmonella and it had made a beeline for my brain. Whatever the explanation for my actions, in retrospect, I certainly should have behaved differently.

But the trouble with hindsight is that it never arrives in time.

So as the shots exploded nearby, I reacted instinctively. I rushed past my boss, the vice president of the United States, and took a running dive headlong into the Potomac.

For a split second before I hit the chilly water, it occurred to me that I might have overreacted. But it was only when I surfaced beside the boat, sputtering and in a fair amount of stinging pain, that I saw the fireworks lighting up the sky.

In my defense, the fireworks had been a shock to everyone, and I noted that several people on deck were still crouched down in reaction to the abrupt explosions. None of them had opted for the extra precaution of taking to the water, but still, they'd attempted some form of self-preservation. Even the Secret Service agents had quickly circled RG, since the initial pops really had sounded like gunshots.

As I doggy-paddled to keep my head above water, I noticed something else about the surprise fireworks. Something besides the fact that they'd just created a mortifying new memory in need of swift repression. It appeared that these were the fancy kind that formed distinguishable shapes. One specific shape, to be exact. As I gaped at the night sky, weighing the pros and cons of drowning myself, the crackling lights danced together in the unmistakable design of a grinning mouse. The Exterminators' calling card.

Didn't these people have anything better to do with their time? They were expending a lot of effort just to put an explosive exclamation point on their latest stunt, making sure we knew whom to credit. The police boats escorting us had cleared this portion of the river of any other craft, which meant that the Exterminators must have set off the fireworks from someplace along the shore. I scanned the riverbank, but couldn't make anything out in the darkness. As the first taunting mouse slowly faded into smoke, another one exploded even closer to the boat, just above the heads of the conga crowd, who had frozen in formation. Suddenly sobered, they all stared up at the pyrotechnic prank that rained sparks down on their paused parade.

I could always slip away and float downriver to a new life, I considered as people began to point me out from the deck. I knew the currents were dangerous, but at the moment, they seemed more inviting than the looks and questions I'd have to navigate back on board.

"Sammy? Are you okay?" someone yelled.

"Physically, yes," I answered weakly.

"What?"

"I'M FINE," I shouted more robustly.

Besides being an idiot, obviously.

As a life preserver clocked me in the head, I wondered how many people had actually witnessed my actions. Probably not many. Most of them had doubtless been looking elsewhere, searching for the source of the sudden gunshot-like noises. Gripping the life preserver, I kicked close enough to make out the faces of those peering down from the ship's railing. There was Lincoln, looking perplexed, and Harry, looking apoplectic. And there was RG, smiling.

Smiling?

I did a double take, and on second glance his smile was gone. Perhaps it had existed only as a figment of my water-logged imagination. Or perhaps it had been real, but only because RG had been enjoying the thought of my imminent firing. Regardless, he was now looking decidedly grim and displeased.

The rest of my ignominious return aboard was a shivering, soggy blur. And before I knew it, the boat was docked and everyone was disembarking. I comforted myself that the tattooed stripper received slightly more stares than I did as I shuffled quickly past the shuttle that had been arranged to return everyone to the West Wing. There was no way I was getting on that bus. I needed some alone time.

As I stood hailing a cab around the corner from 31st and K a few minutes later, wrapped in a towel I'd been lent, a siren bleated behind me. I turned to glimpse the official vice presidential motorcade rounding the corner, and stepped quickly back toward the shadows to do my best impression of an anonymous homeless person.

If I don't look up, they won't spot me, I told myself as I pulled the towel over my head. Through the terry cloth, I heard the siren getting closer. And then:

"Samantha," a voice called gruffly.

So much for my ostrich logic. They'd never struck me as the brightest birds.

I reluctantly raised my head. Oh God, it was RG. Why on earth had he stopped? The Secret Service agent who rode in the passenger seat had leapt out and was now looking around alertly as RG leaned out from the shadow of his car.

"Hello, sir," I squeaked, stepping hesitatingly back into the light.

"Do you need a ride?" RG asked brusquely, indicating the extra SUVs and squad cars that had pulled close to form a protective barrier.

Was this like one of those Mafia ride offers? I wondered. It was more my livelihood than my life that felt threatened. If he was going to fire me, I'd rather know sooner than later. But I felt too weak and disheveled and possibly diseased to weather it now.

"No, sir," I answered. "I'm waiting for a friend."

"A friend," RG repeated.

It did sound implausible.

"A taxi-driver type of friend-stranger," I elaborated lamely. "Um, I'm sure we'll be friends by the end of the ride."

I considered burying my head back in the towel.

"Uh-huh," RG replied flatly. "Well, I'm not going to leave you here alone at night on a deserted street. Climb into one of the support vans. I'll instruct the driver to take you where you need to go."

"Yes, sir," I answered meekly. "Thank you, sir."

I could see the van he was referring to toward the rear of the motorcade. Should I just hustle back there, then? RG was still watching me. Uh-oh, I knew that look. He was weighing a decision. He was an avid hunter and I imagined that this was the look that came into his eyes as he was staring through his rifle scope, deciding whether or not to pull the trigger.

He sighed deeply and my career flashed before my eyes.

"I'm going to tell you something and I'm going to say it only once. Understand?"

His tone was harsh. I knew RG was capable of brutal tongue-lashings, and I steeled myself for one as best I could.

"Yes, sir," I managed.

"Listen to me carefully. You're a smart, capable advisor. You're normally an asset to our team. But God almighty, do you have some blind spots."

I gulped. Here it came.

"So just do me a favor. On your ride home, I want you to focus on one thing." He paused. "No matter what loud noises you encounter, try not to fling yourself from the van. Belly flops on asphalt are a lot tougher to recover from."

RG didn't lighten his tone or break into his teasing grin. I thought I saw the corners of his mouth twitch upward as he leaned back in his seat, but it wasn't until the car was pulling away that I finally found my voice again.

"I'll try to remember that, sir, thank you," I said to the space where his car had been.

But I certainly couldn't make any promises.

Dash

———·———

EARLY THE NEXT MORNING, Derrick was the uniformed Secret Service agent on duty when I approached the northwest gate of the White House. He looked at me blankly through the bulletproof glass. I'd passed through this post countless times in the past year and a half and Derrick had been one of the guards assigned to it since day one. Unless something was very seriously wrong with him, he knew precisely who I was. And yet he persisted in acting as though he didn't.

"Derrick, hi. It's me. Sammy," I said as I held up my pass.

Derrick's through-me stare didn't become any more familiar, but I heard the mechanical hum of the guardhouse door releasing. I hurried inside, put my bag on the belt, scanned my pass electronically, and entered my secret code. After clearing the magnetometer, I picked up my bag and glanced back at Derrick.

"Are you going to remember me next time?" I asked him, more plaintive than sarcastic.

"Depends. Do you plan on being memorable?"

Was Derrick issuing some sort of existential challenge? He wasn't looking at me, he was staring ahead, as uninterested as ever. I got the feeling that he'd intended to be more insulting than philosophical. I much prefer people either liking or even disliking me—I'm not a big fan of indifference. Particularly not from people I interact with every single day.

I shrugged off Derrick's unconcern as I exited the guardhouse and walked down the driveway along the west side of the White House toward the staff entrance. Inside the foyer, I nodded to the uniformed

Secret Service agent at the desk, who smiled familiarly at me. I grinned back, grateful for the recognition, and headed quickly up the two flights of stairs to the office I shared with Lincoln Thomas and his assistant.

When we'd moved into the White House, I'd expected my office to be in the nearby Old Executive Office Building along with most of the vice presidential staff. However, RG had worked hard to make the health care issues I focused on a central part of the campaign he ran with President Wye, and he was apparently just as determined to ensure they were an important part of the administration's domestic agenda. He had arranged for me to work directly beneath Lincoln, an old friend of his from his early days on the Hill. When it came to White House appointments, RG's considerable influence with Wye was evident, as many of the senior staff were from RG's camp. I had heard that other politicians would have kept their primary people closely tied to them, but to his credit, RG was a team player.

Lincoln's assistant smiled at me as I entered the office. His name was Nick and he was brand-new to the job and filled with enthusiasm for even the most minuscule task. He and I shared the outer room, though at least I had a bigger desk. I could see Lincoln in his inner office through the open door, sucking away on a Popsicle. This wasn't a good sign. Cherry Popsicles were Lincoln's only known vice, and any consumption before noon, much less before eight a.m., signaled a problem.

I looked questioningly at Nick. Was my Potomac plunge to blame?

"Frand," Nick replied with wide eyes. "He's holding a press conference in an hour to announce his alternative to the Alzheimer's Bill. He's organizing a big rally to demonstrate his 'moral outrage' over the present course."

Senator Frand was the majority leader of the Senate and a member of the opposition party that unfortunately controlled both houses of Congress, making all of our jobs much more frustrating. Frand continually used his considerable power to thwart the administration's goals while fund-raising for his own White House bid. We were still more than two years away from the next presidential election, and none of the candidates would publicly campaign for several more months, but their ambitions informed every move they made.

Plus, the midterm elections were around the corner, which didn't do much for that elusive bipartisan spirit they were always disingenuously advertising.

"I thought he might be planning something like that." I sighed.

But Lincoln hadn't. He'd actually assured the president that Frand would stay out of the debate on the Alzheimer's Bill and let it be one of those he opposed but didn't expend extra energy on actively defeating. I'd respectfully disagreed and argued that Frand most likely *would* make an issue of the bill. I wished I hadn't been right.

I checked out Lincoln again. He was absorbed in his briefing book, his thin neck curved so that his pointed chin sunk into his chest. It was his stork-in-repose look. Over his left shoulder, I saw his latest miniature cabin, made from the wooden Popsicle sticks he carefully washed after his daily snack. He'd once intimated that he constructed the little buildings as a form of meditation and relaxation, but I'd always suspected his log cabin fascination had a lot to do with his name. I'd never inquired along these lines—I just pictured a young Lincoln introduced to the legend of his presidential namesake and experiencing a come-to-Abraham moment.

"Is that you, Sammy?" Lincoln suddenly called.

I took a breath and made my way inside.

"Right here," I answered.

He looked up from his briefing book and rested his sucked-clean Popsicle stick on the polished stone he kept on his desk for that specific purpose.

"I was wrong about Frand, and we need to cut him off at the pass if possible," he said quickly. "Can you get on it?"

I nodded, taking some papers from my briefcase and handing them to Lincoln.

"I drafted this last week in case he tried to pull something like this."

Lincoln scanned the pages. He looked up in surprise.

"This is great," he said.

His voice had significantly less despair in it. He sounded relieved, which was gratifying, considering I'd stayed up past three a.m. the previous Wednesday night writing a rebuttal that everyone had assured me we wouldn't need. I'd done it because of my stubborn hunch that Frand wasn't going to roll over on the bill, but it had occurred to me that I might be creating more work and less sleep for myself for no good reason other than a soft spot for extracurricular stress. Now I felt vindicated.

"I'll need to clean it up once I get the actual copy of his bill from the Senate liaison," I answered. "This is just based on what I assumed he'd do."

Lincoln nodded. "Well, revise it however necessary and make it an official statement. We'll release it just before his announcement."

Which was in less than an hour.

Back at my desk, I printed out the Frand bill and began churning out a document negating it that would go to the national press on official White House letterhead. If I did my job well, we'd be able to steal back the thunder Frand believed he was taking away.

As I skimmed Frand's alternative bill, I worked to keep my anger in check. I needed my wits about me, but the bill *was* infuriating. It purported to aim for the same goals as the measure we'd been backing and even used a lot of the same language, but it completely failed to provide the scientific community with the means to pursue breakthroughs in the struggle against diseases such as Alzheimer's, Parkinson's, Huntington's, and diabetes. It was just trying to trick people. I hoped I could prevent it from succeeding.

I was polishing up our response when my cell phone exploded to the chords of Led Zeppelin's "Fool in the Rain," which I'd programmed to be Charlie's special ring on a night when we'd entertained ourselves by competing to see who could make the cheesiest relationship move. I actually really liked the song. The cheese factor came from the fact that it had provided the soundtrack to one of our earliest hang-outs. I'd lost the contest anyway when I'd walked into the bathroom to find Charlie standing fully clothed in the running shower, blasting Peter Gabriel's "In Your Eyes" from the battery-powered iPod speakers he was holding over his head and barely clear of the pouring water. His updated, soaked *Say Anything* pose still made me laugh whenever I thought of it.

"Hey there," I answered, very happy to hear from him.

Charlie was a reporter for the *Washington Post* and my boyfriend of twenty-one months. I enjoyed keeping count of the months because they represented a time of my life when I'd gotten at least one thing consistently, completely right. He claimed to feel the same way, which was downright thrilling.

"Did you get any sleep?" I asked.

He'd stayed late at work to meet a deadline. I'd spoken to him briefly before bed to regale him with the tale of the stripper and, less enthusiastically, with that of my river debacle, and to reiterate my need for time travel technology.

I kept a running list of my life's top ten screw-up moments that I planned to return to and fix the instant time travel technology became available. How deeply I cringed when the memory of these moments popped into my head corresponded to how highly they got ranked. My recent river plunge had debuted at number six.

"No sleep yet," Charlie answered, sounding tired. "What about you? Did you sleep okay?"

Actually, no. I'd stayed up talking with Liza, my roommate and closest friend. I'd told her about my night and she'd had several questions about the stripper's tattoos, which had led to a discussion about the difference between a minotaur and a centaur. This, in turn, had led to my having a vivid dream about being attacked by a river otter with the head of George Washington.

"I never sleep well when you're not with me," I answered, sparing him the specifics.

Which was true. I loved falling asleep with my head on his chest. I'd grown so used to doing so that I now felt unsettled in bed without him.

"Listen, can you meet for lunch today?" Charlie asked. "I've got exciting news."

"Really? What?" I demanded.

"I'll tell you when I see you," he answered.

Charlie always preferred to tell me anything of import in person, and I was exceedingly bad at being patient. Conflicts inevitably ensued.

"Lunch is four and a half hours away. Can't you just tell me now?" I pleaded.

"No, this is important."

"Which is why I should be told immediately."

It was a familiar argument. And though I won it all the time in my head, that never translated into actually being told any sooner than Charlie was good and ready. He could be as stubborn as me.

"At least give me a hint," I compromised.

"Meet me in Lafayette Park at one. I'll grab sandwiches. And I'll make it worth your while, I promise."

"Fine, I'll see you then." I sighed, hanging up.

Why couldn't Charlie just tell me things over the phone like a normal person? Of course I wanted to see him, but I hated having to wait unnecessarily for information. And what would have been the harm in at least giving me a hint as I'd requested? But no, he had to do it his way. Unless proposing a meeting in Lafayette Park *had* been the hint. I gasped suddenly. Maybe he was surprising me with a trip to France! If so, it was clearly to propose. I'd never been to Europe, and he knew how much I longed to go. When was he thinking of going? This was fantastic news.

Newly energized, I had just enough time to complete the bill rebuttal and show it to Lincoln for his approval. He scanned my work with a discerning eye.

"Great job," he said. "Let's just run this by Stephanie and then get it out. I gave her a heads-up about it so she's expecting you."

Stephanie Grader was the president's senior political strategist. She was shockingly young for her high post—only a few years older than me. Her youth and ambition and important position made her something of a press darling, though she constantly belittled journalists behind their backs at every internal strategy session. We'd worked together a handful of times, but I still had to struggle not to be completely intimidated by her. It didn't help that she was six foot two and very skilled at giving people the impression that she knew far more about everything than they did. She towered, and the rest of us just scampered about in her shadow. I tried to relax my tensed stomach as I made my way down the stairs to her office on the first floor. The salmonella scare from the cruise hadn't really panned out, but I was distinctly sore from my belly flop. And I could practically feel the toxins from the river wreaking havoc in my bloodstream.

"Goddamn people," Stephanie growled as I walked through her doorway after being waved in by her assistant.

Perhaps this was a bad time. Stephanie looked up before I could back silently out of the room. Too late. I was standing before her, a person, on a day when she apparently disliked people to the point of cursing them.

"I'm sorry to interrupt," I said cautiously.

She scrunched her bangs impatiently. Stephanie had thick, dark red hair that she touched incessantly like it was some sort of power source she relied on for recharging. Today she had the bulk of it coiled into a loose bun, with three different pencils sticking out of it. She looked incredibly agitated. I wondered if one of the pencils might be poking her.

"It's fine." She sighed, releasing her bangs. "I just made the mistake of shortcutting on my way back from a meeting in the East Wing and got caught by a White House tour. They were like animals, clawing at me. Like savages."

Interesting. That seemed a bit extreme. It was definitely bizarre to work in a place that had tours passing through it all day long, so part of me understood why Stephanie was jarred. In the beginning, there had been so many surreal things about working in the White House I'd lost count. As time passed, we all pretended to become accustomed to our situation and acted blasé as we immersed ourselves in the mundane aspects of our jobs. We worked at our desks and made trips to the coffeepot and the vending machine, and collectively engaged in the charade that our job atmosphere wasn't all that different from anyone else's. But the truth was, not a day went by that we weren't acutely aware that we were working in the White House, with momentous events taking place all around us. Some of us might have mastered the art of seeming calm about this reality, but underneath the façades, we were all a little giddy.

And we were all extremely stressed. It was just the nature of the place. Our jobs made us significant, but they demanded significant sacrifice in return. And everyone handled the pressure differently. Some people developed Popsicle addictions. Some people jumped into rivers. And some lashed out at others.

It struck me as overly harsh of Stephanie to react so negatively to a group of people who were excited enough to see the White House that they had waited in a long line for a tour and were subsequently thrilled to get a glance of someone they actually knew about. It also seemed a bit disingenuous, since I had been with Stephanie in the past when she'd been recognized, and had witnessed the gleam of satisfaction that always flickered across her face. She was one of the few on the White House staff who actually was identifiable to the public. Most of us toiled behind the scenes, and only occasionally popped up in the background on random C-SPAN broadcasts. The fact that some of us had overzealous family members who constantly TiVo'd said broadcasts and then combed the footage for sightings wasn't something we readily admitted to. Stephanie didn't have to worry about that. She'd always been one of the young guns close to President Wye who the media tended to profile and invite on talk shows. Plus, she was just physically memorable.

"The price of celebrity," I said lightly.

Stephanie rolled her eyes.

"I don't know how the Wyes do it. I couldn't stand it if I actually had to live here all the time."

I didn't really believe her. I bet she could stand it just fine.

"Lincoln thought it'd be a good idea to get this out to the press in time for Frand's announcement," I said, handing over the document in my hand. "I know our folks in the Senate will have a rebuttal drawn up, but it seems important enough for the White House to go on the record about it."

Stephanie nodded, sliding her eyes over the page. I wondered if she was a speed-reader. I considered speed-reading one of the less splashy, more attainable superpowers, and had been meaning to take a course in it if I ever had any free time.

"Yeah, this looks good. Let's get it to the press office."

Was I the one who was supposed to run this down there? Stephanie had resumed mumbling to herself as she scanned her BlackBerry. I guessed I was. There were assistants who had assistants at the White

House. And there were plenty of interns eager for action. Where were these people when you actually needed them?

"Stay dry," Stephanie called after me as I left.

After dropping off the release in the press office, I took the stairs back to the second floor two at a time and snagged my ringing desk phone just before it went to voice mail.

"Samantha Joyce," I answered, hoping my professional greeting made up for my breathlessness.

"Hel-lo, Samantha!" said a familiar craggy voice.

It was Alfred Jackman, an elderly constituent from Ohio whom I'd gotten to know during my Senate staffer days when he'd testified before RG's committee about the skyrocketing cost of prescription drugs. I'd hand-picked him to talk about his experiences traveling to Canada to procure the medicine he needed at more affordable prices, unaware that along with the Lipitor and Nexium he picked up across the border, he also routinely scored a fair amount of grade-A Canadian weed.

In what went down as one of my most terrifying days as a Senate staffer, I'd met eighty-three-year-old Alfred at the security checkpoint to escort him to the hearing only to find him completely, irreversibly, loopily stoned. After some significant hyperventilation, I'd managed to smuggle Alfred back out of the building, convince the committee he was too exhausted from his travels to appear until later, and then sober him up in his hotel room in time for the postponed testimony. Gratifyingly, his eventual participation helped the bill pass committee and advance to the full Senate, where it finally became law after clearing a few more hurdles.

Given how everything had worked out, I had a soft spot for Alfred Jackman, and we'd stayed in touch. President Wye was due to sign a long-overdue follow-up bill that specifically legalized the importation of lower-cost prescription drugs from Canada this morning, and I'd wrangled Alfred Jackman an invitation to the Rose Garden ceremony, after extracting promises from him and his immediate family members that he would arrive clear-headed and felony-free. It was a gamble, but I had faith.

"Hi Alfred, will I still be seeing you this morning?" I asked.

"Not unless I can post bail and hop a plane in time," he answered.

Did faith enjoy biting me in the ass? I couldn't account for the frequency of the occurrence otherwise.

"What happened?!" I tried to ask calmly.

"Have you seen that movie *Traffic*?" he asked.

Had he? I didn't think he had the attention span for that sort of movie. He'd told me before that his favorite show was *Teletubbies*. I'd assumed he didn't mean his favorite show sober.

"I've seen it," I replied guardedly.

Was this where I should get off the phone to avoid hearing something that would make me some sort of accessory after the fact? I was on a White House phone. Nixon had taped himself out of office very nearby. One couldn't be too careful around here.

"So then you're familiar with border-running," he continued. "Well, a bunch of us couldn't wait for this bill—we've got friends and family who can't make the Canada trip, so we took it upon ourselves to smuggle the medicine they need back ourselves."

I put my head in my hands.

"Any illegal drugs?" I asked.

"No. No ganja. Just regular prescription stuff. But it's illegal to import them, as you know."

"It'll be legal after today. Why couldn't you have just waited?" I implored.

"I could've," he answered. "But the people who need this stuff couldn't. They're already barely scraping by."

This chastised me. I knew about those people. I knew a lot of them were forced into a horrible choice between food or medicine. I knew many of them willed their pills to friends upon their death, to try to help them out a little from the afterlife. The situation was dire, which was why RG had pushed so hard for this bill. But it *had* taken a while. I couldn't deny that.

"How'd you get caught?" I asked with a sigh.

"Irma and I were pulled over for weaving. I think I need a new prescription for my glasses. Anyway, they opened up the trunk and saw all the teddy bears and didn't believe our cover story."

"Teddy bears?"

"Yeah, we took out the stuffing of these cute little bears and filled them up with Lipitor, Prevacid, Fosamax, Nexium . . . you know that controversial drug BiDil?"

"Uh-huh . . ." I managed.

"We stuffed the pandas' noses with that!" he said proudly.

"Have I met Irma?" I asked wearily.

"No, she's just a fling," Alfred answered. "A great companion when you're on the lam, though."

"On the lam" was one of those phrases that had stumped me as a child. When I'd been told that it referred to a fleeing criminal, all I could imagine was a tiny fugitive riding a baby sheep, adorably outrunning the law.

Surely Alfred hadn't tried to flee from any police officers, had he? Surely this was just one of his many figures of speech. I could sense faith licking her chops.

"You didn't resist arrest, did you?" I asked.

"Well, wouldn't you?" was the reply.

My head sank deeper as my elbows slid out farther in defeat. He seemed to pick up on my despair over the crackling phone line.

"Not for long, don't worry," he reassured me. "But I'm eighty-five now and who knows how much time I've got left. I didn't want to spend it in the slammer. Though now that I'm here, it's not that bad," he continued. "It sure beats the nursing home."

I wasn't going to argue with that. Few things depressed me more than nursing homes. They were tied with casinos on the list of things that put me in serious funks. Whenever I thought about them for too long, forget about the horror of actual visitations, I had to force myself to think about daisies and pumpkin pie and Steve Martin to pull me back from the darkness.

"So how long are they holding you?" I asked, returning my thoughts to the crisis at hand.

"Not sure. My nephew's on his way with bail money, but they're saying they won't release me unless I rat out the others."

"Others?"

"Yeah, my posse. My crew. Anyway, I wanted to call because I'm not gonna make it to the ceremony today. I'll watch it on TV if I can convince the guys here in the clink to take a CNN break from the monster truck channel. But I've got a hunch it might be a tough sell." He chuckled.

I could tell Alfred was sort of enjoying himself. I hoped the charges weren't serious, because I imagined the novelty of being in jail might wear off in a few days.

"Is there anything I can do for you?" I asked.

"Just don't forget about me, sweetheart," he said.

There was little chance of that.

I switched lines and intercommed Lincoln to tell him about Jackman and that we now had an extra slot at the signing ceremony. I also called down to RG's office to let them know that they should strike out the mention of Jackman in RG's talking points, and I buzzed Stephanie's office to clue her into the situation as well. I expected to leave a message for her, but to my surprise, her assistant put me right through.

"What's up now?" Stephanie asked.

"A constituent who was coming to the signing today just called me from jail. Should I talk to the press office about it?"

"Tell me the story," Stephanie ordered.

"He was smuggling prescription drugs from Canada. He got busted. You'd think he could've waited a couple days, but he feels a sense of duty. He's eighty-five."

"Impressive effort. Yeah, you might want to tell the press office just in case. If we get dragged into it, we might be able to spin it our way. Dire need for the bill, et cetera."

"Got it," I said, but Stephanie had already clicked off.

As I called the press office and filled them in on the Jackman background, I thought about how my tenth-grade English teacher had told our class never to say "et cetera." She claimed its usage was a sign of lack of imagination rather than busyness. I believe it can be a sign of either or both, and I love when people say it. To my ears, it amounts to an invitation to fill in the blank—it's a canvas of a word. When my mom had sent me to the store to get "ingredients for chili: kidney beans, tomato paste, et cetera . . . ," I'd happily filled the cart with everything my heart desired. I'd made the argument later that Pringles and Hostess dessert products played important roles in my personal interpretation of chili—one that I felt she'd given me license to explore by her phrasing.

In a sign that my mother and I might be psychically linked, she called seconds later while I was still on the line with the White House spokesperson, who was sounding annoyed and thanking me insincerely for the heads-up on Alfred Jackman. I had to let my mom's call go to voice mail. She had my cell phone number, of course, but had a habit of calling me on my work line because she enjoyed hitting the speed dial for the White House that she had programmed into her phone. She was a political science professor at a community college back in Ohio, and an overzealously proud mom. The combination meant that she really couldn't get enough of my current position. She'd been ecstatic when I'd landed my initial job in RG's Senate office. The excitement of the last two years had nearly done her in.

"Hello, my darling White House staffer daughter, this is your mother!" her message singsongily began. "Just calling to see how everything's going. Call me when you get a break from running the country! Buh-bye!"

I'd tried to tell her that I didn't actually have all that much influence and was still a junior member of the White House staff, but she'd successfully ignored me. My father was proud of me as well, but my mom was by far the more aggressive of the two. I was certainly grateful for my parents' support. I'm an only child, and they had bolstered me in every way imaginable my entire life. They were getting older now, which I didn't like to think about, and I was secretly planning to surprise them with a VIP visit to D.C. My mom's a lifelong Anglophile despite being born and raised in the Midwest, so I had my eye out for future visits from the British prime minister. If and when he did come, I imagined there would be some interesting events surrounding his stay. I'd get extra points for anything Beatles-related.

I made a mental note to call my mom later and clicked the TV to C-SPAN to watch Frand's alternative bill announcement. As usual, he looked waxen, wide-eyed, and remarkably like Dick York. And as it always did, this Darrin association prompted the *Bewitched* theme song

to begin running through my head. Senator Frand had chosen to surround himself with parents and their young babies as he lambasted the
hubris of the administration to try to push through an "anti-human
agenda." I failed to see the misanthropy of trying to cure people stricken
with horrible diseases, but Frand seemed pretty positive that he knew
something I didn't. How clever of him to cast himself as the "pro-
human" candidate. He was really sticking his neck out with such an
edgy label.

Luckily, we'd gotten our response out in time for it to be included in
the coverage of Frand's grandstanding. That was the most we could do
at the moment. I glanced at my watch. The Import Bill signing was in
the Rose Garden in fifteen minutes. After confirming that Alfred Jackman's spot could be filled with an unincarcerated constituent, I checked
to see if Lincoln was ready to walk down.

"Oh, yes, almost," he said, seemingly surprised that it was already
time.

I noticed his lips were still stained a cherry red.

"I think you might have a little something on your mouth," I tried to
point out helpfully.

Lincoln blushed a shade that matched his Popsicle as he retrieved a
handkerchief from his pocket. He was one of the few men I knew
who still carried one of those. Even their name is old-fashioned—
"handkerchiefs" seems part of a stiffer, dated version of the English
language. Lincoln blotted his mouth clean, looking up at me questioningly when he was through.

"All gone. Perfect."

He averted his eyes as he nodded.

"Do I look all right otherwise?" he asked.

This was not something Lincoln normally cared about. I tried not to
seem surprised as I assured him that he did.

"Thanks. My mother and Emily are coming to the signing," he explained.

Emily was Lincoln's rambunctious five-year-old daughter. Lincoln's
wife had died in a car accident soon after Emily was born, and his
widowed mother had moved in to help out. Lincoln's mother was a
sweet, unassuming woman who was nowhere close to keeping up with

Emily's energy. Whenever they visited, I usually ended up being the one to entertain Emily for much longer than I could afford.

"That's great," I said enthusiastically. "I can't wait to see her."

Which was true. She was exhausting, but cute. Lincoln smiled and bowed his head as he shuffled some papers into organization on his desk. While I waited, I glanced over at his collection of Popsicle stick cabins and thought about the Abraham Lincoln book I'd just read, which was jam-packed with intriguing factoids. I'd been particularly surprised to learn that Abraham Lincoln's voice—the voice of the man many considered the greatest president in history—had evidently sounded like that of an eleven-year-old girl. I'd made a special trip to the Lincoln Memorial after reading this, and looked over the words engraved on the walls with a fresh understanding of how they might have sounded coming from their esteemed speaker's mouth. For the first time ever, they'd seemed more squeaky than rumbling. But no less resonant.

As I'd stood before his marble statue, I'd felt relieved that President Lincoln had been born well before the advent of radio and television. I doubted he would have been elected otherwise. I could just imagine a clip of his jarringly high-pitched voice being incessantly replayed while talk radio hosts and television pundits took endless, eviscerating shots, doing their gleeful best to reduce him to a national joke. And where would we be now if a far lesser man who'd only sounded better had been handed the reins during such treacherous times?

"Are you ready, Sammy?" my present-day Lincoln asked.

He was holding the door politely, waiting for me to follow him out to the hallway. We made our way down the stairs to the first floor just in time to see RG exiting his office.

"I'll be right back," he said briskly to us as he made his way down the hall toward his private restroom. "And I need to talk to you both."

"Yes, sir," Lincoln and I chimed in unison.

We stood awkwardly in the hallway, waiting for him to return. Lincoln didn't look like he was up for any more small talk, so I decided to give him a break and stick my head into RG's office. RG's three personal aides were at their desks, manning the phones.

"Hey, Sammy, how ya livin'?" Margari said brightly when she spotted me.

I liked all of them, but Margari (pronounced "Marjorie") was my favorite. Her mother had actually named her Margarine because she found the word beautiful, but Margari had shortened it sometime in grade school, not before suffering considerably. Margari had gone on to develop a real penchant for word invention that I found frequently amusing. For example, to ask me if I was happy, she'd inquire if I was "gruntled," since in her head this was the opposite of "disgruntled." I'd also fielded questions about whether things were "mantled" and "combobulated." Margari also claimed to have been the first person to refer to BlackBerrys as CrackBerrys many, many years ago in a nod to their addictiveness. It was impossible to corroborate this, but whoever had said it first, the term had certainly caught on.

"I'm pretty good. How about you? Still seeing that guy?"

Margari snorted.

"He can't handle my schedule," she replied disdainfully in her South Carolina accent. "Said he was gettin' tired of bein' accused of having an imaginary girlfriend. I think it musta struck a nerve with him, 'cause he's the type who woulda made up some out-a'-state girlfriend in college."

"Did you say that to him?" I asked.

I knew the chances were good that she had. To borrow one of her phrases, Margari was "jest as sweet as a lil' honey-covered puppy, till ya cross her." I hadn't crossed her yet, and I didn't plan to.

"A'course, I told him! So that was the end of that."

She waved off my sympathetic look.

"I'll date when I'm old. No time for it now, darlin'," she finished sunnily.

I smiled.

"She's holding out for Speck Johnson," the new aide offered from his desk across the room.

"Oh?" I raised my eyebrows at Margari.

Margari actually blushed, which I appreciated. We blushers needed to stick together. I actually took the blushing a bit too far and sometimes even broke out in a full-scale neck rash, but I'd been trying to control it with creams and scarves.

"He's been calling a lot," Margari explained. "For RG, obviously, but still we get to chat. I think he's coming to D.C. next month."

She couldn't hide the excitement in her voice. When Margari was into something, her vowels tended to draw out even further but also run together in a sort of accent canter. I liked it when she got enthusiastic. It meant exposure to a whole new dialect.

Speck Johnson was a movie star with political aspirations. Those weren't all that difficult to come by in Hollywood, but lots of people restricted themselves to fund-raising and lip service. Speck wanted more hands-on glory. He'd been busy with a movie shoot during the final months of the campaign, but had jetted to Governor Wye's side to lend his star wattage to several rallies in swing states. He was young and handsome, and he thought he was a lot smarter than he actually was.

I tried not to be too critical of him, because he was on our side after all. He probably really did agree with us on the important issues, and he probably really did want to help. So what if he was more motivated by personal ambitions than pure devotion to helping others? Being involved for his greater glory didn't make him all that different from a lot of people in D.C. And really, I hadn't spent much time with him, so who was I to judge? I was also cognizant that my ardent crush on Steve Martin often made me hostile to other alleged Hollywood heartthrobs.

"Well, Speck Johnson's an idiot if he doesn't immediately fall for you," I told Margari.

Because I suspected he was sort of an idiot anyway, this didn't even count as a white lie.

She smiled sheepishly.

"Anyway, he's very charmin' on the phone," she said.

"And he recently saved the world from killer mutants," I pointed out.

Not with the elegance and comic aplomb Steve Martin would have flawlessly brought to the role, but still, it had been a blockbuster.

Before any further discussion of Speck Johnson's oeuvre could take place, which was probably lucky because I had a lot of difficulty pronouncing French words, RG returned. I stepped quickly aside as he barked some orders at the room.

"I'll be back after the signing. Line up calls with Prime Minister Badawi, the head FEMA person on the ground in Alaska, and that

NASA climatologist I met with last week. And get me a whole lot more Mountain Dew."

RG turned again and strode down the hallway. Lincoln and I fell into step beside him.

"Any more news on Frand?" he asked.

"Well, we got the rebuttal out in time, thanks to Sammy," Lincoln answered.

Lincoln was wonderful about giving credit where it was due, which was somewhat rare around these parts.

"What did it say?" RG inquired.

Lincoln turned toward me, most likely because he considered it my right to summarize what I'd written, but possibly also because he was approaching his limit of comfortable human interaction for the hour.

"In a nutshell, we denied that we're clone-loving, human-hating monsters and pointed out the substantive differences in the bills. Hopefully the press will see our side of things," I reported.

"If they don't, we'll just kill them and experiment with their organs," RG replied.

Lincoln giggled quietly beside me.

"Listen, I've been thinking about this Canadian Import Bill," RG continued in brisk, all-business tones.

It was set to be signed in about five minutes, so any changes he was mulling were a little late.

"Yes, sir?" I replied.

RG suddenly stopped walking and turned toward us.

"Don't you think big pharma's been remarkably silent about it?" he asked in a suspicious tone.

They'd spent millions on ads accusing the administration of trying to poison the elderly via unregulated foreign prescription drugs. But despite this aggressive campaign to sink the legislation, it had squeaked past both the House and the Senate, so I'd taken their recent silence to mean they were licking their wounds.

"Well, they sponsored that round of condemnations after it passed," I answered. "And I'm sure they're gearing up to punish anyone who broke rank to side with us. I'd assumed their silence was just temporary. Frankly, I was sort of relieved to have a little time off from them."

RG gave me a sidelong glance.

"Lincoln?" he said pointedly.

"They're probably up to something, sir," Lincoln responded succinctly.

"Look into it. I don't trust it and I *don't* want to be blindsided by anything."

"Yes, sir," Lincoln and I said in unison again.

Perhaps we should try to harmonize next time. I could go bass and Lincoln could further emulate his namesake with a ringing falsetto.

We started walking again, past the Roosevelt Room, Stephanie Grader's office, and the president's private dining room. As we entered the waiting area outside the Oval Office, Fiona Wye rounded the corner from the other direction. Between her Secret Service detail, RG's, and the president's agents already posted outside his office, we now had a small army crowded into the little hall. Occasionally, the White House could feel a bit snug.

"Hello, Robert," Fiona greeted RG with a glossy smile.

I'd had limited interaction with the first lady, but knew that she was a character to be reckoned with. She had a reputation for being fiercely loyal to her husband and aggressively protective of his interests. Among the inner circle, her paranoia was legendary, though her staff did everything they could to prevent outsiders from getting wind of it. Their vigilance was warranted, since from what I heard, Fiona employed some unconventional methods to determine who should surround her husband and who should be kicked to the curb.

Back when Max Wye was governor of Louisiana, Fiona had evidently become very close to a handwriting analyst. She'd come to rely on his assessments of friends and associates and had brought him along to D.C. after the inauguration. I wasn't nearly important enough to have had my scribblings analyzed, but I knew others who were. Fiona would have samples collected with or without the person's knowledge, and then her expert would write up a report rating the person's loyalty, ambition, and intelligence. There were rumors that the recent demotion of a foreign policy advisor had been a direct result of an unsatisfactory review by the handwriting guru. Knowing he was under scrutiny, the person had jokingly begun dotting his *i*'s with little mushroom clouds, and it hadn't gone over well.

"Hello, Fiona. Coming to the signing?" RG asked pleasantly.

"Mmm." She nodded. "It better not be breezy out," she added, with a hand-check of her hairsprayed coif.

Fiona's pronunciation of "out" revealed her Canadian accent. She'd been born and raised in Toronto and had became an American citizen only after marrying her husband, whom she'd met while attending Tulane University. It was a smart idea to have her present at the bill signing since she herself was a popular Canadian import.

I caught a whiff of her heavy perfume and sneezed violently. This wasn't the first time I'd been allergic to her—I'd once been stuck behind her entourage in the back of an elevator and had nearly passed out from the fumes. Fiona really layered on the fragrance.

RG followed her into the outer Oval Office, where President Wye was adjusting his tie in the mirror, seemingly lost in thought. Lingering by the door, I waited for some signal that we should leave and head to the Rose Garden ahead of the principals, but Lincoln didn't make any move. I didn't blame him—it was an interesting scene to observe.

Wye gave his tie another tug as he took a sip of his Diet Dr Pepper. It was in a fancy glass with ice cubes, but I knew it was Diet Dr Pepper because everyone knew the president drank Diet Dr Pepper. Just like we knew he loved peppermint breath mints and didn't care for turnips. It was one of those random, inconsequential details about our chief executive that we'd collectively been made privy to.

"One-minute warning, sir," the president's personal aide called.

She had stuck her head through the doorway that led to the garden. Spotting Wye's mirror primping, she shot Fiona a loaded look.

"You look great, Max, it's about time to go," Fiona said.

He didn't respond and he didn't take his eyes from his reflection. He was shorter and stockier than RG, and not a particularly handsome man, but he had captivating eyes. He himself seemed to have been seduced by them at the moment. I'd witnessed this before on the campaign trail. When President Wye would pass a mirror, he'd become instantly fascinated by his reflection. And if there were few people

around, he was capable of staring at himself for remarkably long periods of time. Though this go-round, he seemed more glassy-eyed and
distant as he gazed at himself. Everyone knew that his father was
gravely ill with Alzheimer's and had recently taken a turn for the worse.
I knew Wye took after his father, at least physically, and I wondered if
his extended self-reflection was actually a meditation on more personal
things. Or was it really just vanity?

"Max," RG said in a deeper tone.

Wye looked over, apparently snapped out of his reverie. He finished
off his drink with a final swig, popped a peppermint breath mint, and
turned toward them with a wide grin.

"Let's get going," he said as though *he'd* been waiting for *them*.

Fiona's tense shoulders relaxed slightly.

Lincoln and I followed President Wye, Fiona, and RG at a distance
into the Rose Garden, where the bill signing was all set up. The desk
with its fifteen fresh pens ready and waiting for their half second of
glory sat squarely in the morning sunlight. The president would use
each of the pens to sign his name to the bill, stopping mid-letter to put
one down and pick up another, in a fairly bizarre routine that ensured
that he'd used all fifteen by the time his name was written. He would
then give the baptized and nearly virginal writing utensils to the fifteen
people who had played the greatest role in helping the bill become law.
Lincoln was set to receive one. He'd offered to share it with me, claiming I deserved it as much as he. I'd thanked him but declined. Sharing
a pen seemed a little desperate, even if it did have the seal and signa-
ture of the president on it. I'd just wait for my own.

Stretching out from the signing table were the rows of guests, with
the raised press platform looming behind them. Soon after we stepped
from the Oval Office, I heard Emily Thomas screech with joyful recognition. Not surprisingly, she managed to get loose from her grandmother without too much trouble and come barreling across the lawn
with impressive speed, her little red sundress billowing behind her.
Luckily the president, first lady, and RG were already clear of Emily's
path. I watched Lincoln brace for impact, but before Emily could

launch herself into her father's arms, she stopped short, a shocked expression on her face.

"B-b-beeeeeeeee!" Emily shrieked in a pitch just beneath what only dogs can hear.

She stared down at her chubby little thigh, where a red welt was rapidly forming, then looked back up with an expression of pure anguish before bursting into gasping sobs. Lincoln rushed to her and scooped her up just as she reached peak wailing volume. Several people had turned to check out the mini-commotion. Lincoln was now purple, and I wondered if he might spontaneously combust from so much unwanted attention.

I certainly couldn't let that happen. Without even really thinking about what I was doing, I took Lincoln's shoulder and guided him and Emily a few steps back inside the West Wing.

"Shhh . . . Emily, it's okay," Lincoln repeated to his seemingly inconsolable child.

"It's not okay! It huu-uurts!!" Emily yelled.

She had a point. It's not okay when it hurts. At least she'd taken the volume down a couple notches.

"I know, I know," Lincoln was saying.

"She's not allergic, is she?" I asked, with visions of EpiPens dancing in my head.

"What? No, no," Lincoln answered. "She's okay."

"NO I'M NOT!!" Emily screamed.

The volume was right back up. It was good she didn't keep things bottled inside.

"We need ice," I said suddenly.

That was the only thing that had helped take away the pain of bee stings when I was Emily's age. I looked around. We were back in the outer Oval Office, where the president's personal aide and assistants usually sat, though none of them were there at the moment. Wye's glass was resting where he'd left it on the long side table beneath the mirror, and there were still a few cubes that hadn't yet melted. I hurried over and grabbed the glass, scooped out a cube, and was about to press it onto the sting when I caught Emily's glance of pure distrust.

"This might be a little cold," I admitted.

"Here, use this," Lincoln said, bringing out his trusty handkerchief once more.

I wrapped the cube in it and pressed the whole thing against the sting.

"Is that better?" I asked gently.

Emily nodded between sniffles.

I caught Lincoln looking out toward the Rose Garden. The ceremony was just getting under way.

"Do you think we can go back outside now?" he asked Emily.

Emily looked as panicked as her father had a few minutes earlier.

"No!" she shouted in horror. "That's where the bees are! And they think I'm a big red flower!" she exclaimed, picking up the hem of her red sundress accusingly.

"They won't sting you again. Can you be brave for me?" Lincoln tried.

Emily was shaking her head so hard I feared for her little neck. And the tears had started again.

"All right, it's okay. We can stay inside," Lincoln said in resignation.

I could tell Lincoln was upset. And I understood why. He was about to miss out on his pen. On his recognition. I turned to Emily.

"Hey Emily, would it be okay if I stayed with you here and your daddy went back out into the garden?"

Lincoln looked from me to Emily, who appeared to be thinking it over. After several long moments, Emily nodded. Lincoln tenderly handed her over to me with a grateful smile.

"I'll be back soon," he promised. "I'm sorry to do this to you," he said to me. "If I can get her grandmother . . ." He trailed off.

"It's fine. We'll see you later," I replied, waving him away.

When Lincoln had made it safely back outside to the ceremony, I turned to Emily. She was sucking her thumb, which didn't seem like a good sign. The Thomases tended toward oral fixations.

"Do you feel any better?" I asked.

Emily looked up at me with wide, wet eyes. She didn't say anything.

"I bet that really hurt," I tried again. "Should we get some more ice?"

Emily looked down at her leg. I shifted her slightly and was reaching for another cube from the glass when I heard someone enter the room.

"Well, hello. What's happening in here?"

I looked up to see the president's personal aide, back from whatever errand she'd been running. She was a very pleasant woman in her mid-sixties with a brown sugary accent straight out of rural Louisiana. She'd always struck me as solid and unflappable, but she presently looked a little startled.

"We're just recovering from a bee attack," I explained.

"What are you doing with that?" she asked sharply, pointing to Wye's glass.

She had a right to be annoyed. We shouldn't have even been in here, much less handling the president's stuff.

"I'm sorry," I answered. "We needed some ice. The president was already finished with it. And we were just trying to take the sting away."

She looked down at Emily's tear-streaked cheeks and softened.

"Oh, I see," she said. "A nasty old bee got you, huh?"

Emily nodded.

"And who do you belong to?" she asked.

Emily looked perplexed and I didn't blame her. I wasn't a fan of questions that made children sound like chattel.

"This is Emily Thomas. Lincoln's daughter," I interjected.

"Oh," she replied, in the sympathetic tone of someone who'd heard the Thomas family backstory.

I peered out into the Rose Garden. Wye was signing away. It looked as though he'd gone through most of the pens. I could see Lincoln waiting expectantly nearby.

"Your daddy's about to get a special pen from the president," I told Emily, who immediately perked up.

"Daddy's getting a present?" she moved her thumb aside to ask.

"Yes, he is. An award. For being so smart," I answered.

"I want to see!" Emily shouted.

"Really? Are you better enough to come watch?"

"Yes, yes!" she assured me.

She did seem completely recovered.

"Okay, then you'll have to be very quiet. And we'll have to go back outside."

Emily looked uncertain.

"I'll make sure no bees get us," I promised. "All right?"

I was not accustomed to negotiating with children. With adults who often acted like children, sure. But real live kids were new territory. Luckily I seemed to be doing okay. Emily nodded grudgingly.

"Great! We'll see you later, then," I said to the president's personal aide.

Over my shoulder, I saw her pick up Wye's glass and walk away in search of a White House steward.

"Remember to be very quiet," I whispered in Emily's ear as we stepped back onto the patio.

She nodded, hushed. She was staring at her father, who was now shaking hands with the president while cameras snapped around them. Wye thanked everyone assembled, put his arm around his wife as he assured the press that the Canadian government was fully supportive of the new law, and concluded the ceremony with a smile and a thumbs-up.

As Wye turned to make his way back to the Oval Office, I took Emily's hand and stepped quickly aside.

"Can we go see Daddy now?" Emily asked.

"Just one second," I answered.

Wye didn't even seem to notice us as he passed. He stumbled slightly on the patio step and the nearby Secret Service agents made a quick move to catch him, but he recovered without assistance.

I led Emily across the garden to Lincoln. He was standing near the first lady, who was granting a few remarks to the eager press.

"How are you feeling, buddy?" Lincoln asked Emily quietly.

"Good. I saw you get your 'ward," Emily replied.

"You did?"

"Yeah. Sammy scared away the bees and we watched from over there."

Lincoln smiled. I felt gratified. If I was forced to play nanny, I might as well be an appreciated one.

"What did you think about it?" Lincoln asked.

"Good," Emily replied succinctly.

"Yeah," Lincoln agreed.

I surveyed the rest of the garden. The wind picked up slightly and switched direction, and I was suddenly hit with a full-force blast of Fiona Wye's perfume.

"Achoo!" I exclaimed.

"Bless you, dear," Emily's grandmother said.

"Thanks," I replied.

I still had Lincoln's handkerchief in my hand. Half of it was soggy from the ice cubes, but I brought the dry part up to my nose as I felt another sneeze coming on. How many coats of perfume did Fiona Wye apply in one sitting? Didn't anyone else notice how much she reeked? She was a walking environmental hazard.

I felt my eyes beginning to water and inhaled deeply to try to stop them. To my surprise, I smelled the unmistakable scent of whiskey. I lowered the handkerchief to get a better sniff. Was someone boozing nearby? And if so, could I maybe get in on it?

No, the air around me smelled like it had moments ago: a muggy August morning being assaulted by Chanel No. 5. The perfume was potent, but it wasn't overtly alcoholic. I raised the handkerchief to my nose again and the whiskey scent returned. Maybe Lincoln washed his clothes in some sort of moonshine detergent. Except the whole thing didn't smell like alcohol, only the wet half. The half I'd wrapped the ice cubes in. My eyes widened as my brain clicked through the facts to the only possible conclusion. Evidently, the ice cubes from the glass of Diet Dr Pepper had actually been ice cubes from a Diet Dr Pepper and whiskey cocktail.

Which meant the president of the United States had been downing a stiff drink at ten on a Wednesday morning.

On the Rocks

————

THIS WASN'T NECESSARILY AS BAD as it appeared, I tried to tell myself as I stood in the Rose Garden sniffing the handkerchief in stunned disbelief. It was true that normal, healthy, clear-headed people tended not to drink hard alcohol first thing in the morning. But many of these very same people had a regular cocktail come five o'clock. And it was past five o'clock in Riyadh, where Wye had spent the previous three days on an official state visit. His body clock just hadn't adjusted yet. That explained it.

The fact that being a teetotaler was a crucial part of Wye's well-advertised personal story made this justification a bit more compli-cated. Wye had battled a serious party-boy reputation when he'd first started out in politics. According to friends and acquaintances tracked down by reporters digging for dirt, he'd been quite the reveler in col-lege at Tulane. One former friend regaled the national press corps with the story of how Wye had once drunk a fifth of vodka a day for a week and tried to get extra credit for it from his Russian Studies professor. Essentially, this painted him as an irresponsible, entitled lush who ped-dled in ethnic stereotypes—really not the sort of personal anecdote the hopeful future leader of the free world wanted widely publicized. Since Wye couldn't escape his very drunken past, he'd decided his only option was to carve out a different sort of future.

And so, a few months shy of his thirty-fifth birthday, Wye had thrown away all the alcohol in his house, turned to his wife, Fiona, and declared himself a new man. Or so the story went. The docu-movie at the convention had featured a gospel rendition of "Ain't No

Mountain High Enough" at this point, which then became a theme throughout the rest of the film, crescendo-ing in a photo montage of Wye hugging various presumably sober children. It had been very effective.

And a complete lie? I didn't want to believe that. Maybe Wye had been a teetotaler since the age of thirty-five and had just recently decided to drink in moderation again while in Riyadh, Saudia Arabia. Where alcohol is illegal. Hmmm.

I was still holding the handkerchief to my face when I noticed RG looking at me strangely. How long had I been standing there, just inhaling? I quickly lowered the handkerchief and slipped it into my pocket. RG had turned away again and was deep in conversation with the secretary of health and human services. I wondered who else, if anyone, knew that the president had started drinking again. That was, assuming Wye's ten a.m. whiskey hadn't been a one-time thing I'd just happened to discover on the only day he'd ever done it.

I hurried back inside the West Wing and up the flight of stairs to the second floor. There, I detoured to the ladies' room and retired to a stall to think. By the time I emerged, I'd determined that there really wasn't anyone I could or should tell about what I'd found. At least not for the moment.

On the professional front, there were very few people I could talk to about this without putting my job immediately at risk. Part of me wanted to speak to RG about what I thought I'd discovered, but even that felt dangerous. If he was one of a few high-level people who already knew, he'd be upset that such potentially damaging information had fallen into the hands of a junior staffer. I really didn't want him questioning whether or not he could trust me. All of that would just complicate and probably detract from the work that we needed to accomplish.

But if RG didn't know, he probably should. If the man who ran the country was boozing at ten in the morning, shouldn't the second in command be made aware?

I suspected the answer was yes, but I needed more time to contemplate and strategize. The best thing I could do at the moment was prove my loyalty as a staffer by keeping the secret to myself.

On the personal front, I wished I could tell Charlie, but he and I had learned that there were certain lines to be drawn in our relationship when it came to our work. The reality was that I was a staffer in an administration that he was frequently investigating as a journalist. We'd had trouble early on figuring out how to be close without sharing everything, but we'd eventually achieved an acceptable balance. I knew that I could tell him about Wye and make him swear not to do anything about it, but that would just be cruel. Better for me to suffer in silence than drive him insane bottling up a story out of loyalty to me. The last thing I wanted was for him to resent me, particularly right when we were about to fly to France to get engaged.

The only other person I wanted to confide in was my best friend, Liza, who didn't even work in politics and could absolutely keep a secret, but it felt wrong to spill the beans to her if I wasn't telling Charlie. I wouldn't tell her, I decided. For a few days, at the very least.

With a semblance of a coping plan in place, I returned to my desk. Lincoln was already back in his office, typing away on his computer. I felt for his handkerchief in my skirt pocket. I needed to remember to have it cleaned—particularly now that it might be in some danger of getting subpoenaed.

I surfed a few news sites and came across a short article about the bill signing that seemed harmless enough until I got to the end, where there was a link to another story titled, "Eighty-five-Year-Old Busted for Drug-Running." Sure enough, it was about Alfred Jackman's Canadian escapades. I skimmed it and stopped short at a surprising sentence:

> According to the popular blog LyingWye, Alfred Jackman was supposed to attend this morning's Rose Garden Ceremony for the Import Bill signing, but was clearly otherwise engaged. Upon hearing the news of his incarceration, a White House aide lamented, "Why couldn't he have just waited a few days?"

That's what *I* had said, in private, to Alfred Jackman on the phone. Had he been giving interviews? Or had someone else in the White House had the exact same reaction, but on the record, to a reporter? Who? And when?

No one I knew would go on the record with anyone connected with LyingWye, which was a blog that had been plaguing the White House since the second month of the administration. LyingWye was just one of several blogs hosted on an opposition Web site owned and operated by a wealthy member of the Exterminators, the group of adversarial pranksters who'd most recently arranged for the surprise stripper and taunting fireworks display. But what distinguished LyingWye from the other blogs on the site was the fact that its anonymous author clearly enjoyed an unprecedented level of White House access. Indeed, Lying-Wye purported to be "a man inside the administration"—a claim he backed up by leaking loads of inside information. He'd reported authoritatively on everything from internal power struggles to which member of the president's Cabinet was distantly related to Charles Manson.

White House chief of staff Harry Danson had nearly had a stroke trying to hunt down and fire whoever was behind the blog, but despite his and others' best efforts, LyingWye had continued operating anonymously and untouched—his identity protected by the owner of the Web site that hosted him.

Just when we concluded that LyingWye couldn't possibly be a White House staffer because no one we worked with could be that disloyal, he would post something new that only someone who worked in the West Wing could possibly know. Such as the fact that Harry Danson was so obsessed with wholphins (the rare offspring produced by whales mating with dolphins) that he had postponed a staff meeting in order to attend the birth of one at the Baltimore Aquarium. LyingWye had posted a headline about it within an hour.

I clicked on the link to the blog and skimmed the snarky summary of the Alfred Jackman story. There was an equally poisonous account of the stripper from last night's cruise, and the fireworks incident. At least I wasn't identified by name.

I wondered if I was going to be implicated in the Alfred Jackman dustup. No one besides my close friends knew about his secret pot history, so no one I worked with knew just how irresponsible it was for me to have invited him to the Rose Garden ceremony in the first place. I hoped to keep it that way.

Just then, Lincoln buzzed me on the intercom.

"The press office wants to know who vetted Alfred Jackman."

All right. So maybe I'd have to face a little music after all.

"Okay, I'll talk to them." I sighed.

"I already did. I said I vetted him. They can't do anything to me, so just go along with it."

I was briefly speechless. Lincoln really was a rare bird. I felt lucky to work with him. And though I didn't generally support casual office deceit, I was willing to do so for my own well-being. I didn't have a hankering to be yelled at for inviting a prescription-drug smuggler to the bill signing, so I was grateful for Lincoln's protection.

"Thank you," I said with real gratitude.

"Sure. And . . . um . . . can you make some pharmaceutical calls to see if you can find out about anything going on?"

Of course I could. And I could see now that Lincoln did get something out of protecting me—someone to interact with the public in his stead whenever possible. I had no problems with our symbiotic relationship.

"I'll get right on it," I assured him.

"Good. Over, roger. Um . . . bye."

As with normal conversation, Lincoln hadn't totally mastered intercom interaction.

I put LyingWye and Alfred Jackman and the president's whiskey out of my head and scrolled through my contacts. It was time to get back to work. I wasn't on super-friendly terms with too many of the paid lobbyists for the large pharmaceutical companies, since we often ended up on opposite sides of issues. Many of them actually considered me an enemy, but there were a few with whom I enjoyed civil relationships.

I called one of them and did my professional best to chat her up. When we ran out of small talk, I became more direct, but tried to keep my tone casual.

"About the Import Bill, a lot of your colleagues have been pretty quiet about it since it passed. Is there any reason for that? I know we were on different sides, but we still really value your input."

"Oh, thanks," she replied.

I could hear the hesitation in her tone.

"And so I'd just love to know where everyone's heads are," I continued in soothing officespeak. "Since this thing is moving forward, we'd like to find more ways to get people on board."

I knew that wasn't all that likely. The pharmaceutical companies were deathly opposed to the Import Bill that had just been made law because it allowed American citizens to circumvent their high-priced medicine for the cheaper Canadian versions.

"All I can say is that some of the folks who have been supporting you on this thing might change their tune in the next month," she replied. "And, of course, one little shift can change a whole dynamic. Like everything in this town, you should be careful what you wish for."

Okay, that sounded sinister. Apparently RG's hunch was accurate. They were definitely up to something. But what?

"Exactly who are you referring to?" I asked. "The AARP? The FDA?"

"You'll know soon enough," she answered.

I couldn't get anything else out of her. I made some more calls and sent some e-mails, but no one was any more forthcoming. I had a troubling sense of foreboding, but no firm guess about what might be on the horizon.

I was surprised when I glanced at my clock and saw that it was five past one. I jumped up and raced down the stairs and out the door to meet Charlie. As I hurried through the gates and crossed Pennsylvania Avenue, I spotted him waiting for me on a bench, reading *History of Aliases,* the book I'd bought to celebrate the 146th anniversary of the revelation that George Eliot was actually a woman.

I make a point of celebrating something practically every day of the year. Ironically, this habit had begun due to my dissatisfaction with the boring and useless holidays that clog up so many commercial calendars. I'd agreed with Oscar Wilde's assessment that "most modern calendars mar the sweet simplicity of our lives by reminding us that each day that passes is the anniversary of some perfectly uninteresting event," and resolved early on to only commemorate things truly worth remembering. I'd applied strict and utterly subjective criteria and before I knew it, my days and weeks and months were filled with personal, satisfying celebrations.

Often, I just noted my holidays with mental tributes, but I sometimes did more. For the seventy-seventh anniversary of the beginning of the carving of Mount Rushmore, I watched *North by Northwest*. For Orville Wright's 136th birthday next week? Perhaps I'd review my airline safety manual collection.

Charlie looked up as I approached.

"Do you know what Ralph Lauren's real name is?" he inquired.

"Ralph Lipschitz."

"Correct. I guess I don't blame him for changing it. There was a kid in my class named Eddie Fajina who nearly had to be committed by the sixth grade. No one but the teachers ever pronounced it 'Fa-hee-na.'"

"Kids are the worst," I agreed.

Charlie put down the book, moved aside a bag of sandwiches, and guided me onto his lap. I felt grateful again that he was taller than me. I'd dated men who were shorter and had never warmed to the feeling of physically dwarfing them.

He kissed me tenderly. My future husband. A little thrill shivered through me.

"Are you cold?" he asked.

"Mmm, no. Just excited to see you," I answered happily. "But we don't have much time, so you'd better tell me what's going on."

I fluffed my hair a little, wondering why I hadn't taken a few extra minutes to try to doll myself up a bit before meeting him. Probably because I had neither the time nor the technology to adequately pull it off. Which he knew. I liked that I didn't have to pose for him.

"Right, okay," Charlie answered.

His face became more serious. He actually could speak a little French, which was going to come in handy. I couldn't even pronounce the French words that had already been incorporated into the English language, like "gauche" and "raison d'être." I lived in fear of coming across one of them when reading aloud to a group.

"You know how I've been pitching that science fraud story to my editors for the past few weeks?"

"Did they go for it?" I asked, already excited for him.

He grinned and nodded. This was an excellent development. Charlie had proven himself a formidable investigative reporter when it came to politics, which meant a lot to his editors at the *Washington Post* but often made things slightly uncomfortable in our relationship. I'd been thrilled when he'd shifted his focus a bit recently. In researching a story about a Senate debate over school prayer, Charlie had become particularly fascinated with the role of a boutique Manhattan research firm whose studies were frequently invoked by members of Congress who tended toward more extremist views. Initial research had suggested that the firm was certainly less than ethical, possibly baldly fraudulent, and undoubtedly connected to several prominent members of the House and Senate. Charlie was convinced he was on the trail of a hot story, and he didn't want to hand it over to anyone else.

"That's amazing! I knew you'd convince them," I said, delighted. "We've got to celebrate! What do you feel like doing? Anything you want!"

I waited for the trip proposal, which was obviously going to be the next thing out of his mouth. And going to France was sure to be wonderful, but maybe a domestic celebration was called for as well, it suddenly occurred to me. I began planning a party in my head. One that would truly be for him instead of me, which ruled out karaoke. I wished there were party places for adults that were as fun as a spot like Chuck E. Cheese's was for kids. When I'd expressed the desire for such places in the past, I'd been told by friends that they already existed, and that they were called "bars," but I was in the market for something with more games. I wanted an adult playdate. I'd heard there was a laser tag compound in Bethesda. Maybe I'd check that out.

"Maybe we should just have a quiet night alone," he said, smiling back at me. "I leave for New York first thing in the morning."

"Oh, okay. Will you be back by Friday?"

I knew there were often airline deals to European cities that left on Saturday morning and returned Tuesday. I could arrange to take Monday off for a good cause. In any case, I was pretty sure my productivity would skyrocket with the energy of being newly engaged, so I'd be able to make that lost time right up.

"Well, that's the other thing," he said, his smile faltering.

He looked away for a moment and his face became serious once more. When he met my gaze again, he was subdued.

"They didn't just authorize me to root out the story," he continued. "They've actually transferred me to the New York bureau."

Come again?

"Come again?" I vocalized.

"They just told me today," he said.

"You're *moving* to New York? For how long?"

"I don't know. I didn't expect this. But it's actually a promotion."

He sounded guilty when he said this. Which was how I realized that there was a part of him that considered this good news. A part he was trying to hide for my benefit.

None of this was supposed to be happening. Charlie was supposed to be inviting me on a romantic foreign trip so that he could propose. He was not supposed to be saying these other things that had no place in the future I'd mapped out for us.

"How could it be a promotion to work in New York for the *Washington Post*?" I demanded. "I think you're being tricked."

Charlie smiled wryly.

"It's a promotion. I'll show you my new card to prove it. Believe me, the last thing I want is to be away from you. Thank God New York is as close as it is. The shuttle takes two seconds. The train a few more. If I have anything to do with it, which I do, we'll be seeing each other all the time."

As Charlie spoke, my thoughts went into fast-forward. The mental scrapbook I'd begun compiling of our trip began to self-destruct. There went the shot of us at the Eiffel Tower, the glint of something new on my finger lighting up the smiles on our faces. It was a predictably conventional shot, but I'd been looking forward to it nonetheless. And there went us on the Champs-Elysées, however it was pronounced. Good-bye charming little bed and breakfast. Good-bye moonlit walk. I watched them disintegrate into dusty figments in my mind's eye.

This scrapbook was immediately replaced with a disturbing motion-picture documentary of our impending breakup. I couldn't seem to help it, I just zipped along through the visualization of our doomed trajectory.

There was the separation and the initial rifts, then they got deeper and less bridgeable. There were the fights and the misunderstandings. There were the postponed visits and the growing distance. Oh Lord, there were the easier connections with people geographically more convenient. I wanted to look away, but couldn't. And then there was the official break, and the crushing sense of loss.

I wanted to erase this mental movie, but it had already played. I wondered if it was inevitable. I'd had other relationships that had ended, one spectacularly so, but none of those had held a candle to what I had with Charlie. Charlie was different. Charlie had been the one. This was going to hurt.

"Even if we've got to live apart for a little while, you know that my home is always with you," I heard him saying.

He was referencing a recent conversation we'd had about moving in together. We felt ready, but I didn't want to inconvenience Liza, with whom I also really loved being roommates. And everything was perfectly harmonious the way it was, so we'd decided to hold off a little longer. But then I'd become insecure that maybe Charlie hadn't argued harder against holding off because deep down, he had doubts about me. Perhaps he no longer felt as strongly as he once had, now that he'd gotten to know me better. When I'd finally confessed this fear after a half glass of wine too many, Charlie had kissed me tenderly and assured me that home to him now meant wherever I was. We'd been sitting side by side in a booth in our favorite Greek restaurant. He'd taken his hand from my face, pressed it down into the fabric of our shared cushion, and declared it our home. He'd continued claiming home ownership on the trip back to my apartment, declaring as our own the sidewalk, our Metro seat, the stoop I'd jumped on to point out the Orion constellation, and the drugstore we'd stopped in for some IcyHot for my stoop-twisted ankle. In each spot, he'd found a different way of saying that since I was there, it was his home. By the time we made it to my place, we were real estate moguls and we celebrated accordingly.

"This will be a temporary arrangement and I promise you we'll make it work," Charlie was continuing. "If I didn't think we could, I never would have accepted the job."

I felt myself nodding. I even attempted a smile. Being needy and petulant was only going to speed up the inevitable rifts. I'd rather have them unfold on my terms.

"Yeah, okay, that's wonderful," I managed. "Um, I guess I should be getting back to the office."

Charlie looked concerned.

"We're going to be okay, Sammy," he said, forcing me to meet his eyes.

I loved his eyes. I loved his black glasses that had reminded me of Clark Kent when we'd first met. I loved that I still broke out in a blushing rash every once in a while when he touched me, though I wished it were a more attractive one.

"I love you," he said.

"I love you too," I answered.

And I meant it. I wasn't sure how I'd ever get over him.

I walked through Lafayette Square and crossed slowly back over Pennsylvania Avenue, feeling tired and wounded. Derrick was still on duty at the northwest gate.

"May I help you?" he asked through the intercom.

I didn't have the energy to get feisty with him. I just held up my pass, which he took his time examining.

"Do you do this to everybody?" I asked wearily.

"Do what?" he replied, releasing the door and waving me onward with a dismissive flick of his wrist.

I just walked past him, too dejected to stand up for myself.

One thing about working in the White House is that it's difficult to be self-absorbed for very long. At least for junior staffers. Perhaps it was easier for some of the higher-ups to maintain self-absorption, but my days were filled with assisting others, which helped keep things in perspective.

I spent the afternoon coordinating Roosevelt Room meetings between RG and various health care constituency groups. I drank too much coffee and unfortunately had to spend a large portion of the final meeting with a delegation from the nurses' union silently negotiating with my bladder. Just when I thought I'd have to excuse myself, which really wasn't allowed, the union's long-winded spokeswoman mercifully stopped talking. But then they wanted photographs. Sally, one of the official

White House photographers tasked with capturing as much of RG's busi-ness and general existence as possible for posterity, began snapping away. All of Sally's photographs would eventually go to the National Archives to comprise a visual day-by-day history of RG's vice presidency. At the mo-ment, she was dutifully recording every single person in the meeting shaking hands with RG. I tried to slip out the door, but one of the union reps with whom I'd worked closely called me to join a group photo. And then after the official photo was snapped, everyone's cameras came out to repeat the process for people's personal albums.

Though Sally was a professional photographer, she wasn't intimately familiar with the ins and outs of the various digital and cell phone cam-eras that were suddenly thrust upon her. Which meant that each new camera brought fresh technical challenges that further delayed my trip to the toilet.

"No, it's the other button—no, the one on the side."

"No, you have to press the flash button. But advance it to the next picture first."

"No, you've got it backward. Turn it around and look through the viewfinder."

I felt like screaming.

"Okay, now everyone stay still," Sally instructed as she politely snapped the final photo.

This was most likely directed at me, since I'd had to start tapping my foot to keep from peeing myself. Finally, finally, I escaped.

I made a beeline for the closest available ladies' room. Stephanie walked in as I was washing my hands, considerably more comfortable. I noted that a ballpoint pen had joined the pencil party going on in her hair. It was getting crowded.

"Oh, hey, I'm glad to run into you again," she said.

Really? Stephanie had never paid me very much attention. I wasn't sure why she'd start now.

"Hi," I replied, returning her smile.

It was nice to be on Stephanie's good side, even if I had no idea how I'd made it there.

"Maybe we could grab a drink sometime in the next couple weeks," she suggested. "I have a few things I'd like to discuss with you."

"Oh, yeah? Like what?" I asked curiously.

"Nothing major. I'd just like your thoughts on some strategy issues."

Could she really want my advice? Or want to be friends? Both seemed crazy, but I was willing to go along with it.

"Sure, whenever," I answered brightly.

"Great." She smiled. "I'll 'Berry you. It'll be good to talk. It's important to be certain who you can trust around here, you know?"

I'd been assuming I could trust everyone. Weren't we all on the same team? I knew there were power struggles and the sort of interoffice politics inherent to any job environment, but I'd never felt personally impacted by them. Clearly Stephanie had.

I got away with a nod and returned to my desk, where I stayed until past nine p.m., absorbing the latest National Institutes of Health reports and outlining the proposal for a White House conference on lifestyle drugs that RG had requested.

I finally packed up and trudged toward home. I rarely get sleepy, thanks to my constant coffee infusion, but I am always aware of the exhaustion lying in wait just beneath the surface, threatening to exploit any chinks in my caffeine armor.

Walking out of the White House at night reminded me that I worked in a place that never really slept. At this hour, there were still lots of people at their desks. I could hear phones ringing and Xerox machines humming. I could smell the grease of the last batch of French fries from the mess. Even when staffers finally did head home for a few hours of sleep, the military personnel stayed on in the situation room monitoring the planet around the clock, and the uniformed Secret Service continued keeping guard. This meant that even in the darkest dead of any night, the building was alive.

Charlie had been held up at work, finishing a hundred necessary tasks before he left for New York in the morning. He had promised to meet me at my place as soon as he could. I felt sad and fatalistic about our relationship all over again, and attempted to scald my troubles away with a therapeutic shower. I would have preferred a bath, but the two-bedroom apartment in Adams Morgan that Liza and I had shared for the past two years didn't come with a whole lot of luxury perks. Long soaks in a tub were something I could look forward to only when I went home to my parents. They were aware of this incentive, and frequently called me with the bathwater running in the background to remind me of what I could be enjoying more often. I'd called my mother out on this tactic a few weeks ago, and she'd pled ignorance.

"What are you talking about, honey? I just like stretching out in this great big tub filled with bubbles while I talk to you on the phone. There's really *nothing* like a bath to rejuvenate you. Oh, and we just got some jets installed. It's like a heavenly water massage. By the way, do you have Labor Day plans?"

Though I saw through my mom's manipulation, it was still fairly effective. If I didn't have to work over Labor Day, I'd probably be on a plane headed back to Cincinnati.

When Liza arrived home, I was curled up on the couch in a fuzzy robe. I'd been working on not crying about Charlie's impending departure and its inevitable repercussions for our heretofore blissful relationship. As with unwanted laughter, trying not to cry generally brought it on even stronger and more quickly. I knew that it often helped to just let it out, but I wasn't prepared to relinquish control just yet. I'd found that distracting myself with mindless, repetitive tasks had helped me avoid unwelcome breakdowns in the past, so I'd spent the last twenty minutes trying to throw pennies into a sneaker that was lying on the floor across the room.

"Bored?" Liza inquired hopefully as she let herself in.

She knew that "traumatized" was the other option.

"I'm reclaiming my childhood," I answered.

She put down her bag and crossed the room toward me, amazingly graceful in gravity-taunting stilettos. We shared the same foot size, seven and a half, but there was absolutely no danger of closet poaching since I lacked the balance and pain threshold to wear any of her infinitely more stylish shoes.

"How's that going?" she asked as she plopped herself down nearby.

Even when plopping, Liza had a natural elegance about her. She always seemed effortlessly put together—all cocoa-buttery skin and mermaid hair and clothes you wanted to touch. Next to her, I was a puffy mess.

"Mmmkay." I shrugged noncommittally as I missed the sneaker once more.

I was very glad Liza was home and I wanted to tell her about everything, but I preferred to do it without tears. So I needed to take it slow.

"When I was a kid, I could entertain myself with simple stuff like this for hours," I began. "I didn't have to spend my time on complicated things, like a stressful job or a boyfriend who announces he's moving to New York when he's supposed to be proposing a romantic engagement trip to Europe."

"What?" Liza caught a penny in midair as it soared from my hand toward the shoe.

"Charlie got a promotion. He's moving to New York tomorrow."

"He works for the *Washington Post*."

"I pointed that out."

"I'm sure their New York bureau is perfectly prestigious, but why does *he* have to go there?"

I shrugged morosely.

"And he expects you to just be fine with this?"

"I think so, yeah."

Liza looked consternated. Telling her had helped, actually. I didn't feel so much like crying. More like getting to the bottom of this puzzling mystery.

"But you're not fine with it, right?"

"Nope." I shook my head. "But what can I do? He's incredibly supportive of my career, and I want to be the same for him."

Liza nodded slowly, sending a long ripple through her dark hair.

"New York really isn't that far," she tried.

"That's what he said."

"And it will give you a great reason to go there a lot."

"With all the leftover cash from my fat government paycheck."

Liza looked concerned.

"I'm sorry," she said simply.

I knew that she was.

"Thanks," I said. "I want to believe it'll be fine. Because Charlie is, you know . . ."

I felt myself tearing up.

"I know he is. It *will* be fine. We'll make it fine. That man loves you more than anything. He'd never consciously jeopardize what you've got. In fact, if you told him not to go, not that you would, but *if* you did, I bet you he'd stay."

I wasn't so sure about that. Liza saw the doubt in my face.

"It's true," she insisted.

"Well, I don't think I should test it."

I believed that Charlie and I had a very good thing going—the best thing I'd ever had, or imagined, in fact—but it was dangerous to pit it against either one of our career ambitions.

"I'm pouring us drinks," Liza said decisively as she leapt up and headed for the kitchen.

Which reminded me of Wye.

"You know, I think I'll just have some tea or something," I called after her.

She swiveled on her heels, which were honestly more like stilts.

"Are you sure?" she asked in a tone that revealed she now thought something was *really* wrong with me.

"Yeah, I'm sure, thanks," I replied. "I'll come get it in a second."

Liza disappeared into the kitchen. I dialed Charlie's cell phone. I'd turned down the drink because I wanted to stay as focused and calm as possible for when he came home, considering this would be our last night together for an undetermined length of time. Charlie estimated he'd be another hour at work.

"I'm sorry. If I could be there any sooner, I would."

"I know. Good luck finishing up," I replied.

"Thanks. I'll be thinking about you. I love your body, Larry."

I smiled as I clicked the phone shut, appreciative of the *Fletch* reference. I'd told him once that I particularly liked that movie, not least because Geena Davis had played a woman with a masculine name. I'd identified with her immediately, as well as with her unrequited crush on Chevy Chase. I'd connected with the unrequited part, that is. Chevy Chase had never done it for me. I was strictly a Steve Martin girl.

Charlie had no problem with my Steve Martin fascination, which predated him by nearly two decades, and luckily understood that it did not give him license to harbor his own crush on someone who was not me.

Charlie fit me perfectly, even with all my uneven double-standard edges. I really didn't want to lose him. I sighed and closed my eyes and said a short prayer to the God of Preventing Separations from Sabotaging True Love.

I'd believed in appealing to extremely specific gods ever since first contemplating the existence of an omniscient spiritual being around age four. It had seemed clear to me then that my chances of being heard by a divine entity who was being simultaneously besieged by billions of other pleas were alarmingly slim. In the midst of so many other requests, how could that one distracted deity really pay much attention to my burning need for a tassled pink tricycle like Lexi Towney's? I was much more confident that the God of Pink Bikes had the time and inclination. And when that glorious piece of cycling perfection had been unwrapped on my birthday, I knew exactly whom to thank. Ever since, I'd relied on a large and expanding stable of very diverse gods to keep me spiritually engaged.

I opened my eyes, feeling lighter again. Maybe Charlie and I could make this work. Maybe the separation would actually make our relationship stronger in ways that I hadn't even considered. It would be foolish not to allow room for that hope. I made my way into the kitchen, where I was further pleased to discover that Cal Ripken Jr. was no longer on the brink of death.

"Doesn't he look great?" Liza said as she put the teakettle on to boil and took a sip of her vodka tonic.

Indeed, he did. He was swimming around perkily in his bowl and his gills had almost completely lost their grayish tint, which was hugely relieving. I knew it was possible that this was only a temporary improvement, since I unfortunately had a long and tawdry history of failed Japanese fighting fish caretaking. There had been a dark period when I'd killed eight fish within the space of eleven months, despite doing everything in my power to keep them alive. I had yet to recover from the emotional scars left by such a murderous streak, but held out hope that I could change my luck.

At first, Cal Ripken Jr. had seemed the fish to do it. He'd hung in

there for a record-breaking thirteen months, living up to the name I'd
optimistically bestowed upon him in the hopes that he'd display an
unprecedented winning streak in the game of life. But then he'd begun
showing signs of fatigue and I'd become alarmed. He'd been headed
for the hall of fame. He couldn't blow it now.

The owner of the new pet store I'd begun frequenting told me Cal
needed more exercise and prescribed once-a-day doses of the mirror
trick. This trick capitalized on the extreme territoriality of the male
Japanese fighting fish by fooling him into athletically flaring out his gills
in a protective response to any perceived intruder—even one that was
actually just a mirror reflection of the ferocious but dim-witted fish
himself.

Problems arose when I began feeling guilty watching him inflate
with rage over his own reflection. It seemed like some kind of perverted narcissistic torture. Plus, it made me feel like I was tricking Cal
Ripken Jr. into hating himself. Having been told in the past that I was
my own worst enemy, I'd wondered if somewhere deep down I took
pleasure in transferring this character flaw to another being. Did it
make me feel less lonely to have a pet with similar issues?

Last weekend, after deciding to replace the mirror with a live ad-
versary, I'd returned to the pet store and immediately spotted Professor Moriarty. I'd been intrigued by his reddish tinge and the way he
emanated a sort of quiet, criminal mastermind vibe. Granted, I might
have been unduly influenced by the large FBI "Wanted" poster tacked
on the wall behind his tank, next door to the cage of an enormous par-
rot named Sherlock, but there was something else about the fish's non-
chalant swimming style that seemed clever and provocative. Since I
was in the market for a nemesis, I'd snatched him up.

For the past week, Liza and I had arranged evil playdates between
Cal and Professor Moriarty by putting their bowls next to each other
for short periods of time. Cal always perked up immediately, egged on
by Professor Moriarty's cool disregard for his frenzied reaction. When
it got to the point where Cal looked like he might explode, I'd separate
them until the next time he showed signs of throwing in the towel.
Then Professor Moriarty would pay another little visit.

"Looking strong, Cal," I encouraged.

"Yeah, he'll make it," Liza said. "He's from hearty stock."

Liza took pride in being part Japanese American. I pretended that it didn't bother me that she had a special cultural bond with my fish that I could never approximate.

"How's that vodka treating you?" I asked. She'd almost finished her drink.

She gave an impeccably manicured thumbs-up. I suddenly realized I hadn't even asked her how she was doing. I was neglecting all my roommates.

"How are *you*?" I inquired.

"Not amazing," she admitted. "It's been a rough couple days."

Just because Liza always appeared put together didn't mean that she actually was. She worked as a catering director for the Mayflower Hotel, but longed to open her own event company specializing in lavish bacchanalian celebrations. Thanks to her classics degree and wild streak, she had a well-researched vision, but lacked the seed money to implement it. In Liza's spare time, she trained for her pilot's license and dated men who weren't good enough for her. She'd elevated this latter hobby to an art form, proving herself uncannily talented at attaching herself to all the wrong guys. Her romantic missteps were completely baffling to her friends, who knew firsthand how much better she deserved. I didn't know whether her bad week was due to personal or professional woes, or some treacherous combination of the two.

"What happened?" I asked sympathetically.

"It's nothing," she said dismissively, waving away the topic. "There're rumblings of another strike and we're deluged with orders and I still haven't gotten up the nerve to ask for my raise and Jakers is giving me grief for not spending enough time with him, and the Red Sox are four games behind." She sighed.

"Oh okay, well, if it's nothing, then . . ."

Liza smiled.

"I'm sorry," I continued, feeling renewed guilt that I hadn't named Cal Ripken Jr. David Ortiz like Liza had wanted. It was so easy to make her happy just by showing the Red Sox a little love.

"Is there anything I can do to help?" I asked.

I wasn't sure what to do about the work troubles, but I'd happily break up with Jakers for her if she'd let me. Though I'd become accustomed to her flow of unworthy boyfriends, I grew alarmed when one of them lingered too long. We were in just such a disturbing holding pattern now with her current flame, whom she'd been dating for ten months already. As time kept marching along, I became more and more concerned that she might slip-slide into settling for him.

On our last double date, Jakers had relayed a story about a gay coworker, assuring us that he didn't have "any problem with the homos, as long as they don't try to hug me or anything." As Charlie coughed and changed the subject, my eyes had whipped to Liza's face, expecting a look of horror or distaste. I'd been unprepared for the glassy, no-big-deal expression that had greeted me instead. It was almost as though she hadn't heard him.

"I'll be okay, let's not think about our problems any more tonight," Liza said. "I am hungry, though," she continued, looking at her watch. "I might have second dinner before bed. Any interest?"

Second dinner was one of Liza's and my favorite meals. It normally involved pancakes, but tonight I lobbied for pasta and pastries. I'd had Clemenza's "Leave the gun, take the cannoli" line from *The Godfather* in my head ever since the fireworks incident. Gunshot-like noises tended to conjure up that classic scene in my mind's eye.

"Hey, it's ten o'clock," Liza said when we were loading up our plates. "Isn't *Piling On* on tonight?"

We raced to the couch and flipped to the channel just as the title sequence began.

Piling On was a new reality television show. It promised to break fresh ground in the fully saturated reality TV market, because its producers had somehow managed to convince the former president of the United States, President Pile, to allow cameras to document his everyday existence after leaving the White House.

Before Wye and RG had swept into office on the strength of the country's desperate hope for a new direction, President Pile had managed to thoroughly mangle things over the course of two disastrous terms. He'd run the economy into the ground, ignored imminent threats to national security in favor of manufactured ones, and almost irreversibly tarnished the country's reputation abroad. When it came to shaping policy goals—whether for protecting the environment, shoring up Social Security, improving education, or reforming health care—the Pile administration perpetually endorsed short-term profiteering over long-term responsibility. By the time he'd wrapped up his seemingly endless catastrophic reign, America was exhausted from his misleadership and relieved to finally be rid of him.

But he would not go quietly into that good night. Reportedly starved for attention, and in quest of funds to build a full-scale aircraft carrier replica on the grounds of his library, Pile had agreed to put his post–White House life on display for the cameras. And thus, we were subjected to *Piling On*, which promised entertainment of the highest caliber. So far, this included pop-up thought bubbles and a running crawl featuring viewers' text-messaged reactions.

This show opened with President Pile astride a lawn mower, ready to tackle the sprawling green expanse that rolled magnificently from his mansion to the banks of a nearby river. He squinted forcefully into the camera.

"There's nothing like a hard day's work to keep a man honest," he intoned.

"Doesn't that huge utility belt he's wearing seem a little unnecessary?" Liza asked.

It did. But Pile had always been a big fan of props. We watched as he revved the engine of his mower, sending a cloud of smoke into the air, which got him coughing.

"Water break," he sputtered to the cameras. "Cut!"

But of course the cameraman didn't cut. He stayed on Pile as he coughed his way back to composure, seemingly unaware that he was still on film. I liked this show.

When Pile finally recovered, he patted down his forehead with a bandana, adjusted his hat, and turned back to the camera.

"Okay, action!" he shouted.

The camera kept rolling.

"Watch out grass, here I come!" he whooped.

The show went into a speeded-up montage of Pile mowing his enormous lawn. When his lawnmower blades snagged on a fallen branch, he called over one of his Secret Service agents to help extricate it.

Moments later, he ran over a quail's nest, which was mercifully empty at the time.

"Whoops! Heh, heh, heh, I'm bulldozin' settlements!" he said to the camera.

He continued laughing to himself. Liza and I stared at the screen, speechless. As Pile bent down to extract the mangled nest from the blades, a thought bubble popped up that read, "This is for the birds!"

It cut to a commercial for Viagra just as Charlie showed up. He gave me a kiss before loading up his own plate of pasta. I'd already resolved to act like everything was fine between us, and that the New York sojourn he was making in less than twelve hours was no different from his other work trips.

"Has he had his mower mishap yet?" Charlie asked as the show returned.

Charlie had watched an advance copy of *Piling On* at work the previous week. His review had been our main reason for tuning in, though I probably would have checked it out once anyway, just out of curiosity.

"Which one?" I asked.

"If you don't know, then it hasn't happened yet," Charlie assured me.

On-screen, Pile was becoming frustrated trying to mow the fence line. It was a task that seemed to require a bit more patience and skill than he possessed. After stomping his foot into the mower a few times, he just gave up.

"Time to tackle the river!" he exclaimed.

Distracting his audience away from an incomplete, failed project with enthusiasm for a new mission was a tried and true Pile tactic.

The scroll of viewer e-mails seemed to have been hijacked by hard-core lawn mower aficionados spurting out facts about different models. It was difficult to read them and follow what was happening on-screen. Pile was now mowing just along the river's edge. As he got to a steep section, the mower began to teeter. Liza gasped, which was when I realized I was on the edge of the couch. And we both held our breath as Pile launched himself from his seat just before the mower toppled completely into the river. This was compelling television.

"That's the one," Charlie said.

"He really could have hurt himself!" Liza replied.

Which was true. But he hadn't. And the cameras had captured everything, including Pile's decision to just leave the mower in the river for the moment.

"Someone else can clean up this damn mess," he muttered as he limped toward the house.

Which pretty much summed up his leadership philosophy.

We all clapped as the show went to credits. I immediately ordered a TiVo season pass. I normally didn't have time for any television besides news programs, but this was a show I planned to follow.

"I'm heading to bed," Liza announced, standing up abruptly. "You kids don't stay up too late."

She smiled at us both and disappeared into her room. I knew she was calling Jakers, and the thought made me shudder involuntarily.

"Are you okay?" Charlie asked.

"Yeah," I lied.

We had our own issues. There was no need to dabble in other people's. Charlie touched my face.

"Listen, is there any way I can entice you to New York for the weekend? I'll have to run around a lot setting things up, but I'd love the chance to pitch some woo in another city."

I considered. It wasn't France, but it was a start. Still, I felt insecure that he was just proposing this because I'd had such an adverse reaction to his original announcement. I didn't want him to invite me to New York because he was worried about me. I wanted him to invite me to New York because he knew his life would feel empty and meaningless away from my side.

"Actually, my woo-catcher's mitt is still at the shop, so maybe we should wait a bit," I answered.

Charlie looked briefly surprised, but eased through the moment as usual. Did he look relieved as well? Or was that just my imagination showing its cruel streak?

"Okay, sure, I know you're swamped with work. I'm sorry I just sprang all this on you, but it was a surprise to me as well," he said, running his fingers from my hairline down to my chin.

I loved it when he did that. Although it always made me feel sort of like a cat, which was not an animal I easily identified with. I'd always considered myself a lot more canine, in need of near-constant attention and affection and unafraid to display my love and dedication in all its goofy transparency. This now struck me as immensely unattractive. Maybe it was time for some adjustments. Perhaps I should try to channel some feline mystery and aloofness to keep Charlie interested.

"I'll try to make it work for next weekend," I said. "But I've got a lifestyle drug conference to set up and the usual roster of craziness."

Charlie looked a bit crestfallen.

"Maybe with our work schedules, this whole move is actually going to be more difficult than I thought," he said slowly, turning the words over in his mind before letting them out of his mouth.

He finally seemed to be grasping the tragic scope of our impending separation. It was about time. I was getting tired of all his positive thinking.

"It's going to be tough," I agreed.

Charlie grimaced. I felt a guilty pang. Though I wanted him to feel some sadness and trepidation over this ill-advised move, I didn't want to make him unhappy on our last night together before who knew when. Instead of fostering a feeling of doom, I should really be reminding him of why what we had was worth holding on to.

"Maybe they'll invent instant transporters soon so we can just beam ourselves to each other whenever we want," I suggested lightly. "You should look into that."

Charlie smiled.

"I thought I was supposed to be spending all my free inventing hours on time travel," he replied.

"True. But your multitasking ability is one of the things I love about you," I responded.

"Stop it. You know your dirty talk drives me wild."

I giggled as Charlie jokingly mauled me.

"Tell me more about my multitasking, baby," he growled in my ear.

Not surprisingly, the pretend making out evolved fairly rapidly into the real thing. I was just about to redirect us to my room when Liza burst out of hers. Charlie and I composed ourselves as quickly as possible.

"Oh God, I hate it when I feel like your mother," she said.

She turned to retreat to her room but Charlie and I both called out to stop her. She turned back.

"I'm sorry," she said. "Although I guess your mother wouldn't be on her second vodka tonic on a school night, huh?"

Charlie shook his head.

"She prefers gin," he replied.

Liza laughed. She headed to the kitchen, and Charlie and I relocated to the privacy of my room.

"Should I rave about your filing prowess to get us back in the mood?" I asked.

Charlie was a proficient organizer, which was further proof that opposites attract. He smiled as he hit the lights and pulled me toward the bed.

"I have a pretty good idea of where we were," he said as he slid his hand inside my robe.

I closed my eyes.

"I think it was right about here," he said softly.

Yes, I think it was.

Cheap Shots

———·••·———

THE NEXT MORNING, I arrived at the office ten minutes late after miscalculating the time. This was due to Charlie. On the whole, we were stunningly compatible, but there were a few areas of discord. One egregious one was his confusing relationship with time. Despite my frequently expressed objections, he persisted in setting his watch ten minutes fast. I knew he wasn't alone in this habit. I knew that there were actually lots of people who did this. And I also knew that they were all very deluded.

Charlie had reiterated the basic rationale several times. I got it. He wanted a built-in buffer time and had calculated that ten minutes was the average zone of delay. So even when his watch told him he was ten minutes late, he was actually on time. But there was an essential flaw to this whole thing that screeched to be acknowledged. I argued that he couldn't trick his brain with a scheme that his very same brain had concocted. He knew about the buffer zone, so when he needed a little more time to do something, he could just dip into it without guilt. But if he went over the ten minutes, all of a sudden he had to do arithmetic to figure out just how late he was. His watch said twelve minutes, but that was actually just two real minutes late once you subtracted the ten fantasy minutes. And then how long could it be before he decided his buffer zone should be twelve instead of ten? It was a slippery slope.

It got worse. In addition to the ten-minute-fast thing with his watch, Charlie liked to set his alarm for an hour before he actually had to get up. He'd explained that he really loved feeling good about everything first thing in the morning, and nothing made him feel better than the knowledge that he still had another hour left to sleep. I thought he was showing early signs of senility, but he insisted the alarm trick was something he'd done since he was fourteen and had to get up before dawn for swim practice. I told him that if he would just let us sleep in peace until it was actually time to get up, I would be well rested and grateful enough to ensure that he felt very good first thing in the morning. Better than any alarm could. This had gotten his attention. We'd eventually agreed to a compromise, and he now used his alarm trick only on days when he felt like he'd really appreciate it.

Unfortunately for me, this morning had been one of those days. I didn't share Charlie's ability to instantly fall back asleep after being roused by a jarring noise. Instead, I always stayed awake, staring at the ceiling, listening to the ticking of the clock blending with Charlie's steady, peaceful breathing. In these moments, part of me enjoyed the still calm of the stolen hour, but most of me was cognizant of how much more I would benefit from the sleep that so regularly eluded me.

The trouble this morning began when I'd stayed awake for fifty-six minutes, from the time the fake alarm sounded up until four minutes before the real alarm was scheduled. Somewhere in that fifty-sixth minute, I'd managed to finally sink back into a very deep sleep. Which had made the subsequent rousing all the more painful.

I'd never fully recovered and had stumbled through my morning routine with my eyes half shut and my brain half off. When I'd kissed Charlie good-bye on the street, too disoriented to be upset that he was headed to New York, I'd realized I'd forgotten to put on my watch. Charlie had told me it was seven twenty, which really meant seven ten, which meant I still had thirty-five minutes to get to work at my normal time. Since it normally only took me twenty-five, I'd lingered at a nearby newsstand, skimming *The Economist* and *Newsweek*, and sheepishly eyeing some less reputable magazines that tended toward the softer side of news. Speck Johnson was gracing the cover of one advertising a list of the "Top Twenty Bachelors Who Haven't Been to Rehab."

I was embarrassed about my fondness for celebrity gossip magazines. I knew most of them were trashy, and I knew I should spend my extremely limited free time on more noble pursuits, but it was really difficult not to flip through one of them if it was just lying in front of me. However, I knew the human brain has only so much space for retention of information, and I'd been alarmed to recently discover that though I could recite the names of Demi Moore's children, I no longer had any idea what the Treaty of Ghent was. I'd subsequently put a moratorium on any consumption of celebrity news, and had started rereading my history textbooks from high school.

I was successfully upholding the ban, though admittedly feeling tempted (who were those other nineteen unrehabilitated catches?), when my phone rang with a call from Lincoln's assistant, Nick.

"Hey, Lincoln needs you to come in as soon as you can," he said.

"I'm on my way," I replied, walking quickly away from the newsstand.

It was when I clicked off the call and saw the time on my phone that I realized something had gone wrong. It was now seven thirty, which meant Charlie had actually told me the real time, not his crazy mixed-up time. This also meant that I had only fifteen minutes to get to work. I couldn't make the bus or the train move any faster than they normally did, so I resigned myself to the fact that I would be ten minutes late. This wouldn't be a problem if I wasn't now worried that there was some sort of crisis going on. I'd already learned that at the White House level, ten minutes could easily mean the difference between a close shave and a full-blown catastrophe.

I was breathless when I burst through the door. Nick looked up from his computer. He was a slight man of twenty-four who was outgoing and excitable. Really the opposite of Lincoln. He'd started only a few weeks ago, after Lincoln's long-time assistant had left to join the Peace Corps in Paraguay. Nick had been interning in our office and was beside himself with delight over his promotion.

"He wants you to go right in," he told me eagerly.

Lincoln was pacing behind his desk when I entered his office. He looked up when I cleared my throat.

"We have a problem."

"Okay," I said calmly, waiting for him to elaborate.

"The three largest pharmaceutical companies have informed the Canadian government that they will no longer be supplying their country with medicine."

I sank into a nearby chair. Lincoln continued.

"Minister DuBois called the president half an hour ago. As you can imagine, she was not pleased."

This was swift, direct, and extreme retaliation for the bill signed into law yesterday. The pharmaceutical companies had been furious all along at the thought of how much money they would lose as soon as American citizens were allowed to legally import cheaper Canadian drugs. Having lost the legislative battle, they were evidently willing to take excessive measures for revenge.

"They really cut them off?" I asked in disbelief. "Completely?"

"Not completely," Lincoln replied. "They cut off the five most popular drugs that don't have generic equivalents."

"How could they do this?" I protested. "I've never thought they were just evil. They're willing to deprive an entire country to protect their bottom line?"

"They are businesses, Sammy," Lincoln replied. "Canada is a relatively small market that they can afford to lose if it means preventing significant damage to the larger, more lucrative American one. They blame us for messing everything up. In their view, each market can support a different price, and now we've meddled by legislating access to lower ones. They feel we forced their hand."

I understood all that. And of course it made sense that successful companies went to considerable lengths to protect their markets, but *still*. Didn't they take anything else into account?

"I'm going back down to strategize with Stephanie and the president about this in fifteen minutes, and Secretary Harlow's called an emergency meeting for ten a.m. Pull together anything you can that could help us before then."

"Yes, sir," I said as I hurried out the door.

Secretary Harlow was the head of the Department of Health and Human Services. I'd watched RG talking with her the day before in the Rose Garden, celebrating the signing of the bill. I imagined she was in a far worse mood today.

The news hit the wire later that hour and the Canadian parliament went into an uproar, with many in the opposition party blasting the prime minister for going along with the importation agreement. They accused her of placing a higher premium on genial relations with the United States than on the health and well-being of her own citizenry.

All along, we'd considered the Canadian Import Bill just a temporary solution to the larger problem of the prohibitive cost of prescription drugs. But now this plan that we had touted for years, this bill we'd fought passionately to pass, had completely and utterly backfired and spiraled into a messy international brouhaha. We should have been more careful what we wished for.

By evening, protests had swept across Canada over the immediate shortage of medicine. President Wye held a hastily arranged press conference to announce that though the bill had just been signed into law, the FDA-approved import companies would not open for business. He vowed to help Canada fight the pharmaceutical companies' ban and search for other sources for the drugs they needed. He proclaimed this search to be one of his top priorities.

Which led to my being told that I'd be leaving for India the following week.

For the past several months, I'd been steadily lobbying to use RG's scheduled visit to India as an opportunity to initiate substantive trade relationships with the subcontinent's red-hot biotech industry. I'd written two different reports about the urgent need to partner with a country that was so clearly on the cutting edge of research and drug manufacturing. And after months of getting pleasantly brushed off by Stephanie and others who believed RG should spend his limited time in India pursuing more national security–related goals, all of a sudden I became indispensable to the mission.

RG personally asked me to accompany him on the trip. I was flattered and terrified. Were there not a major crisis going on with Canada, Lincoln probably would have been the one to travel with RG. But as things stood, he needed to work closely with Secretary Harlow to mitigate the damage. Which meant I was on my way.

The next evening, I was picking up some Bollywood DVDs after work when my phone exploded into Led Zeppelin. I'd tried hard not to be too obvious about punishing Charlie for his insensitive move to New

York. In actuality, I was very upset about it, and certainly angry, but I was pretending to be lighthearted and supportive of the whole thing. And there were even moments when I managed to convince myself it wasn't the end of our relationship. I loved New York and had always wanted to spend more time there. Now I had a great excuse for doing so. I could imagine romantic walks through Central Park, fun nights out in the Village, lazy Sundays curled up in bed listening to the sounds of the street outside the window. I could imagine these things, but I always returned to an overall sense of doom. If Charlie was really committed to our relationship, being hundreds of miles away from me wouldn't have struck him as an opportunity to grab.

"Hey," I answered in a deceptively even-keeled tone.

"Hi, just checking in. I've got a lead on an apartment."

"Oh? That's great. Where is it?"

"Brooklyn. I'm headed there now to check it out. It belongs to a copyeditor whose roommate took off unexpectedly, which means I could move in right away."

"Who's the copyeditor?"

"Someone named Amanda something. We haven't met yet. I figure I should at least check it out."

I didn't want to jump to any conclusions, particularly considering my own name, but I imagined it was fairly likely that Amanda was a woman. I'd never heard of that name going either way, like Lindsey or Pat. So unless Charlie had said "Armando" really fast with a new accent he'd recently acquired, it seemed as though he was about to start shacking up with some hussy from work.

Should I voice my dismay and disapproval now or later? How sexy was jealousy?

"You still there, Sammy?" Charlie was asking.

There was no time like the present.

"You know, I'm sort of embarrassed to mention this, but I'm actually not that wild about you living with some random woman."

"Okay, I can understand that. But you know you have absolutely nothing to worry about, don't you?" Charlie answered. "How many different ways do I have to convince you that there's no one I'd rather be with? Don't make me get sappy here. We'll both just feel dirty afterward."

I smiled. I knew he was sincere. But I was concerned that he re-fused to acknowledge the risks of separation. I'd sung along to "Love the One You're With" one too many times to feel entirely comfort-able.

"Just indulge me for a second and imagine this was the other way around," I implored. "What if I suddenly left town and moved in with a man? How would that make you feel?"

"Scared and confused. Like a little fawn. Would this man be a hunter?"

"All right, enough of your lip. Can you just promise me one thing?" I sighed.

"Anything. Always."

"Promise that you won't take the apartment unless it's really great."

"Done. But how are we defining 'really great'? This is New York City real estate we're discussing. Some people think really great is executive broom closet–sized. I just want to make sure we're on the same page about what's acceptable."

"My current definition of the apartment being really great is that its owner is incredibly unattractive and unlikable."

"Got it. I'll keep you posted."

After saying our good-byes, I hung up the phone, conflicted about whether or not honesty was really the best strategy when dealing with these jealousy issues. Charlie seemed to be taking my attitude in stride, but I wondered how far I could push him before it started getting old.

"Pretty far," Liza asserted, her brown eyes flashing. "The only woman he should be moving in with is you. You're being much cooler about this than you have to. I'd demand that he find someplace else."

Sitting across from Liza at Toledo Lounge as we nursed some beers, I tended to agree with her. I'd called her after hanging up with Charlie and she'd met me immediately at one of our favorite local bars. Liza adored Charlie and was in the habit of congratulating me on having found the love of my life, but her soft spot for my man didn't pardon him for bad behavior, no matter how unintentional. I appreciated her loyalty.

"Isn't it discriminatory and pretty paranoid to insist that he elimi-nate half the population when considering roommates?" I asked.

"Your point?"

I smiled. I always loved hanging out with Liza.

"Look," she continued. "Charlie's completely in love with you—anyone who spends any amount of time with the two of you can see that. So since he cares about you so much, he should really respect your wishes on something as major as where and who he's going to live with."

My thoughts exactly.

"Particularly considering what you've been through in the past," she added.

And that was the crux of the problem, whether I chose to admit it or not. The truth was, most of my unease and trepidation about Charlie's move and potential roommate situation existed because I'd been so brutally betrayed by my previous boyfriend.

I had fallen hard for Aaron. Somewhere in the midst of our tumultuous relationship, I'd realized that I was more addicted to him than in love with him, but that discovery hadn't compromised the passionate intensity of our connection. He was charming and handsome and ambitious and insensitive. And he'd cheated on me throughout our six months together—a betrayal that I'd discovered after some suspicion-fueled sleuthing. To make matters worse, in addition to romantic infidelity, Aaron had inflicted political treachery as well. It was still sometimes difficult to comprehend all the deceit he had perpetrated. And though I'd managed to enact some revenge, I could still feel a raw part of my heart that hadn't completely healed.

My time with Charlie had been blissful in comparison to the wild ride with Aaron. But now I was being forced to confront the fact that my residual emotional scars were informing my reactions to this entirely new and far superior relationship. Though Charlie and I had been together almost two years, we'd never had to weather any serious arguments or other relationship disruptions. It was almost creepy how happy we'd been. I should have known it couldn't last.

"Charlie knows all that Aaron did to me," I replied. "He was there for most of it, one way or another."

It still amazed me that it had taken the time it did for Charlie and I to get together. Thank goodness we'd wised up before completely missing the boat.

"I think it would disturb Charlie to imagine that Aaron could even have any effect on me at all anymore," I went on. "He knows how intense my relationship with Aaron was, and I think he sometimes wonders whether . . ."

At this, I trailed off. I'd inadvertently stumbled into territory with which I was definitely not comfortable. I'd started down a path I'd only suspected lay somewhere in my semiconscious musings about my relationship.

"Whether what?" Liza gently prodded.

I hesitated. It wasn't that I wanted to keep something from her. It was that I might want to keep it from myself. But it was too late for that, I realized. Liza was gazing patiently at me.

"Oh, I don't know," I began. "It's not something we've ever talked about, and I could be completely wrong. I was going to say that I think he sometimes wonders how our connection compares, on a passion level. Whether it's as good. What I had with Aaron was so fundamentally screwed up, but it *was* intense. In every way."

Liza nodded before asking what I'd dearly hoped she wouldn't.

"*Is* it as good?"

Damn her. Part of me wanted to scream, "Of course it is! It's far beyond what I ever experienced with that twisted bastard who doesn't deserve to be talked about in the same conversation as Charlie!" But then there was another part. A smaller, quieter part that didn't say "No, it's not as good," but, rather, repeated the question over and over, trying to make up its mind. I hated that part. It felt disloyal and ungrateful and honest and mean.

All I could do for a moment was shake my head.

"I don't know," I finally answered helplessly.

She nodded again and didn't press me any further. But my brain had entered a tailspin all its own. Why didn't I know? And why had I been so drawn to Aaron in the first place?

I'd had plenty of warnings that he wasn't worthy of my devotion, and yet somehow I'd wanted him all the more. I wasn't alone in this mistake. I knew lots of amazing women who fell for awful guys, Liza being a prime example. Why did this happen? Could there possibly be some evolutionary reason? Deep down, did we revolt against the assumption that a good man is always the right choice because we suspect that this way of thinking might just be the product of a pampered society? Did we instinctively understand that good men didn't necessarily ensure our survival in the wild, whereas bad men—men devious enough to deceive and betray us—possessed the traits necessary to make it in a rough-and-tumble world?

If so, this was stupid. I'd learned that for myself. I was grateful that I'd progressed beyond this possibly primal, definitely misguided mindset. I felt lucky to have found Charlie, who took care of me in more evolved ways.

"I was never in love with Aaron," I needlessly reminded Liza. "And I never, ever felt safe with him. That's something I feel deeply with Charlie. Which is wonderful and rare, but I think it maybe bothers him a little bit when I try to express that to him."

"How come?" Liza inquired.

"Maybe because safe can be boring. But not to anyone who's already lived unsafe."

"So he worries about the day when you want to feel something dangerously exciting again," Liza concluded.

"Possibly." I nodded. "Though he's never said that in so many words. And I've never really thought it through till this conversation."

"Well, addictions are usually lifelong battles, right?" Liza said. "Charlie knows there's no chance you'd ever go back to Aaron. But maybe he worries that you'll relapse to that type of guy."

"I'd never do that," I said hotly. "At least not as long as Charlie will have me."

Liza looked at me for a long moment.

"Just don't make it too difficult for him then, okay?"

Where had the loyalty gone? I glared back at her.

"What does that mean?" I demanded.

Liza lifted her shoulders in a nonconfrontational shrug.

"I'm on your side here. And I think you have every right to be upset about this Amanda apartment. I'm just reminding you to be aware of where some of your other reactions might be coming from."

My BlackBerry buzzed before I could think through a response.

To: Samantha Joyce [srjoyce@ovp.eop.gov]
From: Charlie Lawton [lawtonc@washpost.com]

```
Subject: Apartment
Text: It's a really old two-bedroom with enough room
for three. And it's got an uninspired nose, terrible
body odor, and thinks Led Zeppelin is a type of car.
We couldn't be more incompatible, except it's right on
the F train and remarkably cheap.
P.S. I'm a horrible man. Please delete this message
immediately.
```

I showed Liza.

"Are you okay with his taking it?" she asked.

I thought about everything we'd discussed, and nodded. For the sake of the relationship, and my feeling like a reasonable person, I had to be. I typed a quick reply to Charlie.

```
To: Charlie Lawton [lawtonc@washpost.com]
From: Samantha Joyce [srjoyce@ovp.eop.gov]
Subject: Re: Apartment
Text: Thanks for the report. Sounds like a good match.
I hope it won't mind all the blown-up pictures of me
that will soon be decorating it. XoSammy
P.S. Note that I maturely refrained from writing
anything inappropriate about the F train.
```

I resolved to discover Amanda's last name and do some anonymous Google sleuthing at the first available opportunity to further ease my mind. Liza and I finished our beers, left a big tip, and headed home.

I spent most of the weekend working, though I did find some time to try to understand Bollywood. I was by no means successful, but I was wildly entertained. I had never actually sat down to purposely watch a Bollywood film before. I'd been generally aware of what the films entailed and had glanced at a few that had been projected onto the walls of Indian restaurants. After some initial confusion about what exactly I was watching—was it a very long, very foreign music

video?—I'd enjoyed the little that I'd glimpsed. They were fun to look
at as I wolfed down korma and naan. They were enjoyable diversions
when I was dining with someone sort of boring or hard to talk to. I'd
heard that no one was allowed to kiss in them till very recently, which
I'd found intriguing. I definitely had positive feelings toward them, but
limited exposure.

This changed on Sunday night. Liza was out with Jakers, and Charlie was still in New York. I microwaved myself a burrito and sat down
on the couch to introduce myself to a cultural phenomenon.

From the beginning, I was entranced. There's something very soothing about melodramatic story lines and flashy dance numbers. Having
started a Von Trapp family fan club in the fifth grade and composed a
Star Trek comedy opera in the seventh, I knew a thing or two about
musicals. Still, I'd never seen anything quite like the spectacle that unfolded before me. Who could have guessed that twins separated at
birth and reunited on a picturesque mountaintop wearing identical se-
quined outfits and sunny dispositions would break into such a catchy
tune about their love triangle with a humble musician who turned out
to actually be a maharajah. And the fact that *he* would end up also being a twin—oh my!

I was still whistling a melody from the movie when I arrived at work
Monday morning, but stopped self-consciously in the face of Derrick's
blank stare. I doubted he was a Bollywood fan, and I knew for sure that
he wasn't a fan of mine. I sighed and held up my pass to the glass. He
took a full twenty seconds to examine it. Twenty seconds doesn't sound
like a long time, but if you actually stand in one place and let twenty
seconds tick by, particularly when you should have been allowed to
move onto something else seventeen of those seconds ago, it tends to
drag. Derrick was slowly looking back and forth from my face to the
pass photo.

"Hi, Derrick. It's really me. Sammy," I tried through the intercom.

"Sammy?" he questioned, as if he had never heard the name before.
His voice sounded mechanical through the static.

"It doesn't say 'Sammy' anywhere," he continued. "It says Samantha
on the badge and that means you're Samantha to me. If you *are* the
person in this photo, that is."

"Oh for God's sake, of course that's me," I snapped.

I wanted to stay polite toward him, but this was getting ridiculous. Derrick looked from the photo to my face and back again once more.

"Maybe so," he conceded. "I guess everyone has off days."

What was that supposed to mean? Was today my off day, or was my photo taken on one? If he meant today, was he implying that I'd let myself go?

"What are you saying?" I inquired.

He stared straight ahead as if he hadn't heard. But he released the guardhouse door. I sighed in exasperation and continued through the security-clearing motions. After I'd electronically scanned my pass and typed in my code, Derrick once more turned his head slightly in my direction. I stopped, waiting for him to answer.

"You need to keep moving"—he squinted at my pass—"Sepatha."

As I walked along the west side of the White House toward my usual entrance, I debated whether Derrick was the product of an unhappy upbringing who was now unleashing his pent-up animosity on the world, or whether there might be something medically wrong with him. Could it be that Derrick was dismissive and indifferent to cover for a malady? Some sort of short-term memory loss condition that would explain why he never seemed to know me? Like Korsakoff's psychosis! This occurred to me in a rush and suddenly made a lot of sense. I'd recently read about Korsakoff's psychosis; Derrick certainly exhibited many of the symptoms. I should know, because I had been displaying a fair amount of them as well.

I had a history of forgetfulness and preoccupation. I'd once worn two separate shoes to work and not noticed until I was on the subway, pulling up to my stop. Scoffing coworkers had questioned how anyone could not notice the difference between a shoe that tied and a shoe that buckled. In fact, both could be slipped on, particularly if one was in a rush and didn't turn on the closet light. Maybe incidents such as that had been the early signs of my disease.

Lately, I'd been more scatterbrained than usual. Not when it came to my job, but certainly when it came to issues of personal appearance and comportment. It was odd how my brain managed to separate the two. I could find an obscure work file instantly, but I couldn't tell you where my keys were every other morning. And when they turned up on top of the cottage cheese container in the refrigerator, I couldn't tell you why they were there. I hated cottage cheese.

Liza and Charlie had assured me I was just overtired from too much work. They urged me to sleep more and read fewer medical journals. They claimed my short-term memory loss would fade away. I hoped they were right, but I had my doubts. And so I planned to start a secret regimen to prepare for the worsening of my condition. Blueberries and regular crossword puzzles and helpful reminder Post-its all figured into my strategy.

I decided to postpone telling Derrick my diagnosis of his condition till later. It could be delicate, because many people don't want to confront the existence of an illness. Even when gently told of it by a co-sufferer. But perhaps by making the disease relatable, I could win him over. Maybe we could even go through treatment together. If we could remember our appointments.

I had a chance to inquire about possible treatments that afternoon, when I went to the Old Executive Office Building clinic for my inoculations for the trip to India. I was surprised and pleased to run into Dr. Humphrey, the president's personal physician and a relatively new friend of mine. We'd bonded during a White House Conference on Mental Health after being seated next to each other. The conference guest on the other side of Dr. Humphrey had mistakenly referred to him as Dr. Huxtable, and after assuring her that though he was a black doctor he had none of Bill Cosby's comedic timing, he'd spent the rest of the time talking to me.

"Well, hello Samantha, what brings you by?" he asked in his pleasant, reserved way.

"I'm here for my inoculations," I announced. "And I should warn whoever's going to give them to me that I'm not all that reasonable about needles."

To be precise, I loathed them. They made me dizzy, short of breath, and very, very sad about the fact that I was about to be stabbed with sharp metal. Why no one had invented a more painless way of getting the necessary goods was a source of consternation. I'd been waiting to outgrow my needle aversion for a good fifteen years now, but it had stubbornly stuck with me. And the last time I had convinced myself that I was too old to be such an unbelievable wuss and steeled myself for a very courageous performance, I'd promptly had blood drawn by a new doctor who "couldn't seem to find the vein." It turned out that I was not too old to sink to the floor in a dead faint. My track record wasn't strong, so I wasn't overly confident that this whole inoculation mission would come off without a hitch.

"Would it make you feel better if I gave them to you?" Dr. Humphrey asked.

Of course it would. He was the most senior person in the White House Medical Unit, tasked with keeping the president healthy and well. I'd assumed I'd be treated by someone much more junior, but it looked as though Dr. Humphrey was taking pity on me. And though I normally didn't enjoy being pitied, in this case, I welcomed it.

"All right, you won't feel a thing," he assured me. "Except for a very sharp, stinging pain. But it'll be brief."

I wished I could say I appreciated his honesty. I tried to distract myself while he readied the first shot.

"Do you happen to have any familiarity with Korsakoff's psychosis?" I inquired.

Dr. Humphrey gave me an odd look.

"Why do you ask?" he replied, his voice slightly off his normal pitch.

Did he already know I suffered from this and had he been hoping to keep it from me because there wasn't any cure or chance of improvement? I felt the emotions welling up. I should probably call my parents first, though Liza could more immediately sympathize in person. And Charlie—wouldn't he feel bad for being so much farther away than necessary? He should have fully appreciated and enjoyed me while I'd been in my prime.

"Well, I read an article about it and thought I recognized some of the symptoms," I began.

"Really."

Dr. Humphrey's voice was curt. Not the most effective bedside manner for confirming a patient's suspicion of her condition. I didn't want to be critical, but really, I expected a bit more compassion.

"Yes," I replied, slightly more hesitant. "I mean, I just seem to be forgetting a lot of things lately and I think—"

"You're talking about yourself?" Dr. Humphrey interrupted.

"Well, yes. And . . . possibly one other person."

"What other person?" Dr. Humphrey asked quietly.

I suddenly felt weird revealing my suspicions about Derrick. It wasn't really up to me to out a fellow Korsakoff's psychosis sufferer, now that I thought about it.

"No one," I said quickly. "Forget I mentioned it. But what would be the course of treatment for it?"

Dr. Humphrey stared at me for a moment before looking down at the shot in his hand. When he spoke again, his voice had returned to its friendly, casual pitch.

"Oh, there are all sorts of new pills that can help something like that. I seriously doubt that you've developed it though, Sammy. Unless you have some bad habits that no one knows about."

"Like what?" I inquired.

"Like chronic alcoholism," he answered smoothly.

I remembered now that chronic alcoholism had been mentioned in the article I read as a cause of Korsakoff's psychosis, but it was clearly linked to the very severe cases. The more mild forms of the disorder, which I suspected myself of having, had nothing to do with that.

"Oh, no, I wasn't even thinking of that," I said as I shook my head. "I was referring to the more mild strains of the malady."

"Ah, of course you were," he responded. "Well, I think you're most likely not afflicted with any of those. Most short-term memory loss oc-curring in people your age is a result of too much stress and too little sleep."

Which pretty accurately described my existence.

"Okay, I just wanted to double-check," I answered.

"Are you ready for this?" Dr. Humphrey asked as he brandished the needle.

I felt my heart sink stomachward and my body tense for a possible blackout.

"No," I answered.

Dr. Humphrey smiled.

"It'll be fine," he said as he tightened a rubber tourniquet around my biceps.

I felt it cut into my skin.

"How did you come to be reading an article about Korsakoff's psychosis anyway?" Dr. Humprey asked.

I was too much on edge to shrug.

"That's just what I do, I guess. I read medical journals for work, but also get sidetracked by anything that strikes me as being of personal interest. I can't seem to help it. There's just so much to learn about when it comes to the body and brain and all that can go wrong with both," I replied.

"Mmm-hmmm," Dr. Humphrey said. "And have you ever considered that you might be too inquisitive for your own good?"

With that, he pinched me hard on the shoulder. I yelped in surprise and before I knew it, my arm had been released from its rubber trap and Dr. Humphrey was scooting back toward the counter on his rolling stool, like a crab on a skateboard.

"Sorry about that, I just wanted to distract you," he said over his shoulder.

Mission accomplished. And I didn't throw that phrase around recklessly even to myself—I'd really barely felt the shot. My shoulder throbbed from the pinch, though. We had two more to get through before I'd be allowed to fly to the Indian subcontinent, so there was still ample time for pain. The trip itself was only three days. One enormous needle for each. I reminded myself that this whole uncomfortable experience was worth it to avoid contracting typhoid or diphtheria or hepatitis B. I closed my eyes as Dr. Humphrey scooted back in my direction armed with another needle and rubber tourniquet and tried hard not to shake. Despite my best efforts, everything was a bit unbalanced. And as far as I could tell, getting inoculated felt a lot like getting assaulted.

I was worn out by the time I left, fully vaccinated and a little unsteady from my interaction with Dr. Humphrey. I was supposed to be at Andrews Air Force Base at six the next morning to leave on *Air Force Two* for India. What I wanted to do was go home and talk to Charlie and get as good a night's sleep as possible. What I ended up doing instead was working until eleven on a briefing, having a short, unsatisfying conversation with Charlie on my cab ride home, and falling into bed without having packed for the trip.

When the alarm sounded at four a.m., I had a fantasy that Charlie was beside me and that we still had an hour or more before we actually had to get up. I snuggled up to this delusion and drifted back into a happier sleep, only to jolt awake later with the certainty that something was wrong. Which of course it was. The pillow I was hugging wasn't Charlie, and I had let myself oversleep. I was about to miss my plane.

Fight or Flight

AS I LEAPT OUT OF BED and raced around, throwing things in a bag and searching for my diplomatic passport, I cursed myself for failing to pack the night before. I was now incredibly short on both time and fully operational brain cells. I had an uncomfortable hunch that I was packing a suitcase full of surprises that, when opened in New Delhi, would hammer home the knowledge that I'd been very disoriented when I'd tossed in those soccer shin guards.

The cab ride from the city to the suburbs of Maryland was a race against the clock, with a driver who was thankfully up to the task. He took full advantage of the empty streets and the early hour, and after breaking several traffic laws, we made it to Andrews with no time to spare. I tipped the cabdriver gratefully, successfully cleared security, and hurried to join the others already aboard the plane.

Besides me, the staff contingent for the trip consisted of the deputy chief of staff, the trip director, a press handler, a military aide, an NSA staffer, a doctor and a nurse, a spokesperson, a personal aide, the official photographer, and two foreign policy advisors. None were close friends of mine, but I liked all of them just fine. One of the foreign policy advisors was a woman named Sofia whom I hoped to get to know better because she was around my age and seemed smart and interesting. I was also happy to see my favorite Secret Service agent, a big, affable guy named Doug. The remainder of the plane was filled with other agents, various members of the media, and military personnel.

As I settled into my comfortable, business-class-level seat in the staff cabin, I felt a little thrill of excitement. I'd flown on *Air Force Two* before, but not many times, and never overseas. Through the window, in the predawn dusk, I could make out the lights of *Marine Two* on its approach to the landing pad. RG took the helicopter from his official residence at the Naval Observatory to Andrews Air Force Base to both shorten his commute and avoid tying up the roads with his long motorcade. As he exited *Marine Two,* a motorcade pulled up beside him, ready to drive him the extraordinarily short distance from the landing pad to the plane. This always struck me as ridiculous, and RG invariably waved off the motorcade and walked, but I supposed the Secret Service had to have the option available should he ever feel like the drive. Or if the weather was unreasonably bad.

Several members of the press clustered on the tarmac, shooting photographs of RG's good-bye wave, before hustling up the back stairs of the plane as soon as he disappeared into the front. Once RG was settled in his private cabin, the plane was ready to take off in less than a minute.

Before my *Air Force Two* experiences, I'd assumed that every flight I took was going to crash, but I felt safe on this aircraft. Somewhere in my head I knew that this didn't make sense—that a plane carrying the vice president would actually be much more of a target than a regular commercial airplane. But I persisted in my feeling of security. I trusted the military to protect us and to prevent us from crashing into the ocean.

The military stewards who ran the plane requested that everyone wear their seat belts, but they didn't enforce it, so very few people did. Even during taxiing, takeoffs, and landings, people were walking around talking to one another. We weren't purposely flouting the rules, it was just that we were a mobile office with other things on our minds.

Two hours into the flight, RG summoned Sofia and me to his private cabin for a strategy session. All of the scheduling details had already been worked out, but we still needed to finesse our methods of melding foreign policy and health care goals for RG's summit meeting with the Indian prime minister. Walking beside Sofia in the narrow airplane corridor, I tried not to bump into her. She was a substantial woman— pretty in an expansive way. She was loud and opinionated and I found myself fascinated by her confidence.

Once in RG's private cabin, we powwowed with him for nearly an hour. Finally, after reviewing everything for the third time, RG seemed to feel good about the plan. He signaled the steward and told him that he'd like to watch a movie.

"Have either of you seen *Gandhi*?" RG asked.

I hadn't, and I was more than happy to rectify that immediately.

"It's an amazing film, sir," Sofia said. "Very compelling."

And long, from what I'd gathered. This was welcome, though, considering how endless the overall flight seemed. Any time we could burn would be less time spent feeling claustrophobic.

"I promised Jenny I'd watch it," RG replied distractedly as he sifted back through some notes.

RG's wife, Jenny, often made him promise to do things that would give his brain a needed rest. She was skilled at tricking him into relaxation—the only person capable of saving her husband from himself when he was nearing burnout.

The screen was now lit with the *Gandhi* DVD menu. I gazed up at it, eager for the entertainment to begin. I'd heard such good things.

But then Sofia cleared her throat and I turned to see her standing by the door and RG staring at me like I was some sort of alien. Actually, an alien probably had more of a legitimate expectation of kicking back and watching a movie in RG's private cabin, particularly if the alien was some sort of high-up representative of his species. I, however, was a far more lowly representative of mine, and had been idiotic to think that I was actually invited to stay for the viewing.

I jumped up.

"Sorry. Just got a little too comfortable," I said with a smile, hoping that joking about the truth would go over better than just sheer embarrassment.

RG nodded but his face remained tight. Out in the hall, Sofia turned to me.

"Did you really think we were invited to stay?" she asked.

Her tone was disbelieving, but also a bit scolding, which I resented. Position-wise, we were peers on equal footing. She didn't have the credentials to talk down to me, though I knew such behavior was more frequently an issue of ego than title.

"My mind just wandered for a moment," I explained.

"Maybe you should keep it on a leash when you're not on your own time," she retorted.

Now she really was crossing the line.

"Excuse me?" I replied hotly.

Were we going to get into a fistfight at thirty thousand feet? Would I win it?

"I'm just teasing you," she answered with a smile.

But I didn't really believe her. Why was Sofia being so hostile, even if she was pretending not to be? It could be just stress and sleep deprivation. I decided not to take her attitude personally, if possible. Not taking things personally was one of my ongoing challenges.

Back at our seats, the rest of the staff was playing poker. They offered to deal Sofia and me into the game, but we both declined, choosing instead to break out our work. The others looked annoyed, as if we were showing them up in some way. I wasn't sure when this flight had started taking on such a competitive vibe, but I hoped it would dissipate before someone lost a limb.

I worked for a few hours and then managed to nod off and sleep through the short refueling stop in Germany. Soon after I woke up, dehydrated and disoriented, the press handler returned from the back of the plane and reported that the journalists covering the trip were in a combative mood, which didn't surprise me. Something was in the air.

When it came to the media's attitude toward this visit, however, there was definitely more going on. The trip to India had been postponed several times and had been in danger of being shoved all the way into another term, should Wye and RG be reelected. There were certainly several pressing reasons to make the trip, but it was a sensitive undertaking due to a scandal that had nearly sunk Wye's chances in the final month of the presidential campaign two years previously. I'd been right there as the scandal had unfolded. And it hadn't been pretty.

A few weeks before election day, Charlie had broken an incredibly damaging story in the *Washington Post* revealing that portions of then Governor Wye's stump speech had been largely plagiarized from the speeches of an obscure Indian politician named Tilik Kumar. As the article had proven, entire sections of Wye's standard speech were copied directly from this eloquent local leader who was largely unknown outside a small but populous region in the south of India. Charlie and I were acquaintances and even friends at the time, but overnight he became persona non grata to the campaign. In a further twist, Wye's stump speech had been written by Aaron, my deceitful ex-boyfriend, with whom I'd been forced to work in close proximity on the campaign on account of his status as a hotshot speechwriter. Albeit one who apparently appropriated others' material whenever possible.

This bombshell, care of Charlie and Aaron, had sent shockwaves through the campaign. Wye and RG had been enjoying a slight lead over their opponents, but their poll numbers quickly plummeted. Wye had tried his best to explain that though his stump speech was a deeply personal reflection of who he was as a person and candidate, he had been completely unaware of the plagiarism perpetrated by one of his employees, but the American people seemed weary of qualified apologies. Just as we had all begun feeling paralyzed by the suddenly real possibility that the campaign was beyond recovery, RG had stepped in.

RG's presence on the ticket had provided a stabilizing influence from the moment he'd been tapped to be Wye's running mate, and he capitalized on his integrity credentials to appeal directly to the American people. He'd gone on a media blitz, explaining over and over again how Wye's only mistake had been to trust a staff member who had turned out to be dishonest. He declared that of course Wye had approved speech passages extolling the virtues of empowerment and civic leadership, for those were the very things Wye believed in. That obviously Wye had been eager to speak about the need for common understanding and transcendence of one another's differences, because that was what his campaign was all about. His only crime had been wanting to inspire our great country to be better. And clearly, this made him a fantastic leader.

RG took his case to anyone who would listen, urging everyone to focus on what was really important: namely, that he and Wye were intent on shaping the kind of future people wanted and deserved. Luckily, enough of America was persuaded by RG's passionate appeals. The election had been close, but it had gone decisively in our favor.

Since taking office, any dealings with India had inevitably raised the

specter of that nearly fatal scandal and offered journalists and opponents the opportunity to remind people that their president had been
guilty of plagiarism. The administration had understandably sought
to minimize the chances for this to come up. But we couldn't avoid a
country as big and vital and important as India for very long. Having
Wye make the official trip had been deemed inadvisable, so RG had
stepped in once again.

We were all aware that the trip represented the first huge demon-
stration of the importance of our relationship with India, and we were
equally cognizant of the eagerness of the press to watch for any tension
caused by Wye's infamous campaign stumble.

"Are there any reporters whom you're particularly concerned about?"
I asked the press liaison.

"Chick Wallrey's a little too amped up for my comfort," he replied.

That wasn't too surprising. Chick Wallrey was a reporter for the
New York Times who'd decided somewhere along the line that Wye and
RG were spawns of Satan. I'd initially been skeptical of others' de-
scriptions of her bitter bias, since I was among the segment of the population who held the *New York Times* in very high regard and liked to
believe that it was an institution that did its best to present thorough,
unbiased, and meaningful reporting. Once I'd begun reading Chick's
columns, this belief had been tested.

Everything the administration did was described in the darkest and
most cynical terms. RG and Wye were never meeting with constituents;
they were "trolling for photo ops." They weren't responding to sudden
crises or proposing needed reforms; they were "laboring to mask their
panic" and "peddling harebrained schemes."

It was truly stunning. The rest of the paper seemed to be held to its
traditional high standards, but she continued to get away with some
criminally unobjective reporting. I couldn't quite understand how she
managed to hold on to her job there. The press office posited that
Chick was deeply unhappy in her personal life and bitter toward everyone, but just happened to be assigned to this administration. I didn't
know one way or the other. Every once in a while I wondered whether
Chick might have been made aware of something horrible about the
administration that the rest of us knew nothing about, but I suspected

that was because I tended to hold on to some outdated notions about integrity. It was more likely that she simply had her own agenda and, unfortunately for us, we fell on the wrong side of it.

After many more hours of work and another fitful nap, I awoke suddenly to find the plane descending. The entire trip had taken a little over sixteen hours. As we coasted to a stop on the foreign tarmac, I looked out the window at the cameras, crowds, and lined-up cars. I knew that these arrivals often walked a line between festivity and security. If the Secret Service could have their way, we'd land in the dead of night in a remote location known only to them. However, that mode of operation just wasn't politically viable. I looked around at the agents as they tightened themselves into readiness.

Except for the trip director and RG's personal aide, the staff deplaned from the rear, along with the journalists and the baggage. And the journalists' baggage. I eyed Chick Wallrey as she lined up with the rest, ready to observe and question RG during the media avail that normally took place upon arrival on trips such as these. Chick was short and rotund, with dyed black hair and raccoon eyes courtesy of heavy eyeliner. She favored long dark skirts and layered necklaces and generally gave off a Goth vibe. As I walked with the others toward the staff van, I inhaled a big whiff of hot air. It didn't smell the way I'd imagined it would. It was light on spice and heavy on sewage. There must have been some sort of spill nearby.

I watched RG greet the assembled Indian officials and listen attentively to a song sung by girls from a local school. Now bedecked with marigold flowers, he posed for dozens of photographs. After completing the ceremonial greetings, he and the prime minister climbed into the waiting car and our long motorcade pulled away.

My previous experience with New Delhi was confined to a small delicatessen around the corner from my apartment in D.C. that was run by an elderly Indian couple who believed they'd given their establishment a very clever name. They served great roast beef sandwiches so I gathered they didn't feel strongly about the whole vegetarian, sacred cow issue. Perhaps that was Old Deli thinking.

Not surprisingly, I was fascinated by the fact that India is a country of countless gods. According to my Wikipedia research, there are more

than 330 million deities that are considered separate and unique mani-
festations of an overall supreme force. I obviously felt a special kinship
with this sort of spiritual landscape. I thanked the God of Foreign
Travel Opportunities for the chance to experience this extraordinary
country for myself.

Since I was eager to soak in as much of India as possible, I took advantage of my window seat in the staff van and let the chatter of my
colleagues fade into the background. I planned to treat their murmurs
as a soundtrack for the sights and shapes about to unfurl before me, but
before we could even pull off the tarmac, I felt my eyes grow heavy.
The sun beating through the window didn't do much to revive me. The
truth is, riding in cars on sunny days knocks me out faster than anything else can. If someone could bottle the sunny-passenger-seat
effect, they'd revolutionize the sleeping aid market.

I drifted off into a half-sleep and then slowly came to a while later,
just as the motorcade pulled into the back entrance of a hotel that
looked like a shiny space saucer that had crash-landed on its side. Lined
up like bowling pins, the advance team was waiting to greet us. They
had been in New Delhi for two weeks already, setting up everything we
would need for our trip. For all intents and purposes, they took the
place of the hotel staff: they distributed keys and security pins, arranged
for our luggage, and escorted us up to the cordoned-off top two floors
of the hotel, where our rooms were labeled with our names on signs
stamped with the vice presidential seal. RG was in the penthouse suite
and attended by a Navy steward from the vice presidential residence
who had packed everything for him. Had the steward included soccer
shin guards? I wondered. If not, I could probably hook him up.

After checking out my room and confirming that I had in fact packed
extremely poorly, I headed down to the staff office on the second floor.
The advance team had transformed a large ballroom into a first-rate
workspace, complete with laptops, printers, copiers, faxes, phones with
direct lines to D.C., and plenty of coffee, sodas, and snacks. I grabbed
a bag of chips and sank into a plush chair by the far window to review
my trip binder. RG was meeting the following morning with the drug
companies with whom we most wanted relationships, and I was responsible for ensuring it all went well.

I soon found myself dozing off yet again, and was excited to realize that this meant I was officially a victim of jet lag. Since I'd never traveled outside the United States before, jet lag had always struck me as a status symbol. In the past, when people I knew had complained about it, all I'd heard was bragging. But now I'd joined their ranks. I celebrated by giving in to it.

I couldn't tell how long I'd been napping when I woke suddenly, startled by the sound of an infant crying nearby. I looked around, disoriented and confused. As I remembered where I was and how I had gotten there, I turned toward the baby squalls that were still sounding close and loud. My heart skipped a couple beats, and I gripped the arms of my chair and blinked to make sure I wasn't spotting a remnant of a dream. Outside the window, seemingly floating in the dusty air, was a baby. It looked like a girl and she was very young, swaddled and screaming. I leapt up for a closer look. How was this possible?

The answer didn't comfort me. I saw that the baby was actually strapped into a basket lashed to a long pole that was being guided by two women on the ground a story below. I shrieked in unison with the child, threw open the window, and leaned out, motioning for the women to please carefully lower the baby. Or guide her closer so that I could grab her out of gravity's way and carry her back down to her mother unscathed. Was one of those women really her mother? Would a mother do such a thing to her child? If so, why?

The women kept the infant out of arm's reach but made some gestures that I at first couldn't decipher. Not until I noticed a tiny tin cup tied to the baby's leg did I understand what the women were trying to communicate. They wanted money. And it looked as though they wouldn't lower the baby until they got it.

As the pole swayed scarily, I scrambled for my wallet and pulled out some bills, barely looking at what I was about to give away. Once the women could see that I was going to pay, they bobbed the baby close enough for me to make my deposit. As soon as I'd stuffed in the bills, the women started lowering their shrieking bundle, just as hotel security rushed out onto the sidewalk and began yelling at them in Hindi.

Traumatized, I closed the window and turned away. I was alone in the large ballroom, and I no longer wanted to be. I crossed the polished floor quickly and exited into the hallway, in search of less disturbing human contact.

Doug was manning a Secret Service post in the hall.

"You're just in time to run and grab me a beer," he said with a grin.

I liked Doug. He was hulking and jovial, and managed to stay professional even as he joked around about things that would get less popular agents fired by their supervisors. He was just what I needed at the moment. I smiled back at him.

"How many promotions will it take before people stop treating me like a cocktail waitress?"

"You say it like it's a bad thing," Doug replied.

Before he could say more, he touched his finger to his ear to better hear an incoming message. I wished I were privy to it. I coveted earpieces, but had yet to have any professional reason to wear one. I'd sport them just for fashion, but I didn't want to be labeled a poseur.

"Roger. Talon is alpha. Over," Doug said softly into his cuff.

Having him so promptly repeat the incoming message was the next best thing to having my own earpiece. I wondered if he did it for my benefit. By now, I knew enough to decipher the message. "Talon" was RG's Secret Service code name. He and Jenny and their twin boys had been tasked with choosing permanent code names around the time of the inauguration. Their only guidelines were that the names had to begin with *T,* since the Secret Service had already dubbed RG "Talon" during the campaign. RG had agreed to remain "Talon," and Jenny had selected "Tracer." As for their four-year-old twin boys, RG and Jenny had made what some staffers and agents considered a mistake by allowing Jack and Jeffrey to choose for themselves. The boys had been extraordinarily enthused about the assignment and had babbled in twinspeak for several minutes before triumphantly announcing their choices, which were "Tinky-Winky" and "Twerp." They were understandably quite pleased with themselves.

Jenny didn't want to go back on her promise that they could pick their own names, but she also didn't want to subject the Secret Service to daily discussions of the movements and status of Tinky-Winky and Twerp. After lots of back and forth and a little bit of Pudding Pop bribery, Jenny talked Tinky-Winky into "Trotter." This was a considerable victory, marred only by the fact that Twerp held firm. He admitted that "Transformer" was a cool alternative, but insisted that it was too long. Which I actually agreed with when Jenny relayed this whole story to me later. So Twerp remained Twerp in a show of the stubbornness that occasionally caused him to live up to his hard-won name.

"At least neither of them chose 'Turd,'" I'd pointed out.

They'd recently learned this word from a dog-owning neighbor and had displayed a distressing fascination with it. Jenny hadn't even considered that possibility. She'd agreed that the family had escaped worse fates.

"So RG's on his way back, huh?" I asked Doug when he'd finished muttering into his sleeve.

"Yeah. I hope *he* has a six-pack."

I smiled and returned to the staff office to collect the belongings I'd left when fleeing the baby horror. I also picked up a copy of the *International Herald Tribune* and skimmed a couple of the stories I'd already read, quizzing myself to test how much I'd retained. That plus the crossword puzzle would cover my brain-strengthening assignment for the day. I wasn't going to surrender to Korsakoff's psychosis without a fight.

The sounds of commotion in the hall signaled that RG had returned. Moments later, Sally the photographer joined me, still loaded down with camera equipment. I counted three different cameras and four large bags draped across her neck and shoulders in crisscross designs. I often wondered how she managed to get around so nimbly when burdened with so much.

"Hey." She grinned at me. "Surviving so far?"

She opened a soda and plopped down in a nearby chair. I nodded.

"How's the evening gone?" I asked.

"Good!" she replied cheerfully.

Sally was often the happiest person on staff. Maybe lugging all that equipment meant a steady release of endorphins. My BlackBerry vibrated with an incoming message, which surprised me at first. They hadn't been set up to work overseas and the communications team had been laboring since we got here to enable them. I'd gotten all too comfortable with the calm of being off grid, but now I'd just been buzzed back in.

The message was from RG's personal aide, telling me that RG was asking for me. I hurried toward the door and when I looked back to wave good-bye to Sally, she clicked a picture of me. She was very quick on the draw.

I tossed Doug a bottle of Coke on my way past him, though I knew he wasn't allowed to drink it until he got off shift.

"There'd better be rum in this," he called after me.

I took the elevator up to the top floor and made my way to RG's suite at the end of a hall protected by a phalanx of Secret Service agents. I showed them my preapproved hard pin, which worked like a magic charm at any checkpoint. Hard pins were given out to people with clearance to provide easy shorthand for agents trying to keep an area secure. As expected, the agents outside RG's suite nodded and moved aside to let me pass.

The navy steward opened the door for me. Inside, RG was on a secure phone in a heavily padded, soundproof phone booth placed in the far corner of the living room of his suite. The White House Communications Agency, known to everyone as WHCA (pronounced Wah-kah) was responsible for this and all other phone, fax, and computer communications on foreign and domestic trips. WHCA was a military operation, and I was frequently amazed at the sheer number of phone lines they left in their wake. Due to the pronunciation of their acronym, I often thought of them as a giant Pac-Man-like organization, gobbling up free space and civilian communication lines wherever they turned.

RG looked up at me through the glass window of his booth. The booth provided a protected line for any extremely sensitive calls— WHCA's somewhat bizarre solution to the challenge of making uneavesdropped-upon calls in foreign countries where we didn't really have that much control over the basic infrastructure of the places we occupied. I'd been instructed by the trip director to assume all the rooms were bugged. He'd told me of a recent trip to China during which the staff members noticed that after taking hot showers, the bathroom mirrors would fog up except for a large oval in the middle. The placement of these concealed cameras seemed unnecessarily perverted, since as far as we all agreed, discussions of national secrets normally did not take place nude in hotel bathrooms. Though maybe they should. That sounded pretty exciting.

I planned to fog-test my bathroom mirror later and speak aloud to whoever was monitoring the listening devices in my room, just to let them know that I knew they were there. That I was on to them. Maybe I'd throw around some slang words to keep them on their translating toes. Maybe I'd even rap a little, if they were lucky. Ice-T's "Colors" was one of my specialties.

RG finished his call and exited the booth.

"Hello, sir. You wanted to see me?"

He nodded.

"The president's been trying to reach me. He's apparently called three times in the last hour, but when we've tried to patch in, something's gone wrong. He did leave word that he has questions about a specific drug that one of the companies we're meeting with is manufacturing. I may not know all the necessary information, so I wanted you here in case he asks something I don't have the answer to."

"Yes, sir," I replied, ready to be of service.

I secretly relished the moments when RG relied on my particular expertise. I was continually amazed at how much he knew about a vast range of subjects, but every once in a while I was reminded that I played an important role by being a resource for the details he couldn't retain precisely because there was so much else that occupied his attention. RG knew how to delegate, but that didn't prevent him from being intellectually curious about virtually everything. In my mind, this was a crucial combination. Were he only obsessed with acquiring knowledge but devoid of the ability to empower others, he would end up an ineffective control freak. Conversely, were he an intellectually incurious expert delegator, he would just be spreading around ignorance. Which was really the one thing we didn't need any more of.

A WHCA operator stuck his head in the door.

"The line's ready again, sir," he informed RG.

RG nodded and turned to me.

"Come into the booth with me," he ordered.

I nodded and followed him in. There was room for two, in case an interpreter was needed. Inside, the air was tight and lifeless. I willed myself not to be claustrophobic. I couldn't afford to be. Not when I was about to be invited to join a private call between the president and vice president of the United States.

"If I need you to get on the line, use that extension," RG instructed, indicating another phone I hadn't noticed at first.

"Yes, sir," I answered.

RG picked up his receiver.

"This is Vice President Gary. I'm waiting to be connected to the president," he said into the receiver.

"Hello, Max," RG said a few seconds later.

A moment of silence followed. RG had his back to me so I couldn't see his expression, but I watched his shoulder tense.

"I'm not familiar with that, sir, but I do have the health care advisor here with me. Should I bring her onto the call?"

Wye must have said yes, because RG motioned for me to join. I quickly picked up the other phone.

"Sir, Samantha Joyce is now on the line with us. I think she'll be able to answer your specific questions."

"Samantha, are you there?"

Wye's voice sounded very far away.

"Yes, Mr. President, how can I help?"

"Well, you can tell that sonuvabitch Dr. Humphrey he's fired, for starters!"

Wye started laughing. I didn't understand the joke. RG didn't appear to either.

"I'm just pulling your leg," Wye said when he stopped laughing. "It's not his fault he can't get some of this stuff," he continued, his voice suddenly serious. "Tell me what you know about Focusid."

Focusid was an experimental drug that had initially been developed as a type of anti-ADD medication, but had evolved into something much more powerful. According to overseas reports, Focusid had successfully enhanced human mental capacity for memory and concentration by up to 30 percent for a period of four to six hours after ingestion of the recommended dose. These results were astonishing, and had produced a rush of excitement over the potentially groundbreaking applications of such a miracle drug, but unfortunately they didn't come without a hitch.

In addition to its stunningly positive results, Focusid had also been shown to cause dangerous side effects, including strokes and liver failure, which was one of the reasons it was currently unavailable in the United States. However, despite these serious risks, Focusid had been growing in popularity in India, Korea, and Japan. One of the Indian drug companies we were scheduled to meet with produced Focusid.

I summarized as much for the president, wondering to myself why he was so curious about this random foreign drug.

"Someone told me it helps with Alzheimer's," Wye said. "That true?"

There was in fact a recent Japanese study that claimed Focusid drastically slowed the onset of Alzheimer's. Of course. This explained the president's interest. His father had been getting rapidly sicker with the disease.

"According to the Japanese, it is, sir," I replied. "But no U.S. studies have been conducted. The FDA considers the drug too risky."

"Well, I need to get my daddy on it right away. So bring some of it home, will ya?"

I looked at RG, whose brow was furrowed with concern.

"So you'll be signing your father up for a clinical trial, sir?" he asked. "A confidential one?"

"Yeah, yeah," Wye replied impatiently. "I've got Humphrey working on it. But we need the actual drug. The damn FDA's too slow."

RG nodded. Like me, he obviously sympathized with the president's desire to bend the rules and speed up a clinical trial. Wye was trying to save his dad.

"We'll get to work on it," RG replied.

"Yes," I echoed. "We'll be sure to come back with some."

"Good girl," Wye rejoined, sounding lighthearted once more. "People call you Sammy, don't they?"

"Yes, they do, sir," I answered.

"Sammy, Sammy, bo-bammy," he half-sang. "Tell me, Sammy, Sammy, bo-bammy, what makes Sammy run?"

At this, RG looked up and met my gaze. I was at a complete loss, and I could tell RG was somewhat thrown as well.

"Samantha has to go now, sir," RG said firmly but politely, as he motioned for me to hang up the line.

Though I was relieved to be rescued from the confusing question, I wished I could stay on just as a listener. I wanted to know what Wye might say next. As I moved to return the phone to the receiver, I got my wish.

"Bobby, bobby, the no-fun snobby. Lemme tell ya—" I heard Wye slur as I hung up the receiver.

Good Lord, the president was drunk.

I sat in shock and listened as RG spoke for a few more minutes. When he finally hung up the phone, he looked as though he'd had the wind knocked out of him. The WHCA operator rapped on the door of the booth and then stuck his head in.

"All done, sir?"

"Yes, I think we are," RG answered.

Day and Night

———·•·———

A MINUTE LATER, RG and I were still sitting in silence. I'd considered leaving, but felt utterly immobile. I wondered if the White House operator who'd facilitated the call and most likely stayed on the line to monitor the connection had realized that Wye was drunk. I really hoped not. I also prayed that we were the only people Wye had reached out to. The idea of the president drinking and dialing made me shudder, which caught RG's eye. He finally looked up at me.

"What time is it?" he asked.

I checked my watch.

"Twelve thirty a.m. New Delhi time," I replied.

Which made it around three in the afternoon in Washington. I thought about floating the Riyadh theory, but I was pretty sure it wouldn't hold up. It was time for me to tell RG about my discovery. Judging from his reactions during the phone call, it seemed he hadn't already been aware of Wye's drinking.

"Um, sir?"

My voice sounded much higher and more frightened than planned. Now that I thought about it, I *was* scared. This was an extremely disturbing situation.

RG reached over and shut the door that the WHCA operator had left just slightly ajar. The air in the soundproof booth felt tight and lifeless once more.

"Sammy, I know this is a lot to ask, but I'm going to anyway. I'm going to ask you to please not speak to anyone—*anyone*—about the conversation that just took place."

RG's voice had become suffocatingly stern. I nodded vigorously in response, eager to prove to him that he could absolutely trust me.

"I know you and Charlie Lawton have gotten very serious," RG continued.

It still threw me when RG remembered details about my personal life. He of course knew Charlie, but it was still bizarre to have my boss fully cognizant of my love life. Given the trouble Charlie's reporting had caused in the past, though, his concern was understandable.

"Charlie will never know about this from me," I said instantly and very convincingly.

RG nodded slowly. I could tell that he believed me, and for this, I was grateful. I hurried to speak before he could continue.

"Sir, a few days ago at the bill signing, President Wye wasn't drinking just Diet Dr Pepper in the Oval Office," I said quickly. "He was drinking a Diet Dr Pepper and whiskey."

"How do you know?" RG asked.

I took a deep breath.

"I was back in the Oval Office a few minutes later and used some ice from the glass for Emily Thomas's bee sting. The ice reeked of whiskey."

"Did you tell anyone else about this?"

"No, sir," I replied.

"Why didn't you tell me?" he inquired.

I looked down.

"I thought you might already know and be upset that I had discovered it. I really didn't know *what* to do, sir."

RG nodded.

"Well, we shouldn't jump to any conclusions."

"Right. He could have been having a little whiskey for health reasons or something, and just now on the phone, he could have just been . . . giddy," I offered.

RG ignored this. He was deep in pained thought and his creased concentration made him look a decade older. I sensed he was puzzling his way toward a coping strategy for this new crisis, but suddenly his shoulders sagged. I felt my hopes droop with his posture.

"This is a catastrophe," he said in a tone of finality that surprised me.

What happened to not jumping to conclusions? I'd signed on to that plan. And now that RG had turned doomsday, there was no going back. I hated how helpless he sounded. Witnessing his vulnerability frightened me as much as realizing that Wye had fallen off the wagon.

Yet I agreed with his diagnosis. It was unquestionably a catastrophe. Even if it were three in the morning in Washington instead of three in the afternoon, a drunken president was never a good thing. Besides the obvious danger involving the ability to begin a war, there were thousands of other disasters he could perpetrate with very little effort. A wayward utterance could send shockwaves through world markets. Misplaced bravado could trigger radical repercussions. The truth was, a president's good judgment was the perpetual defense against any reckless endangerment of the country. With that impaired, we were in serious trouble.

Before I could find anything at all hopeful or reassuring about this situation, RG stood up. I could tell from his demeanor that I was now dismissed. For the time being, there'd be no more talk of what we'd just experienced.

Somewhere on the trip back to my room the gravity of what was happening hit me and I had to slow down for a moment and run my hand along the hallway wall for support. I knew from a college history course and my own extracurricular reading that the country had already weathered presidents who had incapacitated themselves while in office, whether by drink, drugs, depression, exhaustion, or stroke. I just hadn't expected to be working for the latest future cautionary tale. I didn't always agree with President Wye and I certainly felt a far greater connection with RG, but I'd always taken Wye's essential competence for granted. Knowing that I couldn't was extraordinarily jarring. And how long could we keep it a secret? How long should we?

I reminded myself that this could still be isolated, curable behavior. The president's recent indiscretions could very well be a result of the stress and pain of his father's worsening illness on top of the crushing everyday burdens of the job. I'd overheard RG once talking about the nature of the challenges that confronted the chief executive. He'd said that the problems and decisions that made it to the president were the toughest ones imaginable, because were they even vaguely solvable, they would have already been handled by those below him. When Cabinet secretaries, military commanders, and chiefs of staff couldn't decide what to do, the buck was passed to the president. And there it famously stopped. RG had said that the toughest of the tough challenges also had a knack for arriving in clusters, so that extremely wrenching decisions almost always had to be made in the company of other, equally agonizing ones. It took steely resolve and renewable will to withstand this perpetual onslaught of pressure. RG had talked of decision-making muscles that grew stronger the more they were exercised and stretched and torn.

So it was feasible that perhaps Wye had just felt recently, briefly overwhelmed. And he'd needed an escape hatch in an office that didn't come with one. Willie Nelson's "Whiskey River" ran through my head as I rounded the corner toward my room and nearly collided with a co-terie of staffers headed in the other direction.

"We're getting some late-night grub. Come with us!" Sally chirped.

I'd forgotten about dinner. My stomach now reminded me of how empty and neglected it felt with an audible growl.

"Wow, that was right on cue." Sally laughed.

"Yeah, but I can't come, unfortunately," I lamented. "I've still got some work to do."

"Oh, will you stop showing off," Sofia said as she rolled her eyes.

What was with this woman? She had made her voice somewhat joking, but mainly accusatory. Did she really think I was trying to make myself seem more important than I actually was? I was well aware of my relative insignificance. I didn't need her there to reinforce it.

"Well, if I'd gotten my work done on time like the rest of you over-achievers, I'd be allowed to play too. It's my own fault," I replied.

Very graciously, in my opinion. The others smiled.

"Good luck!" Sally said.

Back in my room, I ate a couple PowerBars, which I'd learned to bring on every trip for emergency food and work fuel, and sifted through some file folders. I hadn't made it very far when my Black-Berry buzzed with a message from Charlie. This reminded me of my promise to RG that Charlie would never know anything about Wye from me, and I suddenly felt very lonely. I gave myself a quick slap to beat the self-pity away. My face stung as I read.

```
To: Samantha Joyce [srjoyce@ovp.eop.gov]
From: Charlie Lawton [lawtonc@washpost.com]
Subject: my little lambikin korma
Text: I wonder if this will get to you in India.
How's it going, my intrepid lady love? Just writing to
let you know that I'm on the planet, missing you. And
bulking up to punch out any international men of
mystery who try to woo you away. Please don't leave me
for a Bollywood hunk. ya, c
```

When Charlie had first begun signing his e-mails "ya, c" I'd been very confused, but hadn't wanted to ask him what it meant for fear that I was already supposed to know. I'd been burned in the past for similar things. For someone as obsessed with noteworthy anniversaries as I was, I frequently forgot to celebrate personal, romantic ones. Besides tracking the amount of time Charlie and I had been dating down to the day and even hour, I hadn't paid a lot of attention to other landmarks of our relationship. The first summer we were together, he'd given me a brand-new pair of stylish soft-soled sneakers and taken me to dinner at our favorite restaurant. He'd been surprised that I didn't know the occasion for a celebration and informed me that it was the year anniversary of the day we'd actually met. Which had been the morning of the Alfred Jackman hearing, when, amid the stress of covering up for a constituent who was too stoned to testify, I'd tripped on a camera cable and fallen onto Charlie, who was covering the hearing for the *Post*. I'd injured him with the hard heel of my mismatched shoe.

Charlie hadn't been upset that I didn't remember, just surprised. And so I'd resolved to stay on top of our romantic anniversaries as much as possible. Then he'd gone and started signing messages "ya, c" every once in a while, and I'd racked my brain trying to figure out the explanation while also worrying that I was possibly supposed to sign messages back to him the same way.

I finally cracked the code when I combed through all the e-mails and letters Charlie and I had ever exchanged. I found my answer in a note he'd written me about how he wished there were other ways to say that he loved me because I deserved consistently intriguing declarations of devotion. He'd made a list of all the ones he could think of and asked me to put checks next to the acceptable ones. Most of them were intentionally inappropriate. At the end, he'd signed the letter very simply: "Yours always, Charlie."

"Ya" didn't sound quite as lyrical, but I loved what it stood for, once I knew. And I'd fallen into the habit of mimicking the sign-off on my return missives. Occasionally I'd invent a new acronym to offer him the same sort of confusion he'd provided me.

```
To: Charlie Lawton [lawtonc@washpost.com]
From: Samantha Joyce [srjoyce@ovp.eop.gov]
Subject: Re: my little lambikin korma
Text: Can you come get me? I'm sleepy and I'd like to
come home. I haven't lost sight of how amazing it is
that I'm actually in India, but I've pretty much just
been trapped in a hotel room with the curtains
closed. Have you ever been stalked by babies on
sticks? It's incredibly scarring. I miss you.
dfhmylm, s
```

His reply was almost instantaneous.

```
To: Samantha Joyce [srjoyce@ovp.eop.gov]
From: Charlie Lawton [lawtonc@washpost.com]
Subject: Re: my little lambikin korma
Text: "desperately freakishly hauntingly missing you
lover-man"?
```

Funny, but no.

```
To: Charlie Lawton [lawtonc@washpost.com]
From: Samantha Joyce [srjoyce@ovp.eop.gov]
Subject: Re: my little lambikin korma
Text: "don't forget how much you love me," actually.
```

Maybe I should have made it about my feelings for him rather than a demand for more attention, but it was already done.

The next morning I woke up hoping that the scandalous phone call with the president had actually been a silly dream. But alas, my brain wouldn't go along with the ruse. I consoled myself with a hot shower, once I managed to free the complimentary soap from its shrink-wrapped plastic, which was a remarkably difficult thing to do. Such packaging really discriminates against short-fingernailed people. We may not look as polished, but we still deserve a chance to be clean.

I saw from the revised schedule slipped under my hotel door that we were now leaving a full day earlier than originally planned—most likely because RG felt the need to return to D.C. after last night's call with the president. The meeting I'd organized was still happening, but we now had only an hour to arrange for India to supply us with the lower-cost prescription drugs our country needed. There wouldn't be time for any gaffes. I scanned the protocol procedure sheet that had been passed around on *Air Force Two*. Apparently, I needed to remember to use my right hand for everything, since the left one was considered unclean. And on the topic of dirty body parts, the feet were even worse. If I pointed my feet at an Indian person, or, horror of horrors, actually brushed up against one of them with my foot, I would be committing a grave insult. I had no plans to play footsie with anyone, but I wasn't used to keeping tabs on where my feet were pointed. Did the person who prepared this briefing really know what they were talking about? It occurred to me that it all might be an elaborate prank.

I tried not to dwell on it, but I was actually a little disappointed that the meeting was taking place in a conference room in the hotel. RG had other events scheduled in much more fascinating places. I saw from his itinerary that he would be visiting the Presidential Palace, the Parliament House, and the gorgeous Jama Masjid, which was India's largest mosque. I'd seen photos of this holy site and had hoped to witness its red sandstone and marble up close in person, along with the Lodi Garden and the Old Fort, but sightseeing didn't seem to be in the cards for me this trip. Particularly now that it had been so drastically shortened. It was looking like I'd endured my inoculations only to be holed up in a hotel my entire trip. Oh well. Perhaps I'd make it back to India in some other lifetime.

Despite some trepidation about the appropriate placement of my feet, the meeting went very well. The representatives of the drug companies with whom we desired much stronger trade relationships were extremely friendly and cooperative. And they all had sharp British accents, which were fun to listen to when I wasn't thinking about their oppressive empirical origins.

Within our allotted hour, we'd gotten almost everything we'd asked for, including the supply of Focusid, which we'd requested confidentially by hinting that the NIH wanted to conduct some top-secret trials to pave the way for eventual FDA approval. Since we were merely hinting at this, we weren't outright lying, but I still felt misgivings about the transaction. I reminded myself that were helping the president try to save his father. It was a noble cause.

At the conclusion of the meeting, RG excused himself to head to his other appointments, leaving me to lay on more elaborate thank-yous and good-byes. The worsening condition of the president's father had even made the newspapers in India and several of the drug company representatives offered their sympathies as if I were directly related to him. I promised to pass the sentiments along.

Several others also inquired after ex-President Pile. They'd seen *Piling On* and were convinced that Pile was either mentally unstable or severely in debt and desperate for cash. What else could explain his behavior? I demurred that I really couldn't speak for Pile, but assured them that most of America shared their relief that Pile was no longer in charge of anything more important than a lawn mower.

Mythri Patel stopped me on my way out the door. She was an executive at the company that produced Focusid. It was the second-largest biotech company in India, and we had spent many hours on the phone together.

"How do you find India?" she asked me politely.

I beat back the Rodney Dangerfield urge to answer "Just turn left at Thailand"—where did that urge come from anyway, and could it please be banished forever?—and instead I smiled and replied that I felt incredibly privileged to be there. Which was true.

"What have you seen so far?" she inquired.

"To be perfectly honest, I haven't left the hotel," I replied.

She looked horrified.

"I know, but there's just too much work to do," I continued. "I'll have to come back sometime on my own schedule."

"What are you doing now?" she pressed.

I'd been on my way back to my room to type the follow-up documents from the meeting and send off some e-mails bringing Lincoln and Stephanie up to speed on what we'd accomplished. India would be providing us with several drugs at a much lower cost than our domestic companies, which was welcome but controversial news. The solution we'd brokered called for a careful strategy of unveiling the plan on our terms. This would be tricky since the U.S. pharmaceutical companies with a presence in India had gotten wind of our meeting and were starting to ask pointed questions. We needed to outsmart them if possible. We didn't want another Canada debacle on our hands.

"You must come with me to lunch," Mythri continued. "If you can spare the time."

I probably could, since RG was going to be tied up for the rest of the day with his other meetings in more exciting locations. If I wasn't going to make it to the Jama Masjid, I could at least make it to a real Indian meal.

"I'd like that," I agreed.

Mythri beamed.

"I'm meeting my cousin at a restaurant right around the corner. Are you ready now?"

"Yes, thank you."

Ten minutes later, Mythri was introducing me to her cousin Tara, who looked like an even smaller version of Mythri.

"Nice to meet you," I said.

"Back atcha," Tara replied in a Bronx accent.

I was slightly taken aback.

"Are you from the United States?" I asked.

Tara shook her head.

"Nope. Born and raised in Delhi," she answered.

Okay.

"It's just that your accent is so . . . American," I said.

Mythri sounded British, like most of the Indian people I'd inter-
acted with. I'd just been reflecting about how much my mom would
love it here. But now Mythri's cousin sounded completely different.

"It's on account of my job," Tara explained.

"Tara works at a call center for a large software company based in
America. Her dialect coach was from New York and taught her to speak
like a native."

He certainly did.

"Wow, that's amazing," I replied.

"Some of my friends got different coaches," Tara continued in her
jarring inflections. "This one girl who sits next to me had a coach from
Arkansas. All day I'm listening to 'Now, how ken I help y'all? Jest tell
me, y'hear?'"

I almost spit out my tea at Tara's dead-on mimicry of a deep Southern accent.

"You should be an actress," I replied.

"Oh, no, I'd miss answering phones too much," she answered, back
to her normal Bronx voice.

I sort of missed the Southern one, to be honest. It was less sarcastic.

"So would you classify yourself as a telemarketer?" I asked.

I had a serious soft spot for telemarketers. I actually loved talking
with them and called them back all the time. I was infinitely curious
about who they were, how they got into their line of work, and whether
they felt they were more verbally abused than people in other profes-
sions. I rarely bought anything from them, but I always enjoyed the
conversations.

One in particular, whom I'd befriended after she'd called to tell me
about better long-distance rates, had become a close friend and confi-
dante over the years. Her name was Zelda. I had her work extension on
my speed dial and I spoke with her frequently. I wondered now if her
job was in any danger of being outsourced to India. And then I wondered whether it already had been. Maybe Zelda didn't live in Florida
like she'd always claimed. Maybe she wasn't even American. Armed

with this new information from Tara, I realized that Zelda could actually be a well-coached Indian woman who'd been masquerading as a Daytona-based working mother of two all along. What deception that would be! I determined to have a word with her when I returned home.

"A telemarketer?" Tara asked. "You mean the people who call during dinner? No way. I don't do the calling," Tara continued. "People call me. Or actually, they call the software company's help line and get patched through to me and then I handle their questions and complaints."

"Oh," I said, trying to cover my disappointment.

I was saddened that Tara seemed so offended by the notion that she might be a telemarketer. Was telemarketing considered lower caste work?

"Well, that's still pretty interesting," I offered. "So you have to be a computer expert, then."

Tara nodded. Computer experts intimidate me. They're like alien royalty, lording over a world I could never truly understand. I need them, and I revere them, but I can never really relate to them. Our brains are too different. Even with all my gadgets, I have an extremely rudimentary understanding of how technology actually works. I wondered if Tara could tell I was in awe of her.

We ate tandoori chicken and roti and talked about our lives in the awkward way of women who don't know one another and will probably never meet again but feel some urge to connect despite these obstacles. After lunch, we said our good-byes. Mythri was late for a meeting, but wanted to make sure I knew my way back to the hotel. I thought that I did. I always pay extra attention when being led around strange places because I hate feeling lost. I spent enough time feeling like that at home.

"It's such a shame you can't see more of Delhi. And outside of it. It's almost irresponsible of you to return to America without knowing more," Mythri said.

I felt like I was being scolded. I agreed with her, but my schedule really wasn't my fault.

"I know," I agreed. "But my time's not my own this trip."

"We could send her back on a camel," Tara said playfully.

Mythri's face lit up.

"Brilliant plan!" she said. "Hold just a moment."

And she disappeared into the street before I could react. I turned to Tara, who was looking very pleased with herself.

"There are camels around here?" I asked uncertainly.

I thought they were mainly outside of Delhi, in the desert.

"Oh, there's everything in Delhi," she replied, leading the way out the door.

To prove her point, Mythri soon returned with a two-humped camel that was being led by a rope by its owner. She grinned excitedly at me before speaking quickly with the camel owner. They seemed to be negotiating the price.

"Thank you, but this really isn't necessary," I said a bit frantically. "I don't even have any money on me. Really, I can just walk."

Mythri waved away my protestations.

"It's our treat. And I've told him where to drop you."

"Terrific," I said, trying to make it sound sincere.

I'd seen plenty of camels before, but mainly on television. I'd certainly never been this close to one. It had knobby limbs, scraggly hair, enviable eyelashes, and what seemed to be some kind of abnormal growth above its right ear. But the most notable thing about it was that it looked completely pissed off.

I didn't know camels could be so expressive. This one looked like it wanted to kill someone. Anyone. Certainly someone stupid enough to make it lug extra weight around on a hot, dusty day.

"I don't think it wants to be ridden," I tried.

Tara laughed.

"What are you, scared?" she challenged.

She actually sounded like a bully. The accent didn't help. I shrugged. I supposed I was scared, but I was mainly just unenthused. I like to think of myself as adventurous and game for new experiences, but some things just don't appeal to me. Recreational riding of animals falls into that category. I didn't even enjoy riding horses because I could never shake the feeling that they would much rather be doing something else. It would be one thing if I *needed* to ride them, for transportation or herding or anything besides just a human entitlement to be entertained. But I didn't have any genuine need to ride them. And I was positive that they knew and resented this.

"It's just unnecessary," I replied.

"It will help you remember India," Mythri insisted.

She said something to the owner, who induced the camel to seesaw itself down to the ground.

"You can climb on him now," Mythri prompted.

So it was a he. I'd been too preoccupied with other thoughts to check. I gingerly put my hand on his neck and tried to beam an apology to him. If animals could sense fear, maybe they could perceive remorse as well. The camel responded to my empathic appeal by noisily passing gas.

Tara laughed again. She really seemed to be enjoying this whole debacle.

"They are very rude, these camels," Mythri said as she moved clear of the assault. "Watch out for the spitting as well."

"Uh-huh," I said.

And they bit too, didn't they? The only upside of this whole experience was that it justified my inoculations. I knew there wasn't any way to get out of this gracefully. I took a deep breath, which was a mistake.

"Just throw your leg over and sit in the saddle," Mythri instructed.

"Saddle" was a generous term. It was more like a little rag covering for what turned out to be an incredibly uncomfortable seat.

And before I could even settle in it, the camel was getting back up with plenty of complaining grunts and groans. It took all of my knee-gripping strength not to pitch over the top of his head as his hind legs shot me forward. And then his front legs whiplashed me back. That was enough of a ride. I could get off now.

"Have fun!" Tara smiled evilly at me from too far below.

There weren't any reins for me to hold. I just had to grasp at whatever camel body parts might stabilize me.

"Um, yeah, good-bye," I said a bit breathlessly.

I wondered if these would be my final words. They hadn't been all that eloquent. But this ride required all my powers of concentration. We moved off down the crowded street. This is fun, I told myself. This is exciting. Enjoy this.

I just couldn't. It was painful and smelly and unforgivably touristy. I felt extremely conspicuous. And already chafed.

The camel man ignored my repeated yelps to please let me down. I knew he didn't speak English, but I was communicating in the international language of distress. He ignored me nonetheless. I was internally berating myself for ever agreeing to this ride in the first place and strategizing about how to best fling myself off the camel before we made it in sight of the hotel and any colleagues who might glimpse me when someone called my name. I looked over to see Doug taking my picture with a disposable camera. He was evidently off shift at the moment and looked delighted to have stumbled across me in my current predicament. I grimaced.

"Can you rescue me?" I called to him. "Tackle the camel man or something. Anything."

Doug grinned and came to my aid after snapping a few more photos. Through some friendly sign language, he successfully persuaded the camel man to release me from my forced ride. I slid from the saddle feeling grateful and smelly. And mildly concerned about the possible harm done to my reproductive organs during the short and miserable excursion.

"Nice form," Doug commented.

"Yeah, thanks," I said. "I'll give you some pointers sometime."

As we walked back to the hotel, I had to concentrate on not hobbling. It was a relief to be reunited with air-conditioning, though the artificial cool seemed to slick the camel odor to my skin in a more permanent way. I thanked Doug and headed for the shower, feeling like a chastened athlete just cut from tryouts.

Hours later, after scrubbing myself clean and reporting to Lincoln and Stephanie back in D.C., I was headed toward the staff room when RG and his entourage rounded the corner. Sofia was briefing him on something as they walked. She gave me a dark look as if I were an unexpected obstacle to be trampled, and I stepped back against the wall to clear out of their way. But RG stopped walking.

"Sammy, can you join us for our next event?" he asked.

"Of course," I said immediately.

They were headed to Parliament. Perhaps there was some health care tie-in that hadn't been obvious to me. RG liked to be prepared for anything and everything.

Sofia seemed exquisitely displeased by the invitation. I reminded myself to investigate just why this woman seemed to hate me so much. Perhaps I could steer her toward some other pursuits.

We took the freight elevator down to the garage level, where RG's motorcade was waiting. He always entered and left through underground garages, since the Secret Service wanted to eliminate as much of his unscheduled public exposure time as they could. I imagined it had been years since RG had seen the actual lobby of a hotel. By this point, he was much more familiar with kitchens and back halls and service routes—the unglamorous innards of prestigious places.

I clambered into the staff van along with the others and congratulated myself on the fact that I'd once again scored a window seat. I stared outside as we drove through the city, trying to take in as much as I could without knowing exactly what I was observing. It was a familiar, unsettling feeling.

As we drove past an outdoor market on a traffic-cleared road, I saw a sizable crowd gathered off to the side, holding welcoming signs aimed at RG. He must have seen them as well, because the motorcade suddenly stopped. It seemed RG wanted to get out. I watched the Secret Service agents spring into action with tense alertness. They despised this kind of spontaneity, but they had to endure it.

Doug had once told me that most of the legitimate threats to RG's safety came from people with a plan, however psychotic that plan might be. This meant that unscheduled stops such as these provided agents with the small comfort that anyone trying something dumb would be doing it in the moment, without a thought-out strategy for success. And *should* anyone try something, they would find themselves up against a well-armed and armored counterattack team that traveled in the SUV "war wagon" in the motorcade. This counterattack team was deployed on all international trips, traveling everywhere with the vice president, ready to engage in warfare at any moment.

RG was now greeting the crowd, much to its delight. But it couldn't remain a quick and simple gesture, because with him, any unexpected move set off a chain of reactions. Sure enough, I could see the press leaping out of their van toward the rear of the motorcade and racing to both capture the moment and shout some questions at RG. I watched the press handler arguing with Chick Wallrey, trying to coerce her back toward the van. I couldn't hear her response but I could tell it was shrill. She brushed him off and hurried forward to lie in wait by RG's car. Doug motioned for her to stand some distance away.

The rest of us jumped out to see if we could be of any help in handling the situation as RG continued posing for photos and signing autographs. I was relieved that it seemed to be a totally friendly crowd. Complete with another camel. Its owner was now asking RG to take a photo with the beast. RG smiled and complied. And it was at this moment that Chick managed to slip closer to him.

"Is it true that the president is incapacitated with grief over the rapidly worsening condition of his father?"

RG acted as if he didn't hear her as he shook another hand. What did she mean by "incapacitated"? Did she have any inkling of his drunken phone call? Lord, I hoped not. Determined not to let RG get away again with the time-honored "Sorry, I can't hear you" hand-cupping-ear move, Chick decided to scream her next question.

"When the president's father dies, will the president write the eulogy himself or will he just plagiarize it?"

If the day had an old-school soundtrack to it, I would have just heard the record scratching to a stop. Everything seemed to freeze as RG turned and stared hard at Chick, who waited shamelessly, holding her mini-recorder out in the air toward him. He didn't say anything, he just stared her down. She must have known she was out of line, but she didn't falter. She'd yelled out her question to get a reaction, so perhaps in her mind she'd won.

The moment seemed to be holding its breath. We all stared from RG to Chick and back again, feeling like we were witnessing a modern-day showdown. Even the camel man was entranced, wondering along with the rest of us just what would happen next. His camel had been startled by Chick's screamed question, and now looked supremely irritated.

"Well? Will he?" Chick asked shrilly.

I watched the camel give another little start. And then, as if divinely inspired, he spat—a stream of disgusting greenish liquid straight from one of his three stomachs—directly in Chick's face. I'd heard of camels spitting when they were annoyed before, but I didn't know they were capable of so perfectly demonstrating what humans around them were feeling. It was as though he absorbed all of the ambient hostility toward Chick and channeled it into a single, dazzling gesture. The camel spit for all of us. I instantly felt much more warmly toward these animals.

Chick shrieked and staggered back. Several of the cameras turned to film her, reminding me of a *National Geographic* special I'd watched about sharks who eat their own. Someone finally came to her assistance and helped her back toward the press van. I noticed that RG seemed to be trying not to smile as he waved a final time to the crowd and ducked back into his armored car. The people in the market continued clapping and waving their signs. The camel looked bored. I made my way back to the van, surprised at what had just happened and unsure of exactly how to react. The protocol sheet hadn't covered this one.

I thought about Chick later in my room, after the trip to Parliament that had resulted in some impromptu U.S. health care policy PR and an evening spent catching up on all my work. I wondered how she'd recovered from her assault and how much it was going to worsen her coverage of our trip. From what I'd read of her, she couldn't really get more hostile. But I knew that underestimating her was dangerous.

And in actuality, there was a lot for her to be hostile about, should she uncover the secrets we were endeavoring to hide. I sighed, helped myself to a Flying Horse beer from the minibar, and reflected on the road ahead. I usually avoided projecting too far into the future because individual days tended to overwhelm me and contemplating an endless stream of them stretched out before me made me completely exhausted. But there were so many questions to consider. What was going to happen with Wye? To RG? To Charlie and me? Just to me? I hated not knowing.

The last time I'd been home in Ohio, I'd listened to a local radio show that had featured a woman who'd advocated turning to the Bible for any and all answers. She'd meant this quite literally. If she couldn't decide whether to buy whole milk or 2 percent, she'd take out her pocket Bible and open it. She'd claimed that whatever page she landed on inevitably contained very specific guidance. The radio host had requested that she demonstrate, so she'd asked aloud what she should make for dinner. I'd wondered at that point if the majority of her questions were sustenance based. In the presence of the host, she'd then opened her pocket Bible and read a passage from Corinthians in which St. Paul instructs the church at Corinth to allow people to speak in tongues. The radio host had posited that the passage was about tolerance and inclusion of people from other cultures, which could be a message that she should make some sort of ethnic food. Or order Chinese or Indian takeout, both of which had sounded good to me. However, the woman insisted that she'd been instructed from above to make boiled tongue for dinner. I'd retched at the prospect. The radio host had argued with her for a while and then answered calls. I'd been surprised to hear that most of the callers agreed with the woman. In fact, the only one who hadn't was a young girl who'd lobbied hard for Chinese takeout. The caller had turned out to be the woman's daughter trying to disguise her voice. It had been an entertaining show.

I didn't have a Bible handy, but the room did have the standard hotel binder of services. I held it in my lap and asked in a whisper, "Will Wye get a handle on his drinking or are we destined for scandal and failure?" And then I flipped it open. My finger landed on a paragraph about the sauna in the hotel fitness center and spa. A place where one could dry out and be restored to peak health. A fantastic sign! Though, come to think of it, a sauna was also very hot, possibly purgatory-like. Great, we were going to hell in a handbasket. I tossed the binder on the bed with a sigh and cracked another beer. In the door of the minibar, I spotted a pack of Camel cigarettes, which I grabbed on impulse. If I was going down, I might as well go down blazin'.

Visitation

———•◦•———

I MADE IT BACK to the States irritable from nicotine withdrawal. Having decided that we might not be completely doomed, I'd determined that I wanted to live after all and attempted to nip my new smoking career in the bud. I tried not to think about cigarettes and focused instead on how proud I was to be jet-lagged. Still sleepy on my second day home, after work I hurried to my apartment, thinking about how much I'd always loved Fridays in September. They mark the beginning of weekends in a month of other beginnings. The start of fall, the start of school when I was younger, the start of new colors and sports seasons and pangs for pumpkin pie. And on this particular September Friday, Charlie was finally coming home.

He'd been gone only ten days, but they'd been ten days that he'd spent working and settling into another city not that far but still too far away from me. And so it had felt like a month. He was back only for the weekend, but I'd take it.

There were countless other things to focus on—the president's secret problem, the crisis with Canada, the hopeful Indian solution—but I shoved them all aside. Charlie was all I wanted to care about for a few blissful hours. That was my plan, and I had a hunch it just might save me.

I glanced at my watch as I tore it off along with the rest of my work clothes. He was supposed to meet me at my apartment in fifteen minutes. Which was not nearly enough time to turn into the most gorgeous and clever version of myself he'd ever seen. Dammit, why hadn't I been able to get everything done just a little bit sooner?

Maybe self-loathing would add an attractive glow. I'd been looking a bit pale lately, probably thanks to the cigarettes.

"I'm on my way out, I promise!" Liza yelled over the running water.

The shower was taking its time warming up to habitable temperatures.

"Wait, don't leave yet." I stuck my head into the hallway. "I need some help."

I felt suddenly anxious and shy about seeing Charlie. Which was ridiculous, I knew. Luckily, Liza seemed to understand.

"Okay. I'm supposed meet Jakers, but it won't kill him to wait. I was mainly clearing out so you guys could have the place to yourselves for the night."

"I know, thank you. It's just that the time got away from me and . . . oh no," I groaned.

I hadn't factored in Charlie's time disorder.

"I've actually got only *five* minutes till he shows up," I revised. "That's not enough time to fix me. I'm a disaster."

"Oh, sweetie," Liza said in that tone that she used to convey sympathy, support, and an ongoing wonder at my basic ineptitude in matters of personal appearance. "How can I help? Have you picked out what you're going to wear?"

Had she just met me?

"Never mind, I'm on it," Liza said as she waved me away.

It was a relief to have her on the case. When it came to things like this, Liza was a genius. I knew she was applying for loans to start her event company, but if she ever wanted to moonlight as a personal stylist, she'd be one of the best. And then I could feel good about all the worst-case scenario practice I'd provided her. Completely free of charge.

"Don't forget to shave!" she called over her shoulder as I plunged into the still-freezing water.

I cursed myself for not having shaved my legs that morning. But I'd reasoned that they'd be even more freshly smooth if I did them right before I reunited with Charlie, as part of the pampering routine that I'd of course have plenty of time for since I'd finish my work early, no problem. I should never listen to myself.

Four frantic minutes later, Liza was styling my hair and spritzing me with perfume as I stanched the trickles of blood from my razor-nicked knees when the doorbell rang. Charlie had a key, but maybe he felt awkward about using it now. Or maybe he suspected just such preparations might be going on and wanted to give fair warning. He did know me pretty well.

I wished Liza had already left, because I wanted to see him for the first time alone.

"I'm going out the fire escape," she informed me.

She also knew me very well.

"What? No, you can't do that."

"I want to," she insisted breezily. "I've been meaning to break in these new shoes," she said, indicating a pair of platform wedges that made her a good five inches taller than normal.

Unlike me, Liza wasn't scared of heights. In fact, she was currently only thirty training hours away from her pilot's license. I knew that she dreamed of flying her own plane to transport far-flung flea market finds for her Greek- and Roman-themed events.

At the moment, however, she was busy climbing out our window. We'd used the fire escape once after I'd insisted we practice in order to be prepared for potential catastrophe, so we knew for a fact that it wasn't a very comfortable route to the street. Even when one was wearing shoes that actually fit in the ladder rungs.

"Seriously, go out the front door," I said.

"Bye, gorgeous. I'll see you on the outside," she called as she closed the window and turned to the ladder.

I smiled and shook my head as I hurried to the door. Before opening it, I took a deep breath. Which reminded me that I hadn't brushed my teeth and there'd been a late-afternoon beef jerky incident.

"One second," I called to the door in what I hoped was a sexy, come-hither voice.

I searched in my bag but I was all out of breath mints. I'd read a recent study that they decayed tooth enamel faster than almost anything else, so maybe it was for the best. I raced back into the bathroom, squeezed some toothpaste into my mouth, took a gulp of water, and then swallowed the whole thing instead of spitting it out as planned. Blech. Way too much minty freshness.

I rushed back to the door and flung it open. I was a half second away from leaping into arms that I hoped would be ready and eager to catch me when I noticed that those arms belonged to Jakers, who was leaning against the door frame with a bored expression on his face. At least I think he looked bored. It was hard to tell because he was also wearing sunglasses. So maybe he thought he just looked cool, which he didn't.

"You're not Charlie," I heard myself say accusingly.

He was really the farthest thing from Charlie.

"Well, I wish I were tonight," he answered, looking me up and down slowly and approvingly.

I knew that this was Jakers's form of a compliment, but that didn't mean I had to take it that way.

"Liza's on her way to meet you," I said acidly. "You can probably catch her on the street."

"Well, she was half an hour late and not answering her cell, so I thought maybe something was wrong," he answered.

"Yeah, I'm sorry, that was me. I needed her help."

Jakers nodded.

"Okeydokey, I'll track her down. Let me just use your little boys' room for a quick sec," he said as he pushed past me.

I really wanted Jakers out of the apartment. Not least because Charlie was about to arrive.

Thinking of Charlie again, I was surprised to feel myself having the heartbeat flutters I associated with the first few months of our relationship. As we'd gone on together, the flutters had become deeper, more sustained grooves. Still exciting, but in a less anxious way. But here were the flutters again. I felt suddenly thrust back about two years.

Jakers whistled when he walked into the bathroom.

"It looks like a tsunami hit in here!" he shouted with typical tact.

"Can you just hurry, please?" I called. "You irritating moron," I added under my breath.

"Still so ladylike," I heard Charlie say behind me.

I whirled around. There he was in the door, the way I'd been imagining. Possibly even more handsome than I'd been imagining, which was tough, because I tended to build people up. In general, this tendency resulted in let-downs. Charlie had yet to disappoint, though.

"Hey, lovely," he said.

"Hi," I said back, thrown off by the unanticipated need to catch my breath.

"Phew, do *not* go in there!" Jakers said loudly as he exited the bathroom.

He grinned hugely, willing his hilarity to overwhelm us.

"Just kidding. How ya doing, my man?" he said to Charlie as he clapped him on the shoulder.

I felt acutely annoyed that Jakers had managed to touch Charlie before I had. And with a hand that from the sounds of things hadn't been washed.

"Enjoying all those hot New York City chicks?" Jakers asked with a wink.

Okay, now he really had to go.

"Haven't noticed any," Charlie answered easily. "I've got all I need right here."

Finally, Charlie was touching me. He pulled me into him like Jakers wasn't even there.

"Sure, sure, we'll talk later," Jakers replied with an elbow jab and another wink.

Then he put a hand on both our shoulders.

"So . . . what are we doing tonight? Big plans?"

I felt Charlie squeeze me a little tighter. It was nice of him to try to shield me from the horribleness.

Jakers's cell phone began ringing before either of us had a chance to answer. His ring was, oddly, "The Electric Slide." It almost made me like him a little bit.

"This is J to the akers," he said as he flipped open his phone.

And then he had to go and keep doing things like that.

"Hey, babe. . . . Yeah, I know I'm not there. I'm at your place with Sammy and Charlie."

There was a pause. I imagined I could feel Liza's wrath raining down from the cell tower.

"All right, all right, sheesh," Jakers said. "I'm on my way out. Don't get your panties all up in a bunch."

He rolled his eyes at us.

"Yes, I'm stepping out of the apartment right now," he continued in a patronizing tone to try to cover up the fact that he was being reamed.

He turned back toward us.

"That time of month," he mouthed.

Charlie guided me inside the apartment and shut the door. We both burst out laughing.

"I wanted to try to make this a really special night, so I called in the big guns," I said.

"You know that nothing gets me hot like Jakers," Charlie answered.

We grinned at each other. With his arms around me once more, I felt supported for the first time in weeks.

"Hi," I said again.

Maybe I wanted to start the evening over on our own terms. Or maybe I just didn't know what else to say. I felt safe but also slightly awkward. It's amazing what even the tiniest bit of distance can do. Charlie traced his fingers from my forehead down to my chin, which reminded me to be catlike. No blatant doglike dependency for me. Nosiree.

It was a good thing I remembered my new strategy, because I was about to ask him if he'd missed me. Instead, I just closed my eyes like I might be purring.

"I've missed you so much," he said in my ear.

I was a feline genius.

"Oh, yeah?" I replied.

"Mmm-hmmm," he answered, pressing his lips to mine.

We quickly ended up in my bedroom. And two hours later, we lay happily wrapped up in each other. When it got to the point that I knew we could maintain our current positions for only another few minutes before limbs began falling asleep, I broached the topic of sustenance.

"I don't really feel like moving," Charlie confessed.

I didn't either, but I knew that we were going to have to in the next few minutes. We'd at least have to shift. And though I had no desire to leave the apartment or allow Charlie to do so, I also wanted this to be a weekend of complete satisfaction. No hunger of any kind allowed. My grandmother's best friend had told me when I was younger that the way to a man's heart was through food. Even back then, I'd dismissed this as the kind of advice that too conveniently dovetailed with a philosophy that kept women domesticated and homebound. But it had stuck with me over the years and popped into my head whenever I periodically resolved to learn how to cook. I wondered if there was anything to it.

"We can order in," I suggested.

I was great at ordering in. For Christmas last year, Liza had given me a sheer lace apron that read, "I don't make dinner. I make dinner happen."

"Where is that apron?" Charlie asked.

I'd been known to wear it without anything else.

"Pizza? Thai? Mexican?" I pressed.

"Pizza," Charlie said definitively. "And the apron."

In thirty minutes or less, he had his wish. And then some.

Lying next to Charlie later that night, I found myself thinking about chicken pox. It's not my fault that he chose that moment to ask me what was on my mind.

"It's good to know I've still got the power to push you over the edge into blissful, satiated epidemic paranoia," he replied when I told him.

"No, no, I'm not worried about getting it. I've already had chicken pox. I was remembering how horrible it was."

"Oh, good. I feel much better. What other memories of pain and suffering has our reunion brought up?"

I covered his mouth with my hand.

"Let me finish. *If* you really want to know what I was thinking."

He couldn't speak anymore, but he nodded his head.

"Okay. I got chicken pox when I was six and it was the first time in my life I really remember being sick. My parents hadn't gotten me vaccinated because they thought getting it on my own would be a healthier way to go. But they wanted to make sure that I *did* get it while I was still young, so I wouldn't be susceptible to the worse forms of it that can take you down when you're older . . ."

"Adult chicken pox is awful," Charlie tried to say through my hand.

"Exactly," I agreed. "So anyway, when my neighbor Lexi Towney came down with chicken pox, they brought me to her house to get infected. And you think Professor Moriarty and Cal Ripken Jr.'s playdates are demented."

Charlie smiled but I kept my hand in place.

"The arrangement was that she would just touch my forearm, but when our parents were distracted in the other room, Lexi rubbed her hands all over my face and neck before I could escape. And a few days later, I was an itchy, swollen mess."

I removed my hand to better illustrate my story with expressive gestures. Charlie stayed quiet, looking concerned.

"It was horrible. My first real memory of acute misery. And I remember lying there thinking about how I would do anything to not feel so bad. And I was remembering how much more fun it was to not have chicken pox and that was the first time I wished very hard for a time machine."

"A red-letter day," Charlie said.

"True," I agreed. "So at first I was thinking about going back to the time before I went to Lexi's and being much better prepared for her attack, but then I started thinking about going forward in time to when I was all better, and I decided that when I did get well, I would never take my healthy, not-covered-in-itchy-sores skin for granted again."

"Very sophisticated thinking for a six-year-old," Charlie commented.

"I know. But not sophisticated enough." I sighed wistfully.

Every once in a while, I got very down that I'd never ended up being a child prodigy. At anything—I would have taken anything. I'd yearned to be naturally phenomenal, but it just wasn't meant to be. So though I still held out hope that I might be staggeringly brilliant at something I hadn't gotten my hands on yet, like a ukelele, I recognized that I was too old now for the talent to be truly impressive.

Charlie kissed my forehead sympathetically. He was aware of the prodigy longing.

"And then, just when I was finally getting better, our neighbor's dog Zeke was hit by a car," I continued.

"I've never heard about Zeke," Charlie replied.

"He was this big, reddish, sort of scary dog that I'd known my entire life. And we didn't have the best relationship because he was a little snappish around kids, but he was consistently a part of my universe, always around. And then, suddenly, he was gone. Never to return."

Charlie nodded. I took a breath and continued.

"And that's what I remember whenever I think about chicken pox. I think about Zeke. He was always a pain, but I cried and cried when I found out I'd never see him again. When I went back to school it was around Valentine's Day and our teacher told us to draw a picture of something we loved and I drew this calendar that said 'January' on it. And I wrote underneath it that I loved January because in January I'd never had chicken pox and I still had Zeke."

Charlie smiled.

"And you were just remembering all this lying here?"

"I was thinking about the things I take for granted that can just suddenly disappear. And about what I'd draw if I got that assignment today."

He offered his profile.

"This is my best side. I recommend charcoal to really capture the contours. I have a devastating jawline."

I smiled and kissed him and decided not to tell him that drawing him wouldn't be enough. If I was really being honest, I'd have to draw him back in August. And here we were in fall.

Sunday arrived much too quickly. I knew what time the last train left, but I also knew it was unfair to expect Charlie to arrive in New York in the middle of the night just for a few more hours with me.

In the past two years, Sundays had made me happy because they'd meant leisure time with Charlie. Fall Sundays had involved football games and couch lounging and creative betting that led to all kinds of adventures. We'd make brunch or nachos and take walks or go to the movies. We'd rest together, sag into each other, be calm. I'd loved them, but now they were gone. Replaced by a day of departure. All of a sudden, Sundays were depressing again.

It was when Charlie was in the shower that I got the idea of writing him a note and sticking it in his bag to be discovered later. This wasn't the most original idea, but I liked the fact that it gave me something to do besides feel mopey that he didn't live in D.C. anymore the way I'd always foolishly assumed he would. It took a special effort to write him notes because BlackBerrying him was so easy and instant, but I tried to remember to go the old-fashioned route every once in a while for the sake of posterity. There was something about handwritten missives that struck me as romantic in our digital age.

I was just finishing when I heard the water go off. He'd still need to shave, so I had a little longer. I read over the note and thought about how I could spice it up. Possibly with a scent. People did that, right? I grabbed some perfume and sprayed it on the note. The paper moistened immediately and the ink ran together. I tried to salvage it with some quick blotting and waving but it was too late. Hmmm, that hadn't gone as planned at all. Not one bit.

I tore off a new sheet and wrote a much shorter, less eloquent note. It was really more of a crummy cartoon, but I made my points. Then I unzipped Charlie's bag and stuffed it deep inside, underneath his sweater, on top of his book, and beside what felt like some small metal cans. Small metal cans were not a part of his normal repertoire. I pulled them out for a closer look.

Interesting. They were cans of Fancy Feast cat food. I held them up for Charlie's perusal when he came into the room.

"Snack for the train?" I inquired.

I was mainly joking, but I did have a babysitter once who'd snacked on Puppy Chow like it was granola. She'd sworn it did wonders for her complexion.

"Oh, those," Charlie answered. "Those are for Amanda's cat, Delilah. I'm trying to get her to like me."

He meant the cat, I assumed, not his new roommate, Amanda. What did he care if Amanda liked him or not? Then again, why would he care about the cat's feelings? Wasn't that even worse?

"Oh," I replied. "How come?"

He laughed. A bit sheepishly, in my opinion.

"Well, she's this adorable little thing and we share the same space and I'd just be happier if she let me pet her once in a while. But as of now, she won't give me the time of day."

"You're talking about the cat," I said.

I just wanted everything to be very clear.

"Yeah. Delilah."

"Okay, so you're bringing her a present," I surmised.

"Right. Amanda said Delilah really loves Fancy Feast but she only gets it once a year on her birthday or something. So she said if I brought Delilah Fancy Feast, she'd love me forever."

"The cat would," I said.

"Yeah," Charlie said, giving me a look.

I wasn't the one being dense.

"Well, that's really sweet of you," I said unconvincingly.

I thought about whether he had brought me a gift. I didn't have to think long. He hadn't, and it hadn't bothered me until now. It wouldn't have even occurred to me had I not just discovered that he'd taken the time at some point during our already-too-short weekend together to go out of his way to buy a gift for someone else. Not even someone else. Some*thing* else. Something else that belonged to someone else.

When had he bought the Fancy Feast anyway? We'd been together the entire time. Except for yesterday morning, I now remembered. I'd still been sleeping when he'd slipped out to get us coffee and the paper. And a random present for his roommate's furball. He could have easily picked up some Fancy Feast when he got back to New York City—were Amanda and her cat so at the forefront of his mind that he couldn't re-sist impulsively buying them things at any opportunity?

"It's silly, I know," Charlie was saying. "But I just want the cat to like me. You'll meet her. You'll see what I'm talking about."

Uh-huh.

"Well, are you all set?" I said brightly.

"Sammy."

He could tell something was wrong. Though I was making it fairly obvious, I was still in no mood to acknowledge it.

"What?" I said, in my same fake tone.

"Why does the cat food bother you?"

"It doesn't. It's great. I'm sure she'll love it. And then she'll love you forever. Which is terrific. You'll be all set to live there as long as you want. For forever, even."

To my extreme annoyance, I felt my eyes start to well up. I hated not having better control over my tear ducts. Why didn't I? Maybe some-thing was actually wrong with them. Maybe I had some kind of faulty duct disease. Another thing to be upset about.

"Sammy . . ." Charlie reached out for me.

I could have let him hold me. Later, I wished that I had.

"I'm fine," I said aggressively, shrugging away from his touch.

I dried my eyes using more force than necessary. Like I was punishing myself for blowing things out of proportion.

"You're going to miss your train," I said without looking at him.

"Actually, in the shower I was thinking about staying over tonight and catching the five thirty a.m. one."

"I think you should probably just go," I replied instantly.

Why was I insisting on a wreck? Charlie could still save us, I knew. Somewhere inside, I was counting on it.

"Fine," he said shortly.

So much for that.

I expected it to be gray and rainy and cold outside to match the mood I had brought about. But it was warm and balmy, which made everything even worse. We walked in silence to the Metro stop.

"I'm sorry about the cat food," Charlie said tersely. "Which you happened to find when you were rifling through my things."

Now apologies were turning into accusations. This was spinning out of control. I took a deep breath and struck out for higher ground.

"I was hiding a note in your bag," I said simply. "Listen, I'm sorry if I overreacted. It's just very hard having you so far away."

"Really? Then why don't you want me to stay longer?"

His voice was tight and angry. He had a right to be annoyed.

"I do want you to. But not if you're going to be resentful tomorrow when you have to wake up at the crack of dawn and get on a crowded train and then be sleepy and irritable all day. I don't want you associating any of that fallout with me."

"You'd prefer I associate this fallout with you?" he asked.

I hated it when Charlie got sarcastic. It really didn't become him.

"Yeah, I guess." I sighed.

"It really feels like I'm the one making all the effort here," Charlie continued.

"You're the one who left," I retorted.

Now it was Charlie's turn to suck in all the air around us so that it felt too tense to breathe or move.

"I'm not so sure about that," he answered after a long, suspended moment.

He walked down the Metro stairs without looking back.

Rejuvenation

LATER THAT NIGHT, the president's father died. As I read the breaking news, I felt my eyes well up again—instantly—as if they'd been
spring-loaded for tears.

I didn't know Ernie Wye well, but I felt a great affection for him. He
had been diagnosed with Alzheimer's more than a decade ago, and
though his physical and mental health had been rapidly declining in the
past few months, he'd been well enough during the campaign and the
beginning of the administration to make a strong impression on everyone he came across. He'd always carried a supply of Fireballs with him
and had passed them out to all the people he'd happily chatted with.
He was an incredibly kind man who had somehow avoided the bitterness and frustration I'd witnessed in so many other Alzheimer's patients. Or perhaps he'd just already passed through that phase by the
time we all got to know him. Whatever the explanation, he didn't seem
too upset by his inability to remember names or faces. He just seemed
very excited to meet everyone repeatedly for the first time. He brought
an infectious sense of joy to each encounter, though he seemed less
childlike than he would have had he not managed to retain a deep quiet
dignity. He'd managed to turn living in the present moment into a
blessing rather than a curse, though it must have been hard not having
a choice.

When he'd visited his son, he'd liked to wander the halls of the West
Wing, and the president's staff sent out word to let him do just that.
They'd arranged for an agent to accompany him but had let him roam
wherever he pleased.

I'd returned from lunch one day to find Ernie sitting at my desk. He'd smiled up at me, offered a Fireball, and told me I looked like a butterfly. When I'd answered that it was better that than a caterpillar, he'd laughed and wanted to talk about bugs for the following hour. He'd told me the story of the ant and the grasshopper three times, but I really hadn't minded. Eventually, he'd wandered off.

Though we'd all been expecting him to pass away, his death was destined to feel premature. I wondered if he'd even had a chance to start the secret Focusid trial. Evidently he'd been too sick for anything to do much good. Technically he'd died of pneumonia but it was the Alzheimer's that had left him ravaged and weak and vulnerable to deadly infection.

I let myself cry for a while and then lay awake in the darkness of my room. Later, very late at night, I picked up the phone and called Charlie. It went straight to his voice mail. After leaving a contrite message, I noticed I had new voice mail of my own. It turned out that Charlie and I had called each other at the exact same time, and left similarly apologetic messages. And then we called each other at the same time again, after listening to those messages. This synchronized calling had actually happened before. Charlie had tried to convince me that it was just a coincidence, and not proof of extrasensory perception as I claimed. But I knew better.

After calling each other at the same time for the *third* time, I decided to end the shenanigans. I hung up and this time waited for Charlie to call again, which must have been what he was doing. Just when I was about to snatch up the receiver and dial, my cell phone began rockin' to Led Zeppelin.

"Hi," I said in relief.

"Hey. I got your message."

"I got yours."

"Yeah, I wish I'd waited on that till after you took all the blame."

I smiled.

"Unfortunate timing," I replied.

"That seems to be our forte these days," Charlie answered.

Which reminded me of something I'd just read.

"Did you know that 'forte' is technically pronounced 'fort'? Not 'fortay.' Unless you're referring to the Italian musical term."

"Are you trying to piss me off again?" he asked good-naturedly.

I smiled again.

"No, I pronounce it 'for-tay' too. I'm just telling you that we're both wrong, apparently."

"I don't mind being wrong about that. Pronunciation is not my 'fort.' See how lame that sounds?"

"I do," I replied.

There was an awkward pause. It had been easier to apologize to each other's electronic surrogates. But it was cowardly not to reiterate the sentiments now that we were talking live.

"Did you hear about Ernie Wye?" I inquired instead.

"Yes, that's really sad. He seemed like a good man."

"He was."

I stayed silent for a long moment. I'd already cried for Ernie Wye. I needed to deal with Charlie and me.

"Do you really think our timing is off?" I asked.

"I do," Charlie replied. "But it's understandable. We got knocked out of our rhythm. We just have to reorganize to a new one."

I was struck by an image of our relationship as a marching band, which didn't make it seem all that cool. Unless it was one of those hip-hop-ified ones that were redefining the genre. I wouldn't mind being compared with one of those. They were often more entertaining than the games at which they performed.

"I'm sorry I've made things more difficult for us by going to New York," Charlie continued. "I really am."

I appreciated that. But I was also at fault.

"I'm sorry I'm having so much trouble with it," I said. "I'll work on it," I promised.

I had to. And I had to stop being such a baby. We were bound to encounter larger, more shattering obstacles in our life together. I needed to look at this separation and all the uncomfortable emotions it provoked as practice. If we could stretch our coping muscles now and still come together in the end, we'd be that much better prepared for the unknown challenges that lay ahead.

"I think I just get a little insecure," I admitted. "Worried that you moved away from me too easily. And that the distance will just feed on itself."

I could hear Charlie listening. His breathing took on a slightly different pattern when he was carefully taking something in. It was almost like an air metronome, counting out the beats of my syllables. I curled up in my bed and turned off the light while I waited for him to speak. I liked being with him in the dark. He took his now-I'll-reply breath.

"I was offered a promotion a year and a half ago. To the London bureau," he began.

What?

"I didn't tell you about it," he continued. "And I turned it down because I knew I didn't want to go that far unless you came with me."

"Maybe I would have! You should have asked!"

"Really? Would you really have left your job in the White House in the first year of the administration?"

Well, no, now that he put it that way. I couldn't have left. I saw his point.

"Probably not," I answered sheepishly.

"Right. So I said no. And I didn't tell you about it because it wasn't an issue. I've never regretted that decision."

"Oh," I said. "So I should be grateful that it's just New York?"

"That's not what I mean. I don't do anything without thinking of you. And I don't think that makes me weaker. I feel stronger because of it. My decisions feel more right because of it. I love you. And I want our lives to work together."

I blinked at the darkness in my room. My eyes were just beginning to adjust to the point where I could make out a few familiar shapes.

"I love you too," I answered. "Too much for your own good, probably."

I thought about bringing up Amanda and the jealousy issues, but it was now almost three a.m. and we both had busy days ahead. I'd save it for another time, and if in the meantime I worked them out on my own, all the better.

We got off the phone. I curled tighter into the blankets and fell asleep wondering if there was enough time to dream before I'd have to wake up.

The next week brought preparations for the president's father's funeral. Ernie Wye had served in the Second World War and had requested to be buried in Arlington National Cemetery instead of in his hometown of Gibsland, Louisiana. The funeral was to take place at the National Cathedral on the Monday eight days after his death. The morning of the funeral, I woke up thinking about black.

Personally, I prefer the tradition of using wakes to celebrate a person's life with festive colors and happy stories. My grandmother had worn a bright purple dress to my grandfather's funeral, and the sight of her had prompted smiles through the tears. But I knew official funerals weren't as progressive as my grandmother, so I reluctantly donned an appropriately somber outfit. I comforted myself by ceremoniously eating some Fireballs bought in tribute to the memory of Ernie Wye, then gathered my things and headed for the door.

A glance toward Cal Ripken Jr. revealed that he was swimming perkily in his bowl. I'd arranged a Professor Moriarty visit the week before, just after returning from the disastrous Metro walk with Charlie. Watching Cal flail about in a wild display of fighting aggression had helped cure me of my own lingering belligerence and moved me toward the remorse that motivated me to call Charlie and apologize. I was pleased to see it had also resulted in a health boon for Cal.

The West Wing was humming with activity as usual, but the buzz seemed muted in deference to the funeral. I worked for several hours before climbing into a motor pool car with other staffers attending the funeral. For a moment, it seemed like a school field trip, but I immediately felt guilty for the association. School field trips had always been welcome escapes from routine, particularly when they'd involved aquariums or grown-ups dressed in colonial costumes. But I wasn't attending this funeral to get a break from work. I was going to pay my respects to Ernie Wye.

"I feel like we're playing hooky," Margari said unhelpfully.

As our staff procession of black minivans pulled onto Rock Creek Parkway, I noticed that the trees had almost all changed color. I'd always been fascinated by this chemical process. When I was eleven, I'd trained a video camera on the branches outside my bedroom window for several hours to try and capture the exact moments when a leaf would leap from green to brilliant orange or yellow. I was thrilled with the subsequent footage. My mother was less so after discovering that

I'd taped over my reading of a poem at her first cousin's wedding. It had taken years for her to fully forgive me. But frankly, I'd never been a gifted orator and that cousin was already divorced.

The number of cars headed to the National Cathedral had created a backup. Our driver drove past the cathedral and the line, and let us out at the next intersection. We walked back past the Cathedral School for Girls and I wondered what it would have been like to attend an all-girls school. Particularly one affiliated with the cathedral. Were they all little Episcopal priestesses in training? Somehow I doubted it.

"Are you with us, darlin'?" Margari asked with a tug at my sleeve.

She tended to treat me like a younger sister she occasionally had to keep in line, but it was a fair question. I'd been lost in my own thoughts since leaving the West Wing. Not only about trees and cathedrals, but about the problems facing us that were just as colossal. The booze, the leaks, the lifestyle drugs. It amounted to a tawdry catalog when I tallied it all up. Those troubles and dilemmas were there, festering, demanding to be dealt with. I worried for all of us.

"Yeah, sorry, I'm just a little out of it," I answered.

"Sammy's our little daydreamer," Sofia said in a tone devoid of affection.

"It's because she's so smart," Margari said protectively. "She needs her thinking time. Like Lincoln here. The silent genius."

Lincoln blushed and didn't say anything.

As we rounded the school building, we could see the cameras lined up to film people arriving at and leaving the service. They were outside and a respectful distance from the cathedral doors, but their presence still struck me as unseemly.

I knew that the president had to live his life on camera, but I wished he could be given a break on the day he buried his father. I got the feeling that very little of this funeral would be private and personal. How could it be, really? There was too much interest in it.

"Do you mind if we ask you a couple questions?" a man with a microphone asked as we passed.

Where was a spitting camel when you needed one? I saw Sofia straighten up and run her hand through her hair. But Margari spoke indignantly before Sofia had a chance to claim her cameo.

"Yes, we do mind, actually," Margari said. "This is a *funeral*. Where are your manners?"

I was happy that Margari agreed with me, but wondered if we ought to be a little nicer to the press. The guy was only trying to do his job. He didn't seem fazed, or at all shamed. He just turned to some other attendees with the same question.

"Honestly, I do not understand some people," Margari complained exasperatedly.

"No kidding. That was ridiculous," Sofia added disingenuously.

In my mind, I rolled my eyes.

We cleared the Secret Service post with our preapproved hard pins, passed through the magnetometers to prove we weren't armed, and found seats in a back row. We had a good view of the altar and of the reserved seating areas. I tried to keep my thoughts on the solemn event at hand, but I was quickly distracted by the fact that so many people were doing otherwise.

I watched Senator Bramen and his wife, Pamela, shaking hands and greeting people as they moved toward their seats. Bramen was tall, lanky, and arrogant, with impressively bouffantish hair. In the last presidential campaign, he had lost the nomination to then Governor Wye after leading the pack of his party's contenders for many months. Wye's surprise upset had been a shock, and one from which Bramen had yet to recover. To add insult to injury, Wye had then passed over Bramen and picked RG to be his running mate instead. Ever since, Bramen had pretended to be a helpful ally of the administration, but I suspected he would welcome any opportunity to discredit the current leadership and then ride to the rescue of the country.

Not far from the Bramens, Senator Frand was making his own entrance into the cathedral. As usual, he looked as though he might be made of wax. He had his Dick York smile on and the *Bewitched* theme song kicked off in my head. Frand's wife, Kathryn, trailed slightly behind, exchanging gentle hand clasps with the people who greeted her. If I'd thought about it beforehand, I would have concluded that of course Senator Frand would attend the funeral. He was the majority leader of the Senate and this was one of those events at which bipartisan respects were dutifully paid. Still, he had been campaigning vigorously against the administration's Alzheimer's Bill, promoting his own sham alternative in its stead. Ernie Wye had suffered mightily from and ultimately died with Alzheimer's. I imagined that most other people would have felt awkward about this set of circumstances, but Senator Frand appeared as cool and calculating as ever. The midterm elections were a few weeks away and he had a majority to retain, by whatever means necessary.

Senator Frand and his wife slowed suddenly and looked back toward the entrance with strained smiles on their faces. I followed their gazes and saw former President Pile and his wife. The *Piling On* cameras weren't allowed inside the cathedral, but even devoid of a camera-wielding entourage, Pile seemed determined to lasso the spotlight. He looked practically giddy as he glad-handed anyone of import within arm's reach while scanning the horizon for bigger prey. His exuberant demeanor was wildly mismatched to the situation. I realized that he hadn't been to an event with Washington's elite since leaving office, but I was still stunned that the fact that he was attending a funeral didn't seem to dampen his pleasure at being back in the mix. He didn't seem to notice that no one was happy to see him.

To the right of the Piles, I saw an old friend of President Wye's who was now a highly paid lobbyist doing a terrible job of hiding the fact that he was typing on his BlackBerry as he waited for the service to begin. I almost nudged Margari to point out this egregious behavior, but thought better of it. She might march over and give him a lecture, and we didn't need to create a scene. Other people had that covered.

A horrible thought flashed through my mind. No one caused a scene like the Exterminators—what if they tried to pull some prank during the ceremony? I instantly dismissed the possibility. Not even they were that low. Though the fact that the idea had entered my head made me realize how frequently I anticipated their sabotage. They did an irritatingly impressive job of keeping us feeling perpetually insecure.

As everyone slowly settled into their seats, RG and Jenny slipped quietly in. I watched various people crane their necks and position for eye contact, but the Garys kept their heads bowed slightly as they walked to their places in the front row. I wondered if they could feel everyone staring at them. Not just today, but every day.

President Wye and Fiona joined them a moment later to a similar reception and the service began. It was very grand, which I appreciated for Ernie's sake. I listened to the prayers and hymns and speeches extolling Ernie Wye's virtues while gazing at the light coming through the huge rose window above us. The cathedral knew how to send people off in style.

President Wye stood and delivered a short and eloquent eulogy. I hadn't expected any slurring or stumbling, but I was still relieved to see that Wye seemed completely back to his regular self. Maybe the terminal stage of his father's illness had just briefly pushed him off the wagon, but wouldn't cause any more problems. I fervently hoped that Wye was back in control for good. I could tell that he was sadder, of course, but this just added an air of pathos to his talent for performance. He was charming and introspective as he recounted his father's character and life.

Ernie Wye had been born in a depressed part of Louisiana and had worked his way up to a position of considerable wealth and influence. After putting himself through school by working as a traveling salesman, he'd volunteered for the army at the start of World War II. He'd distinguished himself in combat and returned to his hometown a war hero. There, he'd married, begun a family, and started building what would eventually become an extremely lucrative grocery store empire. By the time President Wye was born, the family was well on its way to becoming rich and established. Ernie Wye had made something of himself to ensure that his family wouldn't want for anything. This didn't mean that his son had gotten off easy, though, President Wye assured the congregation. His father had continued to believe in the value of hard work and had forced him to put in long hours at his stores when he was growing up. The president recounted a few endearing stories of the lessons his father had imparted, before talking briefly about the disease that had claimed his father's memories and then his life. I was not the only person who stole a glance at Senator Frand during this part. I watched several other heads turn toward where he sat, his expression calm and undaunted. I wondered if it masked any shame at all.

The president ended the eulogy with an emotional good-bye. As he took his seat, a choir from Ernie Wye's hometown assembled on the steps behind the altar to perform one of his favorite folk songs, which evidently featured an extended whistle chorus. And the choir members didn't just purse their lips to get the required sound. They all actually took out small metal whistles and blew the melody. It was a jaunty tune that made me smile, but what made me almost burst out laughing was the sight of so many of D.C.'s elite struggling to mask their distaste for the performance. Kathryn Frand and both Bramens looked like they'd swallowed something sour. Their expressions were mirrored by many others who clearly considered the folksy performance inappropriate to the cathedral's majestic traditions. The president's friend wasn't even glancing at his BlackBerry anymore. Everyone was just staring at the whistle-blowing choir, wishing they could shut them up.

The performance ended eventually, of course, to the relief of many. After the recessional, we shuffled along with the rest of the crowd out into the autumn sunlight and climbed into the motor pool van to return to work. The president and the more important funeral guests were headed to Arlington National Cemetery for the private burial service. They were then scheduled to return to the White House for a reception.

Derrick examined all our passes before letting us into the guardhouse, but he distinctly smiled at Sofia, Margari, and Lincoln. His face went blank when he got to me. I waited until we were through the gate and walking up the driveway before inquiring about the treatment.

"Is Derrick usually nice to you?" I asked Margari.

"Derrick, the guard back there?" she clarified. "Sure, he's a real sweetheart. Works too many shifts in my opinion, though."

Mine too. But she considered him a *sweetheart*? Really? Was I the only person he tormented? Why? My brow furrowed as my tongue explored the beginning of a canker sore on the inside of my cheek. Ouch. My early-morning Fireballs were coming back to bite me.

Lincoln's assistant, Nick, seemed out of breath when Lincoln and I walked back into the office.

"Have you seen the news?" he asked.

His voice was a mixture of excitement and dread—a telltale sign that whatever had happened was bad but titillating. I was very sensitive to the way people talked about disastrous events. I couldn't help but notice that they often seemed more alive and engaged when they discussed them, or had the perverse pleasure of informing others about them. I hadn't worked out what it meant about human nature, I just knew that anyone who ever told me about a deadly earthquake or mass bombing or horrific crash seemed very energized by it. It gave me the creeps.

"No. What is it?" Lincoln asked.

Nick pointed to his computer monitor, where a breaking news headline read, "Woman Claims Ernie Wye Fathered Her Infant." I looked to see whether Nick was on the Web site of the *National Enquirer* or the *Weekly World News*, because it was surely one or the other. Except it wasn't.

"This can't be serious," I said aloud.

"It is," Nick said, making an effort to control his thrilled tone. "LyingWye first reported it on the Exterminator Web site but then someone legit confirmed it and it hit the wire twenty minutes ago. It's been picked up a dozen different places."

"Well, it can't be real," I insisted. "The woman's obviously just making it up—why would they take her seriously?"

I commandeered Nick's computer and clicked through various articles. From what I could tell at a cursory glance, the woman in question was the niece of a patient who resided in the same high-end nursing home where Ernie Wye had lived and received Alzheimer's treatment for the past ten years. She was in her late thirties, and had allegedly enjoyed a romantic relationship with the seventy-six-year-old Alzheimer's sufferer. She'd given birth to a healthy baby boy two months ago. There was even a photo of Ernie Wye holding the infant in his arms with a big smile on his face. Though that was the way he had greeted all the people he didn't recognize.

I felt sick to my stomach. If this was true, it seemed like some sort of sexual abuse, with Ernie Wye as the victim. I looked over my shoulder to observe Lincoln's reaction, but he had retreated to his office and was deeply involved with his own computer. I noticed Nick beside me, handling the fact that I'd shoved him aside and taken control of his chair very well.

"Have there been any reports of a paternity test?" I asked him.

He'd had longer to surf the Web for the pertinent details of this story. And I could tell he enjoyed being treated like an expert on it. He nodded.

"Apparently she's had one. The media are trying to verify it."

I sighed. I bet they were. I wouldn't put it past them to dig up Ernie Wye's body for a hair sample if they had to. This fresh scandal was set to drive many a news cycle.

"Well, I guess we just have to wait and see where this goes."

I walked to my desk and tried to focus on my work but all I could think about was Ernie Wye and our insect conversation. He'd been a sweet, gentle man who'd been forced to live only in the present moment when all his other moments had receded beyond his grasp. But at least he'd enjoyed himself despite the limitations. Maybe he'd even enjoyed romance. I wanted to imagine that was the case, rather than the ugly alternative that involved the president's father being manipulated and taken advantage of by someone desperate for fame.

It didn't take much time for more information than the average person could ever possibly want to know about this budding scandal to come to light. The woman's name was Rosie Halters and she was described by friends and colleagues as a quiet, unassuming woman devoted to her ailing aunt and her charity work. She operated a small art supply shop and spent all of her free time volunteering at the nursing home. Not exactly the profile of a money-grubbing media whore. But could her friends and colleagues really be trusted? Apparently so. Rosie hadn't been the one to seek out the press attention after all—she had simply answered honestly when asked about the incident. And she'd evidently been surprised to have been asked, as she'd considered her relationship with Ernie Wye an intensely private matter.

A caregiver at the nursing home who'd been aware of the romance and the child had called media outlets with the story. He'd been just respectful enough to wait until Ernie Wye had passed away before alerting the world to the news. And he had apparently been the instigator of the paternity test as well, to ensure that his revelation to the press packed the greatest possible punch. I wondered if he'd been compensated for his sensational scoop by anyone connected to the Exterminators. Even if they hadn't been involved, they were sure to make the most of this bombshell.

I switched on the television and watched the long-distance coverage of the burial at Arlington National Cemetery. Had President Wye already known about his baby brother before the news had hit? Or had he found out about it the way the rest of us had? This was shaping up to be quite a day for him.

CNN switched to a press conference outside Rosie Halters's house. The caregiver who'd publicized the story, a male nurse named Bruno Long, was holding court. Rosie didn't seem to be participating. The curtains of her small house were drawn. It wasn't clear whether she was even inside or not.

"How did Mr. Wye and Ms. Halters meet?" a reporter asked.

Bruno smiled.

"Rosie's aunt and Mr. Wye both enjoyed their painting class, which Rosie conducted every Tuesday and Thursday morning. Rosie believed Mr. Wye had real artistic talent. He did a butterfly series that's still hanging in our halls."

I smiled despite my overall mood.

"What is the child named?" another reporter shouted.

"I believe his name is Bernard Wye Halters," Bruno replied. "And he really is a cute little thing. Looks a lot like the president, as a matter of fact."

If this baby was Wye's half brother, that would make him the president's closest living birth-family relative. Wye's mother, Ernie's wife, had passed away four years ago, just before the family had been thrust on the national scene. And up until now, Wye had been an only child.

"What is your relationship with Rosie Halters now?"

Good question. I turned up the volume slightly, since the sound had become a bit staticky.

"She's cut back on her volunteering hours since having the baby, so I haven't seen her in a while. But I took that photo when she brought little Bernard to meet Mr. Wye. I call the baby Bernie Junior. Rosie and I have been friendly for years."

I doubted Rosie felt all that warmly toward him now. But that was just a hunch. I really couldn't know the truth of the situation. At first, I'd wanted Rosie hunted down and locked up for sexual abuse since I'd assumed she'd sought out this bizarre relationship for personal gain.

Then I'd fallen completely for the subsequent stories that suggested she was upset by the attention and had never planned to publicize her liaison with Ernie Wye. And maybe these stories were correct, but most likely no one had gotten the whole picture. I wondered how long it would be before Rosie herself would take the stage.

Not long. Behind Bruno, the door to the little house opened and a petite woman with a head full of tiny tight curls exited and walked toward the cameras. As the assembled press reacted, Bruno glanced over his shoulder.

"And here's Rosie now!" he exclaimed, as if he should be congratulated for conjuring up her appearance. "Hi, Rosie, how ya doing?"

Bruno moved to give her a hug. Rosie ignored him completely and addressed the cameras. Without taking my eyes from the screen, I called out to Nick.

"Are you watching this? Is Lincoln?"

I didn't get an answer and I didn't really care. If they were watching, they probably wanted total silence in order not to miss anything. Although anything sensational was destined to be replayed ad nauseam for the next few days. Possibly years. Still, I shut myself up and raised the volume even further.

"My name is Rosie Halters and I do not want to talk to any of you. I did not organize this gathering and I'm very sad about the way things have gone. Today is Ernie Wye's funeral day . . ."

At this, she became choked up but managed to recover. It didn't seem like acting.

"And I'm asking you all to please go away and respect his memory. He was a wonderful man."

I noticed that she was wearing black and having trouble holding back tears.

"That is all. I hope—"

"Ms. Halters, is the baby really his?" a reporter interrupted.

Rosie closed her eyes briefly, conveying extreme disappointment. When she opened them again, she simply turned around and walked back into the house. There was a brief hush from the assembled journalists, but a couple of them recovered their wits to yell more questions at the closing door.

Bruno seemed only too happy to regain the mike.

"That's Rosie for you. A classy lady," he said, acting as if she hadn't completely snubbed him and didn't clearly despise him.

"Why did you break this story against Ms. Halters's wishes?" someone asked.

Bruno looked offended. How dare his integrity be called into question! He was a model human being, obviously.

"There is no way that this was going to remain a secret. Absolutely no way. I wanted it to come out in a manner that would be the least painful for Rosie."

I switched off the TV. Curious that Bruno thought the least painful way for the news to come out would be to release it on the day of Ernie Wye's funeral. That struck me as one of the more painful times for it to come out. In actuality though, it was shocking that the secret had been kept for as long as it had. Rosie Halters must have been incredibly discreet, because there were hundreds of people constantly combing for any whiff of scandal when it came to the president and his family.

With some effort, I tore myself away from the developing scandal and forced myself to refocus on my work. An intimidating amount of it had piled up just in the hours I'd taken off for the funeral. But before I could immerse myself too deeply in it, Lincoln appeared, looking flighty.

"We should go to the reception," he said abruptly.

Really? Were we invited? I certainly wasn't. The reception was for the dignitaries who had attended the funeral and burial service. It was for family members and senators and Cabinet secretaries and foreign leaders. It wasn't for junior staffers.

"I don't think I'm expected," I said mildly.

"Well, I am," Lincoln replied, with a hint of dread. "And I'm bringing you. I need to pay my respects, but I can't talk to anyone."

And he expected me to handle any of that pesky human interaction that came his way. I stared at him, wondering again just how RG and Lincoln had become friends. RG could be remarkably introverted, but he still enjoyed people and the different experiences they provided. Lincoln, on the other hand, clearly preferred policies to humans. He was starting to appear panicked again, and his dark suit looked rumpled, like molting feathers.

"All right, but I don't want anyone to think I'm crashing the party," I replied.

We made our way down the stairs and through the West Wing reception area. The four couches in this room were usually filled with an eclectic group of people waiting to meet with the president, vice president, national security advisor, or chief of staff. On a given day, you might see the president of Bolivia chatting with Bono, while the gold medal–winning Olympic bobsledding team was ogling Stephen Hawking, who was waiting next to the envoy from the archbishop of Canterbury—all of them mingling in this one little space. It was almost always a crazy scene.

We continued past the Roosevelt Room and the communications office through the holding area just outside the Oval Office and Cabinet Room, then turned left and nodded at the uniformed agent behind his desk. He nodded back, confirming that he knew who we were and wasn't planning to take us down. Reassured, we turned right into the hallway that angled us down to the ground level. We passed the entrance to the press briefing room, pushed through the swinging French doors, and exited onto the outdoor walkway under the colonnade that ran along the side of the Rose Garden. As I almost always did, I reflexively glanced to the spot where the famous photos of JFK and RFK conferring during the Cuban Missile Crisis were taken, and got a thrill that my feet were covering the same ground. Lincoln and I kept walking straight along the path, pushing through the doors at the other end of the colonnade and entering the ground floor of the residential part of the White House.

We passed the White House Medical Unit, the dentist's office, and the Diplomatic Reception Room, where FDR had given his fireside chats. We turned left and climbed one flight of stairs to the Cross Hall. Down the Cross Hall to my left I saw the ornate stairway to the main living quarters on the second floor; the East Room; and the entrances to the Green, Blue, and Red Rooms. None of the color rooms were all that comfortable or fun—but they made one feel like it might still be 1800, which was an interesting sensation. Plus, they were chock-full of busts, paintings, and decorations of American historical significance.

Lincoln and I passed a group of Secret Service agents and turned right into the State Dining Room, where the reception was under way.

I noticed Lincoln shrink a little into himself and glance up at the pensive portrait of Abraham Lincoln above the mantel, possibly in an attempt to draw strength from his namesake.

Beneath the portrait, President Wye stood sipping a cup of tea and talking quietly with the king of Jordan, who had flown to D.C. for the funeral.

Wye didn't seem overly traumatized, but then again, he never did. I trusted that someone had briefed him on the breaking news stories about his infant brother already. I didn't imagine the king of Jordan had brought it up with him.

I turned and nearly bumped into Jenny Gary, RG's wife. She looked very stressed.

"Hello," I said. "Sorry I nearly rammed you."

"It's okay, it's fine," she said, shaking her head.

She was clearly very preoccupied with something. Most likely the breaking news. I knew that of course no scandal was good for the administration, but this wasn't one that really involved anything the rest of us were doing. It was a personal family matter. It didn't even reflect badly on President Wye. It was just sensational, which was enough to whip everyone into a frenzy of curiosity for a while, but I didn't see how it could really have any long-term negative impact on us.

I followed Jenny's gaze. She was looking at President Wye with genuine concern. And just like that, I saw the long-term negative impact. If this new scandal drove the president to an even worse place than he'd been in the past couple months, then of course it was a tremendous problem. Of course it was troubling. Was there anything else in that tea he was drinking?

"Jenny, you're always such a breath of fresh air," I heard someone say behind us.

I turned to see Senator Bramen placing his long arm around Jenny's shoulders. It always struck me as very presumptuous of a man to assume every woman he felt like hugging was receptive to his embrace. I happened to know that Jenny greatly disliked Senator Bramen. Surely, he must have had an inkling of this as well. But they occupied a world where like and dislike didn't have a whole lot of impact on who they associated with.

"Hello, John," Jenny said politely.

I stepped back slightly, clear of their interaction. I was accustomed to being ignored by Senator Bramen and others of his ilk, and I didn't want to make Jenny feel rude for not having me included in the conversation. But I was still close enough to hear them talking.

"Jenny, Jenny, Jenny. I always tell Pamela, you're the best of this bunch," Senator Bramen continued. "And I mean it."

I winced inside at his condescending tone and backhanded compliment.

"Oh, well, like the rest of the country, I think the others are pretty great," Jenny replied with a smile.

"You're too sweet," Senator Bramen replied. "It's good to see you. You keep smiling that pretty smile."

I let myself imagine what might happen if I turned and slugged him. The negatives would most likely outweigh the extreme satisfaction I would feel. Maybe I could injure him in some way that looked like an accident instead. I stuck out my foot a little to see if I might trip him as he moved away from Jenny, but he managed to avoid the trap.

In fact, there seemed to be a little spring in his step. He was probably quite pleased about the Ernie Wye scandal. I'd observed in the past that anything that caused the president pain always made the corners of Bramen's mouth lift upward ever so slightly in the direction of a smile. Often he was vigorously asserting his loyalty and support for the administration, but that tiny hint of a smile gave him away. At least to me.

Jenny had already moved on. In the corner, I spotted Lincoln and RG in conversation. Lincoln's head was cocked as he listened and his hands were clasped behind his back. As I made my way toward them, RG nodded and moved off.

"How's it going?" I asked Lincoln a moment later.

I hadn't done the best job as his wingman. I'd been off observing things on my own.

"We can leave now," he replied, obviously ready to take flight.

I'd just glimpsed Senator Frand across the room and would have preferred to stay and watch his awkward interaction with the president and RG, but Lincoln was already headed for the door. When he was done, he was done.

"Are you ready for battle?" Lincoln asked me as we walked briskly through the dignitaries gathered in the Cross Hall.

"A specific battle or just in general?" I asked.

I liked to know what I was getting into before agreeing to wage war. It seemed like a pretty basic prerequisite, but it distinguished me from more than a few lawmakers.

"The president wants the Alzheimer's Bill passed before the fall recess," Lincoln clarified.

That must have been what Lincoln and RG had been conferring about. It would take a miracle to get Congress to move that quickly. Despite the recent chatter about the bill, most people on the Hill expected any action to be postponed until after the midterm elections, since no one was clamoring to go on the record on such a controversial issue before then. Accountability often took a backseat to showmanship during intense campaign months. The idea that we might force people to deal with such important legislation against their wishes appealed to my defiant streak.

"Sounds good to me," I said enthusiastically.

The bill would naturally get more coverage due to Ernie Wye's passing. We needed to capitalize on that, as tactfully as possible, to leverage for more overall support. And we were sure to run up against substantial opposition from Frand and his pro-human legions.

"I'll ready the robot armies," I said aloud, when I meant to say it in my head.

Lincoln seemed understandably confused.

"Ahem . . . well, good, then."

He knew we needed whatever help we could rustle up.

Thin Walls

———•••———

I HAD LAUNCHED MYSELF into the Alzheimer's Bill battle and was updating our list of its congressional supporters the next afternoon when Zelda called me on my cell phone. I gave only my absolute favorite telemarketers my cell phone number and Zelda topped that list. I'd meant to check in with her since returning from India to confirm that she was in fact a working mother from Daytona, Florida, as she'd claimed, and not a foreign telemarketer with a flawless American accent.

"How's the weather in Daytona?" I asked, quickly checking it myself on the Internet.

"Weird," she replied. "We've been getting a ton of rain. Don't you feel like nature's going nuts lately?"

I did. And it was in fact currently raining in Daytona, according to Google research. I decided to give Zelda the benefit of the doubt.

"How are the boys?" I asked more affectionately.

"They're great," she replied. "A handful as usual, but I guess they're worth it. They just better take care of me in my old age or they're gonna regret the day they were born."

Zelda had a transactional take on parenthood. She often talked about what she expected in return for the caretaking she shouldered now. I imagined she was also one of those mothers who brought up how painful childbirth had been when giving her kids guilt trips.

"How are you doing? Missing Charlie?" she continued.

"Like crazy," I answered.

She clucked sympathetically. Zelda was a Charlie fan, for which I was grateful. They'd even spoken a few times when he'd answered my phone for me. I'd learned to trust Zelda's opinions of people over the years. She'd never liked Aaron and had warned me about him long before I'd been willing to listen.

"Have you been up to visit him yet?" she asked.

"No. But it's only been a few weeks. He comes back here," I answered.

"Hmmm . . ."

That was her disapproving "hmmm." Fine, I'd go visit him. I knew it was important for me to see his new space. I'd just been too busy. And now I didn't feel like discussing it. I opted to change the subject.

"So listen, it's not looking so good for you guys in terms of the registry," I said. "I'd rather you heard it from me first, but it looks like the thing's gonna stand."

I was referring to the National Do Not Call Registry, the bane of telemarketers' existence. It allows people to register their numbers on a list that is then deemed completely off limits. Several large companies had launched a challenge to the registry, but it enjoyed far too much popular support to be revoked.

"I figured as much." Zelda sighed. "TAPAS definitely has our work cut out for us."

TAPAS was an advocacy and support group that was formed in response to the National Do Not Call Registry. Zelda was one of the charter members of the group, which stood for "Telemarketers Are People Also. Seriously." They had monthly conference call meetings over small plates and sangria.

"How's the deletion push coming?" I asked.

TAPAS had discovered that the only way to recover people from the registry was to convince them to voluntarily delete their numbers from the list. This obviously involved a larger effort to rehabilitate the image of telemarketers in the minds of potential deleters. TAPAS had been organizing a "Be Sweet, Please Delete" campaign for the fall.

"It's pretty slow," Zelda answered.

That didn't surprise me. Sadly, most Americans did not share my love of telemarketers, but I was convinced they'd be a lot happier if they did. A recent high-profile study had revealed that "a quarter of Americans have no one to confide in." A quarter of Americans! That was a lot of lonely people. The study showed that this represented a marked change from just a couple decades ago. For various reasons, people in this day and age were living much more isolated existences. Enter telemarketers! They offered a convenient, built-in solution for anyone feeling a little too alone. They were instant confidants. People shouldn't be trying to avoid them. They should be embracing them.

Zelda appreciated my support. She and I spoke for a couple more minutes and I promised to call her later in the week. She reminded me to make plans to visit Charlie. I bristled at the nagging, but knew that she was right. I'd gotten in trouble in the past when I'd ignored her advice. Soon after ending the call, I took out my BlackBerry and sent off a message.

```
To: Charlie Lawton [lawtonc@washpost.com]
From: Samantha Joyce [srjoyce@ovp.eop.gov]
Subject: i hear that new york place is a swell city
Text: hey guy, i'm missing you. and wondering if i can
pester you this weekend to check out your new scene.
people tell me i won't be totally bored by nyc. i
think i should probably be the judge of that. what say
you, mr. fancy feast? ybbilamylc, s
```

There. It was all true sentiment-wise, and now Zelda couldn't accuse me of not holding up my end of the relationship responsibilities. Plus, I was excited to go to New York this weekend. Hopefully, Charlie would feel the same. We'd talked a lot since our fight, but seeing each other in person would help make us feel like we were really back on track.

He wrote me back within a minute.

```
To: Samantha Joyce [srjoyce@ovp.eop.gov]
From: Charlie Lawton [lawtonc@washpost.com]
Subject: Re: i hear that new york place is a swell city
Text: fire of my loins, get yourself up here asap.
seriously, quit your job and hop a train. i should
```

```
warn you that nyc is closed this weekend, actually.
everyone's just staying in their bedrooms—mayor's
orders. so that's what we'll have to do unless we want
to get arrested, which we don't obviously. though come
to think of it, handcuffs might make an appearance.
ya, c
p.s. ybbilamylc="your busty babelicious intoxicatingly
lovely and magnificent young lady caller"?
```

I smiled and wrote quickly back.

```
To: Charlie Lawton [lawtonc@washpost.com]
From: Samantha Joyce [srjoyce@ovp.eop.gov]
Subject: Re: i hear that new york place is a swell city
Text: "you better believe I love and miss you like
crazy," actually. but yours was good too. ya, s
```

I cut things off there, because if I let myself, we could BlackBerry back and forth all day. And given the direction this e-mail exchange was headed, I didn't feel good about spending taxpayers' money on it. Instead, I checked some online news sites before getting back to work. As expected, the press was in a frenzy over the Ernie Wye scandal. Rosie Halters still refused to talk to anyone, but Bruno Long had happily provided the details of the paternity test, which did indeed confirm that Ernie Wye was the father. Bruno had apparently convinced Rosie that there was a new blood test that could determine whether her baby was at risk for developing Alzheimer's in his later life, and Rosie had let him administer it. Bruno had used the baby's blood sample to independently confirm Ernie Wye's paternity. It had been a betrayal of Rosie's trust and friendship, but a godsend to countless reporters and talk radio hosts. Not to mention the Exterminators, who had already sent the White House a five-foot-tall giant plush Mickey Mouse as a baby present. They'd also paid for a full-page ad in the *Washington Post* officially welcoming little Bernard to the world.

President Wye had yet to comment on the matter. The White House spokesperson had held journalists at bay by reminding them that the president was still very freshly mourning his father and wouldn't be commenting on personal matters for the time being. Though he was of course very capably up to running the country, if there were any inquiries more directly related to that. I trusted that would hold them for about five minutes. Chick Wallrey would have to attack soon. She wouldn't be able to help herself.

LyingWye posted more about Ernie Wye's paternity scandal, alleging that President Wye had actually known for several months about his father's relationship with Rosie Halters, even before the baby was born. According to the blog, Bruno had contacted the White House and told an unnamed White House administration official that the baby bombshell could probably be contained in exchange for a presidential pardon of Bruno's brother, who was serving a twenty-year prison sentence for several violent robberies. According to LyingWye, Bruno's offer had been rejected and several Secret Service agents dispatched to deal with him. Bruno had escaped arrest, most likely because the administration wanted to avoid getting him any attention. They'd counted on intimidating him away from the story. But it hadn't worked. Bruno had gone public anyway.

I didn't know whether to trust the accuracy of LyingWye's account or not. Most of the time the blog was filled with baseless lies and accusations, but it also sometimes got explosive scoops before anyone else. It had been the first to report on the existence of Ernie Wye's infant son, after all.

But if Wye had known about his dad and Rosie Halters for several months, I imagined that he would have told a few trusted staff members and ordered some sort of plan for dealing with the story. Yet I'd neither seen nor heard any evidence of such a plan. So maybe he'd been in denial about it, believing that they could keep it from coming out; or that if they just ignored it, it would go away. Or maybe Wye had known that it couldn't be contained, felt helpless in the face of it, and begun self-medicating with whiskey.

Whatever the truth, the facts were that President Wye had a new baby half brother courtesy of the father that he'd just lost to Alzheimer's disease. And whatever other emotions the president was grappling with, he had made it very clear that he wanted the Alzheimer's Bill passed, and soon. We'd all gotten the message that he felt passionately about this. Perhaps it was a way of channeling his grief and rage into something more productive than a bender. All I knew was that I needed to do everything I could to help pass this bill.

I shook my head to clear it and returned to my list of bill supporters. We had enough votes in the House, but were still lacking in the Senate. Damn Frand and his majority party. We had to find some way to make this happen.

Though it was called the Alzheimer's Bill, it actually covered much more than that one disease. It offered increased funding to help find a cure for Parkinson's, Huntington's, and diabetes as well. The controversy lay in the means to achieve the necessary breakthroughs toward cures. Opposition groups claimed that the pathways supported by the bill would open up doors to human cloning and other thorny moral issues. And the truth was, they probably would, if they weren't intelligently regulated. But so would a lot of other things. In my opinion, we needed to address these controversial issues head-on, rather than throw up roadblocks to progress out of fear. History had been pretty definitive about the merits of choosing innovation and advancement over frightened retreat. Rather than endorsing ignorance as some kind of moral ideal, we needed to put the necessary safeguards in place, and then embrace the use of scientific technology to save lives.

Nick intercommed me from Lincoln's office.

"Congressman Gracie's got a sister with Parkinson's."

I kept my voice even.

"Interesting. So is he on board?"

"Not sure. Lincoln thought you could give him a call."

Of course he did. Any time I could make a call instead of Lincoln, it became my responsibility. If he wasn't such a policy genius and a genuinely good guy, the resentment would have built up long ago.

So Congressman Gracie's sister had Parkinson's. We'd discovered that the most effective way of garnering the needed support for this bill was to directly appeal to lawmakers who had a personal investment in finding the cures. Since Senator Frand's alternative bill also claimed to work toward better treatment and eventual eradication of these diseases, we had to find an "in" with people who had a personal stake in understanding the significant differences between the two bills. This led to research efforts to determine which members of Congress had loved ones struggling with one of these conditions. The whole process was tearing me up inside because it involved my feeling a sense of accomplishment when I identified further suffering. It just wasn't healthy to have an impulse to high-five when you find out someone has Parkinson's. I was pretty sure only people headed for eternal damnation felt such urges.

"Thanks, I'll get on it," I told Nick.

"I'm only happy to know that Congressman Gracie's sister has Parkinson's because I know that we can help her with this law," I reminded myself as I looked up Gracie's office number.

I was up to about ten of these little mantras a day, and they were starting to take on the rhythm of ritualistic atonement. But I didn't really believe they were enough to absolve me of my sins. I said another small prayer to the God of Preventing Me from Going to Hell. The chances were high that I'd be driven to therapy before this bill got passed.

I managed to set up a meeting with Congressman Gracie for the following morning. Even with members of the opposition party, being affiliated with the White House got me in the door a whole lot faster than if I'd worked anywhere else. Everyone enjoyed feeling like they were needed and important, and I counted on this truth to grant me access. Occasionally I felt like my time in politics had been one long course in ego management, complete with the regular trampling of my own.

Stephanie stopped by to see Lincoln the next afternoon. As the chief political strategist, she was necessarily involved in any legislative push. I counted twelve different barrettes in her hair. They were the kind worn by little kids—the type shaped like pink and green bunnies and birds. I'd known other people my age who wore these sorts of hair adornments, but they were all far more hip than me. I hadn't placed Stephanie in that category yet. More accomplished, more respected, possibly more intelligent, sure. But not more hip.

"Nice barrettes," I commented.

"Oh, thanks," she said absentmindedly. "How'd it go with Gracie?"

"I think he's on board," I replied.

"Great." She nodded. "Let me know if I need to do a follow-up."

"I will. Thanks."

Stephanie and I still hadn't gotten that drink we'd discussed before the India trip. I wondered if she'd forgotten about it. Or reconsidered her idea of becoming friends with me. I tucked my hair self-consciously behind my ear, feeling suddenly plain.

That night, I stayed at work past two a.m., helping Lincoln and the rest of the domestic policy staff strategize and lobby for the remaining votes we needed. And as I survived the next day with a steady intake of black coffee, both the House and the Senate took up final debates. I was reeling a bit from how speedily we'd managed to focus attention on this bill. I credited Wye and RG, who had really leaned on people, personally calling in favors. Plus, Ernie Wye's funeral had provoked a widespread outpouring of grief over the toll Alzheimer's was taking on individuals and families across the country. Many lawmakers had heard from constituents desperate for help with this painful illness. They talked not only of the emotional cost, but also of the crippling financial burdens of caring for their ailing loved ones.

In response to this pressure, and demonstrating a shockingly fast pace, the House passed the bill by the following morning. It was now up to the Senate, which by the latest count was divided exactly in half. However, we'd gotten word that one of the swing senators had a nephew with juvenile diabetes and another had a stepaunt with Huntington's. So that was good news. Sort of. I said another prayer and flipped on C-SPAN to watch the debate.

Senator Frand had the floor. He seemed to have gotten an even worse haircut, if that was possible. Dick York was probably rolling in his grave. I watched in silence as Frand spoke out passionately against the bill.

"I know I speak for the entire country in offering my condolences to the Wye family for the recent loss of their patriarch to the Alzheimer's disease. Our hearts go out to Ernie Wye's sons and other loved ones . . ."

I gave a little gasp. Frand had used that phrase very deliberately to evoke the scandal of the illegitimate baby while pretending to express sincere sympathy. He'd even given a little smirk as he'd said it. He was the real bastard.

"Indeed, my heart goes out to all the families in America who are suffering because of one of these terrible illnesses. We must find a way to cure them. But it must be a way that doesn't rip the moral rug out from beneath our feet, that doesn't open the door to more insidious plagues on mankind—the sort of ethical outrages that do more harm than we can possibly imagine."

Thanks to Senate rules that had clearly been made by men who loved the sound of their own voices, Frand was allowed to speak for as long as he wanted. Mercifully, after another forty-five minutes, he reluctantly yielded the floor to his colleagues by urging them to listen to their hearts and vote their consciences. And to never forget about the babies who were struggling to be born. It was something of a free association wrap-up.

I glanced at the time as another senator launched into her speech. It was already noon, and there were still dozens of people on the docket to speak. I hadn't really anticipated that we would be in this position when I'd made my plans to visit Charlie. I'd assumed we'd still need another week or two at least to get Congress to the point they were at now. So I'd hoped to finish work early and catch the seven p.m. train to New York. At this rate, I'd be lucky to make the ten p.m. I groaned. Should I call Charlie? Or just glare at the screen and will the wheels of democracy to uncharacteristically speed up even further to better accommodate my love life? After glaring for two minutes with no discernible impact, I picked up the phone.

"Hey, I was just getting supplies for the weekend," Charlie said when he answered. "With the city being shut down, I want to make sure we've got everything we need. You like chocolate syrup, don't you?"

"Preferably Magic Shell," I confirmed.

I still felt the same sense of wonder I had as a child when it came to Magic Shell chocolate sauce. It really was uncanny how quickly the syrup formed a hard shell over ice cream. It was instant poor man's crème brûlée (a dessert whose pronunciation I had to practice in my head before I ordered it in restaurants; sometimes I got away with pointing). I considered Magic Shell to be one of the greatest inventions of the twentieth century. Certainly beneath the microchip, but still up there.

"Actually, Magic Shell opens up whole new sculpting possibilities I hadn't even envisioned," he said. "How early can you get here?"

"Well, that's why I'm calling. They're debating the Alzheimer's Bill and until it goes to a vote, I really can't leave."

"Okay, so late tonight?"

I didn't reply. I was still hoping my answer might change.

"Tomorrow?" Charlie asked.

"Yeah, probably tomorrow," I conceded. "But hopefully really early. I swear I'll make it up to you," I promised.

"Okay, good luck."

"I'll call when I know more. I love you."

"I love you too."

I felt very frustrated as I hung up the phone. I wasn't accustomed to resenting work. I was used to feeling lucky and privileged to be able to do whatever I was doing. Having my personal life regularly hijacked by professional duties hadn't felt like a problem when my personal life had been more geographically accessible. For the past two years, I'd had to work unexpectedly and late all the time. So had Charlie, for that matter. But for most of that time, we'd been just minutes away from each other. So that whenever we did get finally finished, reunions took very little effort. Now they were hard, inconvenient work.

I couldn't catch a break from the Senate. They continued debating late into the night and then all of the following day. Charlie told me not to feel bad, and even claimed to have come under a work deadline himself. I suspected he was lying to make me feel better, but I couldn't be sure. I didn't have a whole lot of time for moping, since we were working the phones and everything else to try and swing senators to our side of the argument. President Wye and RG personally made about a dozen calls apiece. When the vote was finally called on Sunday afternoon, fifty senators grumpy about sacrificing their weekend voted in favor of the bill, and fifty grumpier senators voted against it. A dead tie.

I was wearing the same clothes I'd come to work in on Friday morning as I waited with RG over in his Capitol Hill office, which was just a few steps from the Senate chamber. We'd relocated because we'd determined a couple hours before that the vote would result in a tie. As president of the Senate, RG got to cast decisive tie-breaking votes. He looked tired, but his face lit up when the result was announced.

"Showtime!" he exclaimed.

I understood his excitement. It had to be good for the ego to know that whatever team you supported was guaranteed to win.

"Congratulations, sir. I brought a coin to toss if you can't decide which way to go."

RG grinned as he straightened his collar. His phone rang. He picked up the receiver with a little flourish.

"Hi. . . . Yes, put him through," he said into it. "Hello, Max."

It was Wye. Though I knew the president had been instrumental in the bill lobbying, I hadn't actually seen him in several days. Not since the day of the funeral, in fact. His schedule put him in the Oval Office for most of last week, but he must have been working mainly from the residence.

"Yes, sir, of course. Congratulations, this is a good law. . . . I think he would have been proud too, sir."

RG hung up the phone and looked over at me. We hadn't spoken of the president since India. RG looked as though he were about to say something, but then thought better of it. He left the room instead, and walked onto the floor of the Senate.

An hour later, as I rode back to the West Wing while the sun set on our jam-packed Sunday, Lincoln called my cell.

"I forgot to bring the B file down to Stephanie before I left, and she should really get it as soon as possible," he said, sounding a bit panicked. "I don't want it on e-mail. It's on my desk—would you mind getting it to her?"

"No problem. Consider it done."

"Thanks, Sammy."

The B file was what Lincoln called the list of things we had promised lawmakers in exchange for their support. It was short for the barter file, which no one ever said out loud. Keeping track of these political chits was understandably important. And sensitive.

I picked up the folder from Lincoln's desk and made my way back down the stairs to the first floor of the West Wing. Alone in the hallway, I suddenly felt a surge of adrenaline over the passing of the bill. At times such as these, my head got flooded with *Footloose* lyrics and I felt the need for a little breakout. I usually indulged in these only in the privacy of my own apartment, but I'd been known to conduct brief solo-dance celebrations in other locales if I was positive no one else was around. I had just completed a Kevin Bacon–esque pirouette when a Secret Service agent rounded the corner, followed by the president and Dr. Humphrey.

"Hello," I said in surprise, wishing I wasn't panting.

I stood up against the wall to be out of their way. Dr. Humphrey nodded, but the president didn't even appear to notice me as they passed. Then he turned around, as if he'd registered my presence a little late.

"You're Samantha, right?" he asked.

"Yes, sir," I answered. "Some people call me Sammy."

I couldn't help but add the "Sammy, Sammy, bo-bammy" in my head. The president nodded.

"Right. Robert brought you with him from the Senate."

"Yes, sir," I confirmed. "I work with Lincoln Thomas."

The president nodded. We'd met dozens of times and he was usually very good about recalling people. Still, I didn't expect him to remember me.

"Well, keep up the good work, Sammy," he said with a smile.

He didn't seem at all inebriated. Just personable.

"Thank you, sir. I'll try."

"No," he replied unexpectedly, staring hard at me before flashing his famous smile. "Do or do not. There is no try."

He didn't use the Yoda voice, but I recognized the timeless wisdom of the grizzled green Jedi when I heard it. Maybe Wye was a little tipsy after all. But if he wanted to get into a *Star Wars* quoting contest, he honestly had no idea who he was up against. I'd put him in his place faster than the *Millennium Falcon* could make the Kessel Run.

Perhaps this wasn't the time.

"Yes, sir." I smiled. "Wise words, sir."

He smiled back briefly and then walked quickly into his private dining room. Dr. Humphrey followed.

Left alone again in the hallway, I stared after them before moving toward Stephanie's office, which was adjacent to the dining room. The president liked to keep his head political strategist nearby. I felt the familiar flutter of intimidation as I prepared to encounter Stephanie. I looked up to her literally and figuratively, and I hoped for her respect.

Her assistant was gone but her door was slightly ajar, so I peeked my head in to see if she was around.

It turned out she was. More specifically, she was pressed against a far door, her tall frame hunched over and her eye glued to the little peephole that looked into the president's private dining room.

I cleared my throat.

"Um, excuse me," I said uncertainly.

She jumped a little, startled, before turning around. Her dark red hair looked more frazzled than usual, as if it too had been caught doing something it shouldn't.

"God, Sammy, you scared me. Don't you knock?"

"Sorry. Your assistant wasn't there and your door was open," I replied.

Stephanie looked as though she were conducting a rapid internal strategy session. She abruptly smiled and motioned toward the peephole.

"Want to take a look?"

"No!" I said indignantly.

We were both surprised by my self-righteous, scolding tone. I never imagined addressing Stephanie this way, though I never imagined catching her doing something highly unethical. The door that her office shared with the president's dining room was supposed to be treated as an impenetrable wall whenever Wye was in there. The peephole was a relic of days when her office had been used by servants who needed to know when to enter to clear the table or bring another course. It was not meant to help her secretly observe the commander in chief.

"Lighten up," Stephanie said casually. "I'm just checking in on things."

"But that's not right," I sputtered, feeling a little like a righteous kindergartener. "You shouldn't be doing that."

Stephanie smiled patiently at me as she smoothed her hair into submission.

"Why shouldn't I?" she replied. "I consider this peephole a tool that helps me do my job the best I can. I obviously don't keep tabs on everything that goes on in the president's private dining room—I'm way too busy to watch it all the time. I just use it on a need-to-know basis."

That sounded sort of reasonable. Stephanie was good at persuading people to her point of view.

"Okay. So what is it that you *need* to know today?" I asked.

Her smile turned sheepish.

"I suppose I don't *need* to know, but the truth is, I'm really worried about the president. He hasn't been himself at all lately. I know I shouldn't be spying, but I was hoping to find out what's wrong so that I can be prepared to help."

I nodded and kept my mouth shut. I knew a lot more about this than I cared to let on. Probably a lot more than Stephanie did, in fact. She returned to her peeping. In the silence, I could hear the murmur of President Wye and Dr. Humphrey talking.

"Can you actually hear what they're saying?"

Stephanie nodded.

"If you press your ear right up against the door, you can usually make it out. When it gets difficult, I use a glass."

She demonstrated by picking up a glass from a table and putting the bottom of it to her ear. She pressed the open end against the door.

"Come try it," she encouraged again.

Again, I felt like a five-year-old, staring at a coaxing stranger. That made the glass in her hand a giant candy bar. Something I definitely wanted, but that I was pretty sure I'd been warned about.

"No thank you." I resisted.

Stephanie shrugged.

"You could find out some interesting things," she said.

That was true. And maybe if I took her spot right now I could prevent her from discovering something she possibly couldn't be trusted with. It was in RG's best interest that I guard our common secret. Helping him was the only reason I was willing to do this.

"Okay, I'll try it," I said abruptly.

Stephanie smiled. I hesitated once more, and then took the glass. She moved aside for me so I could stand next to the door. Through the glass, I could just barely hear the president's private conversation. I closed my eyes to concentrate.

"A couple side effects," Wye was saying. "A little nausea. Dizziness. Nothing too bad."

"Have you stuck to the prescribed dosage?" Dr. Humphrey asked.

"I've upped it a little," Wye replied. "Just when I've needed that added focus."

This was followed by a pause.

"How much are we talking?" Humphrey pressed. "Have you doubled it again?"

Another, longer pause.

"Yes, I guess I have. I get used to this stuff real fast."

Without even thinking about it, I pressed my eye to the peephole to get a visual for my soundtrack. The president and Dr. Humphrey were sitting catty-corner to each other at the dining table. Several pill bottles were on the table. Dr. Humphrey was making a few notes in his pad as he questioned the president, who sat very upright in his chair. I tried to make out the names of the medicines on the bottles, but they were too small and far away.

I moved away from the peephole to listen with the glass again. Beside me, Stephanie had gotten another glass. There wasn't really any way to gracefully box her out. And it would probably be futile anyway, since she had constant access to this peephole. I could see how the eavesdropping and watching could easily become a regular habit.

"We just want to make sure this doesn't have a chance to become addictive," Dr. Humphrey said at that precise moment.

For a heartbeat, I thought he was addressing his words to us, somehow aware of our presence on the other side of the door, and I felt newly ashamed. But that was silly. He was talking to the president, of course. Which was actually much more scandalous.

"I know how to control myself," the president said sternly.

"Absolutely. But trials on this drug haven't been concluded in the States," Dr. Humphrey began.

"That's just because the damn FDA moves so slowly," Wye interrupted. "When they do get around to clearing it, the American public's going to know that there's a pill out there they can take that will make them a helluva lot smarter. I don't want to do an infomercial here, but damn, Hank, this stuff is incredible."

Good Lord. They were talking about Focusid. The medicine from India that we'd agreed to get for the president's father to combat

Alzheimer's. RG and I had been willing to bend the rules and assist in speeding up a clinical trial in order to help Ernie Wye, and we'd felt terrible that the miracle drug had arrived just a little too late to save him. I'd assumed the trial had continued with other patients, but now it appeared that most of the Focusid we'd procured had in fact become the president's personal supply.

"How much more do you need?" Dr. Humphrey asked.

"How much more can you get?"

I stopped listening and stepped away. Stephanie moved back to the peephole and watched a little longer before turning back to me. Her face indicated that the exciting part of the show was over.

"Want to go get a drink?" she asked.

Yes, I did. Perhaps this wasn't the healthiest response to what we'd just witnessed, but I wasn't going to let that stop me. For her part, Stephanie didn't appear at all self-conscious about proposing we immediately start drinking after uncovering evidence of our president's pill-popping. I watched her as she gathered some papers and put them in her briefcse. Did she even realize the full extent of what we'd seen? The president was addicted to an experimental drug and yes, that was very, very bad. But did she already know or guess the rest? I knew from my research that this particular drug had all the properties to be very effective in compensating for the effects of excessive drinking, and I suspected this was the real reason it had become so indispensable to the president of late. But these facts about Focusid weren't exactly common knowledge. The very existence of Focusid wasn't even common knowledge. President Wye was really on the cutting edge of prescription drug addiction. He was a step ahead, even in vice.

I looked down at my hand and was surprised to see in it the folder that had been the reason for my visit in the first place. I'd forgotten all about it.

"I'm supposed to give this to you," I said, handing over the barter file.

"Oh, yes. The bill for the bill." Stephanie smiled. "I hope no one promised away too much."

"I think we stayed in bounds," I answered.

Promising favors in exchange for votes was a tricky business. Mainly because outright promises weren't directly made. Fine lines of innuendo were constantly tightwalked. I was still learning how to balance, but everyone else seemed to have it down.

"I'll assess the damage tomorrow," Stephanie said as she quickly eyed the file. "Let's get out of here."

Twenty minutes later, Stephanie and I were sitting across from each other at the otherwise empty bar at the Mayflower Hotel. I knew Liza didn't work Sunday evenings now that she'd begun taking a business school course, but I still instinctively looked around for her as Stephanie crossed and uncrossed her ludicrously long legs.

"Dr. Humphrey mentioned the name of the drug before you got there," Stephanie said as she sipped her glass of wine. "It's something called Focusid. Do you know it?"

I nodded.

"I was going to Google it later," Stephanie continued. "What can you tell me about it?"

I took a gulp of my wine while deciding how much to say.

"It's an experimental lifestyle drug, currently only available in India, Japan, and Korea. It was initially developed to treat ADD, sort of like a high-powered Adderall, but scientists quickly realized it had far greater potential. It significantly sharpens concentration and mental faculties, but the side effects can reportedly be quite extreme."

Stephanie took this in. I'd refrained from mentioning the specific research about Alzheimer's or how Focusid might be used to combat the effects of alcoholism, because I wasn't ready for Stephanie to connect all the dots.

"So the president wants medical help focusing," she said.

"I guess so." I shrugged.

Stephanie gave a short, biting laugh.

"Well, Lord knows, he needs it sometimes."

Her bitter tone made me a little uncomfortable. She saw it in my expression.

"Look, I've worked for him for nearly ten years now," she continued. "Besides his personal assistant and a few family members, there isn't anyone more loyal. And there are few who know him as well. So anything critical I say about him, I say from a place of tremendous respect and allegiance."

She kept staring at me. I realized she was waiting for some kind of response so I nodded.

"He has trouble making decisions because he never wants to let anyone down," she continued. "I was particularly glad when he picked RG for the ticket, because I knew I'd finally have real help keeping him on track. It's his one major weakness."

Not his only one. But I stayed silent. I knew most of this already. Anyone who read any amount of political commentary knew this. The knock on Wye was that he wanted to please too many people to be able to consistently take tough stands.

"Well, I think they've made a good team," I offered. "I know RG is very loyal to him."

Which was also true. Along with a productive working relationship, Wye and RG had developed a genuine friendship. They had very different personalities, but had forged a strong bond. In addition to sharing a common interest in their success, they were both aware of just how much they owed the other. They both knew that they wouldn't be in their present positions had they not joined forces.

RG obviously wouldn't be vice president had Wye not picked him. But there was a very good chance that Wye wouldn't have been elected president had he made a different choice. When the plagiarism scandal had evaporated Wye's lead in the final weeks of the presidential campaign, RG's spotless reputation had helped the ticket regain its lost momentum. His integrity had made up for his partner's lack. Wye was smart enough to understand this.

"RG has really stood by him," Stephanie was agreeing. "But that loyalty well had better be deep, because it's going to be steadily drained."

"That sounds very ominous," I said slowly.

"It's just the way Wye works," she replied. "Believe me, I know."

"How bad do you think the drug thing is?" I asked.

Stephanie looked worried.

"It's not good," she said carefully. "But great presidents in the past have had drug dependencies that didn't adversely affect their leadership. Kennedy regularly took steroids and amphetamines because of his Addison's disease, and he was a champ. We just have to take a page from their playbook and keep everything as quiet and private as possible."

"It was easier to do that in the sixties. It's a little harder these days," I replied.

"Which just means we need to be more vigilant," she replied. "We have to protect him, do you understand?"

I nodded that I did.

"So I don't think we should talk to anyone about this," she continued. "Can you keep it to yourself?"

Again, I nodded.

"Good," she said, satisfied.

I wondered if my being in cahoots with her elevated me in her eyes. I couldn't help but hope that it did.

"Given this new development, do you think that it's odd that the White House is about to host a conference on lifestyle drugs?" I asked. "RG wants it to happen in the next month."

Stephanie thought for a moment.

"I think it's good, actually," she said. "The best way for Wye to deal with any personal problem is to intellectualize it. When he was governor, the initiatives he became most involved in were the ones that touched some aspect of his own life. If he spends the time figuring out how the lifestyle drug trend is changing America, he'll think about how his personal use of them is affecting his own life."

"Okay, whatever you say," I replied.

I'd been arguing for the lifestyle drug conference since the beginning of the administration, so I was just happy to have it still on track. America was becoming steadily dependent on and supportive of so many drugs of questionable necessity. Encouraged by multimillion-dollar advertising campaigns, people were obsessed with different pills that grew hair, gave erections, eliminated menstrual cycles, and smoothed wrinkles, to give just a few examples. As a country, we were in danger of focusing too much of our attention on drugs that improved quality of life in a cosmetic or superficial way at the expense of those that actually cured things. And we were becoming experts at misapplying helpful drugs toward questionable ends—like the recent surge in the abuse of human growth hormone. HGH was intended to combat dwarfism in children, but athletes and anti-ageing enthusiasts had quickly found very different uses for it.

We were living in interesting times when it came to breakthroughs in biotechnology, and I hoped that the White House could shine a spotlight on the kinds of choices we faced when it came to the glut of lifestyle drugs. Hopefully people would call on Congress to spend at least as much time funding lifesaving treatments for diabetes and neurodegenerative diseases as they did debating whether Medicare should cover Viagra.

Stephanie ordered another glass of wine. The bartender was pouring two shots of whiskey for a couple at the far end of the bar who looked like these weren't their first drinks of the day. I thought about Wye's drinking and decided I should at least hint about it to Stephanie. Maybe she was already aware of it and had made her own decision not to reveal anything beyond what we both knew for sure.

"What if the Focusid isn't the only thing he's having a problem with?" I asked.

Stephanie looked surprised. And confused.

"You mean other drugs?" she asked.

She didn't know. Or she was a good actress.

"Yeah. Or whatever . . ."

Something was holding me back from just coming out with it. Stephanie was watching me expectantly. I might as well tell her. She wanted to protect the president as much as I wanted to protect RG. Our interests were linked.

"Well, actually," I began.

"Stephanie Ann Grader!" a voice said from behind me.

I turned around. It was the reporter Chick Wallrey, in all her Goth glory. The last time I'd seen her, she'd been covered in camel spit. I avoided eye contact and turned back toward Stephanie.

"Hey, Chick. Just having a drink with a friend. Do you know Sammy?" Stephanie asked.

Chick eyed me.

"You look familiar," she said.

"We were both on the New Delhi trip," I replied.

I hoped to just leave it at that.

"Ah, another administration lackey," Chick said with a laugh.

Her laugh was gravelly and abrasive. I like it when people's laughs match my perceptions of them. It makes things seem in order.

"Getting loaded on the Lord's day?" she asked Stephanie.

Stephanie smiled and touched her hair. I knew she had to deal with people like Chick all the time because of her role in the White House, but it still surprised me how calmly she could handle their bullshit.

"Are you jealous?" Stephanie replied.

Chick cackled again.

"I'd join you myself but I've got to meet a friend. Are we still on for dinner Thursday?" she asked.

"Of course," Stephanie replied.

This was surprising. Stephanie had to put up with people like Chick, but she didn't have to go and be friends with them.

"Great, and don't forget about Kline's party."

"I'll see you there," Stephanie replied.

Were they talking about Jim Kline, the *Wall Street Journal* correspondent to the White House? He was about as friendly to the administration as Chick. Who was now giving a little wave as she walked away.

"Wow," I couldn't help but say. "I had no idea you two were so close."

Stephanie looked defensive for a split second before adopting a blasé attitude.

"Oh, we're not really. We're D.C. friends, not real-world friends. Though Chick's pretty funny when you get to know her. I'm trying to nudge her coverage in a more positive direction, but it's a long-term project."

I nodded uncertainly.

"What were you saying when she interrupted?" Stephanie continued.

I had been about to let her in on the secret of the president's drinking. I didn't feel so inclined anymore.

"Oh, it was nothing," I answered.

"You sure?" she pressed.

Yes, I was. D.C. sure, at least.

Close Calls

———·—·———

BY TUESDAY, I was getting closer to an anxiety attack. Charlie wasn't answering his cell phone or returning my BlackBerrys, and this drove me nuts faster than anything else could. He'd acted so understanding about our thwarted weekend plans. He knew I couldn't be blamed for the timing of the Alzheimer's Bill. And I obviously wasn't making it up—he could have watched all the proceedings on C-SPAN if he'd so desired. Granted, it was unfortunate that he'd called to check in and found me out drinking at the Mayflower bar, but it had been Sunday evening by then and a trip to New York was out of the question. And the bill had finally just passed, which obviously needed to be celebrated. And the president was addicted to an illegal experimental drug, which certainly needed to be processed. I'd told Charlie about the bill but not the drug. And he'd been happy for me. He'd been disappointed, of course, that everything had turned out the way it did in terms of our personal plans, but so had I. And I'd offered to come up the following weekend instead.

So then why had he cut me off? We'd spoken Sunday night and he'd said he'd call Monday. But he hadn't. We were now entering the forty-eighth hour of radio silence. I'd lasted until early afternoon and then left him multiple messages, but I hadn't heard back. For the third time, I replayed our last conversation. It had been short, but normal enough. Comparing schedules, workloads, and loneliness. Wanting to be with each other, then wanting sleep. Saying we loved each other. Had he been lying? Was he angry? Had he been abducted? My imagination and my fear teamed up for all kinds of paranoid explanations.

If I didn't hear from him soon, I was going to need some type of sedation.

It didn't help that my ex-boyfriend Aaron had routinely deceived me with tales of bad cell service and lost chargers to explain his un-availability when he was actually off cheating on me. After that wrench-ing revelation, I'd come to associate inaccessibility with betrayal. Charlie was normally very patient about this. And since I felt so much safer with him, I was capable of not completely freaking out when I couldn't find him for a few hours. But then I'd reach a limit and tip over into crazyland. And neither one of us enjoyed those rides.

I needed a distraction, I told myself. I'd leave another round of messages in an hour, but till then, I needed to take my mind off the spectrum of horrible possibilities that could explain his silence. I paced the apartment. Liza was selfishly out with Jakers, strengthening her im-munity to his terribleness. It was just me and my insecurities and my fish. I went into the kitchen to check on them.

Cal Ripken Jr. was in his third-most alarming pose. His first was floating belly up at the top of his bowl. This was clearly the most dis-turbing because it was the position I expected to find him in when he shuffled off this mortal coil for real. I'd had another fish who'd enjoyed this death pose practicing in the past, so I never immediately assumed Cal was truly gone. And when I'd poke him with the net, he'd give a lit-tle start and right himself and begin swimming around again. Still, it was very unnerving.

His second-most alarming pose was lying listlessly on the rocks as if his little body were too weak and disease-ravaged to even stay afloat. And his third one, which he was currently demonstrating, was diago-nally suspending himself with his head pointed down and his gills mak-ing no discernible flutter. Sometimes he'd entangle himself in some seaweed before taking this pose, which I assumed was for dramatic ef-fect. For a fish so simple in most ways, Cal Ripken Jr. occasionally sur-prised me with his penchant for flair.

"Are you still alive?" I inquired.

No response.

"How about you?" I checked behind the toaster for Professor Moriarty.

He was in his bowl, unflustered and mellow as usual. He stared back at me, gills pumping in rhythmic disregard.

"Time for a trip, Professor," I informed him as I used both hands to carry his bowl over to Cal's counter.

It was small enough to carry in one hand, but I was overly cautious thanks to an unfortunate incident with another fish a few years back. I'd tripped on a book in the living room of my old apartment and sent Elvira's bowl flying. When I'd recovered my balance and raced to the crash site, the bowl had been intact but empty. There'd been pebbles strewn from my desk to my couch, seaweed on the curtain and water flung in three different directions. But no sign of Elvira. I'd searched frantically, careful of where I stepped, but she hadn't been among any of the other refuse. I hadn't been able to find her in the plant or the cushions or the papers piled around. She'd completely vanished. Around minute thirty, I'd given up hope of finding her alive, and my search and rescue turned into a body recovery mission. But I still hadn't been able to find her. Every couple weeks I would poke through piles of books or under a couch cushion, still perplexed by the disappearance. Months later, her tiny skeleton had turned up in the jar of a half-burned scented candle on the second shelf of my bookcase. I hadn't been able to stand the smell of sweet honeysuckle since.

With a firm grip, I placed Professor Moriarty's bowl next to Cal's and took a seat. Cal immediately popped back into a more lifelike stance and zoomed to the side of his bowl to begin the face-off. Professor Moriarty appeared extremely bored. He did manage a halfhearted mane ruffle, which was all it took for Cal to spiral into hysterics. His gills fully inflamed, he tried his best to break through the glass to get at Professor Moriarty. I allowed this to continue for about two minutes before separating them again. Cal Ripken Jr. remained on high alert. No time for death posing when there was a realm to defend. This was life!

That existential fire drill completed, I returned to the living room and flipped on the TV. A new episode of *Piling On* was just about to begin. After its blockbuster debut, it had been moved to the eight p.m. time slot, and Charlie and I had begun watching the show together on the phone. It was sort of an odd long-distance date, but we liked it. We could each curl up with a phone and still feel connected. Did he remember it was on tonight? Would he call in time to watch it together live?

I had my home phone and my cell beside me on a pillow. The opening credits began to the sound of neither of them ringing. Oh well, maybe he was just running a little late. I'd try not to think too much about it.

Piling On was actually an excellent distraction. In this installment, former President Pile had decided to return to his childhood home and roam the grounds with a metal detector in search of lost treasures. He'd evidently buried several toy pistols and a tin box full of keepsakes when he was younger as a sort of time capsule to be uncovered later. He'd recently watched an archaeology special on the Discovery channel, and had decided to go dig them up. His wife tried to talk him out of it, reminding him of his strained back and the doctor's orders to take it easy. But Pile was undaunted, telling her he was "fit as a fiddler." I watched something cross Lisa Pile's face—perhaps the impulse to correct her husband? She'd had plenty of practice stamping down this urge, but maybe the dynamics had changed since he'd left office. Then again, maybe she was just imagining that fiddlers probably did get very defined muscles with all that bow action and foot tapping.

Pile didn't have to travel far to get to his childhood home. He'd been born just a few miles away on a similarly stunning waterfront New England estate. A maid greeted him at the door and handed him the metal detector he'd apparently called ahead for.

"Thanks, Maizey," he said.

"I'm Ella, sir," she said apologetically.

"Are you sure?" he quizzed her. "You look just like Maizey."

Ella stayed quiet.

Pile was wandering off toward the woods and wondering aloud how much his old pistols would get on eBay when my phone rang. It was Charlie. I snatched it up.

"Well, *hello*," I said. "So nice of you to call."

"Hey, I'm sorry I didn't sooner. Things got really crazy at work."

"Is everything okay?" I asked, swinging immediately from annoyance to concern.

"Yeah, it's fine. I just needed to take care of some things."

This was all very vague. I felt myself swing back to annoyance, but tried not to sound suspicious.

"Where are you now?" I asked nonchalantly.

He'd called from his mobile, according to my caller ID.

"Just leaving work. Are you watching the show?"

"Yeah, Pile's looking for buried weapons."

"That sounds right up his alley. Do we know yet if they're imaginary ones?"

"Unclear at this point. Will you get back to your place in time to watch any of it?"

"I'm not sure. There's a chance that—"

I jumped a little as someone knocked loudly on my door.

"Do you need to get that?" Charlie asked.

"I'm not expecting anyone," I answered. "And Liza's not here," I dropped my voice to a whisper.

"So what—you're going to pretend like you're not home?"

I put the TV on mute and tiptoed to the bedroom.

"I think so," I whispered. "I'm sort of freaked out."

I was easily scared, which everyone close to me knew about and the nice ones didn't take advantage of. Whoever it was knocked again.

"Who could it be?" I asked softly.

"I don't know," he answered. "You didn't order any food?"

I usually ordered a pizza on *Piling On* nights, but I'd forgotten to in the midst of my distress about Charlie.

"No, not tonight."

"Maybe it's a neighbor," he offered.

That was unlikely only because none of them had ever stopped by before. Why start tonight when I was alone and scared and weak from lack of pizza?

"I doubt it. And if so, what if he or she is a homicidal neighbor?" I asked. "What then?"

"Good point," Charlie was forced to admit. "I guess to be safe you just really shouldn't answer."

"Exactly," I whispered.

The person knocked *again*. They were certainly persistent. Weren't they getting the message that I wasn't home? But maybe they'd heard the TV before I'd muted it. Or me talking, before I'd muted myself. In which case, they *knew* I was home.

"Why aren't they going away?" I asked aloud.

"Maybe it's some kind of emergency," Charlie suggested. "If you do want to answer, I'll stay on the phone with you."

That was a nice, but utterly useless offer. It allowed me to feel a completely false sense of security as I opened the door, and then subjected Charlie to the sounds of whatever inevitable attack ensued. No thank you.

"I am *not* answering the door," I said definitively. "They're bound to go away soon."

And they did. The knocking ceased. I waited another minute and then tiptoed back into the living room.

"I think they're gone," I whispered.

"Great," Charlie answered. "You outfoxed them."

"Oh, I'm sure they just gave up," I said modestly. "Do you think they left anything?"

Some sort of note or calling card, perhaps.

"It's possible," Charlie said.

Yes, it was. I should probably check.

"Even if they didn't leave anything on purpose, maybe there'll be some kind of clue," I said, feeling my inner Nancy Drew rear her inquisitive head. "Hold on just a second."

I moved to the door and put my ear against it. Total silence. I wished we had a peephole so I could be positive that the hallway was clear. It sounded like it was. I quietly unlocked the door and opened it slowly, and ever so slightly.

To see Charlie, leaning patiently against the hallway wall.

I yelped and flung the door wider.

"Find anything good?" Charlie asked into his phone as he smiled at me.

I dropped my phone and tackled him.

"That was you the whole time?" I demanded.

"Yep. I shouldn't have knocked so loudly and urgently the first time, but I was excited to surprise you. Strategic error."

It certainly had been. We'd just wasted ten precious minutes with those high jinks. I felt myself blush with embarrassment and the excitement of seeing him. I put my arms around his neck and leapt up, circling his waist with my legs. He supported me with his arms and leaned back into the wall to kiss me deeply.

"I can't believe you're here," I said as I squeezed him tightly.

"I couldn't wait till the weekend," he explained. "So I just took the train down for the night."

Why hadn't I thought of that? I could have made a surprise overnight trip to New York. But maybe it was better that it hadn't occurred to me. This was really much more convenient.

I kissed him all over his face as he walked me back into the apartment and shut the door. *Piling On* was still on the TV, on mute. Pile was knee deep in a hole, digging it deeper. Charlie felt for the remote and turned it off.

"Unless you want to watch?" he asked.

I unbuttoned his shirt and began kissing his chest in response.

"Okay, good," he replied.

He kept walking down the hall to my bedroom. I didn't even spend a second stressing about the semi-controlled chaos awaiting us. And once inside, we certainly didn't waste any more time clearing the books and papers and clothes and Fireball wrappers from my bed. Charlie just grabbed the comforter that was already bunched helpfully on the floor and lowered me down on top of it, with him on top of me. He quickly matched my urgency in the clothes-removal efforts and we were naked and happy in no time. And then we were naked and extremely happy a half hour later.

"This was an inspired idea," I said gratefully as I traced my initials on his shoulder.

I wondered if he'd ever have them tattooed.

"Thank God you finally opened the door," he answered.

"How much longer would you have waited?" I asked curiously.

"Without just telling you I was there?" he asked. "I don't know. I wanted you to discover it for yourself."

I started thinking about how I wouldn't open the door until I thought whoever had been there had left and what that meant about me. But I was in too good a mood to let this get me down.

"What are you thinking about?" Charlie asked. "Smallpox?"

I giggled.

"No. Just how lucky I am to have you."

This wasn't a lie, since on some level I was always thinking that when I was with Charlie. He kissed my forehead and played with my hair, which always brought me a very still sort of joy.

"I know it's late, but I actually made us dinner reservations," he said softly. "So that we could have a real date."

Really? That was a nice surprise.

"Where are we going?" I asked.

"Citronelle," he answered. "But only if you're up for it."

I certainly was. Citronelle was arguably the best French restaurant in D.C.—a place I'd never been but had always been curious about. Perhaps our romantic trip to Paris to get engaged was back on. The only problem was that if we went to the restaurant we couldn't remain nakedly wrapped in each other's arms.

"I definitely want to go, I just don't want to move from right here," I said.

"We still have twenty minutes till we'd need to leave," Charlie said.

"Well, we should use them wisely then," I said, sliding down beneath the comforter.

I'd forgotten how fun it was to get ready for a date, I thought as Charlie and I climbed out of the shower and dried off.

"We're going to be late," I remarked.

"I couldn't be happier about that," he replied.

We dressed quickly and headed out the door. As we settled into a cab, Charlie's cell phone rang. He glanced at it.

"It's Amanda," he replied.

Amanda, his roommate. I still had never met or talked to her. And Google hadn't provided very much information at all, which was highly uncharacteristic. Why was Amanda calling Charlie now? I wondered. Not knowing her, it was difficult to speculate.

"Do you think anything's wrong?" I asked.

Charlie shook his head. The ringing stopped.

"She gets worried sometimes that something's happened to me if she thinks I already should have gotten back to the apartment and I'm not there," he said.

"Interesting," I replied. "Well, that's certainly . . . caring of her."

"She means well, but it's pretty annoying," Charlie said.

Good. I was glad he felt that way. He did feel that way, didn't he? Or could he just be saying that for my benefit?

His phone started ringing again.

"Amanda again?" I asked.

He glanced at it and nodded.

All right, now that was getting a little obsessive.

"You should answer it," I said.

Charlie sighed.

"I'm sorry," he said to me, giving my shoulder a little squeeze. "Hi," he said into the phone.

I leaned in a little, without being obvious, to try to make out how she sounded and what she was saying, but the cab turned uncooperatively and tossed me away from Charlie.

"No, everything's fine," Charlie was saying. "I came down to D.C. to surprise Sammy."

Take that, obsessive woman. She was now having some sort of reaction that I couldn't hear.

"It's not anything I can't handle." Charlie sighed. "But thanks for the concern. See you tomorrow."

There was another pause.

"Sure, tell her I say good night. Great. Bye."

He hung up the phone and turned to me, looking a little exasperated.

"Sorry about that. I'm turning my phone off now," he said. "Can you turn off your stuff as well? We shouldn't have any more interruptions."

I nodded and switched off my phone and BlackBerry, completely preoccupied with other thoughts.

"What did she say?" I asked.

"She was worried that something might have happened to me, as usual."

"No, I know, but I mean after you told her you came to visit me."

"Oh. She thought it was a bit rash. And that I'd be really tired at work tomorrow," he replied.

Okay, that was not acceptable.

"Oh, really," I said dryly.

"I know, none of her business, right? She doesn't really get that."

Maybe I could make it more clear to her. But there was something else I wanted to know first.

"Who were you talking about when you said 'tell her I say good night'?"

Charlie looked a little embarrassed.

"The cat. Delilah. We've gotten closer."

"Since the Fancy Feast," I surmised.

"Right. The cat's sweet but Amanda's a little weird about her. Always wanting other people to talk to the cat like she's a person and dressing her up in little outfits and stuff. I feel bad for her sometimes."

"The cat? Or Amanda?" I asked.

It always seemed to get confusing when we spoke about the two of them.

"The cat. But forget it. Do you mind if we stop talking about this? I'm sorry she called, but let's not get off track."

I was sorry she called too. And I didn't want to get derailed either. This night had begun so well.

"Here ya go," the cabdriver said as he pulled up to the curb in front of the restaurant.

As I stepped outside, I imagined I was stepping into a new attitude. This sort of visualization had helped me in the past to change moods in a pinch. Stupid, clingy Amanda. New mood, NEW MOOD, I ordered my brain in a very shrill internal voice.

"You okay?" Charlie asked as he joined me on the sidewalk, sliding his arm easily around me.

"I'm fantastic," I replied, partially to remind him in case he'd forgotten in all the excitement of the female roommate calls.

"Yes, you are," he answered.

Good, he'd picked right up on that double meaning. I was starting to feel a little bit better for real.

But then as we sat down and looked at the menu, I began worrying about prices. Neither one of us had enough money to be at a restaurant like this and still feel like we were being responsible. Whenever we went somewhere fancy to eat, I tried to calm my anxiety by justifying it as a special occasion, and it usually was. But I could never fully shake the uncomfortable feeling that we were paying way too much for something that was essentially just sort of pretentious. It wasn't as though we needed sautéed frog legs and a stunning Riesling to survive. We didn't even need them to have a good time. We'd demonstrated that in the past.

These thoughts flashed through my mind as we looked at what had to be a very overpriced wine list.

"Do you want red or white?" Charlie asked.

"Should we go somewhere else?" I answered. "We passed a Taco Bell down the street."

Charlie put down the list to address the situation. It had arisen before, so he knew what was going on.

"This is my treat. I surprised you and I want to take you out to a fancy restaurant. Plus, my promotion came with a raise, so let me spend it how I want. Don't deprive me of my plans."

He smiled and spoke sweetly, but there was a bit of command to his voice. Which had very little effect on me.

"The thing is, you've already done enough to make this an amazing night," I began. "And it's not like the train tickets and taxi rides are cheap. This dinner will be the equivalent of another round-trip train ticket; wouldn't it be better to use the money for that? Plus, Taco B. has some new steak chimichangas that are incredibly tasty."

"I thought you were avoiding beef until the mad cow scare is completely over."

It was clever of him to use my own arguments against me rather than just disagree with my scheme.

"They have chicken ones too. And I know how you feel about their soft tacos. They don't serve alcohol, it's true, but we've got plenty of beer and wine at home."

Charlie nodded. Our server approached.

"Sparkling or flat?" she asked professionally.

I hated when they strong-armed you into buying water. Buying water depressed me.

"Tap water would be great," I said.

She nodded curtly and moved away.

"Maybe we should leave," Charlie relented. "You don't really seem in the mood for this, so I don't want to force you."

He sounded a little sad. Making him sad had not been my intention at all.

"No, we can stay," I said. "I just don't want you to think that I'm *expecting* to stay."

Charlie now looked confused. I took pity.

"Let's stay," I decided. "It's a special occasion."

Not to put any pressure on him, though this was obviously a perfect setting to talk about that trip to Paris. We could find discount plane tickets and stay someplace reasonable. And I preferred a simple ring anyway. I found the whole diamond business distasteful as it was, so he was free to get me something else. I wondered if he knew that already or whether I needed to clue him in. Maybe I could start a conversation about birthstones without sounding too flaky.

By the time our entrees came, I was completely relaxed. The wine had certainly helped with that, but I was mainly excited to be with Charlie, with whom I was flirting like we'd been together only a week instead of more than two years.

"This was a wonderful idea," I told him. "Every couple should go out on a date like this to remind them that they don't completely know each other."

Charlie seemed amused.

"What don't I know about you?" he asked. "And what do you think you don't know about me?"

There was so much. Where to even begin?

"Well, there's obviously a ton of work stuff you don't know about, and that's the way it has to be, of course. But it's odd, because that's the main thing going on in my life. It's what I spend all of my time doing. And I can't really be honest about it with you."

Charlie turned more serious.

"You can always tell me anything and trust that I'll keep your confidence," he said.

"I know, I know. But there are things that would just be unfair to ask you to keep secret. Big things. Things any reporter would be dying to know about."

Was I trying to be tempting? I just wanted to tell someone who really knew me about all that had been going on with Wye. I wanted to be able to unload. To maybe get some advice.

"I think I'd be able to control myself," Charlie said evenly.

He probably could, but the things I would tell him were so explosive that he'd be dying to find another way to report them. He'd be sorely tempted to seek out independent confirmation of Wye's substance abuse so that he'd never have to consider me a source. But if I didn't tell him, it would never even occur to him to embark on that particular search. And anything that came out was destined to damage the administration and threaten my job. But then again, didn't the American people, the world, in fact, need to know about this?

"Thank you," I told him. "If I ever really need to tell you something, then I'll feel safe doing it."

But I'd have to avoid getting to that point because it was just too dangerous. So here I was, sort of lying. I did lie on occasion. He didn't know that about me, I was willing to wager.

"Well, you can ask me anything you want to know," Charlie said.

"About work or other stuff?"

"Anything," he repeated.

"Could anything you're researching right now impact the administration?"

He hesitated for a moment.

"Yes. In an indirect way. So far, at least."

What was it? Was it connected to the scientific research firm scandal he'd been investigating? He'd moved to New York to pursue the story about a firm that peddled fake science for a price—I wondered exactly what he'd uncovered. According to him, I could ask.

"Will you tell me what it is?"

Charlie shook his head.

"I'm sorry, I can't at the moment."

"I thought you said I could ask you anything!" I said indignantly. I'd been excited about the double standard. I thrived on those.

"And you can. But I can't answer everything," he replied.

"That's a mean trick," I said, embarrassed that I'd fallen for it.

"It's an old one," he answered with a little smile. "It gets you to reveal more about yourself than you'd planned."

Hmm. So I could have asked him anything and I chose to inquire first about something professional that would impact my job. I wasn't sure that I liked what that revealed about me. I decided to follow it up quickly with a more charming personal question, but before I could, the water refill guy approached. Charlie said something to him in French that made him laugh.

"What did you say?" I asked.

"It's too corny to translate," Charlie replied. "Just a dumb joke about what vintage the water was."

"Well, your French sounds great," I noted. "Have you been using it more?"

"Yes, I've been practicing," he replied. "Amanda's family has a place in Paris and she's fluent. We speak French around the apartment occasionally."

How special. I didn't trust myself to say anything pleasant, so I just kept quiet.

"People always told me that the best way to learn a language was to live with someone who spoke it," Charlie continued. "So when I found out Amanda spoke French, I figured I might as well turn the roommate situation into an educational experience."

I'd also heard that advice about learning a language. But the people who'd told me about it had been specifically referring to a romantic arrangement. As in, the best way to learn Italian was to have an Italian boyfriend. I hoped Amanda wasn't misconstruing Charlie's request.

"And actually, she's invited me to visit her Paris place whenever I want. So we should go sometime," he continued.

Not quite the way I imagined he'd pop the Paris trip question, but I remained calm.

"Are you sure I'm invited?" I asked. "Maybe she was only inviting you."

"Well, I'm certainly not going without you."

I hoped not. And I didn't want a little jealousy to allow me to lose sight of the whole romantic basis for a trip to France. He was finally bringing it up. I should seize the moment.

"Maybe we can go for New Year's," I suggested.

"Or maybe in the spring," he answered. "This winter's going to be busy, and spring is supposed to be beautiful there."

Okay. I could wait the extra months to get engaged. The spring would be nice. And if I'd arranged for Amanda's death by that point, we could always stay somewhere else, which I'd prefer anyway. Despite the added cost for the accommodation and the hit man.

"I'd love that," I said.

"I love *you*," he replied.

We smiled and flirted our way through the rest of dinner. I entertained Charlie with my reenactments of the latest encounters between Cal Ripken Jr. and Professor Moriarty. Charlie always enjoyed my impressions of Cal's fits of frenzy. He said I had a fish-impersonation gift. I credited my full lips—they really came in handy for this line of work.

After dinner, we walked halfway back to my place before finding a cab. The sky was too cloudy to see stars, and the lights of the city interfered too much anyway, but the streetlamps were romantic enough. I glanced at my watch and saw that it was just past midnight, which brought a rush of sadness. It was already tomorrow, five hours from Charlie's leaving again. As amazing and necessary as this evening had been, a part of my brain had been occupied the entire time with the knowledge that it would end with his leaving. And that his leaving would be coming soon. Was that the reason I'd created little problems along the way? To distance before he could? I thought about Liza's advice about not making things too difficult. I knew I needed to heed it more.

She and Jakers were back at the apartment but thankfully shut up in her room. I wouldn't have minded seeing her and I'm sure Charlie would have liked to say hello, but neither of us was broken up about missing Jakers. We got some water and tiptoed down the hall so as not to make any noise he'd feel compelled to investigate.

Safe again in my room, I started to clear the huge mess off my bed. Charlie touched my arm.

"The floor worked great earlier. Why don't we just sleep on it?" he suggested.

I grabbed another comforter and some more pillows to make the arrangement softer and we lay down in the darkness.

"I love inside camping," I said.

Which was true. I enjoyed pillow forts as well. I'd spent many childhood hours and a few more adult ones than I usually admitted to on their construction.

"We should go camping for real sometime," Charlie said.

Tonight was evidently the night for vacation planning.

"Where would you want to go?" I inquired.

"Maybe someplace in New Hampshire or Maine in the summer."

Charlie was from that part of the country.

"We've got good camping in Ohio too," I said loyally.

"We could get an RV and take a tour," Charlie offered. "And head out west, to Yellowstone and the Rockies."

That sounded like a nice compromise and a more fun plan. A bit fantastical, since neither one of us would take off enough time from work for the sort of trip that would entail, but it was nice to pretend.

"Maybe not in the next couple years, but we've got a long life together," Charlie said as if reading my mind.

He had a habit of doing that.

"You know, actually, you really can't ever be sure," I replied.

"What's that supposed to mean?" he asked.

It had sounded bad. I'd meant it as a comment on mortality rather than the chances for our relationship. Was that any better?

"All I meant was, how can we be sure of what's going to happen? Tomorrow, I could get killed by an escaped, rampaging elephant. Or a rogue meteor. Or the return of yellow fever."

I had a particular fear of that last one. Charlie squeezed and kissed me. I wondered if he was just trying to shut me up. It was late, after all.

"I won't let any of that happen to you," he assured me.

He couldn't promise that. I wouldn't fall for it. In the end, even as part of a couple, I had to rely on myself. I didn't appreciate his making impossible pledges, no matter how sweet or intentionally calming they were.

"Seriously, I've cast a powerful spell around you," he continued. "It's a protective bubble. Have you ever seen *Bubble Boy*?"

"No, but I think I get the visual. I didn't know you were talented in the dark arts."

"You yourself said there were things you don't know about me," he replied. "So you'll just have to trust me. You're fully protected."

I smiled and dismissed him with a patronizing pat, but the funny thing was that I actually did feel safer. Maybe there was something to his spell. Maybe if someone who really loved me spent a measurable amount of time willing my well-being, it had an effect.

I drifted off to sleep listening for Charlie's breathing to turn regular and REM-beated, but I never heard the change, which meant that he must have outwaited me. I forgot to ask if he'd set his alarm for an hour early, but I woke up at four a.m. anyway, shaking from a nightmare involving a gigantic rabid cat in a beret.

"What's wrong?" Charlie asked sleepily. "You're okay. It was just a dream."

He essentially recited this last part. I guess I did wake up from nightmares fairly frequently. Once a month was a ballpark figure. But I felt like I needed more from him than just rote concern. I was awake now. I was ready for a conversation.

He didn't seem to be on the same page. I thought about letting him sleep, but then I nudged him.

"Did you have any dreams?" I asked.

"Mmm-humph," he replied.

Okay, I should let him be. Though sometimes I could get him to talk in his sleep if I kept at it. That was always pretty entertaining.

"Charlie," I said in a soft, singsongy voice. "What are you dreaming about?"

He opened his eyes.

"I dreamed we were on Saturn," he said very clearly. "Will you marry me?"

He was staring right at me. I stopped breathing for a second. Was this our moment? Was this how we were getting engaged? And was my answer definitely "yes"?

"Yes" had flooded through me, filling up every part of my body the instant the question was asked, so I supposed that it was.

"Of course I will," I finally breathed.

Charlie snored. His eyes were still open, but he was fast asleep. He'd done this a few times in the past and I'd always found it incredibly creepy. This time, I found it humiliating as well.

I shook him a little too hard.

"What? What is it? Are you okay?" he asked as he came to.

"Yes." I sighed.

That wasn't the yes that I'd wanted to say.

"Bad dream?" he asked.

Did he remember anything about the last ten seconds?

"Bad awakening," I answered.

"What are you talking about?" he asked, fighting to stay conscious.

"You were talking in your sleep," I informed him.

"Oh, really? What did I say? Anything I should know about?"

I thought about telling him that he'd proposed. But he'd been asleep; it had been part of his dream state. I didn't want to force him to discuss it awake. I wanted him to do so of his own volition.

"Nothing too scandalous," I said.

"Mmkay," he answered as he rolled onto his side, sliding up against me. "I love you, honey."

He was already falling back asleep. But I knew that this time at least, he was saying something he really meant.

"I love you too," I replied.

He pulled me closer to him. As I settled into his warmth, I closed my eyes but stayed awake thinking. And thinking. And thinking. Which prevented me from falling back asleep. And by the time Charlie stirred again, I'd decided that sex was a crucial part of my plan to ensure that he kept his mind off Amanda and on me. Had I known then what sort of day was in store for me, I might have opted instead for a quick nap to ensure I got even a tiny bit of rest. But you just never know these things ahead of time.

Debuts

"WHITE HOUSE DABBLES in Experimental Drugs" was not the head-line I would have chosen to greet me when I arrived tired but caf-feinated at the office a few hours later. I'd bid Charlie a bittersweet good-bye and promised to visit him that weekend, then rushed into work to discover that Focusid was front-page news. My heart had stopped for a short moment. But it turned out that "White House Dab-bles in Experimental Drugs" was just what Chick Wallrey considered a cute title for an article revealing the trade agreement we'd brokered in India for a cheaper supply of prescription drugs. They hadn't uncov-ered the secret of the president's private stash. The *New York Times* was just profiling the companies that the government had contracted with, and they'd included a sidebar article about their experimental drug studies. Luckily, that was the only reason Focusid was right there in print. I breathed a sigh of relief.

Lincoln was quoted stressing that the experimental drugs were not part of the import agreement. At least not officially, I said to myself as I read. I wondered why he hadn't told me about the article. He must have spoken to Chick yesterday, but I hadn't heard a thing about it. I was accustomed to being in the loop on such matters. We had planned to announce the trade agreements on our own terms in a few days and it was annoying that the news had leaked out ahead of schedule.

Lincoln's mouth was stained Popsicle red when I walked into his office. I saw the beginnings of a new cabin sculpture on the shelf be-hind him.

"Did you lose your purse or something?" he asked me.

No. I'd temporarily lost my keys every day this week, but not my purse.

"Uh-uh. Why?"

"I couldn't reach you on your phone or your BlackBerry last night. I was worried you'd been mugged."

"Really?"

I searched in my bag for both. There they were, right where they were supposed to be. But both were turned off, rendering them completely useless. Whoops. Now I remembered. We'd turned everything off in the cab ride, and I'd forgotten to turn them back on. Charlie's surprise visit had prompted all kinds of unorthodox behavior. I blushed.

"Here they are. I completely forgot I'd switched them off. Sorry about that," I said.

I turned them both on. My cell phone immediately registered several new voice mails and my BlackBerry buzzed for a full minute with incoming messages.

"I hope it wasn't anything too urgent," I said apologetically.

From Lincoln's frazzled look, I could tell that it was.

"Chick Wallrey called me last night looking for comment on the India story. I wanted to let you know about it so we could strategize for today. Because now there's a ton more requests. I got word from Stephanie that I'm supposed to do Carlton Block's show this afternoon."

Carlton Block was a popular CNN anchor. I tuned in to his show as much as I could because I liked his style.

"That's terrific," I said. "I'm sort of jealous, even. Are you ready for it?"

"No. Which is why you're going instead," Lincoln answered.

What?

"No," I said instinctively. "No, I'm not. I don't do TV. I never have. I'd be an embarrassment. I wouldn't be any good."

"And you think I would?" Lincoln asked.

"Of course. I know talking to people isn't your favorite thing to do, but talking about these health care issues is. You know all about the India deal. And you've already done shows like this anyway," I pointed out.

I know he hated doing them, but that was just too bad. It was part of his job to be able to represent the administration when called upon. I watched him unwrap another Popsicle.

"Sammy, I'm your boss. You're doing the show."

Wow. He'd never taken this tack with me before. But he was right and I couldn't argue. I could be incredulous and bitter, but that would get me only so far.

"It makes sense," he added. "You're the one who went to India and actually brokered the deal."

"But what if I say the wrong thing?" I asked.

I hated sounding incompetent or insecure, but I had legitimate concerns. And then Lincoln started giggling. Was he imagining my inevitable screw-up? I'm glad it was destined to be more hilarious than career-ending. Though maybe it would be both. I couldn't be sure Lincoln didn't consider me laughably replaceable.

"What's so funny?" I asked suspiciously.

"Whew." Lincoln dried his eyes.

His Popsicle had begun dripping a little while he'd taken a break from licking to laugh.

"I was just thinking that in any other office within about twenty miles of here, people would be competing with each other about how to get picked for the show. Not how to get out of it."

I smiled. He was right. We were unique in our self-sabotaging shyness. These sorts of media challenges didn't actually come up too often, since Secretary Harlow was generally the public face of the administration's health care agenda. Which was appropriate. It was only when she wasn't available or willing that someone farther down the ranks got called upon. And even then, Stephanie would frequently step up to fill in, since the media thought that everything was all about political strategy anyway.

"I just think the most qualified person should represent the administration when it comes to these issues," I remarked.

"So do I," Lincoln concurred.

He looked meaningfully at me. Surely he wasn't suggesting that I might be that person.

"But I just don't feel like doing it," he continued with a little smile.

That cleared that up.

"And Secretary Harlow's in Vancouver for the day with a full schedule," he went on.

There was still plenty to clean up on the Canadian front. The first lady had already made two separate goodwill trips. Hopefully the deals with the Indian companies would help provide Canada with the prescription drugs they'd been cut off from thanks to their partnership with the United States.

"So the next best person is you," Lincoln concluded. "I'll help you prepare. We'll go over talking points and probable questions and the whole thing. Just be ready to head to the studio at three."

I nodded. There really wasn't anything else for me to do.

Lincoln did help me prepare. He carefully went over the best ways to present the administration's positions and helped me anticipate the challenges the other guests would raise. Carlton Block's show didn't thrive on conflict the way other programs tended to, but it did invite different perspectives in a quest for balance. As Lincoln coached me, I thought about how often I acted as his voice.

"Now, do you have another shirt you can wear?" he asked me.

"What's wrong with this one?"

I looked down at my shirt self-consciously. It was a basic black turtleneck. I considered it presentable enough.

"Someone told me to wear bright colors on TV, that's all," Lincoln explained. "Maybe Margari or someone has something you can borrow. If not, it's obviously no big deal."

He already seemed acutely embarrassed to have brought it up. Or maybe it was the mention of Margari. I'd noticed lately that he stole little glances at her when they were in the same room.

"I'll see what I can do," I replied.

I returned to my desk and immersed myself in work for the next several hours, but I couldn't help but keep worrying about the show. I reviewed my talking points several times. And at lunch, I sought out Margari. She was wearing a deep red sweater. Now that I thought about it, she did always look very vibrant.

I told her about the show and about Lincoln's wardrobe concerns.

"That Lincoln is a trip." She laughed.

And did she blush a little too? I couldn't be sure. Her cheeks were naturally rosy.

"I don't have any extra clothes here, but this sweater has been itching for some national exposure. We could trade for the afternoon," Margari offered.

Which we did. Margari was curvier than me, but luckily both tops were stretchy enough to accommodate our different builds. I returned to my desk looking brighter and smelling like Margari's cinnamon perfume. I dove back into my work, and the next time I checked the clock it was two thirty. Okay, half an hour, I said to myself. There's no need to panic.

I walked as calmly as possible to the ladies' room, where I stared critically at myself in the mirror. Is this what I'd look like on TV? What I said was more important, but its impact could be undermined if I looked like a total slob. A red sweater could do only so much.

What if I pulled a Nixon and started sweating profusely? Or if my neck rash appeared? I'd have to ask them to put some makeup on my neck for preventative cover-up.

I tried to visualize Carlton Block's set, and myself sitting in it. He liked to face his guests, which meant everyone was generally shot at an angle. Would I get to choose which side of myself faced the camera? And if I did, which side would I choose?

I took out a piece of paper from my bag and held it in front of one side of my face and then the other. I thought my left side was probably my better one. Then I covered the bottom half of my face. Then I split it on a diagonal. Then I tore the paper into different pieces and covered various parts of my face. Before long, I felt like a Picasso painting. Dizzy, I walked slowly back to my desk. I was not reassured.

"All set?" Lincoln's assistant, Nick, asked enthusiastically.

I shook my head.

"Oh, you'll be great."

He checked his watch.

"And you need to go."

I sighed.

Derrick did little to boost my confidence as I left the premises. He gave me a bored glance and then shook his head as he returned to his reading. I hoped the American public wouldn't reject me as completely as he regularly did. I called my mom on the motor pool ride to the studio to let her know I'd be on the air. The response was eardrum-shattering. I assured her I'd check in later.

I BlackBerried Charlie and Liza to let them know as well. And I left a quick message for Zelda. I wanted to inform people, but I didn't really want them to watch if I was going to be a disaster. It was a sticky wicket, which was one of my favorite terms for some of my least favorite situations.

The studio was extremely cold. I was offered a hot coffee, but I didn't want to risk a restroom emergency mid-show, so I just let my anxiety warm me.

"Do you know who else is going to be on with me?" I asked the makeup man I'd tried to win over.

I'd attempted to get this information earlier to no avail. I took it that they were throwing together a last-minute panel.

"Some pharmaceutical executive and Dr. Singh, the celebrity medical expert. He's got a new show they're trying to cross-promote."

Dr. Singh was a doctor who regularly appeared on the network to address any issue with health connections. He was a pleasant, energetic man of Indian descent who played up his expert status to the utmost. He'd just launched his own show, which I'd come across when flipping channels the other day. In an interesting move, he bounded out onto the stage to the song "Wild Thing" modified to "Wild Singh." Dumbstruck, I'd watched him lip-synch along to a verse before dancing his way to the couch.

So I'd be sharing the stage with Wild Singh. I was pretty sure I wasn't a match for his showmanship. In the greenroom, I discovered that the pharmaceutical executive was Laura Rakerson, the exact woman with whom I'd spoken when I'd been trying to discover whatever the pharmaceutical industry had up its sleeve regarding the Canadian Import Law. That really hadn't gone all that well.

We exchanged hellos. I took my talking points out of my briefcase and reviewed them again. I'd known all the relevant details even before prepping to go on the show, but I was worried I might freeze up on camera.

"All right, let's get you all set up," an authoritative man wearing a headset said to us.

He identified himself as a producer and he led the way to the set after instructing us to leave our briefcases and purses in the greenroom. Out on the set, Carlton Block was nowhere to be seen, but I recognized the layout.

"You'll be right here," headset man informed me.

With my right side to the camera. Curses.

"And you're next to her," he told Laura.

She settled calmly into her chair, seemingly unperturbed by the arrangement. Dr. Singh also materialized suddenly and sat himself down.

"Actually, Doctor, that's Carlton's chair," the headset man said.

Dr. Singh acted more wronged than embarrassed. But he moved. And then he took out a compact mirror from his inside jacket pocket and stared at himself.

"I'm going to need some more powder," he said to the air around him.

I secretly hoped everyone would ignore him, but the makeup man appeared and did the honors.

"How's that, Doctor?" he asked after a few pats of powder.

Dr. Singh inspected his work.

"It'll do." He sighed.

I looked at Laura to exchange a smirk, but she just stared back at me, expressionless. Were we enemies for the day? That seemed so childish, but okay, if that's the way she wanted to play.

We waited silently and somewhat patiently for a few minutes. And then the camera came closer and the headset man started saying, "And we're on in ten, nine, eight . . ."

But Carlton Block hadn't appeared. I looked around anxiously. When the show began in eight seconds, were we just supposed to talk among ourselves?

"Seven, six . . ."

I saw Dr. Singh eyeing Carlton's chair. I imagined when it got down to two seconds, he'd just launch himself back into it.

But then Carlton came running up to the stage, clipping his microphone on himself. He sat down just as the headset man used his fingers to silently count down "three, two, one," and then pointed to Carlton, who immediately addressed the camera.

"Welcome. I'm Carlton Block and you're watching *Right Now*. This morning, the *New York Times* reported that the White House has proposed a partnership with the Indian pharmaceutical industry to access supplies of lower cost prescription drugs. Here with me to discuss this development is White House health care advisor Samantha Joyce, Seletra executive Laura Rakerson, and, of course, our own medical expert, Dr. Pratap Singh. Thank you all for being here. Samantha, tell us a little bit about what the White House is thinking."

I took a deep breath and heard myself begin to talk. My voice didn't seem all that connected to the rest of me—it was almost as though I were observing myself from above, listening as I incorporated my talking points into fluid sentences.

". . . so these partnerships should benefit everyone involved and bring some needed relief to the American people," I concluded.

I couldn't really be sure of what else I had said. I just needed to trust that it had made sense. Carlton Block was nodding, which was a good sign.

"Laura Rakerson, do you have any response?" he asked.

We both turned toward Laura. But before she could say anything, Dr. Singh jumped in.

"If I could just add to that first, Carlton," he interjected.

He didn't wait for a response.

"India is on the cutting edge of the biotechnology industry and has so much to share with the United States. On a personal note, it's my homeland, and I think that makes me even more of an expert in this matter. The United States has made a very wise move, and I applaud the Wye administration. I am nonpartisan as a rule, but this just makes good health sense."

I appreciated the support, but Dr. Singh hadn't done a whole lot to advance the conversation. If Carlton Block was annoyed, he didn't show it. Laura Rakerson had more trouble appearing tolerant.

"May I speak now?" she asked in a fake-patient tone. "Thank you," she replied to Carlton's encouragement. "This cockeyed scheme the White House has so recklessly put forth is downright dangerous. Sacrificing quality for cost is not a discount America can afford. Plus, these Indian companies have also produced bizarre experimental lifestyle drugs—"

"You'd prefer that our own pharma companies be able to keep their monopoly on that?" I interrupted her.

I hadn't planned to break in. I'd just blurted out my thought. Everyone looked a bit surprised, including me, I imagined. Oh well. I couldn't just stop there.

"I mean, honestly, your company is one of the three largest and most established in the western hemisphere," I continued. "And though you somehow can't provide this country with enough flu vaccine, you'll spend more than a hundred million dollars pushing a drug that keeps people's toenails from turning yellow. Talk about cockeyed and reckless. That's just indefensible."

Laura looked shocked. And extremely mad.

"Toe fungus is a serious problem for lots of people," she sputtered.

Carlton actually laughed, which made her even more furious.

"No, it is," Dr. Singh said supportively. "I'm planning a show on it. We have to erase the stigma."

"The point is, all that money that's going toward the more pointless lifestyle drugs could instead be paying for what people actually need to stay alive," I seized the chance to say. "There's an enormous difference between lifestyle medicine and life*saving* medicine. The large pharmaceutical companies have persisted in refusing to supply our people with the lifesaving medicines we need at an affordable cost, so our government is looking elsewhere."

"Thank you all very much for the insights, I'm afraid we're out of time," Carlton said. "Next up, is Greenland really melting and what does that mean for us? I'm Carlton Block and you're staying tuned."

Wow, it had all gone so quickly. I knew that the show operated in short segments and that guests generally had time for only one or two sound bites, but still, it felt like it hadn't lasted more than thirty seconds. Laura unclipped her mike in a huff and stormed off the stage. Dr. Singh immediately took out his phone and checked his messages as he hurried away. I sat back in my chair for a moment to decompress.

"You did a good job." Carlton stuck out his hand to me.

Shaking his hand shook me out of my reverie.

"Thanks," I replied.

"I hate to ask you to leave, but we've got to get the next guests on," he said with a smile.

Right. Of course. I stood up quickly and hopped off the stage, dodging the headset man on my way back to the greenroom. I looked back once before going inside and saw Carlton Block watching me. He smiled again and gave a little wave. I returned it, grateful that I was far enough away that he couldn't see me blushing.

As I was picking up my briefcase in the greenroom, Dr. Singh came breezing back in.

"There you are, I'd like to talk to you," he said. "I don't have much time, of course, but this is important."

"Absolutely. What can I do for you?"

"You were very good on the show. Very natural," he said.

"Thank you, that's kind. I was really nervous."

"Well, you couldn't tell. Have you done much TV?"

I shook my head.

"No, this was my first time, actually."

"You're kidding!" he said, hushed. "You're a natural!"

I didn't really believe him, but I didn't mind hearing it either.

"I'm very impressed. And I'm not impressed very easily. Have you seen my new show?" he inquired.

"Yes, I have," I answered. "I love the intro."

Which was true. I found it atrociously brilliant.

Dr. Singh beamed.

"It's great, right? Yesterday I added a little hopping move on the final 'I think I loo-oove you,'" he half-sang. "Did you catch that?"

I shook my head.

"I couldn't watch yesterday," I answered.

"Oh, you should TiVo it," he ordered.

"Good idea," I answered.

"Well, anyway, it was a pretty good move. Very Elvis meets OutKast. I'll send you a tape."

I fought back a smile because he was acting so serious about all this.

"Thank you," I managed.

"The show's a hit. Doing really well. But I'm still tinkering with the format," he continued. "Recently, I've been thinking about bringing on a sidekick."

"Oh, really?" I said politely.

I suppressed an urge to look at my watch. There is no easy way to do that. People always notice.

"Yes. And I'd like to get you an audition with the producers. You've got great energy. Real spunk."

This time I couldn't prevent myself from laughing. He looked at me curiously.

"Are you serious?" I asked.

"Very," he replied. "I could make you a star."

I briefly visualized myself dancing through the audience to "Wild Singh." If I was a sidekick, could I get my own tune? "Mustang Sammy" had potential. Maybe we could even add some ukelele riffs and I could kick-start my long-delayed musical career. He was waiting for me to answer.

"I'm really flattered, Dr. Singh," I began.

"You should be!" he replied. "We'd make a great team. And your health care background helps for the show of course. Not that I need any assistance with that part, but sometimes people like hearing about certain things from a woman."

"Thank you," I started again. "But I'm afraid I'm going to have to turn you down. I'm very involved with my work at the White House, and don't have any desire to leave."

Dr. Singh looked surprised.

"But I could make you a star!" he repeated.

I guessed he assumed this was what I wanted. It's funny that some people take for granted that everyone has a desire for fame. Not that I really believed being Dr. Singh's sidekick was a surefire path to glory, anyway.

"I really appreciate the offer," I said.

Dr. Singh was looking at me incredulously.

"But you're saying no?" he said, giving me one last chance to rethink this catastrophic misstep.

"I am," I confirmed. "I'll be sure to tune in, though. Good luck!"

I offered my hand and made my escape.

Back at the West Wing, I stopped by RG's office to return Margari's sweater. We went into the bathroom to make the switch.

"You were fantastic on the show, darlin'," Margari said sweetly. "And the sweater looked good too."

"Thanks so much for hooking me up," I replied as I took one last whiff of the cinnamon scent trapped in the fuzz.

It made me crave cinnamon buns. Which reminded me that I'd skipped lunch in my nervousness about the show.

"I loved how you stuck it to that gal," Margari continued. "Carlton Block seemed to really like you too."

"You think?"

"Yeah, I watch him every day and I've learned his body language."

"I didn't know you were such a fan," I replied.

Maybe I could have gotten an autograph for her. Or a phone number.

"Well, he really knows what he's doin'. And he's easy on the eyes," she added with a grin. "Anyway, when he likes a guest, he always tugs on his shirt cuff while they're talkin'. It's almost sexual the way he does it. And he was tuggin' away for you, honey!"

I blushed.

"Well, all I did was regurgitate everything Lincoln told me to say. So it was really Lincoln who was impressing Carlton."

"No, I think it was you," Margari disagreed. "Lincoln mighta said similar things had he been there instead, but somehow I doubt he woulda filled out this sweater in quite the same way."

I grinned.

"How's it going with Speck Johnson?" I asked.

Margari looked embarrassed.

"Oh, he still calls every other week, but RG's sick of talkin' to him, so I have to come up with excuses for why he's unavailable. Which isn't hard to do, but I feel bad about it. Just pointin' out the fact that RG's the vice president and too busy to talk politics with random movie stars seems a bit harsh. All Speck wants is to be buddies with him."

"Is he still planning a D.C. trip?"

She nodded.

"Sometime in the next couple months. Maybe for a state dinner or somethin'. He told me he's gonna bring me a present."

"Really. Well, that sounds flirtatious. What do you think he's going to give you?"

"Oh, probably a Ferrari," she said airily. "That's what he gets all his girlfriends, right?"

I knew from my former trashy magazine reading days that this was indeed his gift of choice. Just like I knew from my current history refresher course that Napoleon's wedding gift to Josephine was a gold medallion inscribed "To Destiny." Whether this information was more or less relevant to my life than Hollywood trivia was a matter of debate, but I imagined Napoleon's legacy would continue to be significant long after Speck Johnson's box-office glory had faded.

When I returned to my desk, Nick was waiting.

"Hey, Lincoln wants to see you." He indicated Lincoln's closed office door. "Stephanie's in there now, but he said for you to come in whenever you got back."

"Okay, thanks," I said as I crossed the room.

I knocked softly before sticking my head in. Lincoln was perched on the edge of his desk and Stephanie was pacing the room in long, confident strides. One of her profiles had mentioned that she'd been a dancer in college, but she struck me as more of a marcher. I imagined she and Lincoln had been having a strategy talk about the India deal. Would Stephanie have told Lincoln anything about the president and Focusid? They'd never been particularly close and they seemed to collaborate only on policy issues, so probably not. Even though they both reported directly to the president, Stephanie was a part of Wye's tight inner circle while Lincoln was not. It wouldn't necessarily be a bad idea to bring Lincoln into the loop, though. He was the kind of person who could keep a secret.

"There she is," Stephanie said when she spotted me.

Her hair was in two coiled braids. I thought I could see a black Sharpie sticking out of one of them, stashed there for easy access. One could never be sure when a White House report might need to be edited on the fly.

"Come on in," Lincoln encouraged. "You're our new favorite spokeswoman."

I smiled, happy I hadn't messed anything up.

"Seriously, you were pretty good," Stephanie said.

Had the spokeswoman comment not been serious?

"It's all thanks to Lincoln," I replied. "He told me everything to say."

"Oh, please," he said dismissively. "You already knew all that."

Which was true to a certain extent, but Lincoln had really drilled in the points that needed to be stressed. Plus, he was the whole reason I'd been on the show in the first place. Or at least his shyness was.

"The lifestyle drug comments were brilliant. And a great setup for our conference announcement," Stephanie said.

"Lincoln said I should make that link. I hoped to have more time, but everything went so fast."

"You prepped the lifestyle stuff?" Stephanie asked Lincoln. "I should have known."

"I thought it would be good to get in there," he admitted.

"I probably wouldn't have thought of it on my own," I added. "But then Laura gave a great opening for it."

"And you jumped right in!" Lincoln said proudly. "You were great. You controlled the show."

"Well, they were your words."

Lincoln looked as though he was getting annoyed that I persisted in giving him the credit. It did seem like the conversation was going in a bit of a circle. Stephanie looked thoughtful.

"You know, that Dr. Singh character has asked me on his show," she said. "Maybe I should accept to keep this publicity rolling. Or maybe you should go," she said magnanimously.

"It's funny you should say that," I replied. "He actually asked me this afternoon if I would consider being his sidekick."

Lincoln smiled. Stephanie seemed confused.

"You mean on his show?" she asked. "Like a permanent position? Something you'd leave the White House for?"

"That's the idea," I confirmed. "But I turned him down, obviously."

"Thank goodness," Lincoln said. "I don't want to lose my sidekick to Wild Singh."

I laughed.

"No danger of that," I assured him.

Nick's voice came through the intercom on Lincoln's phone.

"The vice president would like to speak with you, sir."

I moved to the door. Stephanie stayed put.

"We need to meet in the next day or two about the lifestyle drug conference," she said to Lincoln. "It's going to be difficult to plan it with all the midterm election work we need to do, but we'll just have to find some time."

"Definitely." Lincoln nodded.

As he went to pick up his phone, Stephanie looked down at her watch.

"Christ," she muttered under her breath before hurrying off without saying good-bye.

She looked like she was headed for a dark mood. I feared for any White House tourists in her path.

Back at my desk, there were five messages from my mom. The first few were in an indecipherable pitch. She'd certainly been excited about the show.

"Hey, Mom, I need to leave room on my voice mail for actual work business," I said when she answered the phone.

"Nothing is more important than a mother's love," she replied. "And I'm just so proud of you! You were terrific—holding your ground, getting in those digs. You showed them who's chief!"

My mother has a tendency to slip into British slang. It's another leftover from her Beatlemania days and a symptom of her ongoing Anglophilia. "Chief" was a part of this vocabulary, as was "gaffer" and "guv'nor." She just as easily might have said one of those.

"Thanks, Mom." I smiled. "It was really Lincoln's doing. He got me on the show and he told me what to say."

"You were ace," she insisted, as if I hadn't spoken. "Really brill."

Okay, now she was getting a little carried away.

"I'm watching it again right now," she continued. "And then I'm going to take a nice steamy bubble bath."

"Okay, sounds good. I should go, Mom."

"Which reminds me that we should talk about Thanksgiving soon! I've been reading up on different turducken recipes. I'm considering a curry twist this year."

I got off the phone feeling pleased about all the positive feedback. This pleasant high lasted another couple hours as I motored through a pile of work, and then promptly disappeared with a trip to the coffee-pot. A new press aide had just taken the last of it. What was he doing up on this floor anyway? I glared at his turned shoulder.

"Oh, sorry," he said when he saw me. "You want this one?"

He offered his cup, which made my animosity disappear. I thought about taking him up on it, but who knew how many germs were in his mug, just waiting to infect me. Besides, I was already holding my own cup—my favorite one with a Magic Eye trick picture of Snuffleupagus on it that I'd won for myself at an Ohio state fair.

"No thanks. I'll just make another pot," I replied.

He nodded and moved off.

"And hey, I hope you're not worried about that LyingWye stuff. Everyone knows it's a crock," he called over his shoulder.

What LyingWye stuff? What was he talking about? I didn't ask this question aloud in time and he'd already rounded the corner. I instantly forgot about my caffeine craving and raced back to my desk, where I clicked onto the blog.

Under a headline that read "Cyrano de Hackerac" was a posting about me. Specifically about my appearance on *Right Now*. As I skimmed the piece, my mouth dropped open. It read:

> White House staffer Samantha Joyce is getting accolades for her cable talk show debut this afternoon, but the praise is misdirected. She was overheard confessing that her superior Lincoln Thomas "told me everything to say," according to an inside source. Wearing a low-cut red sweater in an attempt to distract from her deficient intellect, Ms. Joyce railed against the pharmaceutical industry and hawked the Wye administration's latest hackneyed scheme. One can only hope that the White House will rethink their policy of sticking incompetent bimbos in front of the camera in a transparent ploy to use sex to sell their silly policies. It's an embarrassment.

What?!? I quickly checked the rest of the article, which asserted that the White House had actually researched the effects of "sexual marketing" and had made a calculated decision to use young women as spokespeople even when they weren't the least bit qualified. It was a stupid, silly, offensive piece. Completely sexist and utterly inane. Yet despite all that, it left me shaken and upset. I was trying very hard not to cry as I glanced over at an accompanying snippet that claimed that the cost of transporting the drugs from India erased any presumed savings, since many of them were shipped in heavy, expensive, refrigerated containers. It included a breakdown of shipping and storage prices and compared it to the ease with which medicine from the western pharmaceutical companies circulated within the United States.

Both articles were just attempts to derail the Indian deals. I knew that, but I couldn't help but feel that I'd been unfairly smeared. Except that I actually *had* said that Lincoln told me everything to say. That was a real quote. But how on earth had it found its way to LyingWye? I briefly reviewed with whom I had spoken about the show. My mom, Stephanie, and Lincoln—and Margari, I almost forgot. The supplier of that "low-cut red sweater." Also, now that I thought about it, Nick had probably overheard my conversation with my mom, given that we shared an office. Or he might have even listened over the intercom when I'd been talking to Lincoln and Stephanie. Had he or any of the others talked to LyingWye? *Was* one of them LyingWye? I was beginning to feel nauseous.

I was pretty confident I could rule out my mom, as much as she'd love to consider herself a White House insider. And it couldn't possibly be Lincoln. Could it? No, of course not. He couldn't even handle a conversation with LyingWye. If he was a source for him, then he was an unconscious one. I'd worked closely with him for a while now, and I knew how loyal he was to the administration. He'd also been so genuinely uncomfortable with my giving him the credit he deserved. I crossed Lincoln off and cursed LyingWye for causing me to even momentarily doubt people who didn't deserve any doubt whatsoever.

With Lincoln crossed off, that left Nick, Margari, and Stephanie. Nick just didn't seem sophisticated or dastardly enough to fit the profile. Margari was sophisticated, but she was also always so helpful and sweet. We instinctively related to each other and would probably be closer if we'd had more chances to bond. Any tension we had was like the tension of siblings spaced too many years apart. Stephanie was another story. She and I had certainly become friendlier, but I didn't really trust her. Catching her at the peephole had been a shock, and I still couldn't believe that I'd joined in. Then the revelation that she was chummy with Chick Wallrey had been particularly disconcerting. There was a good chance that she had been the one who leaked the news to Chick about the trade deal before the official announcement. If they were legitimately friends, maybe Stephanie secretly shared Chick's disdain for the administration.

But that just didn't make sense. Stephanie *was* the administration—or an integral part of it, at least. She was Wye's chief political strategist, for God's sake. Tarnishing Wye's star would dull her own glow, and she'd be insane to sabotage her job security and so many important relationships. It would be tantamount to professional suicide. Then again, people *did* commit suicide. Had something driven her to the brink?

There was one thing that especially stood out to me about this latest hatchet job courtesy of LyingWye: it had been typically snarky toward Wye, but I really felt like I'd been the main target. Which meant that whoever had been the source could have been trying to damage the president and the trade deals, but perhaps they were just gunning for me. I tried to think of anyone who obviously disliked me. Sofia sprang to mind, as did Derrick. But I hadn't spoken to either of them about the show. Nick, Margari, and Stephanie were the only ones who made sense. Could Nick be hiding a dark side and a deep-seated resentment toward me? Did Margari just act as though she liked me, but secretly wished me gone? Or could Stephanie possibly feel threatened by me in some way? In my mind, I kept coming back to her. I didn't really believe she was the one feeding information to LyingWye, but I couldn't completely convince myself that she wasn't.

More people told me not to worry about the article on my way out the door that evening. And I caught a few interns pointing me out and whispering, unless I was just being paranoid. Apparently the entire White House staff read this traitor's blog on a very regular basis. I'd always assumed everyone else was appropriately dismissive of it and I'd been ashamed by my own more piqued curiosity. I'd checked it secretly and guiltily, worried that I was providing its Exterminator-funded host Web site with one more hit that it could use to increase its advertising revenue. I'd certainly never made the site a bookmark or anything. I'd kept up the subterfuge that I was a casual reader, even with myself.

The problem was that the blog was almost equal parts trash and truth. Guessing which posts fell into which category inevitably gave credence to lies and cast doubt on some stories that actually were accurate. I recognized that LyingWye often had an inside scoop, as much as I despised what he—if it really was a he—had to say. All the people who were pointing me out and telling me not to worry about the post knew this as well, which meant they might actually believe this latest piece was true. So perhaps people really did consider me a moron who couldn't think for myself. I wished I were still a TV virgin. The whole experience felt dirty now. LyingWye had really killed my buzz.

It was cold outside. October was an unpredictable month in D.C. A sleet storm could be followed by a seventy-degree streak. But tonight was decidedly chilly. I tightened my scarf and closed my jacket against the wind. And I picked up the pace to the Metro stop.

"Hey, Sammy," I heard a familiar voice call out behind me.

I looked back. It was Stephanie, crossing the street with a takeout sandwich. Her long black coat billowed like a cape. She was heading back to the White House. To work later, I presumed. Or maybe just to spy. Or smear.

"Hi," I said evenly, trying hard not to reveal my recent hostile feelings toward her.

"Do you have a second?"

She hurried over to me. I stayed still. If she wanted to talk, she could do the work. As she came to a stop in front of me, I noticed that her nose was red from the cold.

"Hey, I wanted to apologize," she said a little breathlessly.

Was this her confession? I'd imagined a more dramatic moment involving truth serum.

"For . . . ?" I prompted, feigning an ignorance I no longer suffered from.

"For thinking you were LyingWye," she said.

The ignorance came rushing back. In a way, it was comforting to be reunited with it. We spent so little time apart from each other.

"Excuse me?"

"I know, I'm sorry," she continued. "Figuring out who he or she is has been a side obsession of mine. It's initially why I wanted to get to know you better."

Okay. I was vaguely flattered that she'd suspected me of being so traitorous. People usually considered me boringly safe, to my chagrin. Still, this wasn't all good.

"But now that you've been so destroyed by LyingWye, I know it can't be you," she continued. "Because I don't think you're the kind of person who would go that far to cover your tracks. You have too much pride."

There were way too many things to react to here. I wondered if I could call for a time-out to process them. First of all, she thought the LyingWye article had "destroyed" me? Not the term I would have chosen and not one I enjoyed contemplating. Secondly, she thought I had too much pride? Obviously she hadn't spent as much time with my insecurities as I had. But the main thing was that she was probably LyingWye, and this whole conversation was designed to throw me off *her* track. She was the smart, psychotic one.

"I'm not the source," I said quietly. "Though given the quotes in the article, I have to assume the source is someone I talked to about the show. Or who overheard me talking about it."

"Which means who?" she asked.

"My mom, Margari, Lincoln, Nick, or you," I replied.

"And whoever they might have repeated it to," she continued, automatically crossing herself off the list with her pronoun choice.

She appeared deep in thought.

"You'd think we would have caught this person by now." She sighed. "It must be someone no one would ever suspect."

I just stayed silent as I watched her think aloud. Was this all a calculated performance?

"Well, hopefully it doesn't matter too much," she concluded with another sigh. "The site does damage, but none of it's been lethal yet. Just irritating."

"So you thought I knew all that stuff about Ernie Wye as well?" I asked. "About his relationship with Rosie Halters? And the baby?"

Now that I was remembering all that LyingWye had been responsible for, I was sort of pleased that Stephanie had suspected me. Maybe she was right, maybe I was too prideful. Though only when it came to imaginary and questionable accomplishments, apparently.

"Well, you're smart and observant and a good researcher," Stephanie answered. "You could have gotten to the bottom of a lot of that. Somebody did, obviously."

That was nice, but I doubted that she'd honestly suspected me. It just didn't make sense. I felt confused all over again. If this had been Stephanie's goal, she'd done a bang-up job.

Are you sure *you're* not LyingWye? I asked her in my head. I couldn't bring myself to say it out loud. I was a coward. A coward who was currently losing feeling in her fingers.

"It's really cold out here," I did manage to vocalize. "I should get going."

Stephanie nodded.

"Right. Well, anyway, I'm sorry for suspecting you," she said. "And don't worry about the piece. It's a compliment in a sick way. You're worth tearing down now."

I smiled ruefully.

"I think I preferred just being worth leaving intact."

Stephanie shook her head.

"Those people never go anywhere," she said as she waved good-bye with her gloved hand. "Trust me."

I wished I could.

Breaking News

———·•·———

I CALLED CHARLIE as I half-jogged through the morning fog toward the White House. It was only sixteen days until the midterm elections and I felt myself growing anxious, along with the rest of the town. Plus, the Metro trains had been running late and I didn't really have time for this call, but I wanted to hear Charlie's voice for just a second. I hadn't been able to make it up to New York over the weekend despite my promise, since the midterm crunch had set in. And he'd gotten too busy with his story to come down to D.C. again. I wasn't sure when the next time we were going to be physically together would be.

"Hi, love of my life," I said cheerfully when he answered.

"Hey," he replied. "I'm actually right in the middle of something important. Do you mind if I call you back?"

"Of course not," I fibbed.

I asked the same of him all the time, but there was a snobby part of me that felt I was more entitled to do so. I knew he had meetings and deadlines and important work obligations as well, but didn't he really have more control over his time? It's not like he was helping to run the country. He was just helping to criticize those who did.

As soon as I thought this, I felt guilty. I told myself that I didn't really believe it, that it was just a reaction to LyingWye and Chick Wallrey and my recent feelings of besiegement. I respected Charlie's job. And it was silly to invent conflicts.

I just wanted more attention from him. I could recognize that. He'd been appropriately indignant and protective when it came to the recent LyingWye article maligning me. He'd sent me flowers after the show and laughed with me about Dr. Singh's proposition, though he said he agreed that I could have a career in TV if I wanted to. I'd accused him of just trying to make me think I'd be good at something that would almost certainly require me to be in New York. He'd claimed not to have considered that factor.

So in a way, I'd had plenty of attention from him. But none of it had been the concentrated, hands-on kind that I craved. And none of it could make up for the irritating reality that he was presently living with some random woman who saw more of him than I did. Even her cat got more affection from Charlie these days, just by virtue of proximity.

Whenever these feelings of deprivation cropped up, I always turned a little against Charlie. I hoped that the tension it added to our relationship was good for us, that it kept us sharp and aware of the distance we needed to perpetually bridge, but I wasn't so sure.

My phone launched into Led Zeppelin just as someone standing nearby tried to get my attention. I was happy that Charlie was calling me back so soon. I wanted to talk to him, not some random tourist looking for directions. I kept my head down and moved to answer the call.

"Excuse me, it's Samantha, right?"

Now I looked up. At Carlton Block. Not your average tourist at all.

"Hi," I said, surprised.

We were just outside the White House gates. I thought I saw Derrick eyeing us.

"I thought it was you." Carlton smiled.

He had a good smile. And his eyes kept up with it. I thought about Margari's crush. Was she in the office? This was a good opportunity for them to meet if I could gracefully summon her somehow.

"Do you need to get that?" Carlton asked, pointing to my phone.

Of course I did. I flipped it open just as it went to voice mail.

"Just missed him." I sighed.

"Sorry to distract you," Carlton replied. "But I'm glad to run into you again. I wanted to ask you the other day—would you like to grab dinner with me sometime?"

He was asking me out? I noticed that he'd given his shirt cuff a little tug. I tried not to stare.

"Oh, wow, thank you," I said. "I actually have a boyfriend."

"Uh-huh," he replied.

"So I can't." I made it more clear.

In a town where having a husband didn't necessarily mean you weren't up for a date, the boyfriend excuse sometimes fell on deaf ears.

"Well, that's too bad. Maybe another time," he said with a wink.

"Actually, I plan on having this boyfriend for a while," I retorted.

There was no need for me to feel guilty that I'd just been asked out by another man, but I felt like demonstrating my devotion to Charlie anyway, even if it was to the brink of rudeness.

"Is that who was just calling?" Carlton asked.

"As a matter of fact, yes," I answered before thinking that it really wasn't any of his business.

"Interesting," he replied.

"Why?"

"Oh, just that you didn't answer."

He said this very casually and I tried hard not to let it rile me, because I suspected that was exactly the reaction he was gunning for.

"Not really. I would have if I hadn't been distracted by some random guy frantically flagging me down."

Carlton smiled.

"See you later," I continued as I walked past him.

"Bye for now," he said to my back.

I felt empowered for the six feet I walked to the guard post. I held up my pass for Derrick, who buzzed me into the guardhouse a bit quicker than usual.

"Was that Carlton Block?" he asked me.

It took me a half second to register the question because my ears had been trained to identify only insults and snubs from Derrick up to this point.

"Yes, it was," I answered in surprise.

I waited for further communication but Derrick didn't say another word. He just waved me on, back to his indifferent self.

I called Charlie back as soon as I was at my desk.

"Carlton Block just asked me out," I blurted.

"Congratulations," he replied.

Charlie rarely got jealous, which was another thing we didn't have in common. It came in handy for my double standard dabbling, but it was otherwise somewhat frustrating.

I wasn't informing him to make him jealous, I was telling him because I told him everything. Besides confidential work secrets.

"I said no, obviously," I continued.

"That's good to hear."

"It was the oddest thing. I ran into him on the street just now and he remembered me from the other day and then he just asked me out."

"You sound pretty jazzed about it."

"What? No! I'm just not used to something like that happening."

"I assumed you got hit on all the time," he said.

He did? Because that was certainly not the case. And if it was, he'd be the first to know. Didn't he tell me when anything like that happened to him? Had Amanda openly hit on him and he just hadn't mentioned it?

"Sammy?" Charlie checked to see if I was still on the line.

"Yep, I'm here. Um, I wouldn't say I get hit on *all* the time," I replied carefully.

I didn't feel like admitting that it very rarely happened. Or that I told him absolutely everything when it came to this topic, since that evidently wasn't what he either expected or matched in return.

"Well, Carlton Block's pretty hot. You sure you're not interested?"

"Shut up."

"And he's there in D.C. Superconvenient. A dreamy anchorman right at your feet."

"Are you done?"

"You tell me."

"How's the piece going?" I said, opting to change the subject before he got too much on a roll.

I liked that Charlie called me on any silliness, but sometimes he could take it a bit far and then one of us would end up angry for real.

"It's going well," he answered, his voice turning serious. "It might be sort of big," he added.

Charlie was modest when it came to his work, so I took this to mean it would be huge.

"Breaking when?" I asked.

"Fairly soon," he answered.

I stopped myself from asking again about the implications for the administration. I knew it wasn't fair.

"That's terrific," I said supportively. "And then can you come home?"

"I think it's going to be a series," he replied.

It *was* going to be big.

"Well, hopefully I can make it up there to celebrate after the midterms. I'm really sorry about last weekend."

"Stop apologizing. I had to work anyway. And you guys need to wrest the country away from the lunatics in charge."

"Aren't *we* the lunatics in charge?" I asked.

Which didn't necessarily negate his point, it just made it slightly more complicated. And it made me feel like a double agent, which was kind of sexy.

"Not without Congress."

It was true. Not being in control of the House and Senate had made things more difficult than I cared to dwell upon. It was enormously frustrating. Having the opposition in the majority prevented us from getting so much done that we had planned. But now we had a shot at turning the tables. In just sixteen days, we could create another reality.

"Don't jinx us," I said, suddenly very superstitious.

Not that he would want to. Politically, Charlie and I were on the same team. But he practiced being apolitical for his job and hated being accused of having an agenda. Dating me had opened him up to that criticism more than a few times in the past couple years, which I knew drove him crazy. He acted as though he just sailed above it, refusing to distinguish the disparagement with a serious response.

"Are there any races that you're particularly focused on?" he asked.

Yes, of course. There were a frighteningly high number of them in play, which meant that one party or the other could pull off a sweep that might drastically alter the political landscape. Or the two parties might split them, with one of us just coming up slightly ahead. We were in the minority, and we had a lot of ground to catch up, so any visions of legislative dominance seemed premature and irresponsible at this point. It was always important to dream big, but not to the point of suc-cumbing to fantasy.

"A few," I answered vaguely.

It wasn't that I didn't want to tell Charlie, because I did. I just didn't want to right at this moment. I was beginning to feel very nervous about the whole thing.

"Got it. Well, keep me posted. I should get going."

I didn't want to get off the phone. This had been happening a lot lately. Charlie and I would be having one of our normal conversations, even one in which my mind wandered over various work topics instead of staying fully focused on him, but then I'd be seized with sadness and longing as soon as it was time to end it.

"Wait. No," I said helplessly.

"What is it?" he asked.

"I just don't want to stop talking."

"Okay. I have to go into a meeting in five minutes, but we can talk till then."

"That's not enough time."

Charlie laughed.

"Well, can I call you after?"

He was taking my new clinginess in stride. I suddenly had a vision of a large desperate dog slobbering all over him. Ugh.

"Of course. Yes. Good luck with the meeting," I said, trying to pull myself together.

"I miss you, Sammy," he said softly.

"I miss you too."

I didn't care if he was saying it only because he sensed I needed that kind of reassurance and attention. I just lapped it right up.

We got off the phone and I redirected myself to my work. The Conference on Lifestyle Drugs was scheduled for the week after the midterms, which made its organization particularly challenging. It didn't help that the pharmaceutical industry was doing its best to discredit and derail it before it could even get going. My comments on Carlton Block's show had paved the way for the conference and subsequent legislation, but it had also tipped off big pharma as to what we were planning. They understood that the goal of the conference was to point out the frivolity of many of the new lifestyle drugs they were pumping into the market, and to shame them into directing *at least* as much money toward the manufacturing of drugs that people actually needed. If they would just provide these necessary drugs at reasonable prices, the administration wouldn't have to broker import deals with Canada and India.

The pharmaceutical industry was responding by attacking the new trade deal and waxing patriotic about American-made lifestyle drugs. They had just launched several thirty-second advertisements laying out the differences between happy, proven, life-enhancing drugs such as the ones that beat back dreaded toe fungus and keep people's hair from thinning, and dangerous, experimental, life-threatening drugs such as any that come out of India or other countries. The ads didn't address the fact that the deal we'd brokered with India had nothing to do with importing lifestyle drugs (except for the president's secret request for Focusid, which no one else knew about), but was instead all about access to medicine that regular people needed to simply stay alive. Thirty-second advertisements were rarely overly burdened by facts.

That afternoon, several opposition congressmen with strong ties to the pharmaceutical industry announced that they were launching a probe into the import agreement with India. Though the House had given the administration fast-track negotiating authority after RG had personally lobbied for it in a closed-door committee meeting, the pharma-funded congressmen were now claiming they'd been misled about the true purpose of the trade deal. Congress was always opening up probes, but I paid closer attention to this one since I was directly involved. And I didn't want to be probed. It sounded extremely uncomfortable.

RG summoned me to his office soon after the announcement of the probe. On my way, I passed Doug the Secret Service agent in the stairwell.

"Looking strong, Ishtar," he said.

He'd been calling me "Ishtar" since the camel incident. A few days after returning from India, I'd come into the office to find a DVD of *Ishtar* with one of the photos Doug had snapped of me riding the camel taped over the camel displayed on the front cover.

"Hi, Doug." I grinned. "Taken any bullets lately?"

"All the time," he replied. "I steal them from the supply closet and melt them down for mouth bling."

Capped teeth were in these days. And though he was obviously joking, I'd bet there was just such a supply closet hidden somewhere nearby. One night last year, I'd been working late outside of RG's office, keeping Margari company and using one of their office's infinitely faster color printers after their intern had left for the day. I'd looked out into the hallway at what I'd assumed was a broom closet. It looked like a broom closet at least. The fact that it was always locked hadn't really fazed me—I just thought the cleaning staff was particularly protective of their supplies. But then I'd watched two agents walk up, unlock the door, open an interior panel, and check the two shiny black Uzis that were resting on the inside rack.

The agents were just nonchalantly making their rounds, checking up on all the high-powered weapons stashed around the West Wing. It made sense that there would be such handy caches, but I still found it startling to be face-to-face with one that I passed every day and hadn't known existed. I often forgot that I worked in a place that some people spent a lot of time thinking about how they could destroy—and that there was a small army of agents at the ready to battle any possible attack. Were there ever a real scare, I now knew that machine guns would literally come out of the woodwork. And I'd just hide under my desk and hope that Doug was as good at shooting off his guns as he was his mouth.

I eyed this very broom closet as I turned the corner into RG's outer office. Margari looked up as I entered. A coil of her wavy black hair had fallen forward as she worked and was now perfectly blocking one of her eyes. She didn't make any motion to put it back in place as she smiled up at me. I was always intrigued by people who could just go about their business with huge locks of hair stylishly obscuring their vision. I had to resist the urge to tuck it back behind their ears for them.

"I heard you and Carlton Block had a little chat this mornin'," Margari said.

Had she been nearby? I'd wanted to make the introduction. Then Carlton Block could have hit on her instead of me, and everyone would have been happy.

"Yeah, did you see us or something?"

Margari shook her head.

"Derrick told me," she replied. "He's a Carlton Block fan too."

Oh. I wouldn't know. I wondered if Derrick had overheard Carlton's and my conversation and passed a summary of it along to Margari as well. Did she know all that had gone down?

Her phone started ringing before I could investigate. She tilted her head toward RG's closed door as she picked up the receiver.

"He's ready for you," she said.

Even with her head tilted, that hair coil stayed in place. I fought the impulse to reach out and fix it and instead busied myself with opening RG's heavy door. Margari had pressed the button under her desk to trigger the magnetic lock release, but still, the door was hard to open.

On the other side of it, RG was sitting at his mahogany desk, flanked by the collection of standing flags lining the wall behind him. He didn't look up from the memo he was attacking with violent pen strokes. I cleared my throat nervously.

"You wanted to see me, sir?" I ventured.

He paused his editing assault to register my presence.

"Sit down," he instructed.

This was rare. Normally I stood before his desk and received my orders or verbal abuse or whatever he was dishing out at the moment, and then retreated to my office to dive into a new assignment or lick my wounds or just continue as before. RG spent so much of his life being "on" for people, consumed with the constant pressure of a high-profile job that demanded vast reserves of time and energy, that he often just didn't have any to spare when dealing with his staff. I'd figured this out long ago and strove not to take his biting my head off personally. I didn't always succeed.

But RG hadn't just torn into me or barked an impatient command. He'd told me to sit down. Thereby immediately investing the situation with much more gravity.

I parked myself obediently on one of the stately, uncomfortable chairs that formed a little sitting area in front of the fireplace. As I eyed the army of family photos that had conquered a side table, RG rolled back his chair and rounded his desk to sit opposite me. He paused for a long breath, fully shifting himself into the moment. I felt a shiver race through me. It was fear I was feeling. And anticipation.

"I assume you've heard about the probe?" RG asked in his quiet, serious voice.

I nodded.

"Yes, sir. Is it a problem?"

"It could be," he said simply. "They're saying I claimed that we just wanted to *supplement* the stock of drugs we were already getting from American pharma companies, instead of being honest that we were going to strike a deal that essentially *replaces* that supply with the cheaper, foreign one."

I nodded again. I'd learned as much from the press release announcing the probe. What I didn't know was if RG *had* purposely misled them. Was I allowed to ask that?

"It's semantics," RG continued dismissively. "And it's all just because the congressmen who are funded by big pharma are under fire for authorizing the trade negotiation to begin with. So now they're claiming they've been duped."

"But they can still vote against it when it comes before the House," I replied. "Whether they feel they were tricked into authorizing its negotiation or not will be a nonissue—why waste time and money on a probe?"

"To save face with their biggest bankrollers. They feel the need to prove to big pharma that they were conned. And that they're gonna fight this all the way."

I sighed. The games that were played in D.C. sometimes left me exhausted before they'd even really started.

"I'm not that worried about what they say about me," RG continued. "I didn't do anything illegal. If they didn't grasp the vision I laid out, that's their problem."

He sounded definitive and resolute, which helped beat back the shakiness I'd been battling since he'd instructed me to take a seat. But then he shifted and gave me a grave look, which brought my tremors right back. I focused on keeping still.

"But even though the probe isn't justified, it could still do serious damage," he said solemnly. "Because to make a big show of things, they'll ask to look at all internal communication regarding the Indian deal. Including any notes you made in the meeting over there."

RG was looking pointedly at me. I understood now. This was about Focusid. We'd procured the drug in a side deal during the negotiations, asserting that it was for clinical trials. And it had in fact been intended for a special clinical trial involving the president's father. In our minds, we'd only been bending the rules to speed up a process that could ultimately help millions of Americans since the FDA was likely to approve some version of Focusid eventually. But approval could take years, and until then, Focusid was illegal in the United States.

If the probe uncovered the fact that we had obtained some, they would want to verify for whom and why. Which might lead them to the scandalous fact that the Focusid we'd acquired for a clinical trial had somehow become the president's personal supply. I was still having trouble wrapping my brain around this development. Accepting it meant acknowledging that I had unwittingly acted as an illegal drug broker and mule for the president. Not something I planned to highlight on my résumé.

RG must have discovered the president's dependence on his own— I hadn't told him about the peephole incident. Was that an oversight? Should he know? And did he comprehend that Wye was most likely using Focusid to combat the effects of his heavy drinking? I wondered how President Wye had first come to try Focusid. Had he intended to take it all along—to provide it for his father but also try some for himself? Or had he gotten the notion to take it after his father's death? It had occurred to me that perhaps Wye had grown paranoid about early onset Alzheimer's while watching his father suffer so severely. So perhaps he'd wanted to take the drug as a preventative measure and had subsequently realized how much it helped him concentrate and think, even on hungover days. Once this discovery was made, it was easy to see how Wye's use of Focusid might have evolved rapidly into a habit he depended on to manage the symptoms and impact of his alcoholism.

But did RG grasp all of this? Had he thought through this as well? Probably, knowing him.

"So you might want to just go over those notes," RG continued carefully, "and pare them down to the essentials."

I didn't intend to let the pause grow awkward, but I was a bit stunned at what I was being asked to do. It wasn't against the law, but it definitely didn't feel 100 percent right.

"Yes, sir," I replied, barely keeping my voice from quivering.

"No one's issued a subpoena for the notes," RG emphasized.

He didn't add the "yet," but we both knew it was implied. I nodded again. Neither of us was proud about discussing this, but it needed to be done. Tracks had to be covered.

"I am almost positive that there's no recorded mention of *anything* besides the trade deal," I said. "I remember deciding at the time that the president's phoned-in request should remain an off-the-record one."

A ripple of relief passed across RG's features, though they retained their somber cast.

"I'm glad to hear it. But we need to be certain," he intoned.

"I'll double-check everything," I promised. "And I'll touch base with our Indian counterparts to reiterate the confidentiality of that part of the deal. It's in their economic interest to do what we ask."

"Good." RG nodded.

I could tell he wanted to be done with this conversation, as did I. Since the investigating committee hadn't made a request for these documents, what we were discussing wasn't technically unethical. And I wasn't going to let myself accept the notion that this was somehow shady, or a preemptive cover-up. We were simply preparing. And protecting. There was nothing wrong with that. Was there?

At the end of the day, I knew where my loyalties lay. For me, this wasn't about the president, though I certainly had a vested interest in his protection. This was about RG. He had looked at the larger picture and seen the potential dangers on the horizon, and he was guarding against them. He was doing his duty. And he was asking for my help. It occurred to me that I could be witnessing the beginning of something either very noble or very self-destructive. Or possibly both. Sadly, they weren't necessarily mutually exclusive.

"I believe that's all," RG said.

I stood up to leave.

"Um, sir?" I cleared my throat.

"What is it?"

He had already returned to his desk and engrossed himself in his computer. I wondered how long it would be before people just got microchips installed in their brains and they could log on to the Internet with a blink of the eyes.

"About Focusid . . . are you aware of how it could be used to treat certain conditions? Certain dependencies?" I asked.

I knew that he most likely was, but I wanted to make sure. I also planned to tell him that Stephanie knew Wye was taking Focusid. And possibly about my suspicions regarding her.

"I'm aware of all the facts about Focusid," RG replied.

There was sadness and warning in his voice.

"And I don't think we need to go any further into it," he continued. "There are aspects of this situation that should remain undiscussed."

Maybe I'd just tell him about Stephanie later. I nodded in the direction of his downturned head before making my escape.

After reviewing my files for anything incriminating relating to Focusid, I placed a call to Mythri Patel. I'd e-mailed with both her and Tara since the India trip, thanking them sincerely for the lunch and insincerely for the camel ride. They'd encouraged me to come back to India for more adventures and promised to tell me if they ever made it to the States. I wondered how I could repay them. Did Hells Angels give tourists joy rides for the right price?

Since I needed to discuss the Focusid arrangement without leaving any kind of electronic trail, I opted to call rather than e-mail. It was nighttime in India, but Mythri answered her work line.

"Tanbaj Laboratories, this is Mythri speaking," she said in her crisp imperial tones.

"Mythri, hi! It's Sammy Joyce."

"How are you, Sammy?" she said warmly.

"I'm good, thanks. Listen, I know it's late so I won't take too much of your time. I just wanted to check in about the Focusid supply we procured for our research team. As I mentioned at the time, we really need to keep that arrangement between us, given the sensitivities involved."

Mythri, of course, didn't know who specifically had been behind the

Focusid request. We'd simply intimated that it would be used for a test trial and left it at that.

"Absolutely," she replied cleanly. "You can count on complete discretion from us."

That's what I'd hoped. It certainly behooved them financially to keep our confidence, and that was generally the most foolproof insurance.

"Fantastic. Thanks, Mythri."

"Now, I assume you're aware that a Dr. Humphrey from the White House has made requests for additional supplies of Focusid?" Mythri said.

"Yes," I bluffed. "He's affiliated with the National Institutes of Health."

And the president's personal physician, which was public knowledge.

"Well, you don't have to worry," she said smoothly. "No one will hear about any of this from us. A reporter by the name of Chick Wallrey from the *New York Times* was asking about the deal a couple weeks ago, but we commented only on the official aspects of it, of course."

"Fantastic. Thanks so much, Mythri."

I got off the phone slightly short of breath. I couldn't think about all the ways things could go wrong. I'd just keep moving forward.

Joining the midterm campaign frenzy helped with this plan. I didn't like that they were called midterms. The word reminded me of college exams and made me feel anxious about not having studied enough. Which was sort of the case. I'd been following a few races here and there, but I didn't know as much as I should about where it all stood. I'd been distracted by everything else. And there were legions of others in this place whose job it was to know all there was to learn about the upcoming elections.

According to the latest poll numbers, things weren't looking good for the administration. The president's approval ratings were distressingly low, thanks in large part to the beating he'd taken in the latest spate of campaign commercials. The opposition had been capitalizing on people's frustration with the pace of change to link candidates to the president and smear them all with the same critical brush. And it seemed to be working so far.

It didn't help that Wye appeared to be ducking the press. Ever since his father's funeral, he'd kept a very low profile. And he had yet to make a public statement about his newly discovered infant half brother, though the White House was being showered with baby gifts thanks to the Exterminators' exuberant promotion of the baby registry they'd set up in honor of the new arrival.

Wye was scheduled to travel around and campaign for select candidates in the days leading up to the election, and I hoped he was up to the task of winning people over to our side. He was incredibly charismatic when he wanted to be. When he was himself. But there wasn't concrete evidence that he'd been that lately.

"Are you nervous?" I asked Lincoln when we were ten days away from the election.

"Very," he replied.

The numbers had gotten even worse. We weren't looking at a landslide situation, but it appeared the opposition wouldn't have any trouble hanging on to their majorities in both the House and the Senate. And they were now on pace to pad them considerably, which would just make our jobs that much harder for the next few years. We'd been slogging uphill this whole time; to watch the path grow even steeper and rockier was demoralizing.

And then Charlie broke his story.

He called to tell me it would be on the *Washington Post* Web site late at night eight days before the elections. He didn't want to stay on the phone with me while I read it, so I promised to call him after. It was quite a scoop.

Charlie had first become interested in a Manhattan-based research firm called Trojan Lion after it had circulated press releases listing a number of prestigious-sounding awards won by its in-house scientists. Charlie had vaguely recognized the name of the lifetime achievement award recipient and, after a little bit of research, had discovered that it was the same man who'd been sued several years previously by the National Academy of Sciences for using its official letterhead to publish his report on how strip-mining actually helped regenerate and replenish the earth. At that point, Charlie had decided to delve deeper.

As Charlie soon discovered, although Trojan Lion took pains to present itself as a research institution, it actually operated as a corrupt clearinghouse for fake science. The firm paid a handful of "scientists" exorbitant salaries to propagate sham studies that supported the political views of its clients, many of whom had close ties to Capitol Hill. In fact, Trojan Lion studies that claimed global warming was a hoax or that teaching creationism resulted in tremendous psychological benefits for students had been referenced frequently on the House and Senate floors. It turned out that the twelve senators and congressmen who'd most regularly invoked the suspect discoveries of Trojan Lion's crack research team enjoyed embarrassingly extensive financial and ideological ties to the firm and its extremist backers.

Charlie uncovered all of this. His article included scathing condemnations of Trojan Lion's practices from every major respected scientific institution, along with a testimonial from a retired Trojan Lion researcher who admitted that the firm's philosophy was to create as much doubt as possible in the minds of the public on issues that would normally be regarded as fact. Like the addictiveness of nicotine, the reality of a worsening climate crisis, and evolution. Asked whether he'd truly believed that these tenets weren't clearly established truths, the former hired hand wryly noted that there had been way too much money involved to let a little thing like reality get between him and his paycheck.

Of the twelve politicians connected to Trojan Lion, ten were up for reelection in the next week. And all ten were members of the opposition. Overnight, the political landscape changed. The Trojan Lion Ten, as the implicated politicians quickly came to be called, had all been ahead in their respective races. No doubt the cash that had flowed freely into their campaign coffers from the Trojan Lion board members had partly helped them achieve their leads. But now they were steeped in scandal with little hope of dissipating it or clearing their names in time.

Not that their names deserved to be cleared. The article laid out compelling cases against them. From the e-mails that Charlie had managed to procure and the retired researcher who'd betrayed his former employers and become an invaluable source, a solid and sordid picture of corruption emerged. All of the lawmakers in question had sponsored legislation based heavily on Trojan Lion's fake science. And all of them had thought they'd gotten away with it. Until now.

With some assists from the White House, the candidates running against the Trojan Lion Ten jumped all over the allegations. The story spread rapidly, fanned by the media's lust for scandal, and soon it was everywhere. Television, radio, newspapers, magazines, the Internet—there was no escaping it. The politicians who had been so successfully capitalizing on Americans' frustration with the slow pace of change just days before were now scrambling to explain why they'd been recklessly peddling false science for political gain. They were overwhelmed by the story, and by the time the polls opened on election day, the trends in every single one of their races had reversed. Which was all that we needed. The momentum tipped over into other contests and by night-fall, we had won both the House and the Senate.

Both were nearly evenly split, but we had the majorities. I felt our steep, rocky road smooth and flatten. It would still be a trek, but hopefully one with fewer stumbles.

People were in festive moods and a rare, impromptu party came together in the Roosevelt Room, where many of the staff had gathered to watch the returns. As I slipped through the doorway, I scanned the crowd of fifty or so people who were drinking beer and congratulating one another. The long wooden table that usually took up the middle of the room had been removed and three large television sets had been wheeled in for election-result viewing. They were now all displaying various victory acceptance speeches.

Despite the atmosphere of revelry, I couldn't overcome an uneasy feeling. I was certainly thrilled that we'd triumphed in the elections, but I wondered if Wye was in good enough shape to take full advantage of this windfall. I helped myself to a bottle of beer and eyed the portrait of Teddy Roosevelt above the fireplace as I popped off the cap. He was in his Rough Rider uniform, on a rearing horse. I wished I could borrow some of his confidence.

All of a sudden, a cheer went up. I turned to see President Wye entering the room from the Oval Office, smiling and slapping people on the back. RG wasn't far behind.

"Great work, everyone," Wye shouted, beaming.

He was jubilant, and very wired. It was RG who looked drained and stressed. But all eyes were on Wye.

"We've got a lot to celebrate!" he whooped.

I felt the giddiness in the room amp up several notches. Wye's happiness was a precious prize.

"Can I get you a drink, Mr. President?" Sofia piped up eagerly.

A mini-hush fell over the crowd and I had to remind myself that to most of the people in the room, Sofia's offer had just sounded a bit awkward in light of the president's frequently advertised abstinence. Because Wye was such a vocal teetotaler, the mere suggestion of alcohol seemed taboo.

"Like a Diet Dr Pepper," Sofia clarified, flushing. "Or juice or water."

Wye smiled magnanimously.

"No thank you, I'm just gonna soak up all this love in here," he said smoothly. "I'm proud of this team. I knew if we pulled together and really focused, we could do this. And by God, we did!"

There was an enthusiastic chorus of "yes, sirs" and "we got 'ems!" Behind Wye, RG was nodding and smiling his strained smile. I recognized in his expression the somberness I also felt—the somberness of secret worries. To RG's left, Stephanie was leaning her tall frame against the door, observing Wye's euphoria. She met my gaze and raised an eyebrow. I looked away.

Wye happily made his rounds, oblivious as the rest of the group to our silent concern. He was in his element, hugging his staff and openly adoring the moment. He knew he'd been dealt an extremely lucky break. He knew that finally having a cooperative Congress could mean huge things for his legacy. And he was focused on how good all of this could potentially be. Very, very focused.

Paths Not Taken

———·———

SOON AFTER, I slipped out to call Charlie. We'd first gotten together on election night two years ago—the night that Wye and RG had won the presidency. And we'd decided then that election night would be our anniversary, even though it didn't fall on the same date every year. So since it was our anniversary, I was half-expecting Charlie to show up and surprise me. He knew I couldn't leave D.C. I knew that he was extremely busy as well, but I'd been hoping all day that he'd find a way to come to me.

"Hi!" I said happily when he answered.

I wondered if he was on the train. Or maybe he'd taken the shuttle and was already in a cab. I felt a little shiver of anticipation.

"Have you seen LyingWye?" he asked.

Hmmm. Not an auspicious beginning to the conversation.

"Not in the last couple hours," I replied cautiously. "How come?"

"It claims that I'm a hired gun for the administration. You're mentioned."

"You mean that we're together?"

"Yes. You know, I didn't go after this story for political reasons. These guys' party affiliation didn't matter to me at all. The fact that they were linked to a corrupt scientific research firm was the thing of interest."

He sounded so agitated and defensive. Oh, dear. I'd been hoping for romantic and attentive. Maybe I could bring him around.

"Of course," I answered calmly. "That's what turned you on to the story in the first place."

"Right."

"It's ridiculous to question your motives. You're a proven investigative reporter."

"Exactly. And I've broken plenty of stories that have actually *hurt* the administration," Charlie pointed out.

I was all too aware of that. He'd almost cost us the election two years ago when he'd broken the news that Wye's stump speech was essentially plagiarized from the speeches of an obscure local leader in southern India.

"True." I sighed. "But just between us, doesn't it feel better to help out the good guys?"

"No!" he almost shouted. "I wasn't trying to help anyone politically. I was just getting to the bottom of the story. I leave my personal feelings out of that."

Really? I didn't believe him. I knew he was rooting for us. Why couldn't he just admit it? It didn't compromise his integrity. The story was the story—the fact that it had brought about needed change was just a lucky benefit. Which he should let himself be happy about. At least with me.

"Well, I know you always *say* that, but you don't have to pretend with me. You know I won't tell anyone." I dropped my voice to a whisper.

"I'm not pretending," he said angrily.

Okay, maybe I should check out LyingWye before saying any more about this. It must be pretty bad to have affected Charlie this way.

"I'm sorry," I said, changing tack. "I'm just happy the elections turned out the way they did. And I'm happy for you that you pulled off such a huge scoop. I didn't mean to be insensitive."

"Got it," he replied.

His voice was hard. I heard a cat meowing.

"Where are you?" I asked.

"In my room. Why?"

He sounded combative.

"I was just wondering," I deflected, trying to mask my disappointment that he wasn't on his way to me. "I heard the cat."

"You've really got to get over this cat thing."

It was my turn to bristle. It wasn't the cat that was the problem, exactly.

It was the cat's owner, who always seemed to be around. Was Amanda there now, waiting to soothe his anger and celebrate his success?

"Maybe we should just talk later." I sighed.

"You called me" was the indifferent reply.

I was stung by his tone. It was our anniversary. Had he forgotten? Or did it just not matter that much to him anymore?

"My mistake," I answered bitterly.

He hung up the phone quickly. I stood in the hall for a moment, trying to process what had just taken place.

Margari rounded the corner, all rosy and soft.

"What are you doin', girl? Stop lurkin' in the hallway and get back to the party!" she ordered.

"Yeah, I will." I attempted a fake smile. "But can I jump on your computer for a second? I just need to check something."

Hers was so much closer than mine one floor up.

"All yours, sweetheart. No porn is my only rule."

"You're such a stickler," I complained.

She laughed and turned in to the party. I hurried to her desk and logged on to the Web site that hosted LyingWye.

The feature on Charlie wasn't a text post, as I'd been envisioning. It was one of the video blog puppet shows LyingWye occasionally found time to do in order to distinguish itself from the other political blogs. Though his inside access was really distinction enough. I clicked the play button with a feeling of dread.

I'd never seen myself depicted as a puppet. I can't say that it had ever been a particular dream of mine, but there was something sort of thrilling about being mimicked in felt form. There I was, on the little screen, a puppet in a red sweater that was cut to be much more revealing than the original. And my puppet was in a bed with another puppet that must be Charlie, whose glasses were twice the size of his head.

There was some puppet sex implied and then my puppet ordered the Charlie puppet to cook up some stories to help RG and Wye, threatening to withhold further action till he did so. This was all ordered in an unattractive, high-pitched mechanical voice. The Charlie puppet scrambled to comply. In the next scene my puppet was still in bed, but this time with another puppet in a suit. It wasn't Charlie. It looked sort of like . . . RG? I gasped and covered the screen with my hands, though I realized that wasn't going to do much to prevent other people from seeing it. Unfortunately, that just wasn't the way the Internet worked.

I was alone in the outer office. There was no one else around. I slowly peeled my hands away from the screen to see what this horrible blogger had created. My puppet was calling the other puppet "Mr. Vice President," confirming my fears. As the two puppets lounged in bed, post-inappropriate relations, the Charlie puppet entered waving a copy of the *Washington Post*. The Charlie puppet announced in a similarly high-pitched mechanical voice that the election was sealed up and he was ready for his reward, which was apparently to crawl back under the covers. The smutty little show ended with all three puppets in bed together.

There was an accompanying text post about how Charlie was dating me and completely beholden to the White House interest. It called for his editors to censure him due to this relationship, claiming that his credibility as a journalist had been destroyed. Like so many LyingWye pieces, it was stupid and trivial. And yet still hurtful and damaging. I wondered again who was behind this blog. Besides the Exterminator who funded the host site. Who was the turncoat he protected?

I clicked out of the horribleness, but not before confirming that I wasn't the only administration staffer being beaten up. It had felt that way lately, but LyingWye was nothing if not prolific, and there were plenty of others being skewered just as unfairly. We were all targets by virtue of our jobs. We dared to work here, so we had to live with the consequences, even when that meant living miserably. I glanced into the hallway at the broom closet. The Secret Service had weapons stashed everywhere in case of White House invasion. I wished they could protect us from other kinds of attack as well.

I called Liza, who was still at work, overseeing a cleanup at the Mayflower.

"Are you near a computer?" I asked.

"I've seen it," she replied.

"Does that puppet make me look fat?"

She laughed, which saved me. I needed to make a joke to keep from crying.

"So it's pretty bad, right? Charlie's furious."

"Did you talk to him?" she asked.

"Yes, but we spoke before I'd seen it. I didn't really get why he was so upset, because he's normally so mellow about criticism."

One of his other traits of which I was in awe. Occasionally, he seemed to come from another planet. Which I supposed fit in with the whole initial Clark Kent association.

"Yeah, but this doesn't just question his motives. It questions everything. And drags you through the dirt. I can see how he'd be livid," Liza said.

Apparently, LyingWye had gotten his slimy little hands on some kryptonite.

"He seemed mad at me, though," I answered. "Like I was to blame for it."

"I would guess he's just angry in general. Call him back. Can you?"

"Yeah," I replied.

I knew it was good advice. I knew communication was the key to weathering these rough patches, but I hated it when verbal, phone communication was the only option. I wanted to be able to look at Charlie when we were speaking. To touch his arm. I missed him in a visceral way. Even now, after he'd been a jerk.

"This is just a little blip," Liza continued. "The big story is the new majority. You guys won big!"

I wished it felt more like it. I got off the phone wondering whether to reach out to Charlie. Or whether I should wait till he'd had a chance to calm down or cool off or whatever he needed to do. Before I'd determined whether I was simply being wimpy, RG walked into his office. I jumped up from behind Margari's desk.

"Hi. I was just checking something on the computer," I explained too quickly and guiltily. "Congratulations on the elections, sir," I added brightly.

"It's good news," RG replied. "Charlie's article was a valuable piece of reporting."

"Yes, sir," I agreed. "He worked hard on it. I didn't know any of the details until it came out, but it was a pleasant surprise."

"Well, let him know that we're pleased about it too, if you like," RG said.

It was probably best to skip that. I wondered whether RG had been made aware of the LyingWye post. I certainly wasn't going to bring it up. I suddenly felt extremely awkward. It had only been my puppet in bed with RG's puppet, but those kind of insinuations had never even remotely been an issue before. It seemed practically sacrilegious to go there. Just wrong. If RG hadn't been RG, it wouldn't have been so troubling. My reaction had a lot to do with who he was as a person. Those sorts of vibes just weren't a part of his makeup. He lacked the aura of availability and moral flexibility exuded by so many of his colleagues. If it were Senator Bramen or Frand, even if it were President Wye in the puppet show, it would make more sense. The vibes were there with them. But not RG.

"How are Jenny and the twins?" I asked loudly.

"They're fine, they're fine," RG answered distractedly.

He'd been preoccupied, but he seemed to suddenly realize that he didn't actually have to stand here and talk to me.

"I'm on my way back to them now, actually."

Which is what he always did. He worked incredibly hard, and then he went home to his family. Other people found this boring. I found it interesting, if only because it was so different from how almost everyone else in this town operated. The self-important cocktail circuit struck most people as mandatory, but RG had snubbed it from the beginning. I respected him for his choices, but also wondered if he might possibly consider indulging the political society types every so often. As inane as the circuit was, it did serve to strengthen relationships that could come in handy, and I could imagine a future in which RG might wish he had more of these friends, fickle and false as they were. Given recent developments, that future might be closer than we'd bargained for.

"I, um, took care of the India situation," I said uncomfortably.

RG just nodded, but I saw a kind of guilty gratitude in his tired expression as he moved past me into his private office.

"Good night, sir," I said quietly to his back.

I didn't call Charlie back as Liza had suggested. Instead, I rejoined the party and drank more beer in an effort to forget about everything that was bothering me. President Wye had left by the time I returned, but excitement lingered in the air. Even among staffers who saw him on a fairly regular basis, Wye was consistently able to work a unique charismatic magic.

When people started talking about moving the party to a nearby bar, I took my leave. A half hour later, I called Charlie from the quiet, messy comfort of my bed. I was definitely buzzed, and I now felt ready to talk. The only problem was that he didn't answer.

"Just stay calm," I coached myself as it went to voice mail for the second time. "Crazyland is closed for the season."

But I felt the frenzy building within. Unavailability automatically provoked my suspicions, even more so when it came on the heels of an argument. All thanks to my cheating ex-boyfriend, who had really done a number on me. I hoped he'd never know that, wherever he was right now. Someone had mentioned in passing that he'd moved back home to Florida. I wondered what he was doing there.

No, I didn't. I didn't care.

But dammit, I sort of did, I groaned in realization. Why? Why did I care? I hated Aaron. And I was certainly over him. Over, over, over. So, what? Was it just curiosity?

I'd discovered Aaron's cheating after figuring out the voice mail code to his phone. It had been a remarkably easy code, actually, just two digits repeated. And all his saved messages had been from the other woman he'd been sleeping with over the course of our entire re-lationship. Listening to them had made for one of my more miserable evenings. And it had led to an extraordinarily dramatic breakup.

Could he have possibly kept the same code? I wondered. He'd used the same one for his home number and his cell. But there was a good chance that neither number still worked. He'd obviously have a differ-ent home number if he'd moved, and he most likely would have changed his cell phone number in the last few years. Particularly after Zelda and all her telemarketing friends had called it incessantly to tor-ture him in a generous act of revenge on my behalf.

Still, maybe he'd kept it. He was lazy when it came to anything re-motely connected to personal accountability.

I shook my head hard to stop myself from thinking about Aaron, but it didn't work. I was still thinking about him, and now I had a headache. Though that could also be a hangover setting in early.

I picked up my phone and dialed Charlie. Answer, answer, I willed from afar. It went to voice mail yet again.

I hung up. And then, without letting myself really think about what I was doing, I dialed Aaron's cell, pressing *67 to block my outgoing number. It surprised me how easily his number flowed right off my fingertips, as if I'd never stopped dialing it. It rang and rang. I kept my finger on the hang-up button, primed for a quick escape should it be necessary. But he didn't pick up. And it didn't go to a recording telling me the number was no longer in working order. It went to his voice mail.

"Hey, this is Aaron. You know what to do."

I gasped a little as I hung up. It had been such a long time since I'd heard that voice, and the sound of it triggered a rush of emotions and memories. Some truly terrible ones of course, but they weren't all bad. I sat there feeling a little stunned. What *was* Aaron doing these days? Did he think about me ever? Was he dating someone? Married? It had been more than two and a half years since our breakup. So much could have happened that I had no idea about.

I thought about calling back. I didn't really want to speak to him, but if it went to voice mail again, I could test his old code. Doing so was probably illegal and definitely a bad idea. I couldn't really claim it was a crime of passion by a woman scorned if that scorning was more than two years old. But still, Aaron had wronged me so thoroughly that I sort of felt authorized to meddle in his life whenever I wanted for the rest of eternity. I wasn't positive this argument would hold up in a court of law, but it made sense in my head. The four beers I'd drunk might have had something to do with that.

If only Charlie weren't refusing to take my calls, I wouldn't be contemplating something so beneath me. Charlie was the one for me. Where was he? Was it his code I should be trying to crack? I'd told myself that he was different, but was he, really? And even if he was, was I?

I pressed redial on my phone. It rang and rang and then Aaron's voice came on again. And this time, I pressed *5757#, his trusty old voice-mail code. Which turned out to be his trusty current voice-mail code. I couldn't quite believe it. Although actually, I'd never shared with him the details of how I'd uncovered his betrayal, so he hadn't ever been aware that I knew how to break into his voice mail. Which meant that he'd never thought he had any reason to change his code. And now I could listen all over again.

"You have one unheard message," the automated voice declared.

Uh-oh. There was no way to keep this as unheard. If I listened to it and didn't do anything, then it would come up as a skipped message for Aaron. Though maybe he'd just assume he'd skipped it somehow by accident. That happened to me sometimes. It was a drag.

I knew I should hang up, but I was just so curious.

"Hi baby, it's me. Listen, I'm sorry about earlier. I didn't mean to be jealous and of course I trust you. I know Lorraine is just a friend. Call me back to let me know you got this, okay? I love you, baby. I can't wait to get back home."

The woman didn't sound naïve, but she obviously was. I recognized in her voice a familiar tone of subtle desperation. Like she was determined to hang on to something despite all signs that she should run away. I knew what that felt like.

"To delete this message, press two. To reply to it, press three. To save it in the archives—"

I pressed 2 without even thinking about it.

"Message deleted. To listen to your saved messages, press one . . ."

Oh no, no, no. I'd erased it? It was not my place to do that. I'd meant to skip it. How could I have done that?

Probably because when I'd heard that female voice, I'd felt a surge of jealousy. I'd tried to ignore it, and now I was trying to trivialize it. And really, what was so surprising about it? Hearing Aaron's voice had thrust me automatically back to a time when he'd belonged to me, or at least when I'd thought he had. And getting flung back into that moment had briefly arrayed at my fingertips all the emotions that had informed our relationship. Surging, furious jealousy had been one of them. I felt something similar to it when it came to Charlie, but it was diluted by what I assumed was maturity. I was more grown-up now. I had fewer excuses for being utterly irrational.

So perhaps I'd subconsciously deleted Aaron's girlfriend's message on purpose. Maybe my rush of jealousy had provoked sabotage. If

Aaron never got that message, he wouldn't know to call her back, and that might be enough to push her over the edge and break up with him. Which is what I wanted. They weren't meant to be together, I felt sure. I wasn't positive how I knew this, it was just a powerful hunch.

"To listen to your saved messages, press one, to hear more options . . ." The automated voice was repeating my choices.

I pressed 1.

"First saved message . . ."

I was going in deeper. I knew that I should hang up and cease caring about whatever these messages said, but I felt held hostage by a greedy, inquisitive determination to know more.

"Hey studmuffin, it's Lorraine. You left your shirt at my place. I'm actually wearing it now. And nothing else. I want you. Call me."

This was a completely different woman. The Lorraine of the first caller's fears. Lorraine and Aaron's relationship certainly didn't sound platonic, despite what he'd been claiming. Subsequent messages confirmed that they were definitely more than friends, and, furthermore, that Lorraine had no idea that Aaron was seeing anyone besides her. There were also more voice mails from the first woman, who identified herself only as "me." From the sounds of it, "me" traveled a lot but lived with Aaron when she wasn't on the road. She'd evidently found out something about Lorraine, and Aaron had convinced her there was nothing to worry about. I hoped she'd figure out soon not to trust a word that he said. I didn't want to identify with her, but I couldn't help but sympathize. I knew what she was in for. I knew what they both were in for. And it wasn't fun.

I put down the phone, feeling weak and guilty. Was I happy that I'd listened? Was I happy to know that he was still the same?

I *was* pleased. It pleased me that he hadn't devoted himself to another woman. That those who were under his spell now were being just as tricked and manipulated as I had been. Aaron hadn't changed. I supposed men like him never did. I was lucky that I hadn't wasted any more of my time on him, because he was the kind of guy who would eat up your life completely if you let him.

I fell asleep wishing Charlie would call. Finally, around three a.m., Led Zeppelin startled me awake.

"Hey, am I waking you up?" Charlie asked a little too loudly.

"Hi. No. Yes, but it's fine. Where have you been? Are you all right?" I said, stuttering my way back into consciousness.

My mouth felt dry and fuzzy, like I'd been trying to eat a sweater. I took a huge gulp from the glass of water beside my bed.

"I went out with some friends to celebrate and the bar was really noisy. Sorry I missed your calls," Charlie said.

He sounded drunk, which was rare. I wondered who his fellow revelers had been. Had he and Amanda stumbled home together? I stopped myself from investigating because there were more important things to address.

"Listen, I'm sorry about earlier. I checked out LyingWye and I understand why you're so upset."

"Yeah, well, it doesn't really matter," he said with a sloppy shrug in his voice. "By tomorrow it'll be something else."

I didn't want to argue with moving on, but I needed to be sure this wasn't just his buzz talking.

"It *does* matter, if it causes problems between us," I replied.

I imagined what Charlie's breath would smell like were I lying next to him. It would be metallic with beer, or syrupy from vodka. All mixed with his warmth.

"I hated our conversation earlier," I continued. "I felt like you were pushing me away, and I already feel too far."

"I'm sorry," he said, sounding suddenly very upset.

He'd swung rapidly to remorse—the quickness of the trip courtesy of his lubricated state.

"I'm so sorry," he repeated, his voice ragged with emotion. "I just got so angry. I shouldn't have taken it out on you. I'm ashamed that I did."

Sober or not, Charlie was good at genuine apologies. Even in the past when I hadn't been as eager to restore normal relations, he was capable of defusing resentment with one or two true sentences.

"I love you *so much*," he continued fiercely. "I promise you, it won't happen again."

I believed him. It was nice to be able to.

We talked for another half hour. He was a sweet drunk—sentimental and open and almost childlike in his enthusiasm. He wished me a happy anniversary and tried to list his top two hundred favorite things about me. For my part, I was happy to be back on loving ground. I decided not to mention my Aaron episode. It just didn't matter.

A few days later, Charlie published a follow-up article on the Trojan Lion scandal, featuring incriminating e-mails regarding the politicians involved. The lawmakers had evidently attempted to hide their close ties to the ideologically driven research firm, and their correspondence revealed an awareness that it was a fundamentally fraudulent institution. Ever since their connection had been publicized, these senators and congressmen had been scrambling to salvage their reputations. But the damage had been done. They'd lost their elected seats and though they technically held their positions until their replacements were sworn in at the beginning of January, their power had dissipated. Their party's reign had come to an end.

Which meant that perhaps ours could really begin. With our new majority in Congress, we at last had the support we needed for the initiatives we'd been struggling to enact for nearly two years. We finally had the means to deliver real change—to prove that we weren't all talk.

The White House Conference on Lifestyle Drugs was poised to kick off amid this new optimism. I'd spent long hours organizing it, and had high hopes for its impact. I was also looking forward to working with a senator whom I'd long respected. Over the previous two years, Senator Lane Morris had written several bills advocating government regulation of lifestyle drugs. None of them had been passed, but she'd kept at it, trying her best to get her colleagues to focus on this burgeoning industry. This past spring, she'd written a powerful op-ed proposing hefty FDA fines for pharmaceutical companies that paid for sensational and misleading advertisements of their products. Given that every other ad on television lately sought to convince people that they were suffering from a condition that only a new expensive pill could fix, Morris's op-ed had created quite a stir.

She and RG had been friends for a decade and he was counting on her to help energize the conference, as well as to shepherd the groundbreaking legislation it would hopefully spawn. It was my job to work closely with her chief of staff to ensure that we were all in sync. We had scheduled yet another breakfast meeting, and as I sat in the restaurant of the Willard Hotel anticipating my pancakes, I checked my watch. Where was this woman? I was trying to tide myself over with my second glass of orange juice when Senator Morris suddenly pulled out the chair across from me. She was short and compact, looking cool in a gray silk suit that matched her startlingly compelling eyes. And she emanated a sense of purpose like few people I'd come across.

I stood up quickly in surprise. Had there been some sort of miscommunication? Was she under the impression that this was a breakfast with RG? Where was her chief of staff?

"I'm Lane Morris," she said as she stuck out her hand.

I knew who she was. Even before researching her lifestyle drug bills, I had admired her from afar. Since college actually, when I'd first become aware of her work. She was starting her third term as a senator from Wisconsin. She'd gone through an amicable divorce the year before after a twenty-five-year marriage that had produced two children. She'd never been a flashy speaker, but had always worked steadily and determinedly for her constituents, particularly on issues that impacted women and children.

"Samantha Joyce," I identified myself. "I'm sorry, I think there might be some sort of misunderstanding. . . . Vice President Gary isn't scheduled to be here. I thought I was meeting with your chief of staff to go over the conference," I finished as Senator Morris patiently waited.

"Oh, I know," she replied. "But doesn't that seem like one too many steps? I'd rather just talk with you about how we can move forward. I know the vice president has a lot going on. I'll just see him at the conference."

In my short but jam-packed time in D.C., I had never come across a senator who seemed less hung up on power issues. Anyone else would have made damn sure RG was going to be present before showing up for a meeting that could be easily handled by staffers. Senator Morris impressed me. I was flattered, actually. And determined to make the breakfast worth her while.

"Well, let me just let Vice President Gary know that you're here," I said. "I'm sure he'd at least like to have a word with you—he just wasn't aware that this was going to happen," I explained as I started hurriedly punching out a message to Margari.

RG could at least call and say hello. I knew that he was counting on Morris's championing this legislation in the Senate, and I'd been tasked with making sure she stayed happy.

Senator Morris put her hand on my arm to stop my frantic Black-Berrying.

"It's okay, really," she emphasized. "I think we're going to be just fine."

I smiled and stopped my manic typing.

"Okay, if you say so," I agreed.

We ordered breakfast and began talking about Senator Morris's latest op-ed.

"I just don't understand why more of your colleagues haven't seized on the significance of these drugs. Companies are spending more time pushing pills to keep people from going gray than on pills to prevent heart attacks."

Senator Morris nodded.

"Some people are catching on," she replied. "But we need to intensify the spotlight on the issue and frame it in a way that brings out this ridiculous disparity. And we have to be careful how we do it. We can't come off as anti-choice when it comes to the array of medicines the American public is entitled to. Of course, people can spend their money how they like. But they need to be able to see the stakes clearly."

I nodded.

"Well, I know Vice President Gary really values your leadership on this topic," I offered. "He's looking forward to your input and participation in the conference, since you've made yourself such an expert. He thinks it's an incredibly important issue, and hopes to do his part to bring about some progress on it."

Morris nodded.

"I'm glad he's come around on that," she said, though without any bitterness.

It was my job to know RG's positions on all health care issues, and I happened to be certain that he'd always been supportive of Morris's efforts. He certainly hadn't ever voted against them.

I pointed this out to her, and she held up her hand in an appeasing gesture.

"I didn't mean to suggest he wasn't helpful before," she explained. "It's just that he never did more than offer his 'yea' vote. If he's willing to actually publicize it and put a little energy into it, I'd certainly be grateful," she said. "Particularly now that he has the platform that he does."

It was impossible not to like her, even when she was implicitly criticizing RG. I normally defended him with considerable aggression, but I didn't feel the need to combat Morris's easy mix of charm and steel. Probably, because at the root of it, I agreed with her.

"Well, then, let's go forward with it," I said with a smile. "Are you happy with the structure of the conference?"

Senator Morris nodded.

"Yes, it looks fine," she replied. "To be honest, it doesn't really matter all that much what goes on there, just as long is it's not a disaster. The real point is the attention and focus it will bring. We need to parlay that into legislative victories."

"Absolutely," I said, though I felt the conference served slightly more of a purpose than that. But I was biased. After all, I'd been the person primarily in charge of putting it together.

And now I felt a little silly. Like I was naïve to have put so much emphasis on it.

"Could I make a suggestion?" Morris asked, as if I were the senator and she were an aide.

I just smiled stupidly because I couldn't think of any response that wouldn't make me feel out of place. Of course she could make a suggestion. She could probably order me to clear her plate and refill her coffee and I wouldn't bat an eye.

"Why don't we follow up the conference with a dinner on the Hill that evening?" she asked, brushing a stray blond hair out of her eyes. "Something high profile that will hook the people who can't or won't make it to the daytime sessions. It'll send a message that people really need to take this seriously."

I nodded like a banshee, or as I envisioned a banshee might nod—aggressively, to the point of possible injury.

"A dinner event, that's brilliant, great," I answered, trying to ignore her wry smile.

I was a little surprised at the effect she was having on me. I reminded myself that I was a representative of the White House, after all.

"That's great, because the conference is really more of a general showcase," I continued more professionally. "It doesn't target individual lawmakers. For the dinner, we can keep the guest list small and specific."

"Exactly," she replied. "We could invite a couple of the most dynamic conference participants and the twenty legislators we need the most. Why don't you have the vice president call me if he has the time, and I'd be happy to suggest some of the speakers and guests. Now . . . are you happy working in the White House?" she asked.

The check had arrived, she had insisted on paying, and we were definitely in the wrapping-up phase of the breakfast. Was I happy working in the White House? Of course I was. Overall, at least. Things had gotten a bit weird lately, but I mainly blamed the president for that. And I certainly did not need to go into all of this with Senator Morris, who was currently watching me carefully. I hoped my face wasn't giving away my inner monologue. It tended to do that.

"Oh, yes, I love working for the administration," I said sincerely.

I'd just leave out those other qualifiers. Senator Morris watched me for another moment and then smiled.

"I'm glad. They're lucky to have you. I can tell you're very bright. Do you have a card of some sort so I can e-mail you some of my health care contacts? I'm sure, given your position, that you have all the contacts and access you need. But you never know, they might turn out to be helpful for you."

I fumbled for a card and handed it over.

"Wonderful. Well, thanks for a very productive breakfast, Samantha. It's a real pleasure to meet you."

She shook my hand and smiled again before turning purposefully for the door. I followed her with my gaze, feeling like I'd just met someone very important. She struck me as a woman who knew how to get things done. Could I ever be like her? I wondered. She had almost thirty years on me, so there was at least time to practice.

I checked my BlackBerry on my way out of the restaurant. I had a few confused messages from Margari, who had apparently received a jibberish one from me—the result of my initial flailing in the face of Lane Morris's unexpected appearance. Checking my sent messages folder, I saw that I'd managed to send a real winner.

```
To: Margari Pastor [mkpastor@ovp.eop.gov]
From: Samantha Joyce [srjoyce@ovp.eop.gov]
Subject: rgggggg
Text: Senmorris bfast rgcall cannow
```

Very eloquent. Not surprisingly, Margari hadn't been able to decipher my meaning.

```
To: Samantha Joyce [srjoyce@ovp.eop.gov]
From: Margari Pastor [mkpastor@ovp.eop.gov]
Subject: Re: rgggggg
Text: Is this some sort of coded message? I don't get
it. Please explain or write "balderdash" if you are in
some kind of trouble and can't type freely.—Margari
```

I was just exiting the restaurant and reassuring Margari that I was safe and sound and in the business of sending letter-jumble BlackBerries when I walked straight into a newspaper vending machine. Ouch. I really had to stop typing when I walked. I looked down at where my upper thigh had hit the corner of the machine, expecting to see blood. If my leg was going to hurt this much, I wanted to have something to show for it. I had an extra tourniquet in my bag.

But there wasn't any serious damage. I'd just have to put up with the throbbing. I felt a wave of hostility toward the vending machine and thought about calling Charlie to let him know that his paper had indirectly caused me physical harm. But I decided that my rage wasn't worth the cell phone minutes. My bills were already gasket-blowingly high as it was.

Because of the expense and our busy schedules, Charlie and I had scaled back our phone time. We still connected at least once a day, but all too often it was *only* once a day. Our old practice of checking in every few hours had fallen away. And when we did finally reach each other, it was usually late at night and we were too tired to fill in all the gaps in our understanding of each other's days. I tried not to let this new routine bother me. The important thing was that we were still connecting at all.

Happily, RG thought the post-conference dinner was a great idea and told his scheduler to work it into his agenda. He also kicked off the White House Conference on Lifestyle Drugs in eloquent style. President Wye issued a formal statement in support of the conference and praised its goals, but didn't actually make an appearance. I wondered if other people found this odd, considering that it was a White House conference, after all.

Senator Morris led a fascinating plenary discussion, and the conference as a whole was well received, but it quickly became clear to me that the real progress on the issue would happen at the follow-up dinner.

Which, thankfully, proved to be a big success. We'd booked a private dining room at the Hilton and I'd helped arrange for the best of the conference speakers to repeat their presentations at this more intimate forum. A doctor who spoke about the cumulative effects of unnecessary lifestyle drugs on human immune systems proved especially popular. RG and Senator Morris both made compelling remarks followed by lively discussions with everyone involved, and the evening ended abuzz with interest over the pending legislation. I felt gratified and relieved.

Once the room cleared out, I made a round of the tables, collecting any notes or doodles that people had discarded. I felt a bit like a detective, sleuthing my way through people's forgotten reactions to the evening.

I was cross-checking a borderline obscene doodle with the seating chart when I heard someone delicately clear her throat behind me.

"I believe I left something in here," Senator Morris said, waggling a briefcase that she'd just scooped up from the floor.

I swiveled around guiltily. She laughed.

"Why do you look like I've caught you doing something you shouldn't?" she asked.

When I confessed why, she laughed again.

"Well, let's take a look," she said as she sat down beside me and examined the seating chart.

"Ahhh, Congressman Blythe," she said. "Yes, he's a bit of a rogue. But you know, that could just be a drawing of a snake in a basket after all."

Blushing, I agreed. I glanced at my watch.

"Wow, it's past ten already," I remarked in surprise.

The time really had flown.

"Is someone expecting you?" Senator Morris asked sweetly.

I thought about it. No, actually. Not anymore. Liza and Jakers had gone to a NASCAR race weekend in North Carolina to celebrate their year anniversary. And Charlie would be expecting a phone call, but that was about it.

"Just a couple of Japanese fighting fish," I said, with an unmistakable trace of sadness in my voice.

Morris put her hand on my thigh.

"Those are some lucky fish," she said, as she stared directly into my eyes.

Her hand felt warm and soft on my leg. But it was indeed on my leg—high up, on a part of my thigh that was generally off-limits to anyone besides me. And Charlie. I must have looked panic-stricken, because Morris smiled reassuringly.

"Would you like to go somewhere for a drink?" she asked.

I didn't feel any more violated than I did when a man hit on me. It's just that I normally felt slightly more prepared for such an event. I was genuinely stunned by this development. Senator Lane Morris? Of the twenty-five-year marriage to a man? Hitting on me? I felt briefly—if oddly—flattered. Then confused. Was I happy that she seemed to want me? Did that mean I might be gay? I'd never thought that was a possibility before. I considered it for a moment, considered not taking her hand off my leg. What would happen if I kissed her?

But the attraction wasn't there. I imagined that things were about to get even more awkward.

"Um, huh . . ." I laughed uncomfortably.

Morris removed her hand.

"I'm sorry, I didn't mean to offend you," she said quickly and easily. "You're just a very beautiful woman."

I didn't think I was. And at the moment, I was sweating and a little choked for air. Maybe she was into that.

She moved her chair away from mine in an effort to put me more at ease. I gulped in some air, which led to a spontaneous burp. I covered my mouth quickly with my hand. Morris smiled.

"Do you still find me attractive?" I joked.

Morris laughed.

"You're funny," she proclaimed. "But you're not gay, are you?"

No. I was pretty positive I wasn't. But was this something that everyone definitely knew for certain? Could I be a little bit gay, or did it have to be an all-the-way type of thing? I sensed it was probably the latter. In which case, I knew I didn't qualify.

I shook my head.

"Uh-uh," I said, somewhat apologetically. "But I love gay people."

Okay, that was lame.

"Sorry, that's a dumb thing to say," I continued. "I'm sure there are horrible gay people who I wouldn't love. I was just trying to say that being gay, or bisexual, or whatever, is not something that I would be ashamed of, if I were. It's not something I think *anyone* should be made to feel ashamed of."

Was I still sounding as awkward as I felt? Senator Morris smiled kindly at me.

"You're absolutely right," she said. "And I'm not ashamed, but my sexual orientation is something I choose to keep private," she added simply.

"Oh, I certainly won't tell anyone," I assured her quickly.

"I'd appreciate that, thanks," she said smoothly. "I'd just like to keep it under wraps if I could."

That was fine with me. But it brought up some interesting questions. Did I seem gay enough that Senator Morris assumed it was safe to make a pass at me? What was so gay about me? I wasn't mad about it—just curious.

"It's not that you seemed gay," she clarified when I got up the nerve to ask her these questions. "It's just that you seemed so sweet and open. I wasn't sure if you were or not, so I took a chance. But regardless, you did seem trustworthy, so I wasn't that worried about revealing myself to you," she said.

I really did like her quite a bit. She was old enough to be my mother, but had a different sort of assured wisdom about her. In a way, I could relate more easily to her, since we weren't constrained by any specific conventional relationship.

"If I were gay, I'd have a crush on you," I said impulsively.

I immediately couldn't believe I had addressed those words to a United States senator. That sentiment must have been etched on my face, because Morris patted my hand in a comforting and nonsexual way.

"Thank you. I knew you were sweet," she said.

She stood up and smoothed her jacket.

"Do you need a ride home?" she asked. "I promise I won't jump you."

I smiled but shook my head.

"I'm okay, thanks. Um . . ." I hesitated.

I wanted to ask her something, but I wasn't sure what it was. I felt as if something were slipping out of my grasp and I wanted to stop it. Not a sexual relationship, but something else. She looked at me expectantly.

"Uh, can we still be friends?" I asked, somewhat lamely.

What was wrong with me? Lane Morris didn't need me as a friend. She'd wanted a hookup and I hadn't been into it, end of story. She was too mature to be anything but polite about it, but I doubted she wanted to have much more to do with me. I blushed even deeper as I braced myself for a brush-off.

"Of course we can," she said kindly. "I was attracted to more than just your looks. I look forward to working with you and getting to know you better."

She really did sound sincere. And I wanted to believe her.

"Great," I said thankfully.

"See you around, Samantha," she replied, before walking out the door.

She certainly was a compelling woman. I imagined she didn't have trouble finding willing paramours. For a brief second back there, I might have been one of them.

Back at my apartment, as I sat staring out my window at the steady rain, it occurred to me that I should be grateful to Senator Morris for distracting me from all the other things I might have begun obsessing about this night. Like why Charlie was getting harder to reach on his cell phone. Or whether the president was drunk at this very moment and what his stumbles might mean for us all. In addition, I was very happy that my first experience being hit on by a senator had been satisfyingly unconventional and nonthreatening. I was almost proud of it. I sensed a dangerous double standard, but decided not to focus on it.

And so, while I waited for Charlie to return my call and felt my eyes grow heavy with sleep, my thoughts returned to Lane Morris and her crush on me. Sure, our country might be doomed. And the love of my life might be slipping away. But according to a fifty-five-year-old lesbian, I was beautiful. Not everyone had that going for them.

Plans Forsaken

JUST BEFORE THANKSGIVING, President Wye finally issued a long-overdue statement about his newborn brother, welcoming him to the family and asking everyone to respect the privacy of an infant who had every right to remain blissfully unaware of the global media ruckus he was causing. And to respect the privacy of the baby's mother, who was all too aware of the commotion, but should be spared more pain out of common decency. At Stephanie's urging, the Wyes had gone even further and extended an invitation to Rosie Halters and little Bernard to join them at the White House for a Thanksgiving meal. The White House spokesperson assured any interested parties that this would be a strictly private affair, which was really all that Rosie had wanted in the first place.

As for my own recent escapade, I'd been extremely nervous to encounter Senator Morris again, and had been relieved to find that our subsequent interaction had been smooth and professional and devoid of the awkwardness I'd feared. She acted as though nothing out of the ordinary had transpired between the two of us, treating me as warmly and respectfully as she had from the beginning. I enjoyed working with her on the conference bill, which thanks to the dinner had garnered significant buzz.

One person particularly irked by this buzz was our trusty opponent, the waxen Senator Frand. Still stung by his party's defeat in the midterm elections and reportedly having trouble coming to grips with the reality that he would have to relinquish his status as majority leader in early January, Senator Frand was more determined than ever to do whatever he could to foil the administration's plans. He still had a month and a half as the Senate's most powerful member and he seemed hell-bent to use that time for obstruction and revenge.

Toward that end, he had countered our conference dinner with a gathering of his own. He'd targeted senators and representatives who were on the fence regarding our push to redirect attention away from lifestyle drugs and toward lifesaving ones. He'd specifically homed in on the elderly, male members of this group. And for these members of Congress, he'd arranged an evening of food and drink, with a special guest speaker who could testify as to how Viagra had allowed him to maintain his lifestyle as "a full man." The crowd had been very receptive. Senator Frand could wax as moralistic as he liked, but he evidently agreed with many others that when it really comes down to it, sex always sells.

To be fair to Frand, his motivation probably wasn't purely revenge. He was firmly aligned with big pharma, and Viagra was one of their most lucrative drugs. He needed our legislation to fail, to protect his interests.

The gathering he'd arranged was supposed to have been a private event, but I read a snippet about it in *The Hill* e-news bulletin and had received several e-mails from various Senate staffer friends who were concerned that the evening had unduly influenced their bosses. Which was a serious problem. If Morris's bill was going to pass, I had to find some way to win these men back to our side.

The e-news snippet identified Frand's persuasive guest speaker as Ray C. Pullman, and described him as a New Jersey retiree with a vested interest in Medicare's coverage of Viagra. Apparently, he was just an average citizen with a story compelling enough to sway lawmakers worried about their future performances.

Google sleuthing produced very little information beyond a phone number in New Jersey and a photo caption identifying him at a rotary club dinner. After a moment's reflection, I decided to dial the number. I had a hunch that I should try to find out more about this guy.

"Cockard Productions, how can I help you?"

I'd been expecting a residence. The phone had been answered by a young woman with a lisp. "Productions" had sounded like "producthons." I cleared my throat.

"Yes, hello. Is Ray C. Pullman available?"

"Is this personal or professional?"

I felt bad for making her use so many *s*'s. Though she didn't seem the least bit self-conscious. In contrast, her tone was very confident.

"Um . . . professional, I guess. My name is Sammy Joyce. I was just wondering—"

"The transvestite flick is cast. But *Weapons of Ass Destruction* will be starting up right after. Give me your number and we'll call you if we need you."

Due to the lisp, this had come out as "tranthvethtite" and "Weaponth of Ath Dethtructhon." It took me a second to decipher.

"Excuse me?"

This had all taken a very surprising turn. I was getting used to her lisp at least. I could now instantly translate in my head as she talked.

"We don't have anything for you right now, but we're alwayth look-ing. Ith the 'Thammy' thing jutht to be cute or are you acthually a guy?"

"I'm not a guy," I answered.

I felt I could be definitive about that. The rest of it was a bit confusing.

"Great, we've got too many girl-guyth already. Have you been in the buthineth long?"

I assumed the business was porn. And no, I hadn't. This was my first foray. So far I seemed to be showing a lot of potential.

"I'm sorry, is there any way I could talk to Mr. Pullman?"

"He'th a very buthy man."

"I'm getting that impression. Does he run this whole operation?"

"Thtarted it from thcratch."

"Impressive. Well, if you wouldn't mind giving him my number, I'm actually calling from Washington, D.C., and this isn't about one of his movies."

"Oh, okay. I jutht athumed. When you thaid it wath about buthineth."

"No problem. Could you give him the message?"

"Abtholutely."

I left my name and number. This couldn't possibly be the same Ray C. Pullman whom Senator Frand had invited to be the speaker at his dinner. Could it?

He called back within the hour. He sounded old, but full of vim and vigor. And possibly gin.

"Ray C. Pullman here," he announced triumphantly.

"Hi, Mr. Pullman. I was wondering if there was any chance you visited D.C. recently as a guest of Senator Frand."

"Just last week!" he confirmed. "Though I think I was a bit of a surprise guest. Don't tell me, they're already desperate to have me back!"

I doubted that. But you never knew. What exactly had gone down at this dinner? I was having trouble imagining all these pieces fitting together.

"Did you talk to a group of senators and congressmen about Viagra?"

"Sure did! I love the stuff. It's absolutely crucial to my lifestyle, you know. I couldn't run my porn empire without a steady supply to some of my best actors."

I almost dropped the phone. I was glad I didn't, because I didn't want to miss a thing that came out of his mouth.

"I see," I said slowly.

"Yep, it's a wonder drug. Couldn't live without it. Or at least I couldn't live well without it!"

"I see," I repeated.

I needed to come up with some different words.

"And did you talk about all this at Senator Frand's dinner?"

Mr. Pullman started chuckling.

"Well, actually, this little turd of a guy told me right before that if I even mentioned my business, I would find myself in a lot of trouble with the FBI and the IRS."

"But why did they invite you in the first place, then? Didn't they know what you do?"

"There was a little misunderstanding," he replied. "It's kind of a long story. You sure you want to hear?"

Abtholutely.

Mr. Pullman and I stayed on the phone for another twenty minutes so he could tell me the whole tale. Apparently, a staffer to Senator Frand had contacted Mr. Pullman after seeing a clipping of him in a local New Jersey paper that had described him as a Paramus retiree who claimed that Viagra had changed his life. The aide had liked the fact that Mr. Pullman wasn't a paid lobbyist, but just an average citizen who really, really loved Viagra and could talk very persuasively about it. When one of the scheduled speakers at the Frand dinner had a last-minute conflict, this aide had impulsively invited Mr. Pullman to come to D.C. immediately to spread his magic among the targeted lawmakers. They loved a good pitch from an everyman.

Except, it turned out that this everyman ran a porn production company that he'd begun upon his retirement from the cleaning supply industry. It was now a thriving local business, of which Mr. Pullman was very proud. He loved to talk about it. Sadly for Senator Frand's aide, this didn't come to light until about five minutes before the dinner, when the two of them were reviewing last-minute format instructions.

According to Mr. Pullman, the aide had turned completely white and begun hyperventilating. I felt a pang of pity for him. I'd been in similar positions in the past, most notably with Alfred Jackman, my octogenarian pothead friend. And I'd also had trouble breathing. I'd spent months vetting Alfred Jackman, and his marijuana habit had still slipped by me. However, Frand's aide had barely said three words to Ray C. Pullman before inviting him to be one of the featured speakers at the Senate majority leader's private event. So, really, he'd had it coming.

The aide had eventually regained his breath and his color and done his best impression of a caged animal. He'd gotten vicious, threatening Mr. Pullman with all kinds of terrible punishments should he breathe a word of the truth about his business. Had he been thinking rationally, he would have cancelled Mr. Pullman's appearance and immediately told Senator Frand the whole story. But rationality had deserted him, and he thought it somehow more prudent to keep things as scheduled, scare Mr. Pullman into frightened compliance, and not tell the senator a thing. This was why he was no longer employed on Senator Frand's staff.

Mr. Pullman actually had avoided the topic of his professional pursuits and stuck to a persuasive script about the personal wonders of Viagra. About how it made him feel young and rich and vibrant. About how it had changed his world by improving his lifestyle. He simply left out the detail that by "lifestyle" he meant porn industry moguldom.

Senator Frand had discovered this detail after the dinner, and obviously hoped to keep it under wraps. I, however, felt that the larger world really deserved to know.

"Well, thanks for filling me in," I said to Mr. Pullman when he'd finally finished.

"No problem. I went along with it in D.C. because I don't like embarrassing other people, but I'm not ashamed of a dang thing. I was born to be in porn. Do you know what the *C* in Ray C. Pullman stands for?"

I didn't really care to speculate. I tried to just get off the phone as politely as possible.

"Cockard! It stands for Cockard. My mother's maiden name. Now if you pronounce it the right way, it's pretty clear that—"

"I got you, Mr. Pullman. Okay, thanks, bye!" I finished frantically.

It had really been past time to end that call. I took a few silent moments to process all that I'd discovered. Honestly, what was going on around here? I'd always assumed that the Capitol Hill rumor mill was just juvenilely obsessed with sex, but maybe we were all perpetually surrounded after all. I supposed it was one of the few sensational things that everyone could relate to. Whatever the reason for its omnipresence, I suddenly felt utterly inundated.

But I recognized the valuable opportunity at hand and was determined to help maximize this unexpected turn of events to our greatest advantage. I immediately informed the White House political office of the astounding Frand/Pullman connection. They worked to get it on the wire within the hour, which proved exceedingly embarrassing for Frand as well as for all the undecided members of Congress who'd attended Pullman's talk.

Frand's office claimed no knowledge of what they called "Mr. Pullman's abominable hobby," but the abominable hobbyist himself was all too willing to go on record contradicting them. The resulting press frenzy lasted a few days, with Ray C. Pullman reveling in all the free publicity. Cockard Productions was flooded with orders. Thanks to the fallout, more than half of the senators and congressmen who'd attended the Pullman gathering quickly called us to pledge their support to Senator Morris's bill. And the other fantastic upshot was that Senator Frand was finally forced to stop indirectly criticizing the president for what he'd been calling "his father's transgressions." He had his own can of scandal to handle.

I was contemplating how quickly things could backfire in D.C. as I walked with Lincoln from the press office. Our silent strolls always gave me plenty of time for reflection.

"They got a big one this year," Lincoln remarked unexpectedly.

I followed his gaze out the window to the Rose Garden, where the official pardoning of the Thanksgiving turkey was under way. This year's bird *was* large. They tended to pick big, photogenic ones for obvious reasons, but this one seemed particularly giant and droopy as it was placed before the president.

"It looks a little depressed," I noted.

It seemed to actually be hanging its head. I wondered if it would perk up once it got the good news that it wasn't headed for the slaughterhouse after all.

"It's drugged," Lincoln said.

"Pardon?"

It looked a little down, but giving it antidepressants seemed extreme. Were animals now being targeted for lifestyle drugs? Sadly, I wouldn't be all that surprised. In fact, I'd been reading recently about how a lot of livestock were fed antibiotics to promote growth and produce more meat. Since these drugs helped boost livestock profits, thereby enhancing the farmers' lifestyle, I supposed they counted as lifestyle drugs of a different sort. According to the reports I'd seen, there was increasing concern over the effect that this practice of pumping cows, pigs, and poultry full of growth-promoting drugs such as penicillin might be having on people's ability to resist mutating diseases. The animals were apparently developing antibiotic-resistant bacteria that then got transmitted to the humans who ate them. And nobody liked antibiotic-resistant germs.

"The turkey's been drugged," Lincoln repeated. "All of them are, ever since Reagan was pardoning one and it freaked out and caused a scene."

"I never heard about that. What did it do?" I asked.

"It just flew up into his face and landed a few pecks and scratches before they got it under control."

"Was Reagan hurt?"

"Not really, but it was embarrassing. It didn't make him look very presidential. And it made the turkey seem like more of a rebel dissident than a grateful constituent. So after that, they started drugging the turkeys to make sure they'd behave."

"Seriously?" I asked.

"Completely," Lincoln confirmed. "The guys who bring the turkey give it a sedative before it's led out before the cameras. I talked to one of them about it last year."

I squinted my eyes to look closer at the scene. I wished I had binoculars. The turkey did seem drugged, now that I knew what to look for. It even staggered a little when it walked.

"That poor bird." I laughed in disbelief.

Loaded up for the cameras. I watched as Wye delivered short remarks. Was he loaded up as well?

"I wouldn't feel too bad for it," Lincoln said. "It's not going to be eaten. And maybe it's enjoying its little chemical vacation."

It plopped down suddenly like its legs wouldn't work anymore. I looked around at the people who'd been asked to participate in the ceremony. Several of them were members of Congress who had just been defeated in the midterm elections. In the spirit of the season, the White House had reached out to them with this invitation to honor their service before they left office for good. I'd considered it a kind gesture, but now that I knew about the turkey, I saw everything in a different light. A few lame ducks had been asked to hang out with a drugged turkey. It was a festival of incapacitated poultry.

I told Charlie about it that night on the phone. He laughed that laugh I loved, and I was suddenly overcome with a desire to see him.

"We should spend Thanksgiving together," I said impulsively.

I'd said it the second it had popped into my brain, so I was as taken off guard as Charlie. Thanksgiving was two days away and we both had plans with our families.

"Really?" he asked.

We'd done countless holidays together, but they were all ones that most of the rest of the world didn't celebrate. We'd never shared the big conventional ones. Except for the Fourth of July. And Arbor Day. I considered Arbor Day mainstream, since it was the one that the mainstream joked about being obscure. It had lost its indie credibility.

"Yes. Definitely. This whole separation thing isn't going so well and we need a holiday from it."

"That sounds great. But how do you want to do it?" Charlie asked. "Do you want to come home with me?"

Good Lord, no. My mom would never recover. If I were going to diss my parents, it could never be in favor of someone else's family experience. We had to branch out and do our own thing if this scheme was going to fly.

"No. If it's okay for you not to go home, then I won't either, and we can do whatever we want."

"That's a very interesting idea," Charlie answered.

"Liza's going home, so if you wanted to come down here, we could have the apartment to ourselves."

"Sign me up," he answered.

"Really?"

I was pleased, but slightly unnerved that it had all been agreed upon so quickly. Would this really be okay?

"We're adults, Sammy," Charlie reassured me. "We can do what we want. Of course it will be okay."

It wasn't okay.

"What do you mean, you have too much work?" my mom demanded when I broke the news that I wouldn't be coming home for Thanksgiving.

She was having trouble keeping her voice in a reasonable timbre. I'd used the work excuse to protect Charlie from her wrath, but now I had to handle her fire.

"Are the president and vice president working straight through?" she continued. "Are they not taking time off to be with their families? Because family time is extremely important. And so is your health. Working this much has got to be terrible for your irritable bowel syndrome."

"IBS, Mom. Call it IBS, please."

I should have anticipated that she'd play this card. During the last presidential campaign, I'd developed irritable bowel syndrome, much to my pain and embarrassment. Whoever had named the condition had just been downright cruel.

My first bout with it had landed me in a hospital with unbearable abdominal pain. I was determined to avoid a repeat performance, but since overwhelming stress was the primary cause, I was in constant danger of a relapse. So far, I'd been successfully managing it with a combination of relaxation techniques and stomach tranquilizers. I wondered if the tranquilizers were technically considered lifestyle drugs. For me, they were indispensable.

"Well, you're just asking for trouble if you keep working and don't take a break," my mom warned.

"I know, Mom." I sighed. "I'll be careful. And I'll definitely be home in a few weeks for Christmas."

"Christmas is not Thanksgiving," she replied.

I couldn't argue with her logic.

"Hold on, I've got the solution!" she exclaimed. "You can work here from home!"

This was a trick that I'd fallen for before, when my reason for not coming home really had been too much work. She'd convinced me that I'd have total peace and quiet once I got there, to accomplish everything I needed to get done. She'd claimed they only wanted to glimpse me and have me under the same roof for a few nights. She'd been lying.

As soon as I'd arrived, she'd had all sorts of activities planned. When I'd insisted on working, she'd come and sat in the room and wanted to talk. Any resistance on my part had been met with swift and effective guilt trips. I hadn't gotten anything done.

"No, I really can't," I answered.

"Sure you can! I won't bother you, I promise," she fibbed.

"I actually can't bring the stuff I need to work on. I really have to stay in D.C."

This was met with a long pause. And then: "Well, your father is just going to be heartbroken."

My mom tended to ascribe her emotions and desires to others. If she wanted ice cream, she'd say something like, "Should we go pick up some mint chocolate chip? I think your father would really love some.

Let's surprise him with a couple pints!" I usually just nodded and went along with it, even though I was well aware that my father has always had a mild allergy to chocolate.

Or, my parents and I would be leaving a movie theater and my dad would say something like, "Well, I hope *you* at least enjoyed that. I never knew you were such a big Rob Schneider fan." And I'd be very surprised to discover that he was addressing this to me, and my mom would be walking slightly ahead, whistling and searching in her bag for the car keys. Really, she was a master of manipulation. I hated to think of her being heartbroken, though.

"I hope Dad can understand that I'd be there if I could. And that I can't wait to see you both in a few weeks."

"I'm just not sure he will," my mom replied dramatically.

I got off the phone eventually, convinced that I was a horrible daughter. It wasn't that she'd purposely made me feel that way. Well, actually, she had purposely made me feel that way, but her goal had been to get me to come home, not to make me miserable. I felt guilty that I wasn't being completely truthful about my reasons for staying in D.C., and I hated that she'd taken the news so hard.

Luckily, it didn't take all that long for the excitement of my holiday with Charlie to supplant my lingering feelings of guilt and shame. By the time I met him at Union Station on Thursday morning, I was completely happy.

He'd brought me a tiny Christmas tree to decorate my apartment, and placed a small box beneath it. My first present of the season. I went to open it immediately.

"What are you doing?" he asked. "You can't open that now!"

"Why not? You gave it to me now."

"So that you'd have something under your tree."

"Well, if that's the only reason for it, why didn't you just give me an empty box then?"

"If I'd known you suddenly have no willpower, I would have. Now is not the right time."

"Fine."

"You have to wait till Christmas."

"Fine," I repeated.

We weren't really fighting, but we weren't exactly clicking either. I just had trouble being denied instant gratification for no good reason. I wondered what the present was. It was small, but still a little too big to be a ring box. But he could have put it in something else to throw me off. Not that a ring was all I wanted from him or thought about receiving. Maybe it was one of those stress squeeze dolls! I'd told him about knifing my last one, and he knew how much I relied on them.

"I don't have anything for you yet," I pointed out.

"You've got plenty for me," he replied as he pulled me into him.

There, that was better. Having an empty apartment to ourselves felt like an extravagant luxury. After spending most of the day celebrating our total privacy, we came up with a game plan as it began to get dark outside. We lit candles all over the apartment to make it feel more cozy. I wished we had a fireplace, but Charlie had anticipated this and thoughtfully brought a DVD that simulated one, transforming the TV monitor into warm, flickering flames. It couldn't hook us up in the s'mores department, but it helped to create a nice mood.

We'd decided to make spaghetti, since neither of us had the knowledge or time to prepare a turkey. Plus, after watching the pardoning of the drugged bird in the Rose Garden, I'd been reevaluating my whole relationship with poultry. I'd still eat it, but maybe I'd save it for days when the entire rest of the country was focused on something else, just to do my tiny part to help even things out. We'd next considered a less traditional fish dish, but then I'd glanced at Cal Ripken Jr. and Professor Moriarty and opted instead to make a meal that wouldn't so offend them. No animals would be hurt in the preparation of our supper. For just this once, at least. I wondered briefly how my parents' meal had turned out, and I combated the sharp stab of guilt that accompanied this thought by turning my attention to dessert.

For me, Thanksgiving really came down to pumpkin pie. I ate pumpkin pie throughout the year, occasionally in place of an actual dinner, because I considered it the height of culinary perfection. There was very little on the planet that tasted better to me. I spoke of it in hushed tones—it was my own personal miracle food.

Charlie knew of my affection and was very supportive, though I was aware that he wasn't quite as ardent a fan. He was more of an apple pie kind of guy. He insisted that we have only one pie represented though, so we supplemented it with ice cream and chocolate sauce and strawberries and incredibly cheap champagne.

Much later that night, I was lying beside Charlie in front of our TV fire with several of these dessert items strategically placed on my body instead of my normal (far less tasty) clothes, when someone knocked on the door.

"Just stay quiet," I whispered.

"That's worked so well for you in the past," he replied.

But he'd kept his voice low. Since he was lying beside me, there really couldn't be anyone outside worth opening the door for. Whoever it was clearly disagreed. They knocked again, a bit louder and more urgently.

"They'll go away," I predicted confidently.

Hurry up and go away, I beamed toward the door. I didn't appreciate the interruption. I glanced at the clock on the wall, which showed ten forty-five. Very late for unexpected visitors. Maybe someone was in trouble.

"Sammy? Are you home?" my mom called through the door.

Maybe that someone was me.

"Mom???!!" I asked incredulously, hurrying toward the door.

"Sammy, hold up!" Charlie said.

"Don't worry," I whispered.

I wasn't going to get carried away and fling open the door, looking the way I did. I wasn't a complete idiot.

I cracked the door ever so slightly and stuck my head out gingerly, leaving the rest of me hidden from sight. Sure enough, there were my parents. My mom was smiling eagerly at me, holding an enormous Tupperware container with both arms.

"Surprise!" she exclaimed, leaning forward eagerly to give me a kiss.

As she did so, the edge of the container in her arms pushed against the door, which rammed hard into my toe, causing me to yelp and leap backward in pain.

I often amaze myself, and rarely in good ways. I could convince senators and Cabinet secretaries of the urgent need for obscure provisions in controversial bills. I could organize White House conferences and lobby Capitol Hill for life-changing policies. I could repeatedly fool the president and vice president of the United States into thinking they shouldn't be firing me. And yet I couldn't calmly absorb the pain of a stubbed toe—I couldn't just wince and hold my ground—even when doing so would prevent my apartment door from swinging open to reveal my dessert-stained naked body and similarly attired boyfriend to my parents, who had evidently driven all day to surprise me on Thanksgiving. So much for not being an idiot.

My mother shrieked. My father pretended he'd been staring at the hallway wall all along. I slammed the door in their faces.

"Just one second," I said in a strangled voice.

It would have been so easy to say that *before* overreacting to a stubbed toe and allowing the door to swing open. So much trauma could have been avoided. Amazing.

"Oh my God," I said aloud.

Behind me, Charlie was cleaning up as much as he could. I raced to my room and threw on some sweatpants and a T-shirt. I didn't even bother to try to wipe off the chocolate sauce and ice cream and spilled champagne. I'd just have to wash these clothes later, if I could ever peel them off. I felt disgusting.

Back in the living room, Charlie had succeeded in cleaning up most of the scene of our crimes and had put on some jeans and a shirt himself.

"I am so sorry," I said softly to him as I looked worriedly toward the door.

"I think we're ready for them now," he answered.

He was grinning an uncomfortable grin.

"Should I go in the kitchen or something?"

That was a good idea. I'd already blown the chance to ease my parents into this whole situation, but it still might be better to face them for a few moments alone.

"Sure, can you just clean up a bit in there?" I asked.

Our dessert fiesta had begun on the counter, after all. Charlie nodded and gave my arm a supportive squeeze.

"Just yell if I need to flee via fire escape," he joked.

Another not so bad idea. But no. I could handle this.

I ran a sticky hand through my hair, which only worsened what I had going on up there, and then composed myself as much as possible as I moved again toward the door.

They were leaning against the hallway wall. My dad appeared to be comforting my mom, who was having trouble holding her container. My dad was loaded down with grocery bags. He must have been carrying them before, but I hadn't registered it amid all the lifelong emotional scarring that was taking place. I wished I had one of those memory erasers that always came in so handy in science fiction movies. I was particularly partial to the Tommy Lee Jones special from *Men in Black*. Oh, how I yearned for one.

"Hi!" I said brightly.

Maybe I could blind them with my fake smile instead. They stared back at me. My dad's hair had been completely white for decades, but everything else about him seemed younger than his fifty-seven years. His face was remarkably unlined, except for a long thin scar above his left eyebrow from a tractor accident when he was young. My mom looked like a blond Tracey Ullman—an association she loved. At the moment, both of them looked stunned.

"Surprise," my dad said a bit faintly.

"Yeah, no kidding." I laughed nervously. "Come on in."

They cautiously crossed into my apartment.

"Was that, um, Charlie who's here?" my mom asked as she took in the hastily cleaned up scene.

Of course it was Charlie! What kind of girl did she think she'd raised? Though in her defense, he had been a bit unrecognizable in the split second she saw him. I cringed as I briefly imagined their perspective.

"Yes. He's in the kitchen. He took the train down from New York."

"Why was he in New York?" my dad asked.

Had I really not told my parents about his move? I guessed not, come to think of it.

"He got transferred to the New York bureau so he moved there a few months ago," I said quickly. "I'll tell you about it later. What are you guys doing here?"

My mom handed me the very heavy Tupperware container and sank down on the couch.

"We knew you had to work, but we didn't want you to completely miss out on the holiday. So we just decided to get on the road and bring Thanksgiving to you," she said.

That was very sweet. Incredibly inconvenient given the weekend I had planned with Charlie, but sweet.

"Really?" I replied. "You've been driving all day in this weather?"

"And your mother stayed up all night cooking," my dad added.

He put down the bags he was carrying.

"Wow," I reacted. "You must be exhausted."

"I slept in the car." My mom shrugged. "The weather delayed us, along with all the traffic. So I guess you've already had some sort of meal," she speculated wistfully.

I was acutely aware of the dessert remnants still visible in the room.

"Not really," I ventured. "What did you bring? Curry turducken?"

My mom's face lit up a little as she patted the Tupperware.

"Right in there!" she said triumphantly. "Along with some other goodies. Where's Charlie?"

I imagined in the kitchen, wishing he were elsewhere.

"Hello, Mr. and Mrs. Joyce," he said from behind me. "It's so great to see you."

He shook hands with my dad and put his hand in the air for my mom, who high-fived him. This was how they'd been greeting each other for the past year or so. I was relieved to observe that despite the state in which my parents had found us, they were genuinely happy to see Charlie again. As a matter of fact, Charlie was the first boyfriend my father had ever liked in my entire life. They'd bonded over a shared fascination with windmills and dams—with the different ways humans try to harness the earth.

"I'm sorry I'm not a little more presentable," Charlie continued. "If I'd known you all were coming, I'd have brought out my tux."

My mom giggled. She tended to do that around him, which made me smile.

"We hear you've moved to New York?" my dad said.

"Yes, temporarily," Charlie replied.

"Where are you living?" my mom wanted to know.

She'd always dreamed of living in New York. She'd gotten an offer to teach at NYU decades ago, but had turned it down to stay in Ohio with my dad. My dad ran a dairy farm that had been in his family for generations, and my mom taught at a local community college. But she talked about getting an apartment in Manhattan someday when they retired. It was one of the reasons she regularly played the lottery.

"In Brooklyn," Charlie replied. "Someone at work needed a room-mate and it just came together perfectly."

Not so perfectly, in my opinion, but I kept quiet.

"Do you get along with him?" my mom asked.

"You mean my roommate? It's a her, actually. And yes, for the most part."

"Oh."

It was times such as these that I was reminded that I inherited my inability to prevent my emotions from displaying on my face from my mother. It was currently evident to all of us that my mom thought it strange that Charlie lived with woman. She followed me into the kitchen while Charlie and my dad entered into a discussion of the Hoover Dam and how many unlucky workers' skeletons were encased in its concrete.

"Charlie's living with some girl? Do you really think that's safe?" she asked as I set the Tupperware on the freshly wiped counter.

"I don't think she's an axe murderer or anything," I replied.

Though I couldn't be sure. I added that possibility to my list of objections to the arrangement.

"That's not what I mean," my mom said, sounding frustrated. "I know Charlie loves you, but mistakes can happen when someone's constantly confronted with temptation. Removing temptation is part of the way people protect their relationships."

I sighed.

"I trust Charlie, Mom."

"Of course you do," she replied. "I'm just saying."

It bugs me when anyone uses the phrase "I'm just saying." It's way too dangling and redundant to serve a productive purpose.

"What's the girl like?" my mom asked.

"Her name's Amanda," I replied. "And she has a cat named Delilah that she's creepily obsessed with."

"Well, maybe she just really loves it," my mom said defensively.

At home, we had an ancient cat named Kitty who'd been my nemesis for almost twenty-one years. Kitty was the evil sibling I'd never had. My mom adored her.

"I thought you were on my side on this," I replied.

"Of course I am! I'm just saying, cats can be very lovable. Not that it should matter, but what does Amanda look like?"

I often wondered this myself.

"I don't know. I've never met her."

"Well, you need to change that right away."

I sighed again.

"Yeah, I know," I replied.

I'd been happy not to worry for a little while about Amanda and New York and the distance Charlie and I now had to battle. But my mom had made me completely paranoid again. I felt my shoulders tensing up and my stomach beginning to ache. Was my IBS returning? Or could too much pumpkin pie be to blame? I really didn't believe there ever could be too much.

Which was lucky, because my mom had brought two of them. The largest one was decorated with a frosting photo of the Beatles. I'd never seen frosting on pumpkin pie before.

"I invented it," my mom said proudly.

I decided not to express any doubts.

"The cake store in town started doing these frosting photos on cakes for people's birthdays and anniversaries and stuff, and I thought, why not for pies too?"

"Good thinking," I replied.

"Do you have any more champagne?" my mom asked.

She must have noticed the bottle in the living room.

"I do, in fact. Do you want some?"

I was surprised only because it was now nearing midnight. My parents were usually in bed by this point.

"Don't you think it would be fun to pop it open to celebrate our weekend together?" my mom asked.

She practically hopped around. Maybe she really had slept the entire car ride. Maybe her day and night were now completely flipped.

"Okay," I said.

Were she and my dad really planning on staying the whole weekend?

Surely, she didn't mean here in my apartment. I tore the foil off the cork and prepared to pop it. I got the feeling I was going to need plenty more booze.

I was right.

"Your mother said that Liza was away for the weekend and there'd be room," my dad said a little later as we sipped champagne.

I could tell he was concerned about imposing. And newly distrustful about whether or not my mom really had been telling the full truth.

"That's true, Liza is gone," I answered. "But I'm not sure how she left her room. We weren't expecting visitors."

Which was also true, but I actually had a very good hunch about how Liza had left her room. Most likely the way that she always left it: impeccable. I operated in barely organized chaos. Liza operated in surgical, stylish order and cleanliness. I often wondered how she put up with living with me.

"We can try to find a hotel or something," my mom said disingenuously. "It will be hard at this hour and in this weather, but some sort of flophouse might take us in."

Really, that was unnecessary.

"Of course you can stay here," I replied.

I noticed that Charlie was looking nervous. I didn't blame him. This weekend wasn't shaping up the way we'd planned. In fact, this was just about the opposite of what we'd planned.

"Should I sleep on the couch or something?" he asked softly as he helped me clean some dishes.

My parents were finishing off the champagne and enjoying the video fire. They seemed blissfully content, in a real holiday mood.

"No! Don't be ridiculous!" I replied.

"Are you sure, though? Think about it," he said.

It was a fact that Charlie and I had never shared a bed in the presence of my parents. It wasn't that they were all that conservative when it came to things like this, but like most parents, they didn't love being directly confronted with evidence of their daughter's sex life. So maybe Charlie and I should sleep separately. On the other hand, I'd already done about the worst I could with my memorable greeting, so wasn't it pointless to backtrack?

"Let me think about it," I agreed.

"I'm okay with whatever you decide is best," he answered. "They're your parents."

He kissed me on the forehead before making his way back to the living room. I had the sinking feeling that might be the most action I'd be getting for the rest of the weekend.

Around one thirty in the morning, my parents finally seemed to get a little sleepy. I showed them to Liza's room, which was spotless as predicted, and kissed them good night. My mom stuck her head into the hallway before I could make it too far away.

"Sweetheart?" she said.

I turned.

"It's totally fine with me if Charlie stays in your room tonight," she whispered. "But I think your father might have a little problem with it."

I nodded. For once, I believed that she was assigning the right emotions to the right people.

"And if you've got it, I think your dad would really love a little glass of Baileys to help him get to sleep."

And there she was. Right back.

The weather kept us pent up inside for most of the weekend. Charlie developed a knot in his back from sleeping on the couch, but pretended that he was completely comfortable and fine. I'd always known that my apartment was on the small side, but I became intimate with its inadequacies in a whole new way. By Saturday afternoon, cabin fever had reached epidemic proportions.

"We could go check out the new Imax movie at the Air and Space Museum," I suggested.

My voice had taken on a slightly hysterical edge.

"I hear it's great," Charlie backed me up.

It was about lemmings. Who didn't like a good lemming flick?

"I do want to go to the museums," my mom began. "But it looks so miserable out."

"Oh, I think it just looks worse than it actually is," I replied. "We'll bundle up!"

My dad was already pulling on his coat and hovering near the door. The cramped quarters had gotten to him, as well. My mom was the only one who didn't seem to mind our conditions. We hadn't left the place since Thursday. We'd eaten all the food they had brought and lounged around in the living room talking and watching TV and playing card games. I'd begun to feel like we were being penned and fattened for some other creature's meal. We needed to escape.

"I can lend you some long underwear and a sweater," I offered.

It wasn't as though they weren't accustomed to bitter cold and harsh weather. Winters in Ohio were hardly balmy.

"Oh, okay," my mom agreed, realizing she was outnumbered. "Does anyone want some hot chocolate before we go?"

Which meant that *she* wanted some hot chocolate before we went. She looked pointedly at my dad, the man who was still allergic to chocolate despite the fact that she desired him for cover.

"I'll go make some," he said.

"I've got instant. And traveling cups," I said.

"I'm on it," my dad replied.

Like me, he was determined not to let this delay our departure.

"I'll look for extra boots and hats and stuff," Charlie offered as he beelined for the closet.

I led my mom back to my room to lend her some warm clothes.

"Why can't you keep your room like Liza's?" my mom inquired.

She was looking around at my mess with a disapproving gaze. It was a valid question, but Liza's example was a nearly inhuman one to try to live up to. I didn't understand how anyone with a pulse could be that neat.

"We were trained by different folks," I replied.

I didn't mean to make this a direct dig, but really, my mom couldn't blame all of my bad habits on me.

"Humph," was the reply.

We picked out some warmer layers and found Charlie and my dad waiting for us at the front door, steaming travel mugs of hot cocoa in tow. It did taste good, I thought as we stumbled into the cold wind and snow outside.

It turned out lemmings didn't make for the most gripping movie subject. Their tendency for mass suicide was certainly intriguing, but watching them fling themselves off cliffs got a little old after forty minutes. Lemmings really worked much better as a metaphor than as the topic of an Imax film. They were just too little for that big screen.

And too soon, we were back in my little apartment.

"Does anyone want some pumpkin pie?" my mom asked as we shed our layers.

Obviously.

"Oh, gosh, we're making a mess," my mom continued, looking back at the mud and melting snow we'd tracked in.

"Yeah." I sighed.

One of the reasons neatness didn't capture my fancy was because there never seemed to be a long enough payoff. Things always got messy again so easily. If the losing battle against dirt and disorder could be waged with less effort, I might more enthusiastically engage in it.

"I'll go slice the pie," I offered, heading for the kitchen.

I could at least manage that. I was still pretty excited for pumpkin pie, though my claims that I could happily eat it every day were certainly being tested.

I wasn't prepared for what awaited me in the kitchen. As soon as I saw Cal Ripken Jr.'s bowl next to Professor Moriarty's instead of safely on the other side of the room, I knew that something was terribly wrong. Rushing over, I saw that Cal was now suspended listlessly with his head pointing toward the rocks. His body drifted with a mini-current, but he showed zero signs of life. Stooping closer, I could see that he looked like he'd been roughed up. My kitchen was a crime scene.

I knew exactly how Cal had come to be battered. During his staged encounters with Professor Moriarty, Cal often lunged into the side of his bowl to try to get at his enemy. And even after being stymied by the glass, he'd keep lunging, over and over. I'd often wondered how long Cal would continue to mash himself into the side of the bowl if I didn't stop the self-destruction by removing Professor Moriarty from sight. I now had my answer. He'd continue until death. Suicide by aggressive stupidity. But was he really dead? Or just exhausted and stunned? I felt like I might throw up.

I must have shrieked at some point, because soon everyone was in the kitchen with me, wondering what was wrong.

"What is it?" my mom asked.

Charlie took Professor Moriarty's bowl to the other side of the room. I picked up the net and gently prodded Cal Ripken Jr., waiting for him to give his little start and begin swimming around again. But he didn't. He was lifeless.

"He's dead," I said disbelievingly.

"Oh, honey, I'm so sorry," my mom said soothingly, putting her arms around me. "I know you've had him for a while."

The longest yet. He'd been my champ.

"How did this even happen?" I wondered aloud. "Who put their bowls next to each other?"

I looked at my mom. Perhaps due to proximity, she was my first-choice culprit. But my dad cleared his throat.

"Were they not supposed to be next to each other?" he asked a bit nervously. "I thought fish liked to be near other fish."

My dad was the traitor? Didn't he know about Japanese fighting fish? Hadn't I told him of all my travails?

"You put their bowls next to each other?" I repeated, making it a question so he could still backtrack.

I'd prefer to believe that a stranger had broken into my apartment and cruelly sabotaged my fish arrangement while stealing our things. We didn't have much of actual material value, but there were lots of sentimental gems. Like the rocket-shaped lava lamp in the living room. The thief could have taken that before killing my fish. This was a far superior scenario to the reality that a loved one had just murdered my pet.

"I'm sorry, Sammy, I thought I was doing a good thing. They seemed lonely so far apart. I was going to ask you why they couldn't just share a bowl."

Come on, my dad had to at least know the rudimentary truths about Japanese fighting fish. I was his daughter! The fact that I regularly killed these finicky fish while doing everything in my power to keep them alive was something that he should know. But he didn't. He was looking very contrite.

"I'm sorry I messed things up," my dad said. "I promise I didn't mean to kill him."

"It's okay, Dad, I know you didn't. You didn't know. And I hadn't told you, so it's my fault. Killing them is always my fault, really. I'm distressingly talented at it."

"Well, now we know that you get that from me," my dad said ruefully.

I smiled and started crying at the same time. I didn't want to make this any bigger a deal, but I couldn't seem to help it. Cal Ripken Jr. and I had spent a lot of time together. So the tears were for him, but they were also for my dad and me and the possibility that we didn't know each other as well as we should. The fish misunderstanding was a trivial example in the big scheme of things, but it suddenly represented too much more.

"I'm sorry, I don't mean to cry," I said through my escalating sobs.

Again, trying to stop only extended the session. I laughed in embarrassment, so now I was laughing and crying. I was a mess.

My mom hugged me tighter and Charlie suggested that we head back into the living room. Other than the bathroom, the kitchen was the smallest area in the apartment. It really couldn't support all the people and emotions that were filling up its space.

"I'll bring the pie," my dad said. "Pumpkin pie makes everything better."

So maybe I got that from him too. Along with my eyes and my soft spot for telemarketers. I reminded myself of these things as I silently resolved to spend more one-on-one time with him. I felt guilty for wishing they hadn't come this weekend. Who knew how much longer I had left with them? Moments together like this should be cherished.

We talked for a while as we ate pie and eventually flipped on the television to check the scores of some games. This was when we discovered the *Piling On* marathon. My parents had never seen the show, so we brought them up to speed as we tuned in.

The episode we were watching was from Halloween, and Pile had dressed himself up as the king mascot featured in commercials for *Burrito King*, a new fast-food chain that was currently *Piling On*'s biggest sponsor. Pile at first seemed to enjoy his crown and velvet cape, but before too long, he was making borderline bitter jokes about how much easier life would be if one could just rule for life. To make things worse, he was handing out nickels to the Secret Service–screened trick-or-treaters instead of candy, making the same quip about a tax refund every time. He also went into a brief soliloquy about his personal relationship with Jesus Christ, to reassure any viewers who considered Halloween a dark holiday. His supporters had been known to try to ban it in the past.

"So President Pile actually agreed to this? He wasn't tricked into it?" my mom asked in wonder.

"He signed up for it," Charlie assured her.

"Amazing," she replied.

It was, really. We watched in fascination for the rest of the half-hour episode. I could understand why it had quickly become a hit show. I wondered if Pile truly understood its implications. And that ratings weren't the same as respect.

During the break between back-to-back episodes, Charlie and my mom brought the plates into the kitchen and made some more hot cocoa. I was sitting with my dad, watching him watch TV out of the corner of my eye, when my BlackBerry buzzed. It had been remarkably silent the past few days. I'd worried that my lack of constant working would tip my mom off to the fact that I'd lied about my real reason for staying in D.C. instead of heading home to Ohio, but she seemed to think that she'd just successfully managed to distract me into concentrated family time. I was fine with letting her have that assumed victory.

I picked up my BlackBerry, wondering if I'd conjured up an actual work crisis by gloating over the lack of one. There was no need for the worry. It was from Charlie.

To: Samantha Joyce [srjoyce@ovp.eop.gov]
From: Charlie Lawton [lawtonc@washpost.com]
Subject: How's it going?
Text: Everything's fine in the kitchen. Your mom just
asked me if I know who Pete Best is. Should I take
this as a bad sign? Am I just a placeholder until your
Ringo Starr comes along?

I smiled.

"What is it?" my dad asked.

He'd apparently been watching me out of the corner of *his* eye.

"Oh, nothing," I replied.

He looked disappointed. I immediately felt guilty. I wanted to get closer to him, not add to the distance between us.

"It's just that I think Mom is getting on one of her Beatles jags. She's quizzing Charlie about their early years."

"Well, I hope for his sake he gets some right answers." My dad chuckled.

I did too. I wrote him back.

```
To: Charlie Lawton [lawtonc@washpost.com]
From: Samantha Joyce [srjoyce@ovp.eop.gov]
Subject: Re: How's it going?
Text: You're my Ringo, George, John & Paul all in one.
Show off your sweet air-drumming moves and my mom'll
be putty in your hands. Write if you need rescuing.
```

I didn't even have time to put my BlackBerry back down on the coffee table before it buzzed with his reply.

```
To: Samantha Joyce [srjoyce@ovp.eop.gov]
From: Charlie Lawton [lawtonc@washpost.com]
Subject: Re: How's it going?
Text: You seem funny and cool. Can we hang out
sometime?
```

"Are you and Charlie talking to each other over that thing?" my dad asked.

"We are," I admitted.

Which was a little ridiculous, but it was what we'd had to resort to with my parents on the scene. Charlie and I hadn't been able to talk alone since they'd arrived. But now I felt self-conscious that my dad had picked up on all this. Were we being rude? Maybe I should have been more secretive about it while sitting right next to him.

"And what do you call it again? A blueberry?" he was asking.

"BlackBerry."

"Right, I knew it was a berry. Do you like it?"

Did I? It made my life easier in lots of ways, but it also made me constantly available for work. And it combined my professional and private lives in a very dangerous, recipe-for-disaster sort of way. There were so many horror stories about people sending personal messages to the wrong parties. I myself had a doozy of one that still made me cringe and yearn for time travel whenever I let myself remember it.

"I do like it. But I probably need to wean myself off it a little," I admitted.

I was just asking for arthritis in my typing thumbs. Though I was also making them stronger from the constant workouts. Defined thumbs were not something people normally strove for, but they were so much easier to achieve than defined abs. If only society could start admiring them, I'd really be ahead of the game. I could be a thumb super-model.

"Maybe I should get one and then we can strawberry each other," my dad suggested.

"BlackBerry," I corrected him.

"Right," he replied.

"I'd like that."

He grinned.

"I would too. I'm more of a Post-it kind of guy, but I need to get with the times."

I thought about telling him that I liked him just the way he was, but dismissed this as too cheesy a comment to make. And I didn't want to stand in the way of his technological education. BlackBerrying with my dad would be a new experience. My goal had been for us to talk more, but any strengthened communication would be welcome. Maybe I could get him one for Christmas, and we could deepen our relationship on the plains of cyberspace. It would be like a father-daughter camping trip, but on the Internet. Where we couldn't get rained out.

We all stayed up late again that night, talking and watching *Piling On* and listening to the Beatles, which never grew old. And the next morning, I slept later than I had in a long while. I thought perhaps my clock had frozen the night before at eleven fifteen p.m., and was shocked to discover that it was accurately telling me that it was eleven fifteen in the morning. I peeked into Liza's room on my way down the hall to find it clean and empty, with the bed made not quite as nicely as she had done it, but fairly close.

Charlie was in the living room, reading a book.

"Hey, lovely," he said with a smile.

I'd caught a glimpse of myself in the hallway mirror and knew he was being kind. My eyes were puffy and my hair was in the throes of some kind of static electricity dance. My Einstein hair, Charlie called it. I wished I could emulate the genius to go along with it.

"Where are my parents?" I asked.

They hadn't ventured out alone before. I couldn't understand what would possibly have gotten them to do so now. The view from my window told me the weather hadn't improved.

"They left," Charlie said.

"They *what*?"

I'd basically been waiting for them to leave since they'd arrived, but it still came as a shock.

"They didn't want to wake you."

"Oh."

This meant that Charlie and I had the day together until he had to catch his train back to Amanda and Delilah. So we had some alone time at last. But I felt a real sadness about the sudden absence of my parents. They hadn't even said good-bye. I would have preferred a real good-bye to sleep.

"They left you something in the kitchen," Charlie said.

I hurried toward it. On the counter in a sparklingly clean bowl was a brand-new fish, swimming around vivaciously. A Post-it note stuck to the bowl read: "For Sammy. Love, Dad." My mom had added her own note beneath his, which read: "See, there are lots of fish in the sea!"

"I'm really starting to think your mom has turned against me," Charlie said wryly behind me.

I smiled and leaned back into him.

"She's still high-fiving you, right? That's a good sign."

"Yeah, but she threw out a 'down low, too slow' this morning as they were leaving."

"I wouldn't worry about it," I replied. "You should really just focus on me."

Obligingly, he circled his arms around me and buried his face in my morning-wild hair. He was warm to lean against. We hadn't had the weekend alone together that we'd planned, but we had this moment at least. I collected these kinds of moments. I didn't like it when they slid by me, unappreciated. The only danger in consciously collecting them was that they tended to thrust me into a state of acute pre-nostalgia. As though I were just waiting to look back on this time, to trot out this pretty memory. I consciously plucked it to be part of my remembered past in the future, perhaps to the detriment of total enjoyment in the present.

"What are you thinking about?" Charlie asked into my hair.

"That nostalgia sounds like a disease."

"You are a one-woman romance machine," he replied.

I was also thinking about what I would name my new fish. Maybe Samson.

The Agony and the Ecstasy

GOOD-BYES WERE STILL FRESH in my head the next morning as I read a short piece about the president's Thanksgiving with his newborn brother. They'd kept it a private family event as they'd said they would, but released a statement about the importance of holiday together-ness. I wondered if Wye had self-medicated through the encounter. I wondered if Stephanie had spent any of her weekend pressed to the peephole.

Lincoln had tacked up a new drawing from his daughter, Emily, and had been enjoying a Popsicle-free morning so far. Even despite some alarming health care headlines about senior citizens who were selling their prescription drugs to addicts for extra cash. This made me think about Alfred Jackman and wonder how he was doing. He'd been re-leased from jail and ordered to do community service, and the last I'd heard from him, he was planting flowers outside a local preschool and plotting his return to Canada.

I was alone in the office, organizing some new reports generated by the lifestyle drug conference and wondering how Senator Morris's hol-iday had gone when there was some commotion outside the office door. Nick rushed in, flushed with excitement.

"He's right outside," he said breathlessly.

Who was? The president? RG? Bigfoot? Really, only the last would be an unprecedented event.

It turned out it was Speck Johnson, movie star extraordinaire. His feet were actually remarkably small, though his head was huge. I'd heard that about movie stars—that a lot of them had physically enormous noggins. I'd also heard that they were proportionally very short, but Speck Johnson had some height on him. I knew that celebrities often got a more personal tour of the White House and I'd been waiting nearly two years for Steve Martin to ask for one. Speck was exhibiting none of Steve's endearing humility. Instead, he was looking critically around the room with an imperious air.

His appraising eyes alighted on me.

"And you are?" he inquired.

"Pretty busy. Can you give me just a second?" I said as I calmly finished typing the e-mail I'd been working on.

Nick gasped quietly. I kept my head bowed as I typed and didn't look up till I pressed send. Speck was still there, with a little smirk on his face. For a big-headed guy, he had a very small mouth.

"Hi, I'm Sammy," I said as I stood up and offered my hand. "And you are?"

Nick gasped again.

"Speck Johnson," Speck Johnson said.

"Welcome to our office. Just getting a tour?"

"That's right," he replied, still watching me with an amused expression. "Can I ask you something?"

"Sure," I answered.

"Do you just have an attitude today, or have you always been one of those too-cool girls who pretends not to recognize people she clearly knows?"

I was taken aback. It's true that it was a little cute of me to act as if I didn't know Speck Johnson, but I hadn't expected him to call me on it so blatantly.

"I don't feel like I know anyone if I haven't actually met them, so I was giving you the chance to introduce yourself," I replied. "But you must be one of those too-smug movie stars who acts like a down-to-earth guy but would secretly shrivel up and die if people stopped caring who you are."

I wasn't sure what I'd expected to come of this little speech, but I was definitely surprised when Speck Johnson burst into laughter. And a little relieved, to tell the truth. I didn't enjoy being a jerk.

"What are you doing tonight?" he asked.

"Working," I answered automatically. "Why?" I added curiously.

"I'm going to the state dinner for the president of the Czech Republic," Speck said. "Wanna come with me?"

Nick gasped a third time. I resolved to have a word with him later, but to be honest, I was a bit breathless myself. I'd never been invited to a state dinner before. The idea of going to one was more exciting to me than the idea of going someplace with a movie star.

"I have a boyfriend," I replied instinctively.

"That's fine," Speck Johnson replied. "I'm not really asking you on a date. I'd just prefer to go with someone besides my publicist, and I don't know anyone in this town."

"I'm free," Nick piped up.

He really needed to be calmed down.

"I was hoping to go with someone in a dress," Speck replied with a smile.

"I can do that," Nick answered immediately. "I'll even wear a wig. How does long and blond work for you?"

This was getting a little creepy. From the way Nick had offered, it sounded as though he might already have this getup in reserve. Would I find photos of him in it if I looked up his MySpace page? LyingWye would have a field day with those.

"I'm gonna have to pass, but thanks," Speck told him. "What do *you* say?" he asked me.

What did I say? I'd told him about Charlie, so he knew this wasn't a date, but what would Charlie's reaction to the whole thing be? And what about Margari, who'd been waiting several months for Speck's visit?

"You know, there's actually this great woman who works for Vice President Gary who's much more charming and interesting than me. I think you've talked to her, actually. Her name's Margari. Why don't you ask her?"

Speck looked at me for a moment.

"So you're blowing me off?" he asked.

"No. I'm just suggesting a better alternative," I replied.

"I'm not looking for one. Look, if you don't want to go, I'll go alone. Or with my publicist. I just thought you might enjoy it."

I probably would. I could sense that this was one of those opportunities I should seize. At the very least, to have a good story to tell. He'd just impulsively asked me. I should impulsively say yes. Right?

"Okay, sure. I'll go."

"Well, don't do me any favors," Speck said with a grin.

"I thought that's exactly what you were asking for," I replied.

"I'm staying at the Hay-Adams. Here's my room number," he said as he started scribbling on the back of a piece of paper he presumptuously picked up from my desk. "Meet me there at six thirty and we'll walk over together."

I was scheduled to work way past six thirty. And I didn't keep any ballgowns at the office, so I couldn't just change here. I didn't keep any ballgowns in my closet at home either, come to think of it. I kept them unbought in whatever store sold ballgowns. I didn't have much need for them. I felt a headache coming on. I hated having to worry about appearance. It wasn't my strong suit.

"Sure, I'll see you then," I said.

I'd make it work somehow. For the sake of having a good story to tell, I reminded myself.

As soon as I'd calmed Nick down and was alone again, I called Charlie to run the Speck Johnson non-date by him. He took it fairly well.

"So you're spending the evening with a handsome movie star. Great. Thanks for the heads-up."

"Hey, you know how much I dislike Speck Johnson," I replied. "But it's a state dinner. It's probably my only chance to ever get to one of those."

"I doubt that," he said. "But I understand. It's exciting. You should definitely go."

"Are you sure? I know you were kidding, but if it makes you uncomfortable, I'll call the whole thing off in a second. Seriously. I really don't care that much. I just thought it would be a cool event. You know how much I like Václav Havel."

"Will he be there?" Charlie asked.

"I don't know," I admitted. "Probably not, actually. But he's Czech."

"Yep."

"As is Milan Kundera. And Martina Navratilova. Both heroes."

"Are they attending?"

"Unclear. But even if none of them are, it's still a state dinner."

"With a movie star."

"I can skip it."

"You shouldn't."

"Are you sure?"

"I am. But I might rethink it if you keep asking me."

"Okay, great."

"Is Liza helping you get ready?" he asked.

He knew that was the only way I'd look presentable.

"Hopefully. At the moment, that's the least of my concerns. I have a day to get through first."

"Okay, well, good luck. Call me later, hot stuff."

"You're making fun of me, aren't you?"

"Never. I'm just sublimating my jealousy."

"Oh. Okay. Hey, Charlie?"

"Yeah?

"You would never to do this to me, would you?"

"I'd never get away with it."

True.

"I love you."

"Love you too. Bye."

And we were off. I called Liza next, who signed up for gown duty immediately. I trusted her, but this was a tall order. Hopefully she'd come up with something flattering. That showcased my toned thumbs.

I tried not to feel excited that I was going on a non-date with Speck Johnson, because I didn't like the little flutters of giddiness that started taking hold of my system as the day progressed. I told myself that this was just about the state dinner. And the Czech Republic, for which I had a strong affinity. But whether I admitted it to myself or not, deep down I knew that I was also feeling jazzed that a famous movie star was interested in me. It didn't even matter that he wasn't an actor I particularly enjoyed. Most of the rest of the world enjoyed him. He was one of the top ten hottest bachelors who hadn't been to rehab, after all. That was really something.

Margari sent me an e-mail around three.

```
To: Samantha Joyce [srjoyce@ovp.eop.gov]
From: Margari Pastor [mkpastor@ovp.eop.gov]
Subject: Are you fr**k'n kidding me?
Text: SPECK JOHNSON ASKED YOU TO THE STATE
DINNER??!?! I need an immediate firsthand report. You
better be down here within the hour. Unfr**k'n
believable.
```

Only Margari would feel the need to censor a non-swear word like "freaking." Or "frickin'" in her accent. Both were already PG substitutes—there really wasn't any reason to tone it down. But she had her own special relationship with language. I checked my watch. I cared about Margari's feelings enough to try to squeeze in some explanation time. I felt truly guilty that I'd been asked out by her celebrity crush. I took a painful moment to contemplate what I would do if Steve Martin visited and asked someone else in the West Wing to accompany him to a state dinner. Probably take to my bed in soul-crushing despair. Good God, I couldn't even consider the possibility of such misery. The very idea made me shudder.

I hurried down the two flights of stairs to RG's office. Margari hung up the phone as soon as I entered.

"I'm gonna remain calm as long as you give me every single detail," she said.

"It was the craziest, stupidest thing," I replied. "I guess it just occurred to him while he was standing there that he could go with a real White House employee to this thing and he just sort of impulsively blurted out the invitation. He'll probably call back and say the whole thing was a joke."

Now that I'd said it out loud, I wondered if it really was some kind of prank. Could Speck Johnson be an operative of the Exterminators?

"Oh, not Speck. He's a real down-to-earth guy," Margari claimed.

She'd been fooled along with so many others.

"But I heard you sort of snubbed him," she continued. "Is that true?"

Had Nick blabbed all this to her?

"I guess so." I shrugged. "Speck just waltzed in expecting us all to drop everything and be awed by his presence, and I had work to get done. I didn't love his attitude."

"That's why he asked you out!" Margari cried. "Oh, why didn't I do that? That's brilliant. You played hard to get, and it worked!"

"I wasn't playing anything," I protested. "I really don't like him. No offense."

"Sammy," Margari said seriously.

"Yes?"

"I know you realize that this is a man I put on a pedestal and lust after from afar. And since you know this, you also must realize that it's tough for me that he's taken a likin' to someone who doesn't appreciate him, when I've been sittin' here all along, completely available to attend a state dinner with the man of my dreams."

So maybe I should admit that I was excited to be going, even though that admission made me feel a bit lame. If it would comfort Margari, I'd own up to it.

"I'm sorry. You're right. I am excited. But I told Speck about Charlie and Charlie about Speck and everyone understands that this isn't a date. It's just an experience. Plus, I plan on talking you up the entire time," I assured her. "Anything in particular you want me to highlight?"

"Just my loose morals and home address."

I smiled and checked my watch.

"Get out of here," Margari continued. "I've had enough of ya."

She was handling this all much better than I would've, had the situation been reversed with Steve Martin substituted for Speck Johnson. That would have ended in tears.

"Do you want me to call you after with a report?" I asked over my shoulder.

"Oh, no, I won't be talkin' to you for several months," she responded sunnily.

I opted to believe she was still joking.

On the stairway back to my desk, I almost ran into Doug. I was happy that we'd both looked up in time to avoid a collision. I didn't want to test any instinctive Secret Service combat reaction moves unless I was wearing pads.

"I hear you're eloping with Warren Beatty tonight," he said.

The White House grapevine often turned into the telephone game. What had actually been witnessed or said turned into something completely different by the fifth or sixth telling.

"Isn't he married?" I replied.

Doug shrugged.

"I just liked the poetry of a true *Ishtar* coupling."

I nodded.

"Well, sorry to disappoint. Warren and I aren't destined to cross paths."

"A man can dream, can't he?" Doug replied.

To my relieved surprise, Liza managed to rustle up something that fit me pretty well. It was a beautiful gown. A real thumb-showcaser.

After getting ready at the Mayflower with her expert assistance, I headed to the Hay-Adams. I called Charlie on my way over, but he didn't answer. So I left a message promising to check in later.

I wobbled a little on my way across the lobby thanks to the too-high heels Liza had insisted that I wear. I reminded myself not to have more than two drinks. If balance was already elusive when I was completely sober, there wasn't any need to tempt fate.

Glimpsing my made-up eyes in the mirror as I waited for the hotel elevator, I suddenly felt like a paid escort. Unlike practically everything, this had not been a profession I'd aspired to in my youth. In fact, I'd been the only one of my friends who'd completely hated the movie *Pretty Woman* and felt offended for Roy Orbison for its appropriation of his song. I blamed *Pretty Woman* for years of little girls dressing up as prostitutes for Halloween. Not as the common hooker versions of cats or bunnies or devils, but actual straight-up prostitute costumes. As in a nine-year-old in fishnets and too much makeup proudly telling me she's a whore before grabbing a Snickers bar. All dolled up to turn tricks on a night of trick-or-treating. In my opinion, that movie was a serious disservice to society. But I'd been told by more than one person that I occasionally read too much into things.

And now here I was, all dolled up and headed to the room of a man I'd barely met. Was this really a good idea? I took a breath before knocking on his door. Speck opened it a moment later. His collar was upturned and his tux tie hung loose.

"Hey, come on in. Help yourself to a drink."

I grabbed a beer and drank the first half of it too quickly. I was thirsty but it was dumb to waste one of my two allotted drinks on non–state dinner refreshment. Speck emerged from the bathroom tying his tie.

"Give me a sip, will ya? I need something to wash this down."

He was holding out his hand, which had a few unrecognizable tablets in it.

"Do you have a headache?" I asked hopefully.

They didn't really look like aspirin. Speck chuckled.

"No. But this stuff *will* blow your mind. Have you ever had organic ecstasy before?"

Oh, dear God. I shook my head no. He wasn't really planning on taking that, was he?

I was very unsophisticated and inexperienced when it came to drug consumption. I'd just never really gotten into it. I'd smoked pot a handful of times and never enjoyed it. Which other people had assured me meant that I'd never done it right. Still, I'd given up on it. Everything else I'd stayed completely away from.

"You should try it, it'll change your life," Speck assured me. "So much better than the chemical stuff. You're not going to believe it."

"I don't want any, but thanks," I said quickly.

He looked at me the way I'd assumed he would.

"Ah, a D.C. square, huh?" he said.

"Hanging out with a Hollywood cliché," I confirmed.

He laughed.

"You're funny. It's too bad you insist on being so boring."

"Mmm . . . yeah. It's my fatal flaw."

"No worries. More of the good stuff for me," he said as he downed the pills and took my beer from my hand for a swig.

Good God, he'd done it. There was no going back. I was about to attend a state dinner, as the guest of movie star Speck Johnson, who would soon be tripping his face off.

Maybe he wouldn't be, I thought hopefully. Maybe organic ecstasy was really mild. And maybe he was really used to it.

"Do you take that a lot?" I asked.

I needed to know exactly how accustomed he was to functioning under its influence. I didn't want to be responsible for a complete train
wreck. He flashed me that smile that garnered ten-million-dollar pay-
checks but zero acting accolades.

"I'm a pro, darlin', don't you worry. How does this look?"

He'd finished fiddling with his tie and put on his jacket.

"Not awful," I conceded.

I could see why other women found him attractive. I didn't, I reminded myself. That annoying thrill showed up again. It was only because I was in the room of a famous actor who for some reason had
asked me out. That was inherently sort of thrilling. And now I would
like to stop feeling this way and just act like this was all very normal.

"So, have you ever been to one of these things?" he asked me.

"No, actually. We're both state dinner virgins. Hopefully they'll be
gentle."

"Drink up, buttercup."

Just for that, I didn't finish my beer. Which meant that didn't count
as one whole drink. I could still have two at the dinner and feel like I'd
only slightly bent the rules.

Walking through the lobby, I couldn't help but feel a little special.
Everyone stared at Speck and a few people came up and asked for autographs and pictures. I was accustomed to being with people who garnered this type of response, considering I worked for the president and
vice president of the United States, but it was still a different ball game
with a movie star.

"You must be used to this sort of thing, working in the White
House," Speck remarked after signing another autograph.

I'd kept those internal thoughts to myself, but he might have read
my expression. Even a bad actor had plenty of practice picking up cues.

I nodded.

"Yes, but the Secret Service add another element to it," I replied.

"I'm supposed to have bodyguards, but I don't like them. They make
me feel like I'm putting on airs, you know? I'm just a regular guy."

I was pretty sure regular guys didn't frequently proclaim their nor-
malness. But I nodded again anyway, just to be polite.

"I like D.C.," he continued. "It's a fascinating place. So much power. I've only been here a couple times, but I get a kick out of it. It's like Hollywood for fat and ugly people, you know?"

I didn't stop walking or immediately respond. I was guilty of D.C. degradation occasionally myself, but I hoped I never did it in quite so charmless and unoriginal a way. This was my adopted town. It had its flaws, certainly. Some of them were more inexcusable than others. But I didn't like it being knocked by an idiotic outsider who not-so-secretly dreamed of his own political career after his acting roles dried up.

"That's a good line, isn't it? You can use it if you want," Speck continued, apparently oblivious to the fact that he hadn't been the first one to say it.

He was also evidently clueless to the tension of my irritated silence. I added tone deaf to my list of unflattering adjectives for him. I shivered in the cold air as we approached Pennsylvania Avenue.

"Hey, do people come out and try to round up the homeless in front of the White House?" he asked as he eyed a man lying wrapped in blankets on the street.

He was just going to keep talking. Perhaps he liked the sound of his own voice more than the sound of an actual dialogue. And was he serious about that question? This was Washington, D.C., not Beijing.

"Because it doesn't look so good to have them hanging around just outside the gates," he continued. "I had a homeless dude who'd come rifle through my garbage up at my first house in the Hills and I called the city on him. You gotta protect appearances, you know?"

He turned to me to see if I was nodding. I wasn't.

"I mean we need to help them, of course," he continued, becoming slightly self-conscious. "Homeless outreach and funding for services for the homeless are important parts of any platform," he intoned.

Now who was the boring one? He was just reciting things he planned to regurgitate whenever he did make that run for office. I wondered when the ecstasy was going to kick in. Maybe he'd be interesting then.

"So are you working on any new movies?" I asked.

"Absolutely. Always working, always working. Gotta pay the bills, you know?"

"Anything interesting?"

"Nothing I can really talk about now. But it'll be big. I promise you that. Very big."

He didn't specify with a noun, so I reserved the right to think it might be a big, fat, ugly bomb. Which wouldn't be a first for him.

We didn't enter the White House through my normal gate, so I didn't run any risk of encountering Derrick, which was a relief. Guests for state dinners arrived at the White House via the East Wing, where they set up a D.C. version of the red carpet. I felt my stomach start to flutter as we approached the white-gloved military officer who was announcing arrivals over a microphone.

I eyed the press cordoned off to the side, looking for any familiar faces. Anyone I knew would be shocked to see me here, a staffer dressed up as an official state dinner guest. Just before it was our turn to be announced, Speck put his hands on my shoulders and turned me toward him.

"I just want to tell you that you look truly beautiful tonight," he said sincerely.

He was an actor and this was a line, but it still sort of worked on me.

"Thank you," I replied, trying not to blush.

That couldn't possibly be my neck rash. I wasn't the least bit attracted to Speck. He looped his arm around my shoulders and kissed me lightly on the cheek. And then he started rubbing my shoulder. Perhaps the organic ecstasy was doing its thing. Or maybe there was some other kind of organic process underway. His hands were getting bolder, endeavoring to explore areas south of my shoulder.

Having the military officer announce "Speck Johnson and Samantha Joyce" was incredibly surreal, and it gave me the excuse I needed to get away from Speck's roving hands. As we were escorted past the twittering press and up the stairs to the first floor of the White House, I wondered if Speck was planning on bringing his touchy-feely cravings into the East Room, which was currently brimming with cocktailing dignitaries. D.C. wasn't big on physical contact. At least not in public.

When we entered the room, we were announced yet again, which seemed a little unnecessary. I imagined the band didn't appreciate having to constantly compete with these redundant declarations.

During the reception hour, Speck managed to keep mainly to himself, though he did hold people's hands a little too long during introductions. Most didn't seem to mind—they were flattered to have the attention of a movie star. Even some of the Czech guests were fans, which made me question their taste in movies, but I kept my mouth shut. The truth was, I was happy to let others tend to Speck while I scanned the room for Vaclav, Milan, and Martina. Alas, they were nowhere to be found.

I rejoined Speck just as the president, first lady, and their honored guests were about to make their official descent from the private quarters down the main stairs into the front hall.

"Okay, great, Pammy, just tell me where to stand."

His breath smelled like gin. Gin was my least favorite alcoholic smell. I'd rather breathe in rubbing alcohol than gin.

"It's Sammy," I replied.

"Are you changing your name around on me?" he asked.

He had a go-to flirtatious tone that was wearing a bit thin. I led him over to a marble column outside the Blue Room where we watched President Wye and Fiona, the president and the first lady of the Czech Republic, and—a little behind them—RG and Jenny descend the grand staircase. The military escort carried the American and Czech flags while the band played "The Star-Spangled Banner" and the Czech national anthem. I was surprised to find myself getting misty-eyed as I watched and listened. I chalked it up to a general sense of feeling overwhelmed. I'd never expected to be a part of this experience. And certainly not under these circumstances.

"Will we get a chance to go say hi to Max and Fiona?" Speck leaned in to me to ask.

Yes, but I really hoped he wasn't planning on calling them by their first names.

"We're expected to go through the official receiving line," I whispered. Speck nodded.

"Oh, good. So I'll see Robbie and Jenny too," he said. "Not as important a job—the vice presidency—but still crucial. Just a heartbeat away, right?"

"No one calls him Robbie," I replied.

Speck looked at me.

"I do," he said matter-of-factly. "He needs to loosen up."

He took on a mock-serious face.

"Hi, I'm Robert Gary and I just walk a straight line, which is why so many people can't relate to me," he said in a fairly bad impression of RG.

"Wait a second," he continued, clearing his throat. "How about this: 'As your president, I refuse to make any real decision unless the polls tell me it'll be popular.'"

Now he was doing Wye. That impression was slightly better, but still far from good.

"Mmm . . . funny," I said unenthusiastically.

"It cracks my friends up," he assured me.

We made it through the receiving line without incident, though RG and Jenny were very surprised to see me. I blushed as the photos were taken. Did I look as out of place as I felt? Maybe I should give a thumbs-up to the camera to draw attention to my best asset.

Once inside the State Dining Room, Speck and I were seated at different lavishly decorated tables. Apparently it was customary to split up couples since there were only thirteen tables of ten people each and the White House social office liked to mix it up as much as possible. Though Speck and I might as well have been seated next to each other, since our chairs ended up being back to back. I couldn't turn around without smacking into him.

I watched as President Wye took his seat and a White House butler hurried over to hand him a glass of Diet Dr Pepper. I wondered if anyone besides the White House butler, Fiona, and me knew that there was a fair amount of whiskey in that glass. I looked over at RG, but he was occupied in a conversation. And now Speck was tapping my shoulder. He could really be a big baby if he didn't get the attention he wanted.

"What is it?" I asked, a bit impatiently.

I checked myself. I wouldn't be here if it wasn't for the impulsiveness of this needy, high, somewhat offensive movie star. I should at least attempt to be polite to him.

"I was just wondering what sort of entertainment they were going to have. Do you know?"

It wasn't going to be dancing girls, if that's what he had in mind. Before my ban on celebrity tabloids, I'd read that he knew his way around strip clubs.

"One of the military orchestras plays during dinner and then there's supposed to be a special surprise performance after dinner in the East Room," I told him.

"Sounds groovy," he said, winking at me as he took another pill out of his pocket and washed it down with some wine.

"Vitamins," he said with a wink to the woman next to him.

She didn't seem to know much English. I glanced again at President Wye and wondered if he'd taken any Focusid to be up for this event.

By the time the elaborate desserts were served on plates decorated with a china pattern used during Thomas Jefferson's administration, Speck was sweating profusely.

"Can I smoke in here?" he leaned over to ask me.

"Smoke what?" I asked suspiciously.

Even if it was cigarettes, the answer was no. He had to go outside. Speck opened his jacket to show me the pack of Marlboros nestled in his pocket. I though I saw some Benadryl as well. He was a walking pharmacy, which I could actually kind of relate to. I had my own mini-clinic in my purse. It was one of the reasons I could never carry a clutch—not nearly enough room for medical supplies.

"Join me?" Speck asked.

It was the polite thing to do. And he should probably be supervised. Plus, I was more comfortable in a staffing role anyway. I quickly led the way to the doors that opened onto the South Lawn.

"It's really hot," Speck complained.

No it wasn't. It was actually quite cold outside. I looked closer at him. His face had flushed a spotty red.

"Are you all right?" I asked, concerned.

"I'm not sure," he answered. "Maybe there was something wrong with that E."

Something wrong besides the fact that he took it before and during a White House state dinner? Something wrong besides the fact that he'd washed it down with prodigious amounts of alcohol? Did he mean there was something wrong with the drug itself?

"Is that a possibility?" I asked. "Has that ever happened before?"

I really didn't want to have this kind of problem on my hands. Speck shrugged.

"Sometimes they can get mold on them or something. The downside of organic," he said with a lopsided grin.

He was starting to look really sick.

"Maybe we should get you checked out by a doctor."

"Nah, I'll be fine," he said as he waved me off.

But then he began sneezing and coughing. He looked at the cigarette between his fingers accusingly.

"What's wrong with this thing?" he asked.

There was more likely something wrong with the smoker than the smoked.

"If you're having an allergic reaction, we should get some Benadryl," I said. "Do you have some?"

I thought I'd glimpsed it. If he didn't have it, I knew I had a small packet in my purse, which I'd left back at the table.

"Nope," Speck answered. "Why would I have any Benadryl?"

I opened his jacket and fished out the Benadryl box.

"That's just the box I carry my E in," he said, seemingly enjoying the manhandling.

I shoved it back into his pocket. Earlier, during the reception hour, he'd briefly tried to convince me that organic ecstasy was not illegal. But if that really was the case, then why was he taking pains to hide it? I didn't trust him. Why was I always the staffer stuck with the druggies? Had one of my gods chosen me for this bizarre special purpose?

"Can I get you two anything?"

I looked up to see a White House butler holding a tray. I shook my head, hoping he'd just move along before any felonies became public knowledge.

"I'd love a gin and tonic," Speck said.

I turned back toward him. He was still sweating, and his face was a blotchy burgundy. He didn't look like a man in need of a g & t.

"I'm going to get my purse," I said. "Stay here."

He leaned obligingly against the door frame.

My tablemates looked at me a little inquisitively as I stooped to collect my purse from beneath my chair. It was unusual for state dinner attendees to leave their tables. Most people stayed put and reveled in the experience. I couldn't really explain why we weren't. I just hoped no one beyond our tables noticed or cared too much about our absence.

I needed to make a quick detour to the ladies' room on my way back outside, courtesy of the four glasses of water I'd gulped. I looked at myself in the bathroom mirror as I washed my hands and solemnly vowed not to be a part of a scandal. I'd heard the stories of past state dinners. There had been the one where a football legend had crawled under the table, wrapped himself around the legs of a Supreme Court justice, and proclaimed his ardent desire to take her home later. And there had been the one where the secretary of state's father had insisted on serenading the room with songs from *Les Miserables* in his less than impressive falsetto. The common denominator in all of these state dinner horror stories was alcohol, as the individuals who embarrassed themselves and those around them tended to be overserved. It was an understandable phenomenon, especially among those who drank to ease social tension. For the average person, White House state dinners were social tension central.

Of course, most state dinners passed without incident, but when something scandalous did take place, it was guaranteed to live on forever in White House mythology.

"Nothing like that will happen tonight," I said to myself in the mirror.

I sounded very convincing. I dried my hands and hurried back outside to Speck. His cigarette butt was where I'd left him, but he himself was nowhere to be found. The White House butler from before walked over and picked up his ashy remains.

"Sorry about that," I apologized.

"While you were gone, he was telling me all about how he's 'a butt man,'" the butler replied.

Was this a joke? I couldn't be sure. I laughed uncertainly.

"Charming. Well, do you know where he went?" I inquired.

The butler indicated the doors back into the dinner.

"That way," he replied.

Okay, he was probably just back at his table. Maybe having some coffee and chatting like a normal person with the rest of our companions.

Except he wasn't. My eyes whipped to where he should have been

sitting as I reentered the room. And then they whipped much less enthusiastically over to the head table, which was where he actually was.

Speck was kneeling beside the president, earnestly talking his ear off.
And sweating. Sweating so much that it was really the main thing he was
doing. Even ahead of breathing, which was itself probably just a vehicle
for gin fume distribution to anyone near his airspace. There were Secret
Service agents a few steps away, and I noticed the White House social
secretary hovering, waiting to swoop in and rescue the president. Oh,
goodness.

I thought about just taking my seat and allowing others to handle this.
It wasn't my responsibility, after all. Speck had invited me, not the other
way around. Still, people knew that I had come with him, so anything he
did inevitably reflected on me. If one was innocent until investigated in
D.C., one was also guilty till disassociated. Maybe I could just distance
myself from him quickly.

"Hey, Pammy, come join us!"

Speck had stopped breathing down Wye's neck long enough to spot
me and was now waving me over to their table. So much for distancing.
I hurried over, feeling people staring at me along the way.

"So anyway, it's gonna be a great flick. And I think it really shows my
compassionate side," Speck was saying. "Which will be key for future
endeavors," he said with a wink.

President Wye was being very gracious. Though he'd obviously had
enough.

"Sounds like it," Wye replied. "I'd love to talk to you about it later. If
you'll just excuse me now, I should get back to the president."

Of the Czech Republic. Whom Speck had blocked from Wye's view
with his enormous head.

"Why don't you come with me, Speck?" I asked.

When he turned toward me, his eyes looked glazed. Unlike Wye's,
which were exceedingly focused. For a moment, I wondered if anyone
in the room wasn't on some sort of controlled substance. Even if it was
just vitamin C, or aspirin, or a little wine. It suddenly seemed abnormal
not to be on something.

"Yeah, okay. So we're done for now, Maxie Pad?" Speck asked the
president.

"Right this way." I grabbed Speck's arm and dragged him away.

He was much bigger than me, but I had the strength of a woman in crisis. Like a mother who could lift a car to free her child, I could tug a two-hundred-pound man to avert further scandal. Good Lord, I hoped the Czech translator had exercised some discretion.

With the somewhat aggressive help of the social secretary and a few Secret Service agents, I got Speck clear of the state dinner and on his way back to his hotel.

"Do these things always end this early?" he asked, slicking his hair back with a big sweaty hand as he slumped in the cab.

I'd determined that he wasn't in good enough shape to even make the very short walk back to the Hay-Adams. He seemed to have lost the ability to really understand what was happening around him.

"Frequently," I assured him. "You're not missing anything."

"All right," he said. "Never had a chance to talk to Robbie . . ."

Now he was mumbling. Did he need to see a doctor? I called Charlie from my cell phone and briefed him on the situation.

"How many drinks has he had?" Charlie asked.

Speck now had his eyes closed and was leaning back against the car seat.

"I don't know—six?" I estimated. "In my presence at least. I don't know about beforehand."

"And you saw him swallow four pills?"

"Yeah."

"That's not enough to overdose," he said confidently.

How could he be so sure?

"Hey Speck." I shook his shoulder. "You only took the organic E tonight, right?" I asked him.

His eyes flew open.

"Who are you talking to?" Speck asked suspiciously. "Are you selling me out? I'll deny everything. I'm going to be president one day."

This was all strung together in a paranoid, delusional burst. I tried to keep from rolling my eyes. I didn't succeed.

"It's just my boyfriend, Charlie," I replied. "I called him because I was worried about you."

Speck grabbed the phone.

"Hey Chuckles? Speck here. Your lady looks like a great lay. Lay, lady, lay . . . I'm gonna lay her across my big, brass bed . . ." he sang.

I snatched the phone back.

"Are you there?" I asked, silently praying that the call had disconnected before Speck's outburst.

"Yep," Charlie answered.

Curses.

"I say you just drop-kick him to the curb and leave the rest to fate," Charlie offered.

He seemed markedly less concerned about the overdosing possibilities.

"Good idea," I replied. "I'll call you in a bit."

The Hay-Adams was very close to the White House, just across Lafayette Park, but the cab still managed to do an elaborate turnaround that took some time. I suspected the driver just wanted to eavesdrop for longer. I couldn't really blame him.

"Oh, crap," Speck said as we made our final approach to the hotel.

"What?"

"Paparazzi," he replied.

"No," I responded.

Surely not. We didn't usually have those in D.C. But there they were, all right. Three of them, camped out on the curb. Someone must have alerted them as to where Speck was staying.

"Well, we better give 'em what they want," Speck continued. "How do I look?"

Like a soggy, puffy disaster. And his voice was slurred.

"Can you go around to another entrance?" I asked the driver.

"Sure," he replied, only too happy to keep us in his presence a little longer.

We made it into the hotel through a side door and headed straight for the elevators. Speck started getting handsy again as we waited, which was when I decided to catch the attention of the concierge.

"Could you just see that Mr. Johnson gets to his room?" I asked.

I was done. It wasn't my job to babysit Speck Johnson any further. We were on the hotel's turf now and they could take over.

"Of course, ma'am," the concierge replied as he sized up his charge.

"What? You're not going to come lay, lady, lay?" Speck asked me. He sounded hurt.

"No," I answered firmly. "But thanks for a memorable night."

At least I had a good story to tell my friends. That had been the justification, after all.

"Then give me a hug before you go," Speck said, wrapping his arms around me.

I didn't have a chance to resist. As he pressed me to him, I heard some shuffling feet and cameras flashing behind us.

"Hey, Speck, give us a good shot!" someone called out.

Dammit. At least my face wasn't visible. And it was just a platonic hug being captured. Until I felt Speck's hand move down my back and cup my butt.

Snap, snap, went the flashes.

Slap, slap, went my hand.

And just like that, I had the pictures to go with the story.

Anatomy of an Emergency

———·•·———

BY THE STAFF HOLIDAY PARTY at the vice presidential residence the following week, I had become a celebrity among a very small group of people who didn't get out much. My colleagues. The party was held on a Friday night, and Charlie had come down from New York for the occasion, for which I was extremely grateful. I needed the support. And the chance to further reassure him that I'd done nothing wrong during my evening with Speck.

Unfortunately, *Us Weekly* had just come out with a new issue featuring my anatomy in one of their photo galleries with the caption, "No butts about it—Speck Johnson is off the market!" LyingWye had linked the photo to another one that showed my face, and accompanied it with a snarky snippet about how I'd jilted Charlie once he'd served my purposes and was trying to upgrade to a blowhard Hollywood actor. At least LyingWye had spared me another puppet feature. Those seemed to get under Charlie's skin more than anything else.

"Thanks for doing this with me," I whispered to Charlie as we waited to clear the security checkpoint and be allowed into the party.

I stood on my toes to give him a quick kiss. His lips were surprisingly warm.

"Thanks for inviting me," he replied. "I'll try not to embarrass you."

Was he being sarcastic? I stayed silent.

"I'm no Speck Johnson, but I can grab you inappropriately with the best of them," he added in a more obviously teasing tone.

Okay, good. At least he was keeping his sense of humor about the whole thing.

I needed to know that Charlie and I were solid when everything else felt a little shaky. Given all that was secretly going on with President Wye, feelings of uncertainty and insecurity were understandable. But lately, I couldn't seem to shake the sense of a gathering storm. The feeling of a colossal one brewing filled me with anticipatory dread. I squeezed Charlie's hand to remind myself that for now, we were safe.

Once past security, Charlie and I climbed the front porch stairs and entered the vice presidential residence. The main room was festooned with garlands and pretty holiday decorations and it smelled like gingerbread and pine trees. To the right of the stairs that led to the private quarters I'd never been invited to view was the start of a line that shuffled through the library and into the living room, where the Garys were standing in front of the large Christmas tree, posing for photo after photo with their guests. During the weeks surrounding the holidays, there was some kind of party or two practically every night. And every one of these parties was work, on top of our normal routines. It made the holidays exhausting in a whole new way.

As we took in the scene, I became aware that we were being pointed out and whispered about. I hoped Charlie hadn't noticed, but I knew better. He was observant by trade, which was another thing we didn't have in common. I couldn't tell you the color of my bedroom unless I was actually standing in it.

"Should we get in line?" Charlie asked a little stiffly.

"Let's fuel up first," I replied, steering him in the opposite direction, toward the dining room.

We got some drinks and food and found Lincoln hiding in a corner.

"Lincoln, you remember Charlie, right?" I asked.

He gave a little start. I felt guilty. He looked as though he'd believed he really had been blending into the wall.

"Good to see you again," Charlie said with his hand outstretched.

Lincoln looked at Charlie's hand in surprise for a second before shaking it. And then he cleared his throat with an embarrassed warble.

"Sorry, I was just a bit lost in my thoughts," he explained.

"Don't let us bother you," Charlie said kindly. "We can just use each other to avoid dealing with everybody else."

Lincoln smiled again, more sincerely.

"See, most people here think my girlfriend cheated on me with a hot movie star, so I'm not feeling super-social at the moment either," Charlie continued with a grin.

Did this still count as him keeping a sense of humor about everything?

"How's Emily?" I asked abruptly.

I wanted to change the subject, but I was also genuinely interested. I was actually surprised she wasn't with Lincoln. This was the one party where staffers were expected and encouraged to bring their families. If my parents hadn't just made their Thanksgiving trek, they would have been here as well.

"Emily's sick with a sore throat," Lincoln replied. "I didn't want to leave her, but I was worried it would be rude not to show up. My mother's with her, of course."

"Do you think it's strep?" I asked.

Because if it was, Lincoln was probably contagious. I took a step back. Charlie held my hand, preventing me from fleeing farther.

"No, just a virus, most likely," Lincoln replied.

Most viruses were contagious too. I wasn't reassured. Charlie held on tight to my hand.

"Is she getting excited for Christmas?" Charlie asked.

"She doesn't celebrate Christmas," Lincoln replied.

"Oh, I'm sorry," Charlie said quickly. "Hanukkah, then?"

"Kwanzaa, actually," Lincoln replied with a smile. "We did Hanukkah last year. She learns about all these different traditions at school and insists on exploring them."

A woman after my own heart.

"How old is she?" Charlie asked.

"Almost six," Lincoln answered.

She still had so much time to be discovered as a prodigy, I thought with a stab of jealousy. An ecumenical prodigy.

"She'll probably grow out of it soon," Lincoln said. "Which wouldn't be a bad thing, to be honest. It's pretty tough to keep up. And she demands total compliance."

I'd had a taste of how demanding and strong-willed Emily could be. As I took a sip of my wine, I thought about how long ago that day in the Rose Garden seemed. It was really relatively recent, but it felt like I'd been burdened with the president's whiskey secret for an eternity. I suddenly had the urge to check in with RG.

"We should probably get in line," I said.

The three of us joined the queue, which was moving very slowly. A full thirty minutes later, it was finally our turn for a picture.

"Hi, Sammy." Jenny smiled warmly at me. "And Charlie. It's so nice to see you again."

RG shook hands with Charlie.

"You've been writing some terrific articles," he said.

"Thank you, sir," Charlie replied graciously.

"Are you ready for your close-up?" Sally asked,

She was on duty tonight, of course. I imagined she'd even volunteered. The woman never took a break. As she snapped the photo, I had an uncomfortable flashback to my evening with Speck Johnson.

"Happy holidays, sir. Happy holidays, Mrs. Gary."

RG and Jenny smiled back at me.

"To you too, Sammy," RG said.

I turned to move along, but Jenny squeezed my arm, holding me back. I met her intense gaze with a questioning look. Charlie had already walked a distance away and RG was presently wrapping Lincoln in a bear hug. It was just the two of us.

"I just want you to know that I'm counting on you to hang in there, no matter what," Jenny said quietly. "You're one of the very few we can really trust."

I was a little frightened by her tone. It was so full of portent. Princess Leia's "Help me, Obi-Wan Kenobi. You're our only hope," ran through my head. Did I play so crucial a role in our little universe? It seemed unlikely. And terrifying.

"Well, you can count on me for anything," I managed to reply.

Which was true. I wasn't sure how much of an asset I was, but I did feel fiercely loyal to them. Of course I'd hang in there. I'd do anything to help them.

Jenny smiled briefly and tilted her head in the direction of her husband.

"Let's just hope our knight in shining armor doesn't fall on his sword just because he thinks he has to," she said softly.

With that, she moved on to greet Lincoln. As I stepped away, I could still feel the pressure of her fingers on my arm, where they'd dug in a little too hard.

I found Charlie talking to Sofia, of all people. The foreign policy advisor who hated me for no particular reason. I joined them, a fake smile plastered on my face. I wasn't a person who could pull off fake smiles well.

"So this is your boyfriend!" Sofia exclaimed. "I assumed you guys had broken up. I mean, with the whole Speck Johnson make-out photo and everything."

The verdict was in. Sofia was a truly awful person. Exterminator-level awful. She might be loyal enough to the administration, but she certainly wasn't on my side.

"It wasn't a make-out photo," Charlie replied, putting his arm around me.

He was good about making me feel like we were on the same team in these situations.

"No. It wasn't," I seconded, shooting daggers at Sofia.

"Oh, I'm sorry, I should have known better. Of course they doctor those things sometimes. They really made it look like he had his hands all over you," she said to me.

I stayed silent, opting not to admit that there hadn't been any doctoring involved. I thought I felt Charlie's grip loosen slightly. I'd explained many times how it hadn't been a mutual embrace with Speck. And how I'd slapped him right after, even though they hadn't chosen to publicize *those* photos. And Charlie had understood completely. Hug me again, I shouted in my head at him. But he didn't. I put my free hand on top of his and rubbed it to remind him that he still loved me.

"So you're living in New York now?" Sofia asked Charlie.

"Yes," he answered. "For the time being."

"I love New York!" Sofia said. "But Sammy, you don't strike me as a New York kind of girl. How often do you make it up there?"

She knew that I'd been working weekends the last couple months.

"Sammy hasn't visited yet," Charlie answered for me.

He sounded a little defeated now. And his hand wasn't responding to my advances.

"Really? That's so weird," Sofia said.

"It is, sort of," Charlie said as he slipped his hand completely away.

What was going on here? What had happened to our united front? Charlie should not be taking Sofia's side on anything. And particularly not when it was against me. I struggled to keep smiling.

"Oh, everyone always thinks they want me around until I actually show up," I said lightly.

"Surely not everyone," Sofia replied.

Though this was a technically ambiguous statement, I had no doubt how she'd intended it.

"Well, it's been a pleasure, as always," I said.

There was no reason I couldn't just end this. She couldn't force us to keep talking to her.

"See ya around," she said flirtatiously to Charlie.

Once we'd moved far enough away, I leaned in to Charlie.

"I despise that woman," I confessed. "She's horrible. And she's had something against me for a while now. I don't know what, but it's really getting on my nerves."

Before Charlie could respond, Margari was upon us. She'd been remarkably forgiving about the whole Speck episode, and like everyone else, highly amused by the fallout.

"There's the superstar," she said to me with a big smile. "I'm just gonna need you to autograph this."

She pulled the *Us Weekly* from her bag, opened to the photo page. I laughed a little as I eyed Charlie out of the corner of my eye. He didn't seem quite as amused. I'd been about to go along and sign the photo, but his expression stopped me.

"You know what, maybe another time, okay, Margari?"

She looked from me to Charlie and then stuffed the magazine quickly back into her bag.

"I was just jokin' around," she said apologetically.

"No, I know," I assured her. "We're just in a rush."

"Okay, sorry."

I felt bad for making Margari feel like she'd caused the iciness between Charlie and me. The blame certainly didn't lie with her. Charlie had already turned brusquely toward the door, but I didn't want to leave Margari feeling so terrible. I spotted Lincoln trying to scoot past and impulsively grabbed his sleeve.

"Lincoln, Margari, you guys should really hang out more. You're two of my favorite people in the whole White House. I'd love to stay and chat with *both* of you, but I've got to chase after Charlie. So why don't you two talk?"

They stared blankly at me, then at each other.

"Okay, well, good luck!" I blurted, leaving them and hurrying after Charlie.

Poor Lincoln was probably dying inside. But I didn't have time to worry about it.

"Do you want to leave?" I asked Charlie softly once I'd caught up to him on the front porch.

"Yeah, I'm going to," he replied. "But you can stay if you need to."

He wasn't looking at me. I hated it when he wouldn't look at me. Our eyes could sometimes connect when none of our words seemed to be able to. But he was cutting off that option.

"Let me grab our coats," I replied.

I left him on the porch and collected our things as quickly as I could, noticing in the process that Lincoln was actually managing to talk to Margari in a semi-normal way. On my way back outside, my phone started ringing. Distracted, I answered without even looking at the number.

"Sammy Joyce," I said into the phone.

Where was Charlie? I spotted him down by the gate. He really was ready to get out of there.

"Can you come to New York?"

I didn't recognize the voice.

"Who is this?" I asked.

I was hurrying across the driveway and considering hanging up. No conversation was worth delaying making up with Charlie.

"It's Speck. I've got this premiere and my agent wants you to come out for it. He thinks you've got a cute ass."

I hung up the phone.

"Who was that?" Charlie asked as I joined him.

"No one. Someone stupid," I replied.

My phone started ringing again. I was moving to silence it when Charlie snatched it from my hand. I was completely startled. Charlie never did anything like that. He never had irrational, impulsive reactions. He always gave me the benefit of the doubt. Always behaved reasonably. Always until now.

"Who is this?" he barked into the phone,

I couldn't hear the person on the other end, but I imagined it was Speck.

"What do you want?" Charlie demanded, with venom in his voice.

I watched as he listened, his face a mask of annoyance. And then he tossed the phone back at me. It wasn't aimed to hit me, it was up in the air, but I had to act quickly to catch it. It was a hostile, immature gesture.

"It's your boyfriend Speck," Charlie said as he moved away.

He kept walking through the gate, thanking the guard and not looking back. I stared after him for a moment. And I raised the phone to my ear, not even really thinking.

"Hello?" I said into it.

"Everything will be paid for, if that's what you're worried about," Speck said.

"Don't call me again," I replied.

I hung up and hurried after Charlie.

"Hey!" I said, when I finally caught up to him.

We were passing an incoming crowd. Parties at the official residence were scheduled in waves.

"Have you guys been chatting a lot?" Charlie asked.

"No, that was the first time," I replied.

"You must be excited."

His tone was contemptuous. When had he started hating me? Just this evening? I felt my eyes well up.

"Stop it," I shouted as I grabbed his arm, along with the attention of some nearby uniformed guards.

"Don't make a scene, Sammy," he hissed. "If you can help it."

I didn't let him go. He was being cruel enough to warrant such a move, but I held on.

"I'm not trying to be dramatic," I said quietly. "And I understand why you're angry. Let's get out of here so we can talk."

Charlie sighed.

"That's all we do these days. We talk," he said wearily. "But the conversations aren't even that good anymore."

I stared at him in disbelief. My phone started ringing again. I flipped it open to speaker mode and yelled into it, keeping my eyes on Charlie's face.

"I told you to never call me again and I mean it! I love my boyfriend, whether he believes me or not. You're nothing to me!"

"That's all very interesting, but we need you down here immediately," Stephanie replied.

I snapped the phone up to my ear, taking it off speaker.

"What's going on?" I asked.

"Just get down here. RG should be on his way, and he told me to call you."

I spun around. Sure enough, RG's motorcade was pulling up to the front entrance of the VP residence to pick him up. For him to leave in the middle of the party, there must be something big happening. People usually came to him.

"I'll be right there," I said into the phone.

Charlie was still standing before me. The windchill was punishing. My whole body shivered.

"I have to go," I said helplessly.

Charlie nodded.

"Can I meet you at home?" I asked.

I didn't know how long I'd be. I didn't know if Charlie felt like waiting.

"I'll see you later," he replied.

I didn't want to go anywhere until I knew we would be okay, but I didn't have a choice. RG's motorcade pulled past me, prompting me to start my hurried search for a cab. I spotted one turning from 34th Street onto Massachusetts Avenue and ran to flag it down. As I slid gratefully into the seat, I looked back at Charlie, who was walking up the hill in the other direction. Where was he headed? He didn't look back.

✿   ✿   ✿

Stephanie, RG, and Wye's chief of staff, Harry Danson, were assembled in RG's office when I hurried in.

"Good, you made it," Stephanie said as she closed the door after me.

Her hair was in several different braids, all pulled back tightly. I felt a migraine coming on just looking at it.

I sat down quickly, wondering what on earth was going on. Why had I been summoned to join an emergency gathering of the president's chief of staff, his senior political strategist, and the vice president in the West Wing? And why did we have to be in person instead of on a conference call? I could sense the edginess in the room. And the danger of uncertain dynamics. This was not a likely coalition of people. It had to have been forced together by something gone terribly wrong.

"We have a potential crisis on our hands," Stephanie began. "The president, as I believe everyone in this room now knows, has completely fallen off the wagon."

So Stephanie and Harry also knew what RG and I had been aware of for the past two months. Had we gathered to discuss an intervention?

"Let's be careful here, Stephanie," Harry said.

He took a tape recorder from his briefcase, placed it on the table between us, and pressed Record.

"From here on out, we're on tape," he continued. "There will come a time when the president will want to know the details of this meeting and we need to have incontrovertible proof that all this was on the up-and-up. Now, Stephanie, I really don't think we want to exaggerate the problem. President Wye has started drinking again, it's true. But plenty of people drink."

"Not many who've been publicly sober for more than two decades because they're complete screw-ups when they're not," Stephanie replied, displaying a remarkably reckless disregard for the tape recorder. "And it's more than alcohol, as we all also know."

"He's on some prescribed medication," Harry said evenly.

"Prescribed by who? Indian physicians? Because what he's taking currently isn't legal in the States," Stephanie retorted in exasperation. "Are you trying to spin the people in this room, Harry? Or just protect yourself on the record? Because that's not the most productive use of our time."

I was shocked at Stephanie's tone. Harry outranked her any way you looked at it. But perhaps these were the sorts of frank discussions that took place in these summits of the high command. I wouldn't know, because I'd never been privy to them before.

"We all have reason to feel on edge," RG interceded. "And we all want to help the president as best we can. So let's review the facts. He's been drinking for at least the past three months. He's been taking Focusid for a month and a half. None of this would be much of our business if it didn't affect his behavior, but it does. We've all witnessed it. Whether it's phone calls or CIA briefings or meetings with the Joint Chiefs, it's affecting his leadership. So we need to intervene."

"Who else knows?" I asked.

I'd meant to keep quiet. I was there only because RG had requested my presence. I certainly wasn't important enough to deserve a place in these discussions.

"That's a good question," RG replied. "Harry?"

"His personal aide does," he answered. "The first lady, of course. Various stewards. Perhaps members of his Secret Service detail. And Dr. Humphrey."

"Shouldn't some of them be here?" Stephanie asked. "Not the stewards, obviously. But Dr. Humphrey is the president's personal physician, for Christ's sake."

"He got called away on a family emergency," Harry replied. "We'll talk to him soon."

"And Fiona?" RG said quietly.

"Do *you* think it would be helpful for her to be here?" Harry asked.

RG didn't have time to respond. As if she'd been listening just outside the door for the most dramatic possible cue, the first lady burst into the room looking as if she were searching for someone to wrestle to the ground. I avoided eye contact.

"What the hell is going on in here?" she demanded.

"We're talking about Max because we're all very worried about him," RG said calmly.

His directness seemed to surprise Fiona.

"And we really need your insight, but I didn't want to pull you away from him tonight," Harry hurried to add.

Fiona looked as though she were deciding whether or not to believe this.

"Max is sleeping now," she finally replied.

I snuck a look at my watch and saw that it wasn't even nine o'clock yet. Fiona caught my glance.

"What's she doing here?" she demanded.

It was a valid question. I was the lowest-level staff member here by many, many rungs.

"She's involved," RG said. "Don't worry, you can trust her."

Fiona glared at me.

"She better hope I can," she warned, before turning her attention to Harry. "So now that I'm here," she continued pointedly, "tell me what's happened. What's the damage?"

I was wondering the same thing myself. Something more specific must have happened to warrant this urgent meeting.

"He's been calling people," Harry answered. "And leaving voice mails."

Fiona closed her eyes.

"While intoxicated," Stepanie added unnecessarily. "Noticeably intoxicated."

"I understand," Fiona snapped. "Who's he called?"

I looked at RG. Should we speak up?

"Various heads of state," Harry replied. "A couple governors. And several senators. Senator Bramen contacted me this evening about a message left on his home voice mail."

Senator Bramen was as bad as an opposition senator. The fact that he was a member of our party was practically meaningless. He wished Wye and RG nothing but misfortune.

"What does Bramen want?" Fiona asked icily.

"Plenty, I'm sure," Stephanie replied.

Fiona glowered at her.

"Apparently, Max's message was about what Bramen could expect in exchange for some vocal support on the upcoming budget cuts," Harry said. "There were some inappropriate suggestions regarding call girls. Jokes, I'm sure, but unfortunate ones."

"That idiot," Fiona hissed.

She was referring to her husband, who was by all accounts not an idiot. It felt strange to be speaking of him as if he were a child gone out of control, but his recent behavior had reduced him to almost that. It frightened me how easily his faculties had been compromised by human weakness and bad choices.

"How much is he drinking?" RG asked Fiona.

I wondered the same thing. The president had seemed okay at the state dinner. Certainly in better shape than Speck Johnson.

"Frequently," Fiona replied. "But certainly not all the time."

"Some of the time he's amped up on Focusid," Stephanie pointed out dryly.

"That's enough, Stephanie," Harry said sharply.

But the first lady appeared not to have even heard. She was staring into space, lost in private thought.

"I can talk to Bramen," RG spoke up. "I can keep him in line."

"It'll be difficult, Robert," Harry warned.

"Just give me a little time and I'll take care of it," RG replied. "I know Bramen. He and I go way back."

They certainly did. Bramen and RG had been elected to Congress the same year, and had always been more competitive than friendly with each other. While RG had worked slowly and steadily to serve his constituents as best he could, Bramen had opted for a flashier career that had propelled him toward his ultimate goal: a campaign for the presidency. In the nomination race, Bramen had been the favored candidate, but he'd snatched defeat from the jaws of victory with a series of epic missteps caused largely by his own arrogance. He'd been stunned to watch then Governor Wye swoop past him to secure the nomination, thanks in large part to RG's endorsement. RG's decision to support Wye over Bramen had given Wye the win in the pivotal Ohio primary and sealed up the nomination. Wye had subsequently asked RG to be his running mate. Bramen had never forgiven him.

"Well, don't you dare admit anything to that asshole," Fiona instructed. "I don't care if he has a voice mail. He can't prove anything."

"I'll handle it," RG assured her.

"What are you going to offer?" Stephanie asked curiously.

"I said I'll handle it," RG repeated firmly.

He sounded so confident, I felt calmed.

"Do we know of any other problematic calls?" Fiona asked. "I mean, with fallout."

Harry Danson shook his head.

"I'm getting the logs from the White House switchboard of all outgoing calls they connected for him in the past two days. Would you say he's been, er, not quite himself since the state dinner?"

Fiona nodded.

"He's basically been awake since then as well. Until I finally managed to get him to sleep about an hour ago. You all need to understand that this has been a *very* difficult time for him," she said, looking at each of us in turn.

Her voice had become pleading. Wounded, even. All of a sudden, she sounded the most delicate I'd ever heard her.

"With his father dying. And the baby surprise. And—"

Her voice broke and she looked away. For the first time, I felt very sorry for her. I really couldn't imagine what the Wyes went through every day, just trying to muddle through. Particularly when they wanted so much more than to muddle through. They wanted a legacy to gloat about, they wanted to soar, and here they were simply struggling not to crash.

"It's okay, Fiona, we understand," Harry said as he moved toward her and put a hand on her shoulder. "No one is judging him."

That was a lie. Everyone was judging him. I myself was thinking about how much better off we all would be if RG was in charge. I checked how he was taking all of this. I felt I could watch more of his dark hairs turning gray if I stared long enough. Like the leaves, they marked the passing of a season. There was nothing we could do about it—I knew instinctively that we were headed for bleaker days. The storm had come.

Bombshells

————·•·————

AFTER THE MEETING DISPERSED with plans to regroup the following day, RG sent me a BlackBerry asking me to return to his office. I hadn't had a chance to wander far. I was back outside his door in less than a minute.

"Sir?" I said as I knocked.

He was now sitting at his desk. He looked up and motioned me inside.

"How well do you know Stephanie?" he asked me.

"Not very," I answered. "I don't really trust her, if that's what you're asking."

"You shouldn't," he replied. "She told me she suspects you of leaking sensitive information to the press."

"What?!? That's a lie, sir. That is a total lie."

"Well, it's not a lie if it's what she believes."

"I'm not talking to anyone in the press!"

"What about Charlie?" he asked. "You're obviously talking to him."

Not really, actually, I thought with a pang. But I couldn't dwell on that now.

"I haven't told him anything," I said sincerely. "I promise you. I haven't told a soul."

RG nodded.

"I happen to believe you," he replied. "But Stephanie doesn't, and she has the president's ear more than I do on some things. For whatever that's worth these days," he added dismissively.

"Okay, sir, I understand."

"Everyone is scared at the moment and fear drives people to do stupid, reckless things," RG said ominously. "So just watch out for her, okay?"

"Yes, sir. Thank you, sir."

Once by myself in the hallway, it didn't take long for me to work myself into a rage against Stephanie. How dare she tell RG I couldn't be trusted! That I should be watched. She was the one who was so buddy-buddy with Chick Wallrey and Jim Kline. She was the one who spied and eavesdropped. I marched toward her office, half hoping she was still there so that I could give her a piece of my mind, half hoping she was gone so I wouldn't have the chance to do anything I might later regret.

She was there. I heard her before getting to her door, which had caught on the rug as it closed and was just slightly ajar. It sounded like she was talking on the phone. I leaned close to the door and listened.

"So I told Fiona and Harry that it was only a matter of time before the story got out and that *we* should be the ones to put it out there, so that we could stay in control of it, but they wouldn't listen. The president is drunk and drugged—that's not something that can be kept secret for very long. I don't know how long I can keep doing this. I feel so torn. But I'm just so sick of the lies."

"Everything okay in here?" a voice behind me said.

I turned in surprise. It was an agent on his rounds, but not an agent that I knew.

"Hello?" Stephanie called from her office.

"Just staying at the office too long." I smiled at the agent. "Have a good night!"

I managed to sprint down the hallway and round the corner before Stephanie made it out of her office to spot me.

I didn't stop running till I was out of the gates and down the street. And then when I couldn't find a cab immediately, I kept on running to the Metro stop, only to discover that the last train had left. It was late and cold and I was running out of options. I suddenly felt scared and very, very vulnerable. To events beyond my control, to dangers I couldn't protect against, to frostbite. I needed to get somewhere warm and safe. Soon.

✧　　✧　　✧

"Hello?" I whispered, as I unlocked and opened the door to my apartment twenty minutes later.

Everything in my apartment was completely still. I peered into the kitchen. My new fish, Samson, was looking very strong, and Professor Moriarty was in the pink as usual. I continued down the hall. Liza's door was closed and her light was off. My door was closed as well. Had I left it that way?

I opened it slowly, looking for Charlie's shape in the bed. But the only shape I could make out was the mound of my clean, dumped-out laundry. I wasn't good about putting it away. Organized chaos. That's how I rolled.

So he wasn't here. I glanced at the little Christmas tree he'd given me. It was in the window, its small present hunkering into the sill beneath it. Would Charlie and I still be together when it was time to open it? If we weren't, I'd rather just leave it wrapped. It could be its own little pile of something I wouldn't know what to do with.

I checked my BlackBerry, which was blinking with an unread message. I must have missed its buzz earlier in the commotion of the meeting.

```
To: Samantha Joyce [srjoyce@ovp.eop.gov]
From: Charlie Lawton [lawtonc@washpost.com]
Subject: Tonight
Text: Sammy, Had to head back to NY. I'll call later.
```

And that was it. No "ya, c." No tenderness at all. I took out my phone to see if I'd missed any calls. The voice mail signal was on. I called it quickly and held my breath as I listened.

"You have . . . one . . . new message. First . . . new message. Received at . . . ten thirty-seven p.m."

Just hearing Charlie's voice would be a relief. Even if it was angry, at least he'd followed up with a call. At least he was still making some kind of effort.

"Is this about the ass photo?" Speck's voice came through over the line. "Because you really gotta get over that. Do you have my watch? I lost it the other night and it's on loan from Tiffany's and it's worth a buttload of dough, so whatever, they're breathing down my neck. Just bring it with you to New York."

Charlie did finally call, but not until early the next morning.

"Hi," I said with relief when I saw the incoming number. "Are you okay?"

"I'm fine," he answered.

His voice sounded tired.

"Why did you go back?" I asked.

I had to ask. Even though I was petrified of an answer I couldn't handle.

"Amanda got sick," he replied. "It was sort of an emergency."

Excuse me?

"Is she alive?" I asked bitterly.

Because it had better have been a nearly fatal illness to warrant that kind of response from Charlie. Even then, it was questionable. He should be trying to work things out with me, not rushing back to New York to care for another woman.

"I'm with her now," he answered. "So I'll have to tell you more about it later."

"Oh, good. Well, whenever you can fit me in."

"Sammy . . ."

"I've gotta go."

I hung up and lay down on my bed, trying to feel numb. I strove for numbness when I knew that it would be a far superior feeling to whatever would come naturally. Every now and then, I achieved it.

I was still attempting it when my phone rang again. It was Charlie. I thought about not answering it, but picked it up in the last second before it went to voice mail.

"Hello, I'm here," I answered.

There was no reply. But I could hear some background noise.

"Hello?"

". . . but that's the problem. She doesn't even think of that," Charlie said faintly.

I could barely hear his voice. It was being muffled by something.

"Hello!" I screamed louder.

"Do you mean a selfish stage? Or that she's really just selfish?"

Okay, that was Charlie's voice again. It sounded far off. I suddenly realized that he hadn't meant to dial me again at all. That the phone was in his pocket. The redial button must have been pressed by accident. I'd been the victim of that before. I'd gotten complaints from friends whose voice-mail boxes had been filled with the less than thrilling sounds of the inside of my briefcase for far too long. And I'd been on the receiving end of those kind of messages myself.

So he didn't know that I could hear him. And really, I barely could. I had to strain to listen. I stopped yelling to get his attention, though. That was pointless.

"I don't know. Maybe the interest just isn't there anymore. This whole thing with Speck—"

A much fainter voice interrupted him. It was female, I could make out that much. Amanda. Charlie and Amanda were sitting around discussing me. And not in the most glowing terms, from the sounds of it. "The interest just isn't there anymore"? I leaned back against my pillow, feeling sick.

I closed my eyes to try to make my hearing sharper. What was Amanda saying now? It was something about Speck. I could make out only the cadence. Her voice sounded light and airy, but steady. Relentless. And Charlie was opening up to her about things he hadn't even discussed with me.

"Maybe you're right. Maybe that's what she wants," Charlie said.

Maybe what was what I wanted?! Now Amanda was talking again, no doubt positing vicious untruths about my wants and needs.

"I just can't keep this up, I don't think," Charlie said. "I don't want to feel like a liar. I've got to come clean."

I barely made it to the toilet before I threw up. My stomach had gone into full spasms. Liza knocked on the door.

"Sweetie? Are you okay?"

I moaned and retched again. Then I sagged against the toilet, my head in my arms. Please don't let this be happening. Not again. Not with Charlie.

"Do you have your medicine in there?" Liza was asking. "Do you need some juice or something?"

"Can you ask her to hurry up, I've gotta take a whiz," I heard Jakers say.

"Shut up!" Liza yelled angrily at him.

All of this now sounded far away. As far away as the phone conversation I'd just listened in on. I should have known this would happen. I should have ended things earlier and first, on my terms. My ex-boyfriend Aaron had taught me that much. To expect the worst and to protect against it. I was an idiot.

"Sammy? Sam?" Liza called from the other side of the door.

I didn't have the strength to answer. I glanced at the phone, which was lying beside me on the bathroom floor. It had turned itself off when I'd dropped it on the hard tile. I wondered if it was broken. I wondered if I was broken.

The door opened and Liza hurried in and knelt beside me. She brushed back my hair and offered a wet washcloth. Her voice was full of concern and worry and curiosity. Everyone is always a little excited when things go terribly wrong. Even your best friend.

After telling Liza about Charlie and letting her comfort me and clean me up, I decided that I needed to head to New York immediately. Liza was supportive, urging me not to jump to any conclusions until I had a clearer idea of what was actually going on. An hour later, I was on a train speeding away from D.C.

There are all sorts of ways for a mind to occupy itself when given a four-hour opportunity to run wild. Mine naturally gravitated toward worst-case scenarios, even during the best of times. When I actually had good reason to contemplate catastrophe, the abysses I managed to plunge myself into were depthless. Well before the Philadelphia stop, I'd decided that for Charlie and Amanda's wedding weekend sometime next fall, I would treat myself to a solo trip to Paris, where I would wander the streets, wailing and rending my clothes. I'd eventually pick myself up and move on, sure, but I'd then be one of those people who smirked cynically when others talked about love. I wouldn't miss my naïveté. I'd feel grateful for an end to the charade. I'd be sophisticated. I'd be sad. I'd start a blog.

By the time I got to Penn Station, I'd planned out my deathbed speech to the cousin who would be there only because she felt sorry for me, after I'd managed to isolate myself and push everyone else away.

I'd wheeze out some regrets about my poor choices. I'd try to grip her hand for a last bit of human contact, for the first bit I'd had in years. And then I'd expire in an unglamorous coughing fit. At age thirty-five, the first yellow fever casualty in the States in more than a century.

I BlackBerried Charlie when I got off the train.

```
To: Charlie Lawton [lawtonc@washpost.com]
From: Samantha Joyce [srjoyce@ovp.eop.gov]
Subject: are you home?
Text: i need to talk to you. ya, s
```

I stood in Penn Station waiting for a response before descending into the signal-less subway bowels where neither my cell phone nor Black-Berry would work. I'd planned to take the downtown train to West Fourth Street, then transfer to the F train to Brooklyn. But Charlie wasn't accommodating my plan. When his response didn't arrive after five more minutes, I raced in the other direction and jumped in a cab.

My BlackBerry finally buzzed as we pulled up to his place. I glanced at it as I fished for cash, aware that I might not have enough. I had to stop taking cabs.

```
To: Samantha Joyce [srjoyce@ovp.eop.gov]
From: Charlie Lawton [lawtonc@washpost.com]
Subject: Re: are you home?
Text: Yes. I need to talk to you too.
```

Again, no loving sign-off. But he was here, just moments away from me. I hadn't gambled fruitlessly only to learn that he was elsewhere in the city. I took that as a good sign from the universe. I checked the address on the building, which was a nice-looking old brownstone. A little fancier than I'd been imagining. I'd pictured something more tenement-like, more brothelesque. Though that had probably been mainly due to my feelings about Amanda. I didn't picture her in a legitimate apartment. I pictured her in a den. Of iniquity, of wickedness, of boyfriend-stealing.

I thought about calling before I knocked on the door, but I didn't. Part of me was interested in catching him unawares. I no longer trusted him. How could I when I'd heard the things he'd said to Amanda? I fought back another wave of nausea as I knocked on their door.

This wasn't the time to be sick, I needed to be strong. I needed to know what was going on.

"One second," Charlie's voice called out.

My heart skipped a little. The door cracked open.

"You're here!" Charlie exclaimed.

"Hi," I said.

I almost added a dozen things. About how much I needed to see him, about how sorry I was that this was my first time to his place in New York, and that it was under such distressing circumstances.

"Hi," I said again, instead.

He opened the door farther.

"Come on in."

As soon as I did, a white Persian cat leaned into my leg. Of course she was a white Persian.

"And you must be Delilah," I said, leaning down to strangle her.

I petted her instead. I wondered if the Fancy Feast made her fur so sleek. And voluminous. A few long hairs were floating up toward me. I sneezed violently.

"Oh, no, are you allergic?" a voice from across the room called out.

It was a light and airy voice. A voice I'd heard before. I raised my eyes slowly, prepared to meet my nemesis.

Who for some reason was dressed up like a sickly woman in her early seventies.

"Sammy, this is Amanda. Amanda, meet Sammy," Charlie was saying.

This was Amanda? What?

"Hello, Sammy, it's so nice to finally meet you. I've heard a lot about you."

No kidding. I was just standing there, dumbly. With my mouth hanging open a little. In true dog fashion.

"Hi," I croaked.

I needed water. I closed my mouth and swallowed so I could try again. I'd heard a lot about Amanda as well. I'd thought that I'd heard too much for my liking. But somehow amid all that hearing, I'd missed the crucial detail that she was an old lady. This was insane! How on earth could Charlie have failed to mention this? Had he been *trying* to make me jealous?

"Hi," I said again, much more successfully.

"If she bothers you, we can put her in my room," Amanda was saying, indicating Delilah. "She just loves to be around people."

I nodded, still staring. And then I started laughing. Amanda looked concerned. Charlie was watching me with an odd expression.

"I'm sorry," I said, trying to stop. "It's just . . . I thought . . . I didn't think . . ."

I couldn't figure out how to finish that sentence in any acceptable way.

"It's really great to meet you," I said sincerely.

Amanda smiled.

"I'm sorry I'm not up and about. I had a mini-stroke yesterday and the doctor wants me to stay laid up for a while. Charlie's been a saint keeping me company so that I don't go crazy. I hate not being able to move around. Talking is the only thing that cheers me up."

"I'm so sorry," I replied.

"Oh, I've had them before," Amanda said, with a wave of her hand. "Part of the whole ageing process, I'm afraid. They started the month after my husband died, several years ago. Just about the time that I went back to work at the paper to keep active and social. I hate being alone. I don't know what I'd do if I didn't have boarders."

I just stood there, listening, replacing all my previous assumptions with this new information.

"Oh, but don't let me talk your ear off. I will if you let me! Show her around the place, Charlie. I need to catch up on my book now."

With that, she raised a large-print book up in front of her face to a height that couldn't possibly be comfortable, and proceeded to read. Or act like she was reading, at least. I turned to Charlie.

"I'll show you my room," he said, leading me down the hall.

So many things I'd been worried about seemed so silly now. My clothes could remain unrent on that Paris trip. No weeping would be necessary. Perhaps Charlie might even join me after all. I could make things right between us now.

"Why didn't you tell me Amanda was . . . older?" I asked when we were alone in his room.

"What are you talking about? I did," he replied.

"No, you definitely did not," I insisted. "Believe me, it would have saved a lot of pain."

"First of all, I did. Second of all, what pain?"

"The pain of imagining that you'd end up in her bed!" I nearly shouted.

Charlie looked shocked.

"You really think I'd do that?" he asked.

"Well, no. Not *now*," I said with a laugh. "Not now that I've met her."

Although there had been a trend of young guys with older women lately. And *Harold and Maude* was one of Charlie's and my all-time favorite movies.

"But before, yeah!" I continued. "I was worried. Any person would be."

"Not someone who trusted me," he replied quietly.

"Oh come on, don't get all self-righteous," I answered. "I got jealous. I'm sorry. It's an irrational emotion."

"Even if she'd been young and attractive, I would never do that to us," Charlie said. "I'm not your ex-boyfriend. I'm not Aaron."

Thank the Lord.

"And you're going to have to decide if that's okay," he continued.

What did that mean?

"Of course it's *okay*! It's better than okay. Jesus, I couldn't handle another Aaron. That's my whole point. You're not him! Hallelujah!"

Charlie stared at me. He was clearly not sharing in my giddiness.

"And it's not just that you're not him," I hurried to elaborate. "You're you. I love you. I adore you. I want to be with you."

He nodded. But he didn't seem to echo my sentiments. In my exhilaration about discovering that Amanda was not the woman I'd feared she was, I'd momentarily forgotten what I'd overheard Charlie tell her. Maybe it didn't matter that I wasn't jealous anymore. That I was ready to patch things up. Maybe he'd already made up his mind. He looked like a man who was finished.

"Do you still love me?" I asked, trying to keep the panic out of my voice.

He didn't answer for too long.

"That's not the problem," he finally said.

I begged to differ. It was the only problem, if it was true.

"I love you," he continued. "But I'm not sure I can keep doing all the work."

Well, if that was all!

"I know you've done all the traveling and I haven't visited you till now and—"

"You make me feel like there are a hundred more exciting things you could be doing instead of wasting time with me," Charlie interrupted. "Like there are a hundred more interesting people, half of whom are asking you out, I should add, who you could be spending your time with. I don't want to feel that way. I've never been an insecure person and you're turning me into one."

I was making *him* insecure? This was an unwelcome news flash.

"I am so sorry," I said. "I had no idea you felt this way."

"I know. And that's partially my fault," he replied. "I was stupid to think that the distance wouldn't change things. It has. And I've got to come clean with you. I do mind that Speck Johnson wants you. That Carlton Block asked you out. That Lane Morris hit on you. I act like I don't, like I'm cool with it all, but I'm not. I trust you, but I'm getting tired of people assuming we've broken up."

"Sofia's an idiot," I replied.

"She and the other two million *Us Weekly* readers."

Damn them and their fascinating magazine.

"I am so sorry about that," I replied.

"I know. We've talked about it. But you put yourself in the position for it to happen in the first place. Think about the situation in reverse. It's nearly impossible to, because I wouldn't do that to you."

My double standards had enjoyed a good run, but they were being called out at last. Charlie was right. I knew he was right.

"I'm sorry," I said. "But you acted like it was fine."

"That doesn't mean it is."

I started to say something, but stopped myself. It was best to just let this sink in.

"I'm sorry about how I behaved last night," Charlie continued. "I'm not proud of that, but I'd just about reached my limit. I don't want to be that kind of person. If you need drama, if you need those crazy ups and downs and fights and whatever else, you need to go elsewhere."

I tried not to start crying because I knew that would prevent me from being able to talk, and there were things that absolutely needed to be said. How could I have been so oblivious to all of this? I'd just been push, push, pushing Charlie to the edge.

"I can't believe what a moron I've been without even realizing it," I said.

No sobs so far. Very good.

"I don't want drama," I continued. "I really don't."

I'd had that relationship already. I wanted something more.

"Are you sure?" Charlie questioned.

"Of course I'm sure!"

But I understood why he was skeptical. Because there were synonyms for the things we'd been denigrating that didn't sound as terrible. I could say I didn't want any more drama, but there was passion in drama.

But it was the wrong kind of passion for me. What Charlie and I had was so much stronger, so much fuller, so much more real. Which made it so much more exciting.

Both of our phones began ringing at once. Like alarms. Charlie checked his, giving me license to peek at mine. It was a White House number.

"I should actually take this," I said apologetically.

Charlie nodded, moving to answer his as well.

"Samantha Joyce," I said into my phone.

"This is Charlie," Charlie said behind me.

I moved back into the hall.

"RG's looking for you," Margari said from the other end. "Hold one second."

"Where? On the AP?" I heard Charlie say.

I had the urge to race to a computer. But Margari was soon back on the line.

"He's on with Jenny now. Can you get down here?" she said.

"It might take me a bit," I answered. "What's going on?"

"The AP picked up a LyingWye story that Wye's off the wagon," Margari told me. "All hell's broken loose here."

I sucked in my breath and whirled around to watch Charlie, who was calmly taking in what I imagined was very similar news.

"Has it been confirmed yet?" Charlie asked whomever he was talking to.

"Are you there?" Margari inquired.

"Yeah," I replied. "That's not good."

"It's certainly changed my weekend. RG wants you here. Stephanie's AWOL and there's an angle with the Indian trade deal that's involved."

"I'm in New York," I said helplessly.

"Well stop talkin' and start shuttlin'," she advised.

"Right."

I hung up. Charlie had just finished his call as well. We looked at each other.

"I've gotta . . . ," I began.

"Yeah, me too," he answered.

"Right."

I had to go. I really had to go.

"Hey, Sammy." Charlie took my arm.

It was the first time we'd touched since I'd arrived.

"Yes?"

I looked up into his eyes. There we were. I could feel us again.

"Is it true?" he asked. "About Wye?"

Charlie was breaking one of our cardinal rules. I stared at him. He dropped my arm and pulled back.

"Forget I asked," he replied.

No, no! I didn't want him to move away again. I reached out. I knew that I needed to leave. That I should just give him a kiss and run out the door. But I couldn't stand surrendering to the distance.

"It's true," I said simply.

Charlie was stunned, whether by the news or by my choice, I couldn't be sure.

The only thing for me to do was leave. Which I did, wishing I could rewind.

Outside, the heavens had opened up. It was one degree too warm for snow, so it was pouring freezing rain.

Alarm Bells

———•—————•———

DERRICK WAS ON DUTY when I hurried up to the gate, completely soaked. I flashed my badge.

"Where's the fire?" he asked dryly through the intercom.

"Excuse me?"

"You look spooked."

"Oh. Well, I'm not. I'm just in a hurry. Am I clear?"

He studied me a moment before shaking his head.

"As clear as you're ever gonna be," he replied, releasing the door.

I hurried into the guardhouse and through the rest of the security routine, but turned back before exiting the booth.

"What's that supposed to mean?" I asked him.

But he just shrugged. I got the feeling he was toying with me for his own amusement. And that I'd be better able to dismiss it if I wasn't worried people could just look at my face and tell that I'd done something I shouldn't.

"I'm glad you're here," Lincoln said when I walked in. "Though you look miserable."

I really did. Every part of me was dripping cold water. I grabbed a dry sweater from the back of my chair and tried to stop shivering. When I turned back to Lincoln, I noticed he was frantically searching through some folders on Nick's desk.

"I tried calling you but couldn't get through," he continued.

I'd had to turn my phone and BlackBerry off on the shuttle.

"I was in New York. Unexpectedly. Where's Nick?"

"I didn't call him in," Lincoln replied. "I figured you and I could handle anything that came up. Under the circumstances, I think the less people around, the better."

Under the circumstances. We were officially under circumstances that called for vague, euphemistic phrases. I started feeling a bit claustrophobic. I needed direction.

"What can I do?" I asked.

"Get me all of your stuff on the India deal," Lincoln instructed. "I've been looking through mine, but there seem to be some files missing."

Uh-oh.

"Yeah, I went through them a little while ago and condensed some things down for clarity," I replied.

Lincoln stopped shuffling through the folders and looked up at me in surprise. I avoided his eyes.

"Why would you do that?" he asked.

I cleared my throat nervously.

"Well, they were a mess and I knew we'd be needing to refer back to them if Congress ratified the India trade pact, so I thought I'd make things easier on us. RG thought so too, actually."

Lincoln was staring hard at me.

"Interesting," he replied.

"Yeah. Sorry if I messed something up," I answered.

"Well, it's just that we have lots of new press inquiries about our arrangements with Tanbaj Laboratories," Lincoln said.

The company that produced Focusid. Mythri's company. I'd of course briefed Lincoln on everything that had happened in India, except for the Focusid transaction. That had been secret, at RG's request. I wondered if someone at Tanbaj had started talking after all. Despite Mythri's assurances of confidentiality.

"Inquiries from the legitimate press?" I asked.

"I'm not even sure how to differentiate anymore." Lincoln sighed. "Now that LyingWye is breaking major stories . . . you know the president's drinking has been confirmed by the *Washington Post*," he added carefully. "I assumed you knew that."

"When?" I asked, and I heard that my voice had gone squeaky.

"About two hours ago," he answered.

That was about right.

"The AP already had it, but they were only reporting on the reporting," Lincoln continued. "They weren't confirming. The *Post* was the first to do that, and now it's everywhere."

"Oh, God," I said, sinking into my chair.

What had I done? It was unfixable. It was unforgivable.

"It wasn't Charlie," Lincoln said quietly.

"It wasn't?"

The surprise in my voice was incriminating. But Lincoln acted like he hadn't heard. It wasn't Charlie. Which meant that Charlie hadn't taken the byline; he'd given up some glory for my sake. At least he'd done that.

"The source was an unnamed administration official," Lincoln continued. "And Stephanie resigned this morning. She's already struck a deal to host a morning show."

"You're kidding."

"She sent out an e-mail. About the same time the LyingWye article hit."

"So then people think . . ."

"That she's the source? Yes, I imagine everyone does. Certainly for LyingWye. And it follows that she could be for the *Post*, as well. Let them think that."

Lincoln said this in a calm and forceful voice. His seriousness helped me focus on Stephanie's guilt as a distraction from my own. I'd overheard her the night before on the phone, most likely talking to LyingWye. There wasn't any doubt she was a traitor. A traitor who could save me.

"So Stephanie's gone," Lincoln reiterated. "And we need you here."

He stared at me until I met his gaze, until I acknowledged all our unspoken understandings. I nodded.

"Good," he said. "Then let's tackle this mess."

That was a scary proposition. Even if she'd been a turncoat, Stephanie had also been an extremely effective political strategist whom the president had relied upon to steer him through treacherous waters in the past. And now she was gone, just as we'd been slammed with the most damaging story of our administration's tenure. Who would take the helm? Who could?

328 Kristin Gore

"What do you think is going to happen?" I asked Lincoln with a tremor in my voice.

I hated sounding scared. I wanted to sound calm and sure of myself. More than that, I wanted to *be* calm and sure of myself.

"I don't know," Lincoln answered. "If it's true that the president is drinking again, it's not the worst thing in the world. It's not anything illegal. Just inadvisable. Of course we have to worry about the court of public opinion as much or more than any court of law, but Wye knows that better than anyone. He's too smart to let this get out of control. He'll do something, and probably soon."

He did, or someone did for him, but it wasn't all that reassuring. The White House released a statement refusing to dignify the "scurrilous falsehoods" and proclaiming that Wye was happy, healthy, and wished everyone a very merry holiday. The response was pathetic in its inadequacy. Not the move of a man with his wits about him, or his full complement of top advisors to aid him. Stephanie would never have allowed such an anemic response.

Charlie reached out to me later that evening. I cringed when I saw his name in my BlackBerry lineup, and wondered how long it would take before I didn't associate him with a terrible mistake. I hoped he understood not to ever, ever mention what had passed between us.

```
To: Samantha Joyce [srjoyce@ovp.eop.gov]
From: Charlie Lawton [lawtonc@washpost.com]
Subject: FW: Old e-mail
Text: It took me a while to find, but here's the
proof that I told you about Amanda. Please re-delete
immediately to protect my rep as a semi-nice guy. And
call me later when you get a second.
Miss you. ya, c
————Original Message————
From: Charlie Lawton [lawtonc@washpost.com]
Sent: Friday, August 25
```

```
To: Samantha Joyce [srjoyce@ovp.eop.gov]
Subject: Apartment
Text: It's a really old two-bedroom with enough room
for three. And it's got an uninspired nose, terrible
body odor, and thinks Led Zeppelin is a type of car.
We couldn't be more incompatible, except it's right on
the F train and remarkably cheap.
P.S. I'm a horrible man. Please delete this message
immediately.
```

Interesting. Technically, Charlie was right, but I doubted many people would have interpreted those words the way he'd assumed I would.

At least he hadn't mentioned anything else. I was grateful that he knew not to bring up what I'd done. Not even to allude to it in an indirect way. I wrote him a quick note back in lieu of a call. I no longer felt comfortable calling him from the office. I'd do so from other phones, in other places.

```
To: Charlie Lawton [lawtonc@washpost.com]
From: Samantha Joyce [srjoyce@ovp.eop.gov]
Subject: Re: FW: Old e-mail
Text: You can't send e-mails like that and expect them
to make any sense. You know that I'm easily confused.
I'll call later. Tell Amanda to keep her stinky
claws off you. ya, s
```

I wanted so much to believe that we could work our way back to normal, but I had an uneasy feeling that all the maps of normal were being redrawn.

As I'd feared, the extraordinarily unsatisfactory response from the White House regarding the stories about Wye satisfied no one, and our enemies leapt to the offensive. The Exterminators had of course wasted no time sending over dozens of brochures for rehab centers along with literature from the local chapter of AA. Congress approached the issue more gravely. Even those lame-duck members who'd previously been lying low and trying to avoid indictments zealously pursued the rumors, denouncing the president's presumed misbehavior in long-winded

speeches filled with moral outrage. Unaware or unfazed by their exqui-
site hypocrisy, they relished the chance to focus attention on the alleged
misdeeds of the man they blamed for their downfall. They seemed to
believe that if they could take him with them, all the ignominy might be
worth it after all. There was bloodlust in the air.

Sensing opportunity for long-term damage, and taking full advantage of the final month of his leadership post, Senator Frand announced that there would be only a three-day holiday before everyone
was expected back for a special session between Christmas and early
January to "address this crisis for the country." What Frand proposed
wasn't unconstitutional, but it was ethically questionable. Several members of our party bitterly complained before concluding that they had
no choice but to wait things out. This strategy frightened me. We
couldn't sit around; we needed to make our fate. I didn't like giving in
to destiny. I didn't trust destiny's allegiances.

For the first time in my life, Christmas seemed like an inconvenience, which made me feel old and a little soulless. I needed to watch
A Christmas Story pronto to turn my attitude around. My mom said
that she had the DVD waiting for me at home. She'd also been waxing
rhapsodic about how amazing it was to lie back in the Jacuzzi tub with
some scented candles lit and a cup of eggnog to sip. I promised her that
my nonrefundable plane tickets were way too expensive for me to even
think about bailing on them, and she seemed somewhat relieved. I was
going for only twenty-four hours, but I was going.

"Good, good. But I'm afraid your father won't believe it till he sees it.
So just get here," she'd said a bit sharply, before adding, "My sweet girl."

My BlackBerry buzzed with a message while I was still absorbing my
mother's veiled threats. She was now talking about the stereo system
she'd installed in the Jacuzzi room, and I tuned her out a little as I read:

```
To: Samantha Joyce [srjoyce@ovp.eop.gov]
From: Sammy's Dad [papajoyce48@yahoo.com]
Subject: Don't listen to your mom
Text: I opened this account last week for our double
super secret communication. For the record, I will
```

```
completely understand if you can't make it home. I
know there are some very intense things happening
there now. So I'm just writing to say that I love you
no matter what. And your mom does too. Hang in there.
Love, Dad
```

"Are you still there?" my mom asked.

I'd been suspiciously silent for too long.

"Yes, I am," I said with a smile. "But I'm looking forward to coming home."

Just before I left for the airport, LyingWye struck again. The blog hadn't reported anything explosive since Stephanie had left, further confirming everyone's conclusion that she had been his source on the inside. But now there was a breaking story that claimed that the president had cancelled his trip back to Louisiana to undergo a private detox program. It quoted an unnamed high-level administration official as saying that the president had been drunk for more than a week and was being placed in the care of doctors at Camp David at Fiona Wye's insistence. I looked up from my computer monitor as Lincoln hurried out of his office.

"Have you seen the latest?" I asked. "It's made up, right? Stephanie was his source and now he's just making stuff up."

Lincoln stopped walking, extracted a piece of paper from his briefcase, and placed it on my desk. It was a revised copy of the president's daily schedule. Glancing at it, I was struck yet again at how tightly scheduled the president and vice president were. Down to "12:01pm–12:06pm Meeting with Secretary Harlow; 12:06pm–12:07pm Move to Roosevelt Room; 12:08pm–12:27pm Discussion of Labor Dispute; 12:27pm–12:30pm Return to Second Floor Residence; 12:30pm–12:55pm Lunch with the first lady;" and so on. It was ludicrous. But the other crazy thing about what I was looking at was that the president was now listed as wheels up for Camp David scheduled for an hour hence. As of that morning, he'd been headed back to Louisiana.

"He *is* going to Camp David. But how . . . ?"

Lincoln shrugged and continued his trajectory out the door. I shook my head in confusion. Had LyingWye obtained another source after Stephanie's departure? And if so, who? Had he had multiple sources all along? I didn't understand how he worked. I thought I'd had it figured out, but apparently I'd been wrong.

And did this mean that the detox story was true, then? There was no doubt that President Wye had changed his schedule at the last minute to fly to Camp David instead of to Louisiana, but that could be for a variety of reasons. LyingWye could have just gotten wind of the schedule change and invented the crazy detox tale. It might not be true.

On the other hand, he'd been right about almost everything in the past month. It was very disconcerting to get hard news about where I worked from an anonymous blog. I continued puzzling through the mysteries of LyingWye as I logged out of my computer and gathered my things for the sprint to the airport. I was flying out of BWI in order to take advantage of a slightly better but still criminally expensive flight, and beginning to realize that the hassle of getting to Baltimore in the freezing rain on the day before Christmas wasn't really worth the meager financial savings. I was soaked again, and just boarding my train when "Fool in the Rain" exploded over my cell phone. The song sounded more taunting than romantic.

"Hey," I answered, balancing the phone under my chin and remembering again that I needed to purchase a replacement earpiece.

Maybe I'd even upgrade to one of those *Star Trek* models. I could talk all day on one of those. And be inspired to brush up on my Klingon.

"Where are you?" Charlie asked. "I need a visual."

I preferred to avoid that, actually. I was really at my soggy, disheveled worst at the moment.

"I'm on the train," I replied. "Lounging on the seat in a scarlet teddy."

The woman ahead of me tossed a disdainful look over her shoulder. Jokingly, I winked and held my finger to my lips in a *shhh* gesture. She rolled her eyes. I didn't get the impression we were destined for a close friendship.

"Remind me what a teddy is again?" Charlie requested. "I know they don't involve much fabric."

"Practically none. There's nothing comfortable or sanitary about them," I replied.

"Well, that sort of kills the mood. 'Sanitary' is one of the least sexy words ever."

"Sorry. Where are you?"

"About to hop a train to Penn Station, in a bowler hat and assless chaps," he replied.

"Those can be drafty."

"You aren't kidding. But hey, price of fashion. Will you call me from the airport?"

"Sure."

"Hey, Sammy?" Charlie said.

"Yep?"

"Did you see the LyingWye thing?"

I paused enough to let him know I was pausing.

"Yep," I answered nonchalantly.

"And?" he inquired.

"And what?" I said.

I wasn't hostile yet, but I was on the verge.

"And is there anything to it?" he asked.

I closed my eyes, pained.

"You know I'll protect you," Charlie added softly.

He'd already failed to. Just by asking.

"I don't know anything about it," I replied shortly.

Which wasn't true, but Charlie had no right asking me these things. I felt sad for us. And offended. How much did he want to talk to me because he loved me, and how much was to find out what I knew? How did that exact breakdown work? I hated wondering these things about him.

"Okay. Easy. I just thought I'd ask," he said smoothly.

"Uh-huh," I replied.

There was no way he couldn't know I was upset. He could gloss over it, but there was no doubt that he knew.

"Will you still call me later?" he asked, confirming that he did.

I sighed.

"I've gotta go."

We'd taken a turn. It was both of our faults. The other morning in New York, he'd made the mistake of asking me to do something I shouldn't, that I did, nonetheless. And I'd been foolish to think it couldn't haunt us. It was just one wrong moment, but it had been toxic. And now I could feel the poison spreading. I spent the short and uncomfortable ride toward Baltimore wondering if we could find our way to an antidote in time.

Stephanie was on my flight. I was connecting through Chicago, which was her hometown. I spotted her in the boarding area and ducked my head quickly to avoid being noticed, before taking a seat behind a pillar and occupying myself with *The Economist*, which I'd managed to purchase without flipping through a single celebrity tabloid. Not even the one that screamed from its cover the news that Speck Johnson had entered rehab and converted his Bel-Air mansion into a homeless shelter, much to the dismay of his wealthy, famous neighbors. Not even that one.

Like it was sending electronic kudos, my BlackBerry alarm dinged to remind me that it was the 191st anniversary of the signing of the Treaty of Ghent. I could still recite the names of Demi Moore's children, but thanks to my history refresher course, I could now also safely remember that we'd fought more than one war against the United Kingdom. Among other things, the Treaty of Ghent had established that Canada wasn't ours for the taking.

I was contemplating how best to celebrate the Ghent holiday when Stephanie spotted me.

"Sammy! What a nice surprise! Are you headed back to Cincinnati? Isn't this place a nightmare? Is that seat next to you free?"

"Yes," I replied, reluctantly moving my bag from the chair beside mine.

It wasn't until she was sitting next to me that I really looked at her.

"You cut your hair!" I exclaimed.

This seemed like a very girly and minor thing to get excited about. But with Stephanie, hair was much more than hair. And hers was now incredibly short. Really a pixie cut, which was a bold move for a woman of her build.

"Oh, yeah." She shrugged, running her fingers lightly through it. "There's nothing more to play with."

Which actually might not be a bad thing.

As we talked, I found myself looking around to see if anyone we knew might spot us together. I was curious about her apparent lack of shame. If I felt worried to be observed in her presence, how could she not have some level of self-consciousness about her new radioactivity?

"I hear you got a book deal along with your TV show," I said abruptly.

In fact, the book proposal, along with the amount of her unethically large advance, had been reported the previous week. From the looks of the proposal, Stephanie planned to be incredibly disloyal to President Wye. It apparently paid to be so.

"Yes, thanks," she replied.

I hadn't congratulated her. I'd just been stating the facts. She seemed to suddenly comprehend this and she shifted in her seat, for the first time looking slightly ill at ease. Up until this moment, she'd always been the one to make me feel uncomfortable, and it felt a little exhilarating to switch roles.

"Do you feel guilty?" I asked.

"About leaving?"

"And selling out."

Stephanie's smile became so thin and tired I thought it might fall right off her face.

"I don't really expect you to understand. But walk a mile in my shoes before you judge," she replied.

It was a silly response to an overused expression, but I immediately looked down at her shoes. I hated it when my reflexes made me seem so literal. Plus, she was wearing stilettos. I wouldn't make it ten yards.

"I just couldn't take it any longer," she continued.

I'd gathered that much from the proposal snippets. There'd been something about a therapist and a wrestling match with her conscience. I wondered suddenly if on the night I'd eavesdropped on her she might have been talking to this therapist and not LyingWye at all.

"And I didn't want to be a liar anymore," she continued. "I'm not calling you one," she clarified quickly. "You weren't asked to do the things I had to do. For a while I suspected you of being much darker than you are. But I realized I was wrong. In the end, I was impressed by you. And jealous."

My face must have broadcast my surprise and disbelief because Stephanie laughed. She seemed relieved to laugh.

"Seriously. Not jealous the way Sofia is jealous of you. She thinks you're an airhead who got lucky and keeps people fooled. I know that you're smart. And I know RG relies on you, especially in times of crisis. He described you to me as the girl you want to get on the other line when you call 911. Maybe scattered at other times, but a genius in a crunch."

I didn't know what to say. I was obviously happy to hear that RG praised me to others. And interested to find an explanation for why he treated me like someone way above my pay grade when tough times arose. Sofia's opinion mattered far less. It bothered me, of course, but just in a niggling, unhealthy way I knew I should let go of at the first possible opportunity. Which was now.

"That's nice," I replied. "About RG at least. I was a volunteer paramedic over the summers during college, actually," I offered.

"The reason *I* was jealous of you is because you can still believe. You don't know enough not to."

Hmmm. I didn't enjoy this alleged compliment as much.

"I know more than you think I do," I replied. "And I know at least as much as you when it comes to Wye and his . . ."

I looked around to make sure no one was within earshot. Approximately eleven people were. I lowered my voice.

"His demons," I said softly.

Stephanie smiled again. It was a condescending smile.

"You don't know the half of his demons," she replied. "And you should be ecstatic that you don't."

I stifled the impulse to argue further, because I was starting to have a sinking feeling that she might be right. That she wasn't a villain after all. I'd grown so used to polarities. To categories of people who were with us or against us. I knew that the reality was much more nuanced and complex—that there were decent and shameless people on both sides and at every level, but I'd submitted to the more simplistic worldview of team sports. Others took it further and let unmitigated hatred be their main motivator. I'd known who our enemies were, but I'd tried to focus more on the positive associations. On who we were supposed to rally behind. Which captains we'd chosen and how to revere them. I'd

been into the face paint and the signs and the slogans. And maybe I'd
been fooled.

Stephanie sighed.

"You're a good kid," she said. "You might want to get out while you
can."

Over the P.A. system, the attendant announced the preboarding
process. Next up was first class.

"That's me," Stephanie said as she stood up.

I stayed put. There were a few sections to go before my part of the
plane would be called. Stephanie looked down on me. She seemed im-
possibly tall.

"Do you have any connection at all to LyingWye?" I blurted.

She met my gaze and didn't blink. Like she was making a point of
not blinking.

"I would kill that bastard with my bare hands if I knew who he was,"
she replied.

I nodded. I actually believed her. I'd never trusted her, but I felt like
she'd been more honest with me in the last half hour than she'd been
with most people in the past two years. She was still looking at me.

"You know, if this flight isn't completely booked, I bet I could get
you upgraded," she offered. "First class is a much cushier ride."

She was half turned away from me, her fingers grasping her ticket.

I shook my head.

"Thanks, but I'm all set. I'm fine flying coach."

It had sounded more like a declaration than a polite refusal.
Stephanie held my gaze (was it defiant? I hadn't consciously intended
that) a moment longer before nodding.

"Good luck with that," she said as she moved away.

Eighteen frustrating minutes of pushing, jostling, and overhead bin
negotiation later, I was uncomfortably squashed into my middle seat in
the last row of the plane. Charlie called just as the flight attendant was
making the announcement that all cell phones needed to be turned off.
I could have picked up and said a quick hello, but I didn't. Instead I si-
lenced its song, aware that if I crashed, I'd be leaving an imperfect life.

✲   ✲   ✲

On Christmas, I couldn't stop thinking about LyingWye. I'd been so convinced that his source had been Stephanie, but now I knew the answer wasn't that easy. In addition to instinctively believing Stephanie's denial, there was the fact that the latest Camp David leak had occurred *after* she'd left. So then who had overheard the president's change in plans and passed it along? I was determined to get to the bottom of it and spent hours making lists of suspects and possible motives.

I also drank eggnog, soaked in the Jacuzzi tub, listened to *The White Album* three times in a row, and watched *Modern Times* to mark the twenty-ninth anniversary of Charlie Chaplin's death. I recognized that had I been born a half-century earlier, Charlie Chaplin might have been my Steve Martin.

Late on Christmas night, once my mom had finally left my room after her failed lobby to get me to stay another day, I called Charlie and acted like nothing had gone too wrong between us. It was my present to him. I'd accidentally left the gift that he'd given me long ago under the little tree in my room in D.C., but he said it was better that way, that he wanted to be with me when I opened it. Which was when I heard someone attempting to stifle a gasp. My mom, listening from a phone in another part of the house. She'd eavesdropped on my calls throughout my childhood. I'd been silly to think she'd grown out of it. I sighed.

"What is it?" Charlie asked. "Are you all right?"

He was being sensitive in lieu of directly apologizing for having pumped me for confirmation of the Camp David leak.

"I'm fine," I replied. "But I think there's someone on the line with us."

I imagined my mom had assumed the little present might be a ring, which had led to her unstiflable gasp. The thought had crossed my mind as well, but I'd dismissed it. Charlie and I might have been on the brink of getting engaged a few months ago, but too many things had interceded.

I listened as my mom tried to carefully replace the receiver without making too much noise. Why she hadn't mastered the use of the mute button for her eavesdropping endeavors was a mystery to me. I almost felt like giving her some pointers, if it weren't so obviously against my interests to do so.

I got off the phone soon after and lay on my back on my bed, feeling increasingly troubled. I was certainly irritated with my mother, but I didn't have the strength to confront her. I was annoyed with Charlie too, for other reasons. But I was mainly upset with myself. I felt suddenly overwhelmed by a crushing catalog of personal failings. I'd pushed Charlie away without even realizing it. I'd been half expecting him to betray me, so I'd been too quick to distrust, too quick to distance. Then, in trying to get him back, I'd confirmed Wye's drinking after swearing to RG that the secret was safe with me. In one fell swoop, I'd betrayed the confidence of my boss and blurred important boundaries in my relationship with my boyfriend, creating serious trust issues in both my personal and professional life. I'd messed everything up. I started blinking more rapidly at the ceiling as I struggled to catch my breath. I hadn't intended to become so emotional, but I couldn't seem to hold back the shuddering sobs. Another failing.

After succumbing to the sobs for a few minutes, I resolved to pull myself together. I tried to breathe deeply, calm myself down, and intellectualize the problem. It all really came down to privacy. Had I *ever* really had any? Thanks to my mom, I'd been surrounded by eavesdropping my entire life. And recently, I'd encountered it in other areas. In accidental ways, with Charlie's cell phone mishap, and in completely intentional ways, by peering through the peephole and standing outside Stephanie's office. *My* eavesdropping had been necessary. Important, even. And it had been easy. In the White House, I'd just realized, it was actually remarkably easy.

In a flash, my hours of puzzling over the mystery of LyingWye's sources paid off in a spectacular epiphany. I sat straight up in my bed. Eavesdropping. Of course that was the answer. My despair fled as I was flooded with the elation of sudden discovery.

I was so jubilant I called Zelda.

"Merry Christmas!" I exclaimed when she picked up. "I've got news! But how was your holiday?" I added.

This didn't have to be all about me.

"Getting woken up at five a.m. by two boys hopped up on candy canes is not my idea of a holiday," Zelda replied. "They better remember this when I'm old and broken down and don't have any teeth. I better get the best care around. I want top-notch milkshakes."

"I figured out LyingWye!" I announced, unable to delay with further small talk.

Zelda had been fully briefed about the problem and had assured me that my puppet hadn't looked as trashy as I'd thought it did.

"I know you did. You told me. It's Stephanie," she answered.

"No, I was wrong," I replied. "It isn't Stephanie, or any other single administration official. It's all of us. We're *all* his sources! Through the White House operators!"

"Hold on, hold on. Slow down," Zelda said.

I *had* become a bit manic in the euphoria of my finding.

"How would that even work?" she inquired.

"The White House switchboard handles ninety percent of the calls placed and received by people in the White House," I said, trying not to talk too fast. "Plus, they can see whenever anyone is on any line, and can easily jump onto it if they need or want to. Which means that almost every single telephone conversation can be overheard by a switchboard operator."

"Okay," Zelda replied cautiously.

"The operators have a strong reputation for being full of integrity and completely trustworthy," I acknowledged. "But just like CIA agents sometimes turn to the enemy, some of the operators could probably be lured to betrayal as well."

Zelda stayed silent while she processed what I was saying.

"So let's say the president wants to talk to the prime minister of Mongolia," I posited. "He picks up the phone and relays this request to the switchboard operator. That operator makes the connection and rings the president back when the call is set up. Once the president and the prime minister start talking, the operator monitors the call so that in the event that it drops, it will be immediately reconnected. Operators who stay on the line and listen could learn plenty of interesting things that really aren't any of their business."

"But hold on, aren't all the operators cleared by the Secret Service? Aren't they all professionals?"

I should have anticipated that Zelda would feel a sense of solidarity with people who worked with phones.

"Yes, of course, but they aren't screened for political loyalty," I replied. "I'm certainly not accusing *all* of them," I clarified. "Maybe it's just one. Like I said, I'm sure most of them are honest and upstanding. But there could be a bad apple in the bunch."

"Hmm. Do all the operators turn over when a new administration comes in?" Zelda asked. "Or are there operators working there who were hired by the previous one?"

That was an excellent question. I wasn't sure. I knew a lot of the White House support staff, like the ushers and stewards and even the medical personnel, were held over from one administration to the next. I imagined that a lot of the switchboard staff would probably fall into this category as well.

"I think there are most likely a fair number of holdovers," I replied.

"All right, then it *is* possible," Zelda conceded. "But you have to find out for sure before you go accusing innocent people."

"Right," I agreed.

"So, then, you know what to do."

I did?

"You need to test it out," she clarified.

"Right. Absolutely," I replied. "And, um, how exactly would be the best way to do that, do you think?"

"If this operator has been listening in to your conversations, then place some calls with that in mind," Zelda instructed authoritatively. "Make up something and see if it shows up on LyingWye."

"That's genius!" I exclaimed.

"Just don't place the calls to me," Zelda said. "I don't want to be dragged into some White House scandal."

I didn't either, really. But at this point, I didn't seem to have much choice. I might as well try to be involved on my own terms.

I set my plan into motion the next day. I'd hopped on the early-morning flight and gone straight from the airport to work. Everyone was back in action, thanks to Senator Frand's special session.

I'd already briefed Liza on how to react. Though I normally called her directly from my desk line, I made a point of asking the switchboard to connect my call.

"Mayflower Events," Liza answered in her smooth, professional lilt.

"Hey, it's me," I said.

"Hey there," she answered, still in her slightly fake work voice.

There must be other people nearby, otherwise she would have dropped into her normal, familiar tone. Something was prompting her to keep sounding official. But at least she was speaking clearly. I had other friends who felt the need to whisper and mumble when conducting personal calls at work. This prevented coworkers from hearing what they were saying, but it also prevented me from hearing what they were saying. It was very frustrating.

"Having a good day?" I inquired.

"Mmmm . . . an all-star one. How's yours?"

"Not that great," I replied.

"Really? Is it Charlie?"

She sounded distracted.

"No, it's not Charlie," I replied, a little annoyed.

We weren't supposed to be having a real conversation. Was she too busy to do this properly? Her part wasn't that difficult.

"It's the Stephanie stuff."

"Oh, right!" Liza replied, obviously just now remembering the plan. "Is there anything new with that?"

"Actually, yeah. Guess what she accidentally left behind in her desk drawer?"

"What?"

"A diary."

"No!"

"Yes, indeedy."

I paused for a minute, wondering if my use of "yes, indeedy" might have given me away. I was not a person who employed such a phrase. But I doubted LyingWye knew me that well.

"We're just hoping no one else finds out about it, because it could be potentially really damaging. I mean, what if it got subpoenaed or something? Diaries have taken down plenty of folks in the past."

"Wow, have you read it?"

"No, Harry Danson's holding on to it. So, anyway, don't mention it to anyone, okay?"

"Of course not," Liza replied. "I never do."

We got off the phone with a minimum of chitchat. Liza really did sound like she was in the middle of some kind of important catering coordination; I managed to catch something intriguing about fresh mushrooms and a special sauce.

After replacing the receiver, I thought for a few moments about the chances that the rogue operator had connected or been listening in on that particular call. There were countless more high-level ones to eavesdrop on, so even though I'd been a target in the past, there was no reason to believe I was regularly monitored. Maybe I should call some-one else and repeat the story. But who? Zelda had taken herself out of the running. I didn't feel like telling my parents the whole backstory because there would be way too many questions. And I obviously couldn't rope Charlie into this, because then the story would just be that I was leaking things to a *Washington Post* reporter. I was seeing if I could plant a phony story, not a real one.

My fears that I wasn't important enough to have my privacy invaded by the White House turned out to be unfounded—LyingWye posted a story one hour after my call to Liza, all about Stephanie's diary and the detailed accounts of impeachable offenses it allegedly contained. The AP wire picked it up immediately, though it was only reporting on the re-porting. A convenient protection in case the story turned out to be ut-terly false, which I of course knew it was.

Both Stephanie and Harry Danson immediately made statements refuting the story. Harry made a point of adding that though there was no diary, even if there were one, it couldn't possibly contain any docu-mentation of impeachable offenses because none had been perpe-trated. Stephanie simply stuck to disputing the existence of the diary. I imagined she'd calculated long ago that keeping one would be too dan-gerous for precisely this kind of reason.

I was both pleased and a little frightened at how easily I had planted a completely bogus item. It had been in pursuit of the identity of Lying-Wye, but still, I felt guilty. And I was not to remain unpunished.

Once enough of the legitimate news outlets had dismissed the re-port as false, another LyingWye story appeared claiming that I had planted the diary tale in an act of revenge against Stephanie. I hadn't anticipated this kind of development when I'd concocted my plan, though in retrospect, I probably should have. I wondered nervously how much trouble I was going to get in. I had a chance to find out within the hour, when Harry Danson called me into his office to ask if the Lying-Wye accusation was true.

"Not entirely," I replied nervously.

He raised his formidable eyebrows.

"I did make up the story, but only to conduct an experiment."

"Was the experiment to test how quickly you could get yourself fired?" he inquired.

His pointy head had flushed red and his cheeks had turned hard and round. Amid my fear, I wondered if he'd ever grown a beard to be a garden gnome for a costume party or something. Probably not. I doubted he'd ever had the patience.

"I hope not," I answered. "It was aimed at LyingWye. I wanted to see if a story could be generated by someone listening in on my phone conversation. I had a theory that LyingWye's source might be a White House switchboard operator."

To my satisfaction, Harry found my theory extremely interesting. In all his frenzied efforts to root out LyingWye, it had never occurred to him to suspect the White House switchboard. He'd been so focused on which colleague was a traitor. He'd been too ready to be angry with someone closer. With someone higher up.

"I think we all assumed his source was Stephanie, but it's true that these latest things had to come from someone with access she no longer enjoys," Harry concluded, his eyes bright. "Leave this to me."

Harry worked quickly. A White House switchboard operator was fired the following afternoon. She had worked at the switchboard for seven years, and she hadn't been the only White House employee in the family. Her roommate and second cousin had worked as an intern in the Pile administration. This cousin had evidently channeled her fury over the displacement of her party via the election of our administration into devoted service to the Exterminators, who only existed to perpetrate disruptive mischief. Masquerading as a man with high-level administration sources, she'd begun posting the LyingWye blog on the opposition Web site launched by one of the Exterminators. She'd convinced her cousin to use her switchboard operator access to assist in these vengeful pursuits, promising a cut of any profits if the blog took off. Which of course it did. Paid handsomely for their experiment in cyber-revenge, these two women had continued to wreak more havoc than the rest of the Exterminators put together. Decaying mice and surprise stripteases were irritating, but LyingWye had ruined people.

Within hours, the operator and her cousin were besieged. In addition to the media onslaught, both faced possible criminal charges. The LyingWye blog was put on hold. I suspected another Exterminator operative would step up to fill the void, but with luck they would never enjoy the same amount of access.

Harry Danson took most of the public credit for the discovery and dismantling of LyingWye, though my name was mentioned in several of the articles in an unexpected way. Apparently, the operator had been instructed by her cousin to eavesdrop on a few specific people more than others, in order to set up scapegoats. I had evidently been identified as one of these frame-able fall guys. LyingWye had clearly heard of my relationship with Charlie (evidenced by the puppet show she'd devoted to it), so she'd been aware that there were already natural circumstances in place to help set me up. She'd targeted Stephanie as well, but Stephanie had deserved it. Stephanie had proven her disloyalty in spectacular fashion, though we'd have to wait for the book to get all the gritty details.

I was surprised to discover that I wasn't unreservedly overjoyed by the defeat and destruction of LyingWye. I was congratulated by a lot of people who knew the inside story (Margari had baked me a batch of sheriff badge–shaped cinnamon cookies that smelled as good as the perfume she wore), and I was certainly relieved to know that one massive leak had been plugged in our listing ship. But still, the whole thing left me unsettled. I couldn't put my finger on why.

Sense of Sinking

———·•·———

THE VERY NEXT DAY, Chick Wallrey posted a story from India revealing what RG and I had hoped to keep quiet: that the administration had procured a large supply of Focusid as part of the trade agreement. Mythri Patel had refused comment on the story, but Chick had successfully cultivated another source. She'd tracked down a secretary who had recently been fired from Tanbaj Laboratories for stealing more than fifty thousand rupees' worth of printer paper, and managed to manipulate the former employee's bitterness to her own ends. Unfortunately, this very secretary had helped to fill the Focusid request. She told Chick all about it, along with her suspicions that the supply was for something "the American government was trying to cover up."

In an effort to manage the furor that erupted in the wake of Chick's story, the attorney general appointed an independent counsel to investigate. And thus, what had started out as a Congressional probe quickly turned into something much more deadly. I hoped that we might be able to keep people from discovering that the Focusid supply that we'd procured for a clinical trial had ended up becoming the president's personal stash, but I was becoming accustomed to disappointment. Any way I looked at it, the new reality of an independent counsel was terrible news. Opponents spoke of quick indictments, and pundits on both sides amped up the speculation that the Wye presidency might be in serious trouble. On her new morning show, Stephanie compared President Wye to a man on life support.

For all we knew, she wasn't too far off. President Wye hadn't made a public appearance since around the time of the state dinner. He hadn't even made a private one in the West Wing. Everyone knew that the first step toward dispelling the rumors that he was incapacitated with drink was to hold a press conference in which he was sober, lucid, intelligent, and convincing. Not all that much to ask from the most powerful leader in the world, but it had yet to occur. Wye had been absent instead, essentially confirming all that was being said about him. In the age of twenty-four-hour news cycles, absence was unforgivable. And so it could become the entire story.

The White House press office had fallen back on a flu explanation for Wye's low profile, and attempted to assure the skeptical media that the president was still running the country from his bed and hoping to be on his feet again soon.

When President Wye finally did appear, he looked like a dead man walking. I'd just finished skimming a series of op-eds suggesting that RG was now actually running the country when Lincoln informed me that Wye had called a press conference. I hurried downstairs to watch. I so often saw on TV things that were happening just a couple floors below me or a few yards away, but for this, I wanted a front-row seat. Or back row, as it turned out. Very, very back row. I made myself as small and unobtrusive as possible, leaning against the wall as the White House press corps filed into the small briefing room and filled the theater seats.

Looking around at them, I thought about the fact that they worked in a space that used to be an indoor swimming pool. Nixon had ordered the pool to be drained, covered, and converted into a room filled with cubicles for the press. The idea had been to corral them into a specific room for better control, in contrast to Lyndon B. Johnson's policy, which had apparently been to allow the members of the press to lounge in the West Wing lobby, hanging out and keeping tabs on who came and went. Despite their different approaches, both Nixon and LBJ had suffered tormented relationships with the media. And both had oddly recorded secret tapes of their tenures that had only come back to haunt them. Nixon's tapes were well known, but LBJ's were just as revealing in many ways. According to them, Johnson had been a complicated and at times deeply depressed man who had utterly tortured his vice president, Hubert Humphrey.

The room quieted down as President Wye entered and strode slowly to the podium. I wondered if he was trying to make a show of walking a straight line. Maybe he'd stretch out both his arms, close his eyes, and touch each index finger to his nose once or twice before he started speaking. He looked truly awful. Shell-shocked, even—like he'd been startled and burned by a surprise blast. A living Wile E. Coyote after another Acme product explosion. My heart went out to him. I'd always had a soft spot for Wile E. and an intrinsic hatred of the Road Runner. God willing, Wye could pull this off. I noticed I was short of breath.

Just as Wye reached the podium, I saw RG enter the room and stand off to the side, out of most people's line of sight.

"Good morning," President Wye addressed the room.

His voice was slightly unsteady. He took a sip of water from a mug at the podium. At least I assumed it was water.

"I'm speaking to you today to reassure everyone that I am in fact completely healthy, and doing the best job I possibly can to lead this wonderful country of ours to a brighter, better future. I've had a bout with the flu, which I know many of my fellow Americans can relate to, but I'm pleased to report that I'm on the mend. You got that?" He directed this to the assembled press. "You folks seem to be getting a lot of things wrong lately, so I just wanna make sure you got that."

In addition to looking weak, he was clearly upset, but perhaps that was justifiable. I wondered if he was mainly mad at himself.

"The freedom of the press is a right we all hold dear," he continued. "But when lines are crossed, some breaches cannot go unaddressed. Listen to me here today: I haven't taken a single sip of alcohol in more than seventeen years. I don't condemn those who do. I just know what works for me. And that's the truth."

Oh, good God. Why did he have to go and do that? Why did he have to lie? I looked at RG, who was keeping his face a mask of support. Had something flickered across it in the split second Wye had made his false declaration? Back at the podium, Wye brought his hand down defiantly. Though he looked more withered than a healthy man should, his jaw was alive and tensed and a little vein beneath his left eye was throbbing. With his back against the wall, he was ready for a fight.

"Mr. President, what kinds of medication are you on?" the first reporter called on inquired.

Wye looked as though he wanted to tear the reporter several new orifices, but managed to control himself.

"What medications?" he repeated with a chuckle. "You wanna come look in my medicine cabinet?" He jerked his thumb over his shoulder in an awkward hunched motion.

"Yes, sir, I do," the reporter called back.

Several of his colleagues laughed. Anger flashed through Wye's eyes as he readjusted his half grin.

"I bet ya do," Wye said. "Nice try."

There was a clumsy pause. I knew that Wye had undergone pre–press conference prep with his staff and must have practiced for this sort of question. I hoped he could answer it convincingly.

"Nothing out of the ordinary," Wye continued. "I took some over-the-counter stuff for my flu. And I take vitamins, of course. My wife wouldn't have it any other way. She tans my hide if I don't take those vitamins," he finished, letting his grin out all the way.

He looked around for the appreciative chuckles he was accustomed to hearing after one of his folksy phrases, but none came. His grin disappeared as quickly as it had been summoned.

"Is it true that you have a personal supply of Focusid, a medicine that is currently not approved by the FDA for sale in the United States?"

Wye looked surprised, but he didn't hesitate.

"That is not true," Wye answered. "I don't know where you're getting your facts from, son, but I suggest you find a more reliable source. Yes, Mary."

Wye was calling on Mary Foster, a reporter he could usually count on for friendly treatment. He had a habit of calling on her when he got into tight spots.

"Yes, sir, thank you. What do you think is wrong with some of the media these days, that they insist on broadcasting blatant falsehoods?"

There was an audible groan from Mary's colleagues, but the president seemed grateful for the help. Which was all she seemed to care about. She glowed beatifically as he slammed away at her softball question.

There weren't any more Marys to save him, however. The next reporter asked about the independent counsel and whether the rumors of quick indictments were making him nervous.

"Not at all," Wye replied with confidence. "The findings will show that this is a witch hunt. I've run the most ethical administration imaginable. Perhaps even in the entire history of this country. I speak for myself and my administration when I say that we've done *nothing* inappropriate," Wye intoned. *"Mark my words."*

They were marked. And now so was he.

Wye wrapped up the press conference soon after, still angry and a tad too belligerent. He tried to backtrack and turn on his charm at the end, but most people in the room were too busy scribbling in their notebooks to notice.

I slipped out and hurried back toward RG's office, where Margari and the other aides were fielding calls at their desks. Margari looked up at me and offered a thumbs-up and a thumbs-down with a questioning shrug. I shrugged back. I didn't know which to choose.

"Yes, Ambassador, I understand. I'll make sure he receives the message," she said into the phone.

RG walked in. He didn't even seem to see us, he just headed straight for his inner office. Margari hurried off the phone.

"Sir, Secretary Harlow is wondering whether she could—"

RG paused very briefly at the doorway. He didn't look back, he just held up his hand, and Margari quieted immediately. RG then closed his hand into a fist, walked into his office, and shut the door behind him. We all stared after him in shock.

"What happened back there?" Margari asked in a hushed whisper.

I didn't have a good answer. I just shook my head.

RG stayed in his office for almost an hour. No one dared bother him. I thought about returning to my desk one floor up, but I didn't want to move. I felt like I was standing some sort of guard. That I was proving something, even if it looked like loitering to everyone else.

I wondered what was going through his head. We could see that he wasn't on the phone, so perhaps he was just sitting there. Alone. Thinking.

Fifty-five minutes after going into his office, he reappeared.

"I'm going to need some more Mountain Dew," he said to no one in particular.

He noticed me for the first time.

"Come in for a moment, can you?" he asked.

"Absolutely, sir."

I jumped up from the chair I'd been sitting guard in. My leg had fallen asleep and I stomped and jostled it a little as I crossed the room, but I couldn't shake away the feeling of dead weight.

Inside RG's office, he indicated the couch in front of the fireplace he rarely lit.

"Have a seat," he instructed.

He didn't do the same. He started pacing back and forth behind his desk. RG could pace with the best of them. I knew that he went on morning jogs before coming into the office, but he usually logged enough carpet miles during any given day to keep an average man in tip-top cardiovascular shape. It was how he worked through problems. He walked them through his mind.

"What would you do if you were me?" he finally asked.

"Sir?"

He wasn't really asking me for advice. This was just some sort of crazy test.

"I'm just curious," he continued. "Your partner, your boss, lies to the world. And there's no going back. The damage is done. He doesn't give a crap about your reputation, about your sacrifices, about your plans for the future. He only cares about himself. And he's willing to jeopardize everything we've worked for . . . for what? Why? What do you do?"

Keep your mouth shut, my internal voice instructed. I obeyed, and I imagined RG would too, in the end.

He chuckled unnaturally.

"Exactly," he said.

I'd never looked at RG with real pity before. I'd felt for him countless times, but he'd always projected a strength and self-assurance that rendered pity pointless. This was a new moment for us. Perhaps he'd been lost before, but never so openly, never in my presence. I got the impression I was just there to be a backboard for his self-therapy, but maybe I could offer some solace as well.

"Do you still believe in him?" I asked, as I asked the same of myself.

RG didn't answer immediately. He paced another floor length, absorbed in unexpressed thoughts.

"That question presupposes that I ever did in the first place," he finally replied with jarring bitterness.

"But you did," I rejoined automatically.

I'd seen it. I'd been there when he'd decided to endorse Wye for the presidential nomination three years ago. I'd helped set up the endorsement event and then flown on the campaign plane with the two of them around Ohio. I'd watched them bond. I'd seen the connection. It was real.

RG seemed surprised by my quick answer. By my refusal to let him get away with a revisionist sob story. He stared at me a moment and I wondered if I was about to have my head bitten off. I prepared for the sting.

Finally, instead of yelling at me, he sighed.

"Yes, I suppose I did," he agreed.

That was better. I felt validated. We at least could tell the truth, even if Wye declined to.

"But I didn't realize how weak he truly is," he continued. "It's just amazing how quickly a person you thought you knew can completely disappoint you."

I kept my head down, worried that if he happened to look straight into my eyes he'd be able to tell that he was staring at another disappointer.

"There's no question he means well," RG continued. "And he's brilliant to a point. But he can't seem to get out of his own goddamned way."

I wondered if RG had or would speak like this with anyone else. I felt worried for him.

"And now we're all trapped," he said quietly. "Now he's made us all look like liars."

RG was sent away soon after. First to Ukraine, then China, then Brazil. There were believable justifications for all the trips, but I couldn't help but feel they were a part of a larger banishment plan. I was confident that he felt the same.

The rumor was that Wye had taken to his bed once more with the "flu." With RG gone, I held no hope of being included in the meetings of the high command, but I managed to pick up from others that Fiona Wye seemed to have replaced Stephanie as head strategist. She and Harry Danson were running the show and were therefore behind RG's exile. I wondered if he'd been too honest with them, or if they'd simply sought to neutralize his inherent threat to their authority. After all, he was the one who was supposed to assume power in the event of the president's incompetence. They were all well aware of this, and it made for automatic tension.

In further testament to Fiona's paranoia, several White House stewards and lower-level staffers were abruptly fired. It wasn't clear whether or not Fiona's handwriting analyst had played a role in this purge but I guessed that Fiona was attempting to clear the place of anyone who could have observed the president consuming drink or drugs. She wasn't endearing herself to many in the West Wing as she lashed about, strewing considerable wreckage in her furious wake. Not for the first time, I thought that "Fiona" made for a good hurricane name.

Though Senator Frand's special session finally came to an end in early January when the new crop of senators and representatives took office, a lot of damage had already been done. Even though the president now technically enjoyed majority support in Congress, the scandals surrounding him had turned many reliable friends into skeptical critics. It didn't help that Senator Bramen was chosen to be the new majority leader. Bramen pledged to move the Senate forward to more important business, but he presided over a few more Wye-skewering sessions with barely concealed glee. I wondered if Bramen had saved Wye's drunken voice mail. RG had promised to handle the Bramen situation, but I worried that he'd been sent away before he could.

As the Senate stalled and the media continued to discuss the ongoing question of Wye's sobriety, an air of insecurity and uncertainty descended on the West Wing. People were noticeably frightened and unsure of themselves for the first time since we'd taken office. Though we'd been under attack from the very beginning, we hadn't felt the blows till now. People debated in whispers whether the allegations could be true, despite the president's direct denials. Doubt came to roost, sowing division all around, and our swagger faltered and fell away.

It infected my normally safe sanctum on a late afternoon when RG had been gone for two weeks. I'd been working through some reports about a Dutch company that appeared to have faked their cancer breakthrough findings when I felt someone staring at me. It was Sofia. I'd forgotten that she was scheduled to talk to Lincoln, who hadn't yet returned from a meeting on the Hill. How long had she been standing in the doorway, watching me with that familiar expression of distaste?

"Hi," I said. "Lincoln should be back any minute."

Sofia nodded with thinly veiled annoyance at my existence. Unfortunately, this triggered my babbling reflex. Every once in a while, when confronted with disdain, I talk uncontrollably, as if I could wash away a person's prejudice with a river of words.

"Actually, Lincoln's been running late a lot because he's so swamped lately. We all are, really. You'd think with RG gone, there'd be less to do, but it's the opposite. There seems to be more and more to deal with every day. Do you know what I mean? Or don't you? You switched over to the president's foreign policy office recently, right? Was that like a promotion?"

Sofia didn't even bother to answer my onslaught of questions. When she did speak, it was in a distant tone. As if she were talking to herself and I was just lucky to overhear.

"It has been different with RG gone," she mused. "I wonder if it's true what they're saying about him."

"What are they saying?" I demanded.

My protective tone compelled Sofia to regard me with new interest. She seemed intrigued that she'd gotten a little rise out of me.

"That he's being kept away on purpose," she said evenly.

"Who's saying that?"

"Tons of people," she replied. "He's been gone for quite a while. And they apparently just added Turkey to his itinerary."

They had.

"Well, he's just taking over the trips that Wye can't make on his own right now." I shrugged.

As soon as I said it, I realized how it sounded. And I saw Sofia bristle.

"I mean, not because Wye's incapable or anything. Just because he has to stick around and handle everything," I clarified. "So RG's just pitching in."

Sofia nodded.

"I can't imagine how tough it's got to be on him," she said.

That was more like it.

"Well, I'm sure he'll be back soon," I said mildly.

"I'm talking about President Wye!" Sofia exclaimed.

She seemed outraged that I could have assumed anything else.

"Oh. Yes," I answered, a little uncertainly. "You mean about the rumors."

I still used the word "rumors." I was getting better at pretending I didn't know things.

"They're not just *rumors*," Sofia said hotly. "That makes them sound more harmless than they are. They're awful, vicious lies!"

"Right," I replied, masking the fact that I was so sick of hearing passionate defenses of the president by people who didn't know any better.

I understood that loyalty to him was natural and ingrained, but I was cursed with knowing too much. And this knowledge made others' blind devotion seem suddenly juvenile. It was a lonely position to be in. I was happier before, comfortable in the faithful herd.

"It's amazing how low people will stoop," Sofia continued, shaking her head in disgust.

I agreed with that.

"And I think you're being naïve about RG," she added. "He's obviously being kept away. And do you know *why* he's been sent off?"

Sofia had lowered her voice a bit, a satisfied gleam back in her eye. I could see that she'd returned to repeating gossip that she actually believed in. Making those distinctions about hearsay was a slippery slope toward being a permanently bad person.

I stayed quiet.

"The word is that RG actually *wants* the lies about Wye to be true," Sofia continued. "That he wants Wye to fail so he can step in and take over. And that he made it pretty clear that he was prepared to do so, which is why he's been sent away."

"That's the word, huh?"

Sofia nodded knowingly.

"Has that word been handed down from on high?" I asked.

Dropped from the eye of a hurricane?

"I don't know what you mean," Sofia answered.

"I mean, you must have heard it from someone specific. Unless it's your own stupid theory and you're trying to make it sound more credible. Though I'm beginning to doubt that your petty brain is capable of—"

"What's going on in here?" Lincoln interrupted from the hallway.

It was lucky that he had. Things had been about to turn very ugly. Sofia was staring at me, incensed.

"Nothing." I sighed, embarrassed that I'd sunk to her level.

"Nothing?" Lincoln repeated skeptically.

"I was just mentioning what some people were saying about RG being gone and Sammy jumped all over me," Sofia reported.

Forget the high road. I couldn't let that account stand.

"Sofia was suggesting that RG attempted some kind of coup and has been cast away," I clarified to Lincoln.

"I didn't say *I* believed it," Sofia said dismissively. "I just said that's what the word is."

"All right, all right, calm down," Lincoln said. "It's unfortunate that anyone is spreading that rumor. It's not true. Honestly, we're all on the same team here."

Sofia nodded. "I certainly hope so," she said.

I wanted to punch her.

"We are," Lincoln reiterated firmly. "And we certainly are within this office. Everyone's under a lot of stress at the moment, but let's try to remain clear-headed and cordial, okay?"

Lincoln looked from me to Sofia. Feeling like a child, I nodded contritely. It wasn't until later that I thought about how uncharacteristic it was for Lincoln to take charge so forcefully in the face of human conflict. He had risen to an occasion and in the heat of my animosity toward Sofia, I hadn't even noticed it.

Our office wasn't the only part of the White House in need of mediation. I began to observe serious tension in other formerly harmonious places as well.

"All I'm saying is that if it's true, he should just sober up, admit it, apologize, and move on. It's not like it's against the law," I heard an intern whisper to Nick as they crossed in front of me in the White House mess to pick up lunch orders for their superiors. He then looked worriedly back at me, suddenly aware that I might have heard. His face was strained with an expression of fearful defiance. I smiled neutrally and looked away. This was not how I wanted to spend my time. I decided to just focus on getting my hot dog. They tend to cheer me up.

"A White House divided against itself," I thought to myself as I balanced my tray.

"What's that?" a mess steward asked.

I hadn't thought it. I'd said it out loud. I really needed to be more in control. Especially these days.

"Nothing," I replied, trying to think of something safe to say. "I was just remembering how I used to buy those premade, packaged cheese dogs and how fundamentally gross they were."

It hadn't bothered me as a kid, but really, how disgusting.

"Mmm . . ." was the reply. "Well, we just picked these straight off the hot dog tree, so they should be really fresh."

I laughed. He wasn't making fun of me, right? Or was he? I moved away and was about to take my food back to my desk when I spotted Dr. Humphrey sitting at a table by himself. The tables in the dining room were only for people who'd made actual reservations for lunch. Almost everyone I knew simply called down their order, picked up their food when it was ready, and ate it back at their desks.

Dr. Humphrey appeared to have made a reservation for one. An untouched sandwich lay in front of him while he sipped coffee and stared at the far wall. I moved closer to get a better view of how exhausted he looked. Sensing me, he looked up.

"Hi," I said, acknowledging that I'd been watching him. "How's it going?"

"Fine," he answered, pleasantly enough.

"Thanks for the inoculations a few months back," I continued. "I didn't die from a single disease in India."

Dr. Humphrey smiled. He saw me glance at the chair across from him.

"Would you like to take a seat?" he asked politely.

I would, but was that allowed? I hadn't made a reservation and I had a lot of work to get done over lunch. But I was curious about Dr. Humphrey. I nodded and sat down with my tray.

"Thanks. Not hungry?" I asked, indicating his intact food.

"I'll get around to it," he replied.

I swirled the ketchup and mustard together on my hot dog, hoping to make orange. It was the closest I'd come today to getting some fruit in me.

"How's the short-term memory loss?" Dr. Humphrey asked.

I looked up quickly to check if he was teasing me, but he didn't seem to be. He was too detached to appear very concerned, but I appreciated the checkup nonetheless.

"Better, thanks. I think I'll live. Do you ever worry that you're coming down with things you read about?"

Dr. Humphrey shook his head.

"It's too exhausting to mix hypochondria with a profession in health care," he answered.

Tell me about it. I dealt only with health care policy, and I was perpetually tuckered out. I couldn't imagine what it would be like if I were a licensed practitioner, willingly exposing myself to diseases on a daily basis. I'd never make it.

Dr. Humphrey seemed distressingly sensible to me. I found myself wondering if he had children, and if they still thought he was cool.

"Do you have any kids?" I asked before feeling self-conscious for getting so personal.

But he seemed pleased to be asked. He nodded.

"A son. Five years old. Bert. Goes to the same school as Lincoln Thomas's daughter, Emily."

It sounded more like a diagnosis than a description. Even when discussing things that clearly made him happy, Dr. Humphrey sounded as though he were reading from a medical chart.

"Does Bert know what you do?" I asked.

Dr. Humphrey's eyes seemed to cloud a bit.

"He tells people I take care of the president when he's sick."

I imagined this must have been cuter a few months ago than in recent weeks.

"He must be very proud of you," I said as I brought up my hot dog for a bite.

"You think?"

The plaintiveness in his voice surprised me. The hot dog hovered in front of me, my hand paused by Dr. Humphrey's oddly wistful tone.

"Of course," I replied, hoping I sounded genuine.

For some reason, Dr. Humphrey suddenly seemed like he needed reassuring.

"I hope he is. I hope he will be," he said slowly.

He was staring past me, at the wall again. Something in his preoccupied stare reminded me of RG's pacing, of undisclosed ache.

"Are you okay?" I asked.

He snapped back into the moment.

"Yes, of course," he said smoothly.

I didn't believe him, and I resolved to more artfully probe the thoughts behind his stare. I wondered if there was a subtle way to let him know that I knew the truth about the drinking, that I knew about the Focusid.

"I know it's got to be a difficult time right now," I said carefully. "But you shouldn't blame yourself for anything. I'm sure your son thinks you're a hero, and he's right."

I looked down and took a bite of my hot dog to cover the embarrassment I immediately felt after saying this. I snuck a darting glance back up to see Dr. Humphrey staring at me, just as my teeth crunched into something unfamiliar.

"Uwlk," I coughed into my napkin.

It was a tiny feather. In my all-beef hot dog. A wet, tiny feather. Even had it been a turkey dog, this just wasn't the least bit acceptable. I excused myself and raced to the bathroom, where I rinsed my mouth out with water. And when I returned to the table, Dr. Humphrey had left. I threw away the rest of my food, wondering if anything around here could really be trusted.

After lodging a complaint with an alarmingly unsympathetic mess steward, I climbed the stairs to the ground floor and stepped outside to breathe in some fresh, cold air in an attempt to cure my nausea. I heard the gates closing and turned around to see Jenny Gary's two-car motorcade pulling up the driveway. She had an office in the Old Executive Office Building that she normally visited about once a week, but lately she'd been coming every day, as if trying to make up for RG's absence.

"Sammy, hi," she said when she saw me. "I'm glad to run into you. Do you have a minute?"

"Of course, Mrs. Gary," I replied.

"Please. It's Jenny. You know that," she chided me. "Walk with me to my office."

Once there, her chief of staff diverted her with some pressing scheduling concerns. While they went over their business, I stood outside in the entryway part of the office, admiring the many framed political cartoons that hung on the walls. Jenny was an aficionado and had amassed quite a collection. I lingered particularly over the Garry Trudeau prints. I was a big *Doonesbury* fan.

I was just wondering what kinds of things Garry Trudeau and Jane Pauley talked about over the breakfast table and realizing that I'd been specifically visualizing a breakfast table rather than a dinner one thanks to my association of cartoons with coffee and mornings when the chief of staff walked by me and Jenny called me in.

"Aren't those great?" she asked, with a nod toward the Garry Trudeau prints.

She seemed in a better mood.

"Amazing," I replied. "And I'm assuming you're not just a fan because of the name."

Jenny laughed.

"Though I am partial to all things Gary, I have to admit it's his talent that attracted me."

"Sure, sure," I replied teasingly.

I'd forgotten how easy it was for me to slip into treating Jenny like a friend. I supposed we were friends, on some level, but I imagined that this sentiment had a lot to do with her ability to make everyone feel that way. People enjoyed being around Jenny Gary, and not just because she smelled like baby powder. She was refreshingly unpretentious, which was a rare and welcome characteristic. Even rarer and more welcome, she was fun. Everyone on staff that I knew wished she was around a whole lot more.

"Have a seat," she offered.

"Sugar Magnolia" was playing softly through the speakers in her office. I looked around. There were more cartoons on her wall, plus several photographs of Jack and Jeffrey in various stages of twindom.

"How are the boys?" I asked.

They'd been born the same week I'd begun work in RG's Senate office. Consequently, I'd always felt a kind of primal connection with them. I wondered suddenly if they even knew who I was. I'd held them plenty of times when they were much younger, and I had unwillingly been soiled with a fair amount of their baby bodily fluids, but I hadn't seen them much since the White House days had begun. In the past two years, our link had become anecdotal.

"They're fantastic." Jenny grinned. "Feel free to borrow them whenever you like. If you need any redecorating done and are partial to the permanent marker medium, they're your boys."

I laughed.

"Still a handful, huh?"

Jenny nodded.

"The navy stewards would put them in the brig if they could. We've had to rewallpaper twice in the last four months. And I can't even talk about the rugs."

"Wow."

"I know. I think they've got some permanent marker dealer on the inside. Honestly, I canvass the house from floor to ceiling getting rid of those things and the next thing I know, Jeff is outlining Jack with a Sharpie on the white carpet in the landing. Anyone who walked up to the second floor would think they'd stumbled onto a crime scene."

"Your husband is very partial to Sharpies . . ." I pointed out.

He used them to sign things. Mainly photos of himself with other people who wanted to have them. There were always piles of these to go through every day. I knew RG didn't particularly enjoy the task, but how could he not be flattered?

"Oh, I know." Jenny nodded. "Believe me, I know exactly where to point the finger. I even know which finger to use," she added with a grin.

"Is he doing okay?" I asked seriously.

I knew RG was doing good work from the coverage of his trip. The upside of his banishment was that our foreign relations with four of the countries he'd visited were the best they'd been in years. But that's not what I meant. Jenny sighed.

"You mean, in exile?" she said with a little laugh. "Sure. What's not to love? I think he and the Dalai Lama are going to meet up in Monte Carlo for some blackjack."

I smiled back but it felt forced.

"I wish he'd come back."

"Oh, he will," Jenny replied. "Don't worry. How are you and Charlie doing?" she asked curiously.

I grimaced before I could stop myself. Things certainly weren't perfect between Charlie and me, but that didn't mean I had to go broadcasting our troubles. Jenny was most likely asking about the state of our relationship in light of the *Us Weekly* debacle, but I wondered suddenly if there might be something more to her question. Thanks to the diversion of Stephanie's departure, no one had seemed to suspect that my relationship with Charlie could have been linked to the *Washington Post*'s confirmation of the Wye drinking scandal. But Jenny picked up on things other people didn't. She very likely could have guessed that I'd been the unnamed source. I wondered if she'd wanted to meet with me just to assess for herself whether I could still be trusted.

Before I could explain my grimace, Jenny's chief of staff stuck her head in.

"Sorry to interrupt, but you might want to turn on C-SPAN," she said.

Jenny clicked on the monitor behind her desk. It was programmed to Nickelodeon, but the audio came on before the visual and it took me a second to realize that I was listening to SpongeBob SquarePants and not to Senator Rich Toram. They sounded remarkably alike.

"I had the boys in here the other day," Jenny explained.

She switched the channel and Senator Bramen appeared on the screen. He was addressing the Senate in a voice at least an octave lower than his normal one. Jenny groaned. I smiled. I liked that she couldn't control her dislike. It made her even more relatable.

"So it is with a heavy heart that I say to you tonight that I can no longer support this administration. Not until they come clean. Not until they clean up their act. I won't embarrass them by making public *all* the information I have that has led me to this gut-wrenching decision. Suffice it to say, any other man of honor and integrity would surely reach the same conclusion I have. Above party, above all else, I am first an American. And as an American, I stand here saddened but determined. Determined to represent my fellow countrymen the best way I know how, even when it is difficult, even when it calls for unprecedented courage. Even when it requires a heroic . . ."

Jenny lowered the volume until it was just a muffled buzz. Accompanied by "Uncle John's Band," which was just now starting to play through the stereo speakers. Jenny stared for a few more seconds at Senator Bramen's grave gesticulations before searching for something on her computer.

"Why is he doing this now?" I asked.

Bramen was always ready to turn on the administration, but it seemed like something special would have had to happen to trigger this bold a move. I wondered again about the drunken phone call Wye had placed to Bramen. It seemed that my worries were confirmed— RG evidently *hadn't* had time to handle the situation before he'd been sent away.

Jenny was fully absorbed in her computer. I felt impotent without my own search engine at my fingertips. I tried to search her face for clues to her discoveries instead.

"Apparently, President Wye has been subpoenaed to appear before the independent counsel," she finally reported.

"Can they do that?" I asked.

It was a stupid question, I knew. He was the president, but he wasn't above the law, no matter how much he might yearn to be. Jenny was absorbed in her reading.

"When?" I asked.

"They're in negotiations. This all just hit the wire a few moments ago."

Shouldn't we have found out another way, and earlier? We were in the White House, after all. And though I was just a staffer, Jenny was the second lady, or whatever less demeaning title one wanted to call her. The point was, she was the vice president's wife and should be told about things like this ahead of time.

Jenny was now trying to get RG on the phone. As she waited for the operator to call her back with RG on the other line, she looked over at me. I stood up quickly.

"I should go, of course," I said.

Jenny didn't disagree.

"I hope we can continue our talk later," she said evenly.

She was warm, but she let you know when it was time to go. And really, I should have realized that that time had come several minutes ago. Behind her, Senator Bramen was still pontificating. He raised his arms up and down several times to emphasize his points. His limbs were long enough that any big gestures like these seemed languid. With the volume low, the Grateful Dead provided the lyrics to his slow motion marionette show:

"Got some things to talk about, here beside the rising tide."

I looked from the screen back to Jenny, who was watching me. I wanted her to tell me everything was going to be okay, but she looked as unsure of that as me. We'd been trying our best to weather this storm but we knew we were in trouble. Was our listing ship now officially sinking? There were so many things still to talk about. Like whether we really needed to abandon ship, or if it was premature to contemplate something so drastic. When it came to jumping overboard, I'd been known to leap before I thought.

Wishful Thinking?

—·—

SENATOR LANE MORRIS TOSSED OUT a lifeline later that afternoon. As soon as I heard Senator Bramen say that he was "recognizing the junior senator from Wisconsin," my head snapped up toward the TV in our office that was permanently tuned to the Senate proceedings. There was Senator Morris, standing at the podium, looking around at the nearly vacant gallery. Even during the most heated debates, I was surprised at how often senators were addressing empty seats. It made sense that so many of them seemed perpetually starved for attention. Even in their most accessible arena, their battles were sparsely attended.

Senator Morris didn't seem bothered by the lack of a tangible audience. Everything was on the record, so if anything newsworthy was said on the floor, her colleagues and the public would know soon enough.

She looked as purposeful as ever, her gray eyes flashing with reprimand. I blushed as I recalled the night she'd propositioned me, then struggled to clear my head of the memory to focus on what she was saying now. Where Bramen strove for flowery oratorical heights, Senator Morris was straightforward, almost simple. The contrast seemed especially intentional this early evening, since she was challenging Bramen head-on.

"Too often in these chambers, we lose our bearings," she chastised. "We should certainly be passionate, but we shouldn't be lured into useless drama. The United States Senate can't afford to have a petty agenda or a short fuse. Peddling rumors is beneath us. We must be composed, we must be reasonable, we must be wise. We must be wise *now*. There's been a lot of talk about our president and whether he drinks or not, and how much, and when, and where. This is a waste of both time and dignity. I've listened to so many colleagues express what they describe as 'moral out-rage' over our president's alleged behavior. And as I've listened, I've come to believe that the accusation of impaired judgment more accurately ap-plies to what's happening right here, on this end of Pennsylvania Avenue. Over here, it seems to me, people have grown tipsy from the whiff of blood in the water. So I'm here to sober you up."

She kept going, and I sat staring at her, utterly rapt. She was miracu-lous. Knowing what I did, I couldn't totally agree with her conclusions, but I applauded her perspective. And I recognized that she was what we needed. She was an unlikely champion, a would-be captain who hadn't been picked. As she spoke, I wondered if her words were having the same impact on her colleagues. Did others hear what I heard?

More speakers took the floor once Morris was done. And many of them tried to whip up the anti-Wye frenzy once more. Even those who counted the president the head of their party, since Bramen had em-boldened revolt. Yet one or two cited Senator Morris in their rationale for standing by Wye. In a place powered by talk, this was at least some-thing. Senator Morris had briefly blunted the force of an ill wind that had previously been blowing unchecked.

Soon after, we received word that RG would be returning the follow-ing day. Perhaps Fiona and Harry had decided that they needed him back. Perhaps they were planning another press conference for Wye, and realized that the White House would seem a little too lonely without him standing nearby, clapping, implicating himself with his support.

When I'd mentioned this to Lincoln, he'd tsk-tsked me with a look. I knew that he was as loyal to RG as I was, but he was still aiming for unity, and therefore disapproved of spiteful comments that only added to the turmoil. Lincoln seemed to grow bolder and surer of himself in direct proportion to the unraveling of his surrounding environment. As tensions had risen and divisions entrenched, he'd become ever calmer, anchoring himself in some previously unperceived bedrock.

I felt small-minded and inadequate in contrast. How had RG de-scribed me to Stephanie—as a "genius in a crisis"? I didn't feel that I was living up to that billing. Though I'd been briefly energized by Morris's words and the news of RG's impending return, I couldn't shake a sense of helpless numbness as everyone around me reacted to the fact that our president had been summoned before the independent counsel.

I worked very late, trying to punch through this haze. Trying to feel hopeful, or at least active. But I couldn't quite manage it. I worried that some fearful destiny had taken hold and locked us into an unfortunate path. Near midnight, as I trudged up the outside stairs of my apartment, I slipped on a fresh patch of ice. The slip itself was sudden, but the time between the slip and the impact of my body hitting the ground felt strangely drawn out. Though even with this slow-motion sensation, I still didn't get my arms out in time to break my fall—I just toppled sideways onto the little patio next to the stair.

I didn't consciously decide to stay lying there, but I didn't make any move to get up either. It had been raining nonstop for weeks, with the temperatures hovering just above freezing. It was only at night that the sleet came, and it was falling softly on me now. I closed my eyes and opened my mouth, and pretended that my exhaustion was a blanket keeping me warm. I'd read a short story about what it was like to freeze to death, and it had sounded peaceful to someone who was always sleep-deprived. It had sounded like a nice break.

I wondered how long it would take for someone to notice me if I just kept lying there. Ten minutes later, I decided that it might take all night. It didn't seem like anyone was going to walk by and inquire after my health. The street was empty. People were either asleep in their beds or busy rescuing others. I was on my own.

Grudgingly, I picked myself up and trekked up the stairs and indoors, pausing long enough on my way to Liza's room to check on my pets.

Who were not doing well.

"Oh, no. *No*," I said aloud after flicking on the light.

The symptoms were unmistakable. It was mossy gill disease, and they'd both come down with it. I knew from painful experience that my Japanese fighting fish weren't long for this world. Because once it got to this stage, it was fatal. How had they contracted it? Was I to blame? I'd been too preoccupied with everything else. Maybe I could have done something if I'd only noticed it earlier.

I felt my eyes start to well up. I'd do what I could now, but I knew there wasn't any hope. I walked slowly to their bowls and kissed the glass of each. Samson flared up, ready to attack my lips. At least he still had the strength for that.

Liza was in her room, reading. Alone.

"Did you see Samson and Professor Moriarty?" I asked.

"They were looking a little green around the gills," Liza acknowledged.

I nodded, trying to swallow the lump in my throat.

"Don't worry, they'll perk up!" she encouraged.

She could be so wrong.

"How are things with Jakers?" I failed to ask casually.

Liza shrugged.

"Fine. He's out with his brother tonight. Why?"

"Just wondering. You mentioned things weren't that great the other day. That you guys were having some problems."

Which had overjoyed me.

"False alarm," Liza replied, looking back down at her book.

Perhaps I wasn't as good at masking my intense desire for them to part ways as I thought. She didn't look up again. Feeling unsupported and unsupportive, I turned and slunk toward my room.

"I'm not going to marry him, you know," she called after me.

I turned back toward her. She laughed.

"You don't have to look so thrilled."

I readjusted my face.

"Sorry."

"I know you don't like him," Liza continued. "I don't like him myself some of the time. But I like trying to work things out with him. I'll break up with him eventually, but till then, he's research."

I nodded and fought the urge to ask why she was researching offensive, man-boy Neanderthals. Maybe she was trying to isolate the opposite of everything she wanted in a single person.

"Okay," I replied. "Thanks for telling me. So how long are we looking at? Two months? Four?"

"It's not a prison sentence." Liza laughed again.

I begged to differ.

"It'll happen sooner rather than later," she continued. "I'm not dying to hurt him. He does love me, you know."

"Of course he does! You're the best he could ever dream of having. You're doing him a favor even allowing him within twenty feet of you."

Many times, I'd fantasized about restraining orders for Jakers.

"Well, for now, he satisfies certain cravings and generally makes me feel good, so I just ignore his less savory parts," Liza concluded,

"That's how I used to feel about hot dogs," I pointed out.

Liza threw her pillow at me.

"Not everyone meets the love of her life so young, you know," she said with a rueful smile.

I knew that. I knew that I'd been very lucky to meet Charlie when I did. Though we'd obviously had a fair amount of growing up to do together.

"Not all of us even want that," she added gently, presenting an unexpected challenge to my "I'm so lucky" attitude.

Wow. That was a new way to look at things. I felt as though I was finally understanding something incredibly crucial about Liza that I should have realized long ago. Ever since I'd known her, I'd assumed that we shared the same vision for our futures, the same basic plans and dreams when it came to romance. But I'd been wrong. I'd had my vision and she'd had hers. And hers involved a whole lot more challenge, drama, and action. Years and years more. To her, my desire to be with a good man whom I truly loved must have always seemed somewhat uneventful, but she'd been too polite to say so. She'd let me cluelessly assume that everyone wanted what I did, when I did, simply to keep from disillusioning me. To protect me from realizing that others might look at my amazing good luck and consider it slightly boring and monotonous at this stage of our lives.

"You really *don't* want that, do you?" I said aloud.

Liza shook her head.

"Not yet," she replied. "Eventually, maybe. But there's so much for me to do first. And so many." She grinned.

I smiled back as I nodded in belated, dawning comprehension. I'd been so dense, but I finally got it. I felt like I was really recognizing my best friend for the first time.

"To your research, then," I said, pantomiming lifting a wineglass in toast.

"To your understanding," she replied, mirroring my move.

I was suddenly filled with a rush of love for her. Followed by fear. I depended on her in so many ways and couldn't imagine my life without her, but now that I was aware of our fundamental difference, should I be preparing myself for inevitable abandonment? Liza craved adventure and exploration in a much more visceral way. She was about to get her pilot's license, for God's sake. I'd been assuming she'd be my roommate and best friend for as long as I wanted, but what if she took off?

"Please don't fly off into the sunset," I said urgently. "I understand if you need to, of course, but I'm not so sure I can live in a place without you."

Liza smiled and hugged me.

"I've got plans here for a while," she replied. "And don't worry, no matter where we end up, you'll never be able to get rid of me."

That was a relief. I needed her close.

"Plus, you really never know," Liza added. "You might be the one to go off adventuring first. You got mail, by the way. I put it on your bed."

It was a letter from Charlie. We hadn't been speaking much lately. We blamed it on work, but I knew that when I spoke to him at any length again, I wanted it to be in person. This letter was a surprise. As I opened it, I was overpowered by the smell of musk.

Dear Sammy,

So the man perfume is a joke, but this letter is otherwise serious. I realized that since your New York visit, I've treated you occasionally as a source and not just as the woman I love. And that even though you offered yourself up as one, you're not comfortable continuing that role. I'm not comfortable wanting you to. So this is a letter of apology, very formal and serious and heavenly smelling. I hope you'll accept and embrace all the sentiments and scents enclosed, and know that whenever I think of you (which is all the time), I consider myself the luckiest man on the face of the earth. I hope Lou Gehrig doesn't mind me ripping off his line. And I hope Liza doesn't hate me for loving a Yankee. Let's fix us soon. I'm sorry, and I love you.

Yours always,
Charlie

It was a good letter. Good enough to be an antidote. I breathed in deeply, gratefully, and was thrown into a coughing fit. That was some pungent musk.

Charlie answered on the first ring.

"I got your letter," I said.

"Any typos?" he asked.

"Can you really call them typos when it's handwritten?"

"I dictated it to my robot, who wrote it out."

"Got it. I guess you can, then."

"I was going to BlackBerry it, but that seemed so old-fashioned."

"Mmmm. Well, thank you for it. I don't want to get all serious over the phone, but it means a lot."

"You're welcome. I hope you do forgive me. I'm sorry if I made things weird."

"We both did. What are the chances I can see you this weekend?"

"Excellent."

Which, of course, wasn't really the case. We were being optimistic in the face of an exploding scandal that threatened to swamp us all. RG did make it back to the White House the next day, and disappeared immediately into meetings with the senior West Wing staff. Part of me had expected a message to join them, but none came. Instead, I was e-mailed a breaking news alert that the independent counsel had obtained the testimony of a star witness and was pressuring the president's lawyers to meet with them that afternoon. The identity of the "star witness" hadn't been revealed, but there was considerable speculation that it was Stephanie Grader. Though the story about her diary had been proven fake, it had allegedly given the special prosecutor some ideas. I was grateful my name wasn't mentioned. Being associated with the potential downfall of the president might be a good career move for some people, but it held no appeal for me.

If Stephanie had testified, I knew that Wye had good reason to be exquisitely concerned. I imagined that she would be honest—whether she was beholden to the truth was up for debate, but her devotion to Nielsen ratings and book publicity was unquestionable.

But it wasn't Stephanie. I was talking with Senator Morris's chief of staff about the timeline for the Lifestyle Drug Bill in the event that the Senate ever got around to addressing real business again, when Dr. Humphrey's face flashed on the screen.

"I'm so sorry, I have to call you back," I said into the phone.

I didn't even wait for a response. I just replaced the receiver with one hand and turned up the remote with the other. I felt a craving for a cigarette.

Dr. Humphrey was exiting a car and walking toward a house. It was a fancy car and a large suburban house, and I assumed that both were his. I saw a construction-paper snowman taped to the front door, which I guessed was Bert Humphrey's handiwork. Cameras were chasing his father down, blocking him, tripping him up. His outstretched hand seemed no match for them, but he did manage to jostle his way into his house without responding to any of the shouted questions. It was the middle of the day. Dr. Humphrey was normally here at work, or wherever the president was. He was his personal physician. Didn't that entail some kind of patient-doctor privilege?

Though I supposed Dr. Humphrey had been stripped of his right to invoke this privilege the moment he'd violated the law by condoning his patient's use of an illegal drug. Perhaps the threat of prosecution had compelled him to cooperate with the independent counsel. Or maybe he'd volunteered testimony, willing to risk repercussions because he felt a responsibility to put the interests of the country before the president's or his own.

I recalled the day Dr. Humphrey had pinched my arm too hard and questioned if I'd ever considered that I might be too inquisitive for my own good. I hadn't, actually. I'd subsequently found out plenty about Wye and whiskey and Focusid, but not as much as Dr. Humphrey knew. It turned out that he'd been the one feeling pinched. He'd come to know too much for his own good. I was both impressed and frightened by his decision to speak out, ostensibly for the country's good.

By the following day, details of his testimony had leaked. By whom and how wasn't immediately clear. Leaks spring eternal.

The *New York Times* had a speculative article courtesy of Chick Wallrey, but Charlie and the *Post* had the scoop. I'd gotten a message from him the night before that something had come up and he was on deadline and would call me later. He never did. But here I was now, confronted with the fruits of his deadline. I picked up the paper from our front stoop and read the article with my eyes in a pained half-squint, prepared to close them all the way if necessary. I knew I couldn't have been the source for this because I knew nothing of Dr. Humphrey's testimony, but still I worried I was somehow involved. How had Charlie even gotten the story? He was hundreds of miles away. Charlie and his infuriating ace reporting. He insisted on being tough to love.

According to the article, Humphrey had testified that the president had been drinking excessively for the past six months. A full quarter of his term so far. Humphrey had also apparently confirmed that Wye had been consuming "addiction-level doses" of Focusid for almost as long, supplied to him by Tanbaj Laboratories, one of the Indian pharmaceutical companies with whom the United States had just signed a trade agreement. According to Humphrey, Wye used the Focusid to compensate for the effects of his alcoholism. I already knew most of this, of course, but it was still shocking to see it all summarized and described in damning, succinct, smudgeable print. When the black from the page came off on my fingers, I laughed a little manically after thinking that even the article itself leaked. Or maybe it bled. Maybe that was a more apt association.

Not surprisingly, the news about Dr. Humphrey hit like a tidal wave, slamming heavy and hard. I doubted Charlie could ever be accused of being in bed with the administration again. I could tell from the looks I received at work that most people believed he should never be allowed in my bed again.

But having others expect me to turn against him only drew me closer. I didn't blame Charlie for our chaos. In fact, I wanted to see him and touch him and stay up all night talking to him about what he'd done. I wanted to ask him how he'd gotten the scoop, but I didn't. Maybe he'd tell me sometime, but I'd never press him for it. I knew that a careful understanding of our boundaries had been restored, and I certainly didn't want to jeopardize it. Confronted with the fact that Charlie had just delivered the maximum possible amount of damage to the administration I worked for, I still knew that I loved him. Which is how I really knew. And when it came down to it, Charlie had only revealed things, he hadn't created them. He was good at his job. Now we needed to be good at ours.

He didn't make it easy. His follow-up article contained more revelations from Dr. Humphrey, who had apparently warned President Wye that the trials of Focusid were inconclusive and that there was some evidence that the drug could be very damaging to internal organs already made vulnerable by other behavior. Humphrey had grown increasingly concerned about the president's heart and liver, and had urged Fiona Wye to help arrange an intervention. This had taken place over Christmas, at Camp David, as LyingWye had correctly reported. But after an intense three-day detox, Wye had resumed drinking and popping his experimental pills. Humphrey had apparently reached the end of his rope.

RG called me to his office in the middle of the day. Like most of the West Wing, I was aware that he'd spent the morning with President Wye in the Oval Office. As soon as I got the call from Margari, I raced from my desk, hurried down the stairs, careened around the corner, and ran smack into Doug, the Secret Service agent. Who was evidently made of some kind of rocklike substance.

"Yowch," I yelped, staggering backward.

He caught my arm to steady me. We'd nearly collided once before and I'd been grateful to have averted it. I supposed if something's meant to be, you can't delay it forever.

"You okay, Speedy?" he asked.

I nodded. Nothing seemed to be broken. Luckily the crash hadn't triggered any of Doug's instinctive combat reaction moves.

"Sorry. I'm in a hurry."

"I can see that. But do me a favor. Slow down just a little and watch where you're going to keep from getting hurt," Doug said.

I waited for a joke but Doug seemed very serious. And for the first time, I could see real stress in his eyes. Was he trying to send me some kind of message?

"Otherwise, I'll be up all night worrying my pretty little head about you," he continued. "And lack of sleep is *murder* on my pores."

That was better. I smiled.

"Sorry. I'll slow down and watch out. I promise."

I hurried on toward RG's office. The truth was, no one had been getting much sleep these past few weeks. We all had bags under our eyes. We'd all been hunkered down, nervous, trapped. And we'd all been in spin mode, to concerned family and friends for those of us who weren't called upon to do it as a job. I'd assured my parents that I was fine, that all would be fine. I'd told my friends that there was an explanation for everything. I'd convinced octogenarian troublemaker Alfred Jackman that despite some reports, I didn't in fact have a good lead on where he could get his hands on some Focusid.

At this point, everyone knew that President Wye had lied on national television. That point was undebatable. People could spend time discussing whether the lie was justifiable or prosecutable or distinguishable from countless other statements he'd made. But no one could argue that he hadn't lied. He'd very deliberately been addressing the American public, which had been watching attentively. I imagined LyingWye smiling in its cyberspace afterlife.

One of the many questions now was whether Wye would admit he lied and apologize. Of course he should, but would he? Could he, even? Was he sober and lucid? As I entered RG's office, Margari looked up and indicated that he was expecting me and I should go ahead inside. She was normally so talkative, but she now seemed to have energy only for head movements.

RG was waiting for me. He seemed privately pained, as if he were suffering from a hair shirt beneath his familiar blue suit and tie. I noticed that he was sweating a bit, despite the coldness of the room. Oddly, his desk was preternaturally clean. There were only a few books stacked neatly—I recognized *Leaders Come in Many Forms*, a compilation of Lane Morris's speeches—resting on top. Where had all of RG's piles of paper gone, I wondered. To a shredder?

"Sir?" I said, after a moment of silence.

He had been looking in my direction but didn't appear to see me. He blinked twice and shook his head.

"The president will be testifying before the independent counsel tomorrow morning, and they've requested that I do so this afternoon," he said quickly. "I expect to be asked about all aspects of the president's behavior, and I will be answering their questions honestly and completely, which means that your name will most likely come up. And if it does, it's just a matter of time before they get in touch with you, and I wanted you to know so that you wouldn't be taken off guard."

"Thank you, sir," I replied.

"And so that you know that you should also cooperate fully."

"Yes, sir."

I'd started shaking a bit. I hated when this happened, but there was something in his tone that necessitated shaking. His voice had become as tight as a wire stretched to its snapping point.

"For someone to ask you to do otherwise, to perjure yourself to cover up their mistakes, would be—"

His voice nearly broke at this. From an anger so strong it seemed a separate force. A holy spirit of anger. I'd been looking down, focusing on a fixed point on the floor to prevent my trembling, but I looked back up quickly. His features had clouded with emotion. I watched him struggle to compose them.

"It would be beneath what you'd expect from a decent human being," he finished, back in control.

We were talking about more than him and me, I knew. I stayed silent. His eyes were now sharp and clear.

"That's all, Sammy."

I nodded. It was enough.

RG testified a few hours later. I left my BlackBerry and cell phone at my desk and spent the time in Lafayette Park, contemplating the White House from the outside. Sitting on the very bench where I'd met Charlie for lunch so many months before, when I'd anticipated an engagement trip proposal and learned he was moving away instead. I wondered how I would be taken by surprise today. About what was actually happening that deviated from my fantasies. And about how I would even recognize the deviation if I didn't know what I wanted. What did I want to happen? I closed my eyes and sought stillness, thinking that stillness would have an answer.

Twenty-four months earlier, on the eve of Inauguration Day, I'd been so proud to be a part of something truly new and good. Something that could change our world in ways I'd longed for. A new day after an eight-year nightmare of mistakes and messes. A good morning. People had called me naïve, and I'd felt sorry for them—felt sorry that they couldn't believe in anything but limitations. That they didn't want to be anything but cynical. But who had been right?

What did I want to happen? I wanted not to be foolish.

I stayed on the bench instead of returning to work. I stayed instead of seeking out warmth. I could feel my fingers turning blue from the cold. Even inside my mittens. They hadn't been safe. I noticed Derrick leaving his post at the end of his shift, in his civilian parka and camouflage hat with flaps. He waited at the light for someone, and for a stupid second I thought it was me. It didn't make any sense; it was just the way he was staring in my direction, most likely looking at the leafless branches that stretched above me. They were striking in their bareness—the exposed limbs of stripper trees. I watched a woman run from the gate toward Derrick. She didn't have a coat, and I recognized her as she got closer. It was Sofia. She was gesturing apologetically and pointing back toward the West Wing, and Derrick was nodding. She leaned in to kiss him, then squeezed his coat and ran back inside.

She'd kissed him. Derrick and Sofia were in a relationship that involved kissing. Finally I had a possible explanation for why Derrick was so cold toward me.

"Hey!" I called out to him after he'd crossed the street and was walking past me through the park.

For a second I thought he was going to ignore me and keep moving, but he stopped. I hurried toward him.

"Are you dating Sofia?" I asked.

He cocked his head at me.

"What if I am? What's it to you?"

"She hates me. Why?"

I hadn't completely accepted Stephanie's passing explanation. And though Sofia and I had recently fought, she had hated me long before that. She'd hated me from the beginning. I wanted to know why. I needed to know why. Derrick shrugged.

"You can't help some things."

I thought about this and then I nodded. It was true. I didn't have to be cynical to understand this. Just being human long enough made it clear.

"Do you ever suffer from short-term memory loss?" I asked.

Derrick looked at me like I might be insane. It wasn't as though I hadn't considered the possibility. On particularly paranoid days, I felt like people were just humoring me until the straitjacket guys arrived.

"Only when necessary," he finally answered.

He jutted his chin toward the White House.

"You might want to head back in there," he continued. "Your president's resigning."

I knew, watching the monitor in a room only a few yards above and away from the real-life action, that I'd never be able to forget this night, no matter how hard I might try. Wye wasn't defiant in the end like I'd assumed he'd be. Like I still assumed he would have been, had he let Fiona have control. He just seemed to crumple a little bit into himself. He surrendered. He was done.

He could never please all the people all the time, and he'd come to the brutal realization that he couldn't even please most of the people most of the time. I thought of how he had stared at himself in the mirror that day in the Oval Office. Of how he always stared at himself for too long in mirrors when he had the opportunity. And it occurred to me that he was endlessly fascinated by his own image because he was so driven by his concern with how others saw him.

He wasn't a bad person. His heart was in the right place. But he lacked a strong inner compass and so he looked outside of himself for guidance. He searched elsewhere for cues about how to best be the embodiment of a beloved leader, and for salves and shortcuts when he couldn't be.

Wye admitted that he needed to deal with some "health issues" and apologized for not being truthful about his "relationship with alcohol," implying that his shame had been the reason for his lies. He confirmed that he'd been taking dangerously high doses of experimental medication to compensate for the disorientation and sluggishness brought on by his "other behavior." He revealed that the mixture of the unapproved medicine with the liquor had all but destroyed his liver and announced that he needed a transplant, which was shocking news. He apologized for putting the country through this, and asked for everyone's prayers and forgiveness. He sounded fatigued and looked a little yellow. He stared intensely into the camera, and I wondered if he could see his reflection in its lens.

"So I wishh you a good night and I wishh ush all a good tomarra," he said at the end.

He was just slowing down his final sentence to make it last. He hadn't intended to slur. And I didn't believe that he was currently on any slur-inducing substances, but the effect was unfortunate. Even the word he hadn't slurred had sounded funny with his accent. "Tomorrow" as "tomarra." Rhyming with Samarra. He was done.

RG was sworn in the following day at noon, the appointed time for President Wye's resignation to take effect. Earlier that morning, the special prosecutor announced that RG had been cleared of any wrongdoing. I didn't know if RG had made any deals with the independent counsel and I didn't ask. He was the president now. That was all that mattered.

RG had been loyal to Wye as long as he could, but now he owed allegiance to a higher cause. It was on his shoulders to steer us out of this mess. And as he set out to forge a fresh route forward, he was helped by the fact that he was so different from Wye. The traits for which RG had been previously criticized were now coveted. He was steady and honest and thoughtful. He wasn't a showman, he didn't do tricks. Or at least not as far as most people knew. In fact, accurately or not, RG was being described as an antidote to Wye.

RG nominated Senator Lane Morris to be his vice president—the first female vice president in our nation's history, though probably not the first closeted one. I considered it an excellent choice. Those who agreed with me hailed it as evidence that RG wasn't afraid to make tough decisions and take controversial stands. People speculated that she'd be confirmed quickly, though that remained to be seen.

Inevitably, inexorably, the world moved on. The producers of *Piling On* immediately approached Wye with a pitch to do a reality show with ex-President Pile. Sort of a buddy road trip concept, moderated by Dr. Singh. They were turned down (despite dangling the tantalizing title *Wye Not?*), but undaunted. I imagined it wouldn't be long before they found someone else to fill the role. I'd been reading recently about a burgeoning scandal involving the president of Russia, who would be great for international distribution.

Wye and Fiona took off together on a trip of their own. After boarding the *Marine One* helicopter for the last time from the White House lawn, they made their way to British Columbia to spend some rehabilitation time on Fiona's family property. In addition to some private medical personnel, the president's infant brother, Bernard, and his mother, Rosie, were spotted entering the compound not long after the Wyes' arrival. There were some late-night monologue riffs speculating that Rosie and baby Bernard got invited only after the Wyes learned that the baby's matching blood type might come in handy for the ex-president's liver transplant—creepy jokes that confirmed that Wye was destined to be permanently caricatured as the ultimate user. I hoped that the Wyes didn't watch late-night television, and that their visit with Rosie and Bernard would provide some much-needed family bonding. Besieged by paparazzi, the Wyes asked the local government's assistance in protecting their privacy, and, burying the hatchet, Canada agreed.

Back in D.C., there was a fair amount of staff reshuffling. Feeling drained and unbalanced by all that had gone down, I was taken off guard when RG asked me to be his deputy chief of staff. I thanked him very genuinely for the offer, and requested a day to think about it. He seemed surprised, of course. But unlike Wye, RG wasn't a narcissist. He could understand that I might have something I'd prefer to do than serve him. Than serve the president. What that might be, I wasn't sure.

✿   ✿   ✿

Charlie met me on the banks of the Potomac at one. After weeks of freezing rain, it was a freakishly hot and sunny day. Nearly eighty degrees Fahrenheit, which should have been impossible for January. Climatologists were worried that this hot flash might cause the cherry blossoms to bloom prematurely in confusion, which would make for a ridiculously early and sure-to-be-cut-short spring. Part of me hoped that they would, just to have nature acknowledge that everything had been turned upside down.

Charlie had arrived that morning, and I'd planned to meet him after work, but after my conversation with RG, I'd decided to leave at lunchtime.

"Did you bring them?" I asked once we'd kissed hello.

He held open his shoulder satchel to show me the plastic bags.

"Fantastic, thanks," I said.

I looked out over the water. Downstream, near the Lincoln Memorial, which was my favorite of all the monuments, there was a boat filled with people celebrating something. My own Lincoln had wept when the president resigned. They'd been strong tears, few and sincere. I hadn't cried at all. I'd wanted to, but I'd felt dried up, so I'd been grateful to have someone else express what I couldn't. In exchange for being his voice so many times, Lincoln had shed my tears. I'd hugged him afterward and noticed that he smelled like Margari's cinnamon perfume. Which had reminded me that life went on.

Charlie and I sat down together in the grass. I'd already felt the ground and knew that it was warm. Now that I was closer to it, the blades of grass looked like green full leaves. Green full leaves on a flowering planet.

"Hi, lovely," he said, brushing my hair from my forehead.

"Hi."

I lay down and put my head in his lap. I closed my eyes against the sunlight and watched the dancing dots on the inside of my eyelids. When I was younger, I'd thought those dots were my superpowers.

"I'd like to tell you about Dr. Humphrey," Charlie said.

I nodded. I never would have asked, but I was happy to be told.

"He called me after he testified," Charlie said. "He tracked me down through the *Post* and called me and said he had a story for me.

He didn't want to be directly quoted, but he wanted to tell me everything. He wanted it all to come out on his terms, as much as possible.
He didn't want what he'd done to get twisted by someone else's agenda
before the truth was known. And though he really wrestled with it, he
decided that it had to be known, for the safety of the country."

"That's incredible," I said.

"I know. It's amazing. Probably the most historically significant story
I'll ever be a part of. And I think he chose me because of you."

"How come?"

"Because at the very end, just before we hung up, he told me to
marry you."

At this, my eyes flew open. My superpowers deserted me.

"What?"

Charlie nodded.

"I'd asked him what he would do now that he'd blown the whistle,
what his plans were, where he would go . . . and he said he'd be just
fine. He said he'd retire from the military and move on with his life.
Then he asked if we were still together, and then he told me I should
marry you. That was it."

"What did you say?" I asked.

"I said I'd known that since the day I met you."

"Oh."

In the silence that followed, I imagined I could hear the cherry blossoms straining to burst free.

"You're not proposing right now, are you?" I asked.

Charlie looked into my eyes.

"Not *right* now," he replied. "I feel I owe you some other things first."

I nodded. I felt we both did.

"But I did bring you this."

He reached into a pocket of his bag and took out my present. He
must have fetched it from beneath the windowsill tree. I liked thinking
of him in my spaces even when I wasn't there.

I opened the present. It was a miniature metal music-maker with a
hand crank. The kind of contraption that's normally hidden in a box so
as to be heard and not seen. It looked bare and exposed and perfect in
the sunlight.

I took the little handle between my finger and thumb and turned the crank around, which made the spool with its raised Braille notes revolve. Its motion nudged the adjacent tiny pin-teeth over the bumps, and a delicate rendition of Louis Armstrong's "What a Wonderful World" floated forth. It was just a slice of the song, but it made me smile. As long as I kept cranking, it wasn't allowed to stop. I could force the world to be wonderful.

"I love it," I proclaimed.

"I hoped you would."

"RG asked me to be his deputy chief of staff."

"Congratulations. That's phenomenal."

"But it doesn't make me happy."

"Why not?"

It was a good question. Lately, I hadn't been overjoyed about the things that I should. Even when LyingWye had gone down, my reaction had been bittersweet. Perhaps because although it was a blog driven by hate, it had served an important purpose in our administration. It had focused us on an enemy outside of ourselves; on something that was wrong besides us. When that had disintegrated, so had many of our excuses.

"Do you think truth is a fluid, relative thing?" I asked Charlie.

"Are we getting philosophical now? Should I take out my pipe?"

I smiled.

"I think the truth is, we've let too many things get in the way of us," I said. "It's understandable, given our careers, but our jobs have corrupted us. Or at least co-opted us. We need to be fixed, like you said."

"What are you proposing?" he asked seriously.

I did have a proposal, I realized. I'd been half expecting one from him, when I'd had one all along.

"A time-out," I answered.

He looked stunned. He blinked.

"You mean from us," he said.

Good gods, no!

"No! *For* us. From everything else."

Charlie breathed out.

"Well, that's better," he said. "A time-out," he repeated, considering it anew. "For how long?"

"I don't know, two months? Two months would probably do it."

"So you wouldn't take the job, then?"

I shrugged.

"Not for two months, at least. I don't think I'd be any good till then. What about you? Could you do it?"

"For you? Yes."

He'd said yes. Hallelujah.

"Which casino should we rob first to fund our adventures?" he asked.

I laughed.

"I didn't say it was a responsible plan," I replied.

"Oh, I think it's very responsible," he answered, gathering me up in his arms. "I think it's about the best thing we could do."

We kissed in the afternoon light, with superpowers dancing all around. I was happy. There were things I couldn't help, but there was a whole lot that I could. I just needed a little time. Lying in the leaves of grass with Charlie, I believed again.

It felt like no time at all had passed when the sun began to set. It was odd to have the evening come so early on what seemed like a summer day, but it reminded me of unfinished plans. I opened Charlie's shoulder bag and took out the fish.

Professor Moriarty was in one plastic bag filled with water, and Samson was in the other. They were still alive, but fading. I took them to the edge of the bank.

"Are you sure you want to do this?" Charlie asked.

I nodded.

"I know the river's cold and polluted—I know firsthand, in fact— but it's gotten cleaner, and it's warmer today. The truth is, they're both going to die soon. I'd rather have them die free."

Charlie held on to Samson while I turned Professor Moriarty loose. Then I worked to untie the tight plastic knot of Samson's bag. Once I'd done it, I knelt down, turned the bag upside down, and watched my last little fish plop into the water below. I could only see him beneath the dark surface of the river for a second before he flitted off, but it was enough for his skin to flash a rainbow.